At the Time Appointed

A. Maynard Barbour

At the Time Appointed

The present edition is a reproduction of previous publication of this work. Minor typographical errors may have been corrected without note, however, for an authentic reading experience the spelling, punctuation, and capitalization have been retained from the original text.

ISBN: 978-1-61895-232-5

CONTENTS

Chapter I

John Darrell

Upon a small station on one of the transcontinental lines winding among the mountains far above the level of the sea, the burning rays of the noonday sun fell so fiercely that the few buildings seemed ready to ignite from the intense heat. A season of unusual drought had added to the natural desolation of the scene. Mountains and foot-hills were blackened by smouldering fires among the timber, while a dense pall of smoke entirely hid the distant ranges from view. Patches of sage-brush and bunch grass, burned sere and brown, alternated with barren stretches of sand from which piles of rubble rose here and there, telling of worked-out and abandoned mines. Occasionally a current of air stole noiselessly down from the canyon above, but its breath scorched the withered vegetation like the blast from a furnace. Not a sound broke the stillness; life itself seemed temporarily suspended, while the very air pulsated and vibrated with the heat, rising in thin, quivering columns.

Suddenly the silence was broken by the rapid approach of the stage from a distant mining camp, rattling noisily down the street, followed by a slight stir within the apparently deserted station. Whirling at breakneck pace around a sharp turn, it stopped precipitately, amid a blinding cloud of dust, to deposit its passengers at the depot.

One of these, a young man of about five-and-twenty, arose with some difficulty from the cramped position which for seven weary hours he had been forced to maintain, and, with sundry stretchings and shakings of his superb form, seemed at last to pull himself together. Having secured his belongings from out the pile of miscellaneous luggage thrown from the stage upon the platform, he advanced towards the slouching figure of a man just emerging from the baggage-room, his hands thrust deep in his trousers pockets, his mouth stretched in a prodigious yawn, the arrival of the stage having evidently awakened him from his siesta.

"How's the west-bound—on time?" queried the young man rather shortly, but despite the curtness of his accents there was a musical quality in the ringing tones.

Before the cavernous jaws could close sufficiently for reply, two distant whistles sounded almost simultaneously.

"That's her," drawled the man, with a backward jerk of his thumb over his shoulder in the direction of the sound; "she's at Blind Man's Pass; be here in about fifteen minutes."

The young man turned and sauntered to the rear end of the platform, where he paused for a few moments; then, unconscious of the scrutiny of his fellow-passengers, he began silently pacing up and down, being in no mood for conversation with any one. Every bone in his body ached and his head throbbed with a dull pain, but these physical discomforts, which he attributed to his long and wearisome stage ride, caused him less annoyance

1

than did the fact that he had lost several days' time, besides subjecting himself to numerous inconveniences and hardships, on what he now denominated a "fool's errand."

An expert mineralogist and metallurgist, he had been commissioned by a large syndicate of eastern capitalists to come west, primarily to examine a certain mine recently offered for sale, and secondarily to secure any other valuable mining properties which might happen to be on the market. A promoter, whose acquaintance he had formed soon after leaving St. Paul, had poured into his ear such fabulous tales of a mine of untold wealth which needed but the expenditure of a few thousands to place it upon a dividend-paying basis, that, after making due allowance for optimism and exaggeration, he had thought it might be worth his while to stop off and investigate. The result of the investigation had been anything but satisfactory for either the promoter or the expert.

He was the more annoyed at the loss of time because of a telegram handed him just before his departure from St. Paul, which he now drew forth, and which read as follows:

"Parkinson, expert for M. and M. on trail. Knows you as our representative, but only by name. Lie low and block him if possible.

               "Barnard."

He well understood the import of the message. The "M. and M." stood for a rival syndicate of enormous wealth, and the fact that its expert was also on his way west promised lively competition in the purchase of the famous Ajax mine.

"Five days," he soliloquized, glancing at the date of the message, which he now tore into bits, together with two or three letters of little importance. "I have lost my start and am now likely to meet this Parkinson at any stage of the game. However, he has never heard of John Darrell, and that name will answer my purpose as well as any among strangers. I'll notify Barnard when I reach Ophir."

His plans for the circumvention of Parkinson were now temporarily cut short by the appearance of the "double-header" rounding a curve and rapidly approaching—a welcome sight, for the heat and blinding glare of light were becoming intolerable.

Only for a moment the ponderous engines paused, panting and quivering like two living, sentient monsters; the next, with heavy, labored breath, as though summoning all their energies for the task before them, they were slowly ascending the steadily increasing grade, moment by moment with accelerated speed plunging into the very heart of the mountains, bearing John Darrell, as he was to be henceforth known, to a destiny of which he had little thought, but which he himself had, unconsciously, helped to weave.

An hour later, on returning to the sleeper after an unsuccessful attempt at dining, Darrell sank into his seat, and, leaning wearily back, watched with half-closed eyes the rapidly changing scenes through which he was passing, for the time utterly oblivious to his surroundings. Gigantic rocks, grotesque in form and color, flashed past; towering peaks loomed suddenly before him, advancing, receding, disappearing, and reappearing with the swift windings and doublings of the train; massive walls of granite pressed close and closer, seeming for one instant a threatening, impenetrable barrier, the next, opening to reveal glimpses of distant billowy ranges, their summits white with perpetual snow. The train had now reached a higher altitude, and breezes redolent of pine and fir fanned his throbbing brow, their fragrance thronging his mind with memories of other and far-distant scenes, until gradually the bold outlines of cliff and crag grew dim, and in their place appeared a cool, dark forest through which flecks of golden sunlight sifted down upon the moss-grown, flower-strewn earth; a stream singing beneath the pines, then rippling onward through meadows of waving green; a wide-spreading house of colonial build half hidden by giant trees and clinging rose-vines, and, framed among the roses, a face, strong, tender, sweet, crowned with silvered hair—one of the few which sorrow makes beautiful—which came nearer and nearer, bending over him with a mother's blessing; and then he slept.

The face of the sleeper, with its clear-cut, well-moulded features, formed a pleasing study, reminding one of a bit of unfinished carving, the strong, bold lines of which reveal the noble design of the sculptor—the thing of wondrous beauty yet to be—but which still lacks the finer strokes, the final touch requisite to bring it to perfection. Strength of character was indicated there; an indomitable will that would bend the most adverse conditions to serve its own masterful purpose and make of obstacles the paving-stones to success; a mind gifted with keen perceptive faculties, but which hitherto had dealt mostly with externals and knew little of itself or of its own powers. Young, with splendid health and superabundant vitality, there had been little opportunity for introspection or for the play of the finer, subtler faculties; and of the whole gamut of susceptibilities, ranging from exquisite suffering to ecstatic joy, few had been even awakened. His was a nature capable of producing the divinest harmonies or the wildest discords, according to the hand that swept the strings as yet untouched.

For more than an hour Darrell slept. He was awakened by the murmur of voices near him, confused at first, but growing more distinct as he gradually recalled his surroundings, until, catching the name of "Parkinson," he was instantly on the alert.

"Yes," a pleasant voice was saying, "I understand the Ajax is for sale if the owners can get their price, but they don't want less than a cold million for it, and it's my opinion they'll find buyers rather scarce at that figure when it comes to a show down."

"Well, I don't know; that depends," was the reply. "The price won't stand in the way with my people, if the mine is all right. They can hand over a million—or two, for that matter—as easily as a thousand, if the property is what they want, but they've got to know what they're buying. That's what I'm out here for."

Taking a quiet survey of the situation, Darrell found that the section opposite his own—which, upon his return from the dining-car, had

3

contained only a motley collection of coats and grips—was now occupied by a party of three, two of whom were engaged in animated conversation. One of the speakers, who sat facing Darrell, was a young man of about two-and-twenty, whose self-assurance and assumption of worldly wisdom, combined with a boyish impetuosity, he found vastly amusing, while at the same time his frank, ingenuous eyes and winning smile of genuine friendliness, revealing a nature as unsuspecting and confiding as a child's, appealed to him strangely and drew him irresistibly towards the young stranger. The other speaker, whom Darrell surmised to be Parkinson, was considerably older and was seated facing the younger man, hence his back was towards Darrell; while the third member of the party, and by far the eldest, of whose face Darrell had a perfect profile view, although saying little, seemed an interested listener.

The man whom Darrell supposed to be Parkinson inquired the quickest way of reaching the Ajax mine.

"Well, you see it's this way," replied the young fellow. "The Ajax is on a spur that runs out from the main line at Ophir, and the train only runs between there and Ophir twice a week, Wednesdays and Saturdays. Let's see, this is Wednesday; we'll get into Ophir to-morrow, and you'll have to wait over until Saturday, unless you hire a rig to take you out there, and that's pretty expensive and an awfully rough jaunt besides."

"I don't mind the expense," retorted the other, "but I don't know as I care to go on any jaunts over your mountain roads when there's no special necessity for it; I can get exercise enough without that."

"I tell you what, Mr. Parkinson," said the young fellow, cordially, "you and your friend here, Mr. Hunter,"—Darrell started at the mention of the latter name,—"had better wait over till Saturday, and in the mean time I'll take you people out to Camp Bird, as we call it, and show you the Bird Mine; that's our mine, you know, and I tell you she is a 'bird,' and no mistake. You'll be interested in looking her over, though I'll tell you beforehand she's not for sale."

"Do I understand that you have an interest in this remarkable mine, Mr. Whitcomb?" Parkinson inquired, a tinge of amusement in his tone.

"Not in the way you mean; that is, not yet, though there's no telling how soon I may have if things turn out as I hope," and the boyish cheek flushed slightly. "But I know what I'm talking about all the same. My uncle, D. K. Underwood, is a practical mining man of nearly thirty years' experience, and what he doesn't know about mines and mining isn't worth knowing. He's interested in a dozen or so of the best mines in the State, but I don't think he would exchange his half-interest in the Bird Mine for all his other holdings put together. She's a comparatively new mine yet, but taking into consideration her depth and the amount of development, she's the best-paying mine in the State. Here, let me show you something." And hastily pulling a note-book from his pocket, he took therefrom a narrow slip of paper which he handed to the expert.

"There's a statement," he continued, "made out by the United States Assay Office, back here at Galena, that will show you the returns from a sixty days' run at the Bird mill; what do you think of that?"

4

Parkinson's face was still invisible to Darrell, but the latter heard a long, low whistle of surprise. Young Whitcomb looked jubilant.

"They say figures won't lie," he added, in tones of boyish enthusiasm, "but if you don't believe those figures, I've got the cash right here to show for it," accompanying the words with a significant gesture.

Parkinson handed the slip to Hunter, then leaned back in his seat, giving Darrell a view of his profile.

"Sixty days!" he said, musingly. "Seventy-five thousand dollars! I think I would like to take a look at the Bird Mine! I think I would like to make Mr. Underwood's acquaintance!"

Whitcomb laughed exultingly. "I'll give you an opportunity to do both if you'll stop over," he said; "and don't you forget that my uncle can give you some pointers on the Ajax, for he knows every mine in the State."

Mr. Hunter here handed the slip of paper to Whitcomb. "Young man," he said, with some severity, gazing fixedly at Whitcomb through his eye-glasses, "do you mean to say that you are travelling with seventy-five thousand dollars on your person?"

"Certainly, sir," Whitcomb replied, evidently enjoying the situation.

Mr. Hunter shook his head. "Very imprudent!" he commented. "You are running a tremendous risk. I wonder that your uncle would permit it!"

"Oh, that's all right," said Whitcomb, confidently. "Uncle usually comes down himself with the shipments of bullion, and he generally banks the most of his money there at Galena, but he couldn't very well leave this time, so he sent me, and as he was going to use considerable money paying for a lot of improvements we've put in and paying off the men, he told me to bring back the cash. There's not much danger anyway; the West isn't as wild nowadays as it used to be."

Handing a second bit of paper to Parkinson, he added: "There's something else that will interest you; the results of some assays made by the United States Assay Office on some samples taken at random from a new strike we made last week. I'll show you some of the samples, too."

"Great Scott!" ejaculated Parkinson, running his eye over the returns. "You seem to have a mine there, all right!"

"Sure thing! You'll think so when you see it," Whitcomb answered, fumbling in a grip at his feet.

At sight of the specimens of ore which he produced a moment later, his two companions became nearly as enthusiastic as himself. Leaning eagerly forward, they began an inspection of the samples, commenting on their respective values, while Whitcomb, unfolding a tracing of the workings of the mine, explained the locality from which each piece was taken, its depth from the surface, the width and dip of the vein, and other items of interest.

Darrell, who was carefully refraining from betraying any special interest in the party across the aisle, soon became aware that he was not the only interested listener to the conversation. In the section directly in front of the one occupied by Whitcomb and his companions a man was seated, apparently engrossed in a newspaper, but Darrell, who had a three-quarter view of his face, soon observed that he was not reading, but listening intently to the conversation of the men seated behind him, and particularly

5

to young Whitcomb's share in it. Upon hearing the latter's statement that he had with him the cash returns for the shipment of bullion, Darrell saw the muscles of his face suddenly grow tense and rigid, while his hands involuntarily tightened their hold upon the paper. He grew uncomfortable under Darrell's scrutiny, moved restlessly once or twice, then turning, looked directly into the piercing dark eyes fixed upon him. His own eyes, which were small and shifting, instantly dropped, while the dark blood mounted angrily to his forehead. A few moments later, he changed his position so that Darrell could not see his face, but the latter determined to watch him and to give Whitcomb a word of warning at the earliest opportunity.

"Well," said Parkinson, leaning back in his seat after examining the ores and listening to Whitcomb's outline of their plans for the future development of the mine, "it seems to me, young man, you have quite a knowledge of mines and mining yourself."

Whitcomb flushed with pleasure. "I ought to," he said; "there isn't a man in this western country that understands the business better or has got it down any finer than my uncle. He may not be able to talk so glibly or use such high-sounding names for things as you fellows, but he can come pretty near telling whether a mine will pay for the handling, and if it has any value he generally knows how to go to work to find it."

"Well, that's about the 'gist' of the whole business," said Parkinson; he added: "You say he can give me some 'tips' on the Ajax?"

"He can if he chooses to," laughed Whitcomb, "but you'd better not let him know that I said so. He'll be more likely to give you information if you ask him offhand."

"Well," continued Parkinson, "when we get to Ophir, I'll know whether or not I can stop over. I've heard there's another fellow out here on this Ajax business; whether he's ahead of me I don't know. I'll make inquiries when we reach Ophir, and if he hasn't come on the scene yet I can afford to lay off; if he has, I must lose no time in getting out to the mine." Parkinson glanced at Hunter, who nodded almost imperceptibly.

"I guess that's the best arrangement we can make at present," said Parkinson, rising from his seat. "Come and have a smoke with us, Mr. Whitcomb?"

Whitcomb declined the invitation, and, after Hunter and Parkinson had left, sat idly turning over the specimens of ore, until, happening to catch Darrell's eye, he inquired, pleasantly,–

"Are you interested in this sort of thing?"

"In a way, yes," said Darrell, crossing over and taking the seat vacated by Parkinson. "I'm not what you call a mining man; that is, I've never owned or operated a mine, but I take a great interest in examining the different ores and always try to get as much information regarding them as possible."

Whitcomb at once launched forth enthusiastically upon a description of the various samples. Darrell, while careful not to show too great familiarity with the subject, or too thorough a knowledge of ores in general, yet was so

6

keenly appreciative of their remarkable richness and beauty that he soon won the boy's heart.

"Say!" he exclaimed, "you had better stop off at Ophir with us; we would make a mining man of you in less than no time! By the way, how far west are you travelling?"

"Ophir is my destination at present, though it is uncertain how long I remain there."

"Long enough, that we'll get well acquainted, I hope. Going into any particular line of business?"

"No, only looking the country over, for the present."

To divert the conversation from himself, Darrell, by a judicious question or two, led Whitcomb to speak of the expert.

"Parkinson?" he said with a merry laugh. "Oh, yes, he's one of those eastern know-it-alls who come out here occasionally to give us fellows a few points on mines. They're all right, of course, for the men who employ them, who want to invest their money and wouldn't know a mine if they saw one; but when they undertake to air their knowledge among these old fellows who have spent a lifetime in the business, why, they're likely to get left, that's all. Now, this Parkinson seems to be a pretty fair sort of man compared with some of them, but between you and me, I'd wager my last dollar that they'll lose him on that Ajax mine!"

"Why, what's the matter with the Ajax?" Darrell inquired, indifferently.

"Well, as you're not interested in any way, I'm not telling tales out of school. The Ajax has been a bonanza in its day, but within the last year or so the bottom has dropped out of the whole thing, and that's the reason the owners are anxious to sell."

"I hear they ask a pretty good price for the mine."

"Yes, they're trading on her reputation, but that's all past. The mine is practically worked out. They've made a few good strikes lately, so that there is some good ore in sight, and this is their chance to sell, but there are no indications of any permanence. One of our own men was over there a while ago, and he said there wasn't enough ore in the mine to keep their mill running full force for more than six months."

"Is this Hunter an expert also?"

"Oh, no; Parkinson said he was a friend of his, just taking the trip for his health."

Darrell smiled quietly, knowing Hunter to be a member of the syndicate employing Parkinson, but kept his knowledge to himself.

A little later, when Darrell and Whitcomb left together for the dining-car, quite a friendship had sprung up between them. There was that mutual attraction often observed between two natures utterly diverse. Whitcomb was unaccountably drawn towards the dark-eyed, courteous, but rather reticent stranger, while his own frank friendliness and childlike confidence awoke in Darrell's nature a correlative tenderness and affection which he never would have believed himself capable of feeling towards one of his own sex.

"I don't know what is the matter with me," said Darrell, as he seated himself at a table, facing Whitcomb. "My head seems to have a small-sized stamp-mill inside of it; every bone in my body aches, and my joints feel as though they were being pulled apart."

Whitcomb looked up quickly. "Are you just from the East, or have you been out here any time?"

"I stopped for a few days, back here a ways."

"In the mountain country?"

"Yes."

"By George! I believe you've got the mountain fever; there's an awful lot of it round here this season, and this is just the worst time of year for an easterner to come out here. But we'll look after you when we get to Ophir, and bring you round all right."

"Much obliged, but I think I'll be all right after a night's rest," Darrell replied, inwardly resolved, upon reaching Ophir, to push on to the Ajax as quickly as possible, though his ardor was considerably cooled by Whitcomb's report.

When they left the dining-car the train was stopping at a small station, and for a few moments the young men strolled up and down the platform. A dense, bluish-gray haze hung low over the country, rendering the outlines of even the nearest objects obscure and dim; the western sky was like burnished copper, and the sun, poised a little above the horizon, looked like a ball of glowing fire.

Just as the train was about to start Darrell saw the man whose peculiar actions he had noticed earlier, leave the telegraph office and jump hastily aboard. Calling Whitcomb's attention as he passed them, he related his observations of the afternoon and cautioned him against the man. For an instant Whitcomb looked serious.

"I suppose it was rather indiscreet in me to talk as I did," he said, "but it can't be helped now. However, I guess it's all right, but I'm obliged to you all the same."

They passed into the smoker, where Darrell was introduced to Hunter and Parkinson. In a short time, however, he found himself suffering from nausea and growing faint and dizzy.

"Gentlemen," he said, "you will have to excuse me. I'm rather off my base this evening, and I find that smoking isn't doing me any good."

As he rose young Whitcomb sprang instantly to his feet; throwing away his cigar and linking his arm within Darrell's, he insisted upon accompanying him to the sleeper, notwithstanding his protests.

"Good-night, Parkinson," he called, cheerily; "see you in the morning!"

He accompanied Darrell to his section; then dropped familiarly into the seat beside him, throwing one arm affectionately over Darrell's shoulder, and during the next hour, while the sunset glow faded and the evening shadows deepened, he confided to this acquaintance of only a few hours the outlines of his past life and much regarding his hopes and plans for the future. He spoke of his orphaned boyhood; of the uncle who had given him a home in his family and initiated him into his own business methods; of his hope of being admitted at no distant day into partnership with his uncle and becoming a shareholder in the wonderful Bird Mine.

"But that isn't all I am looking forward to," he said, in conclusion, his boyish tones growing strangely deep and tender. "My fondest hope of all I hardly dare admit even to myself, and I don't know why I am speaking of it to you, except that I already like you and trust you as I never did any other man; but you will understand what I mean when you see my cousin, Kate Underwood."

He paused, but his silence was more eloquent to Darrell than words; the latter grasped his hand warmly in token that he understood.

"I wish you all that you hope for," he said.

A few moments later Whitcomb spoke with his usual impetuosity. "What am I thinking of, keeping you up in this way when you are sick and dead tired! You had better turn in and get all the rest you can, and when we reach Ophir to-morrow, just remember, my dear fellow, that no hotels 'go.' You'll go directly home with me, where you'll find yourself in such good hands you'll think sure you're in your own home, and we'll soon have you all right."

For hours Darrell tossed wearily, unable to sleep. His head throbbed wildly, the racking pain throughout his frame increased, while a raging fire seemed creeping through his veins. Not until long past midnight did he fall into a fitful sleep. Strange fancies surged through his fevered brain, torturing him with their endless repetition, their seeming reality. Suddenly he awoke, bewildered, exhausted, oppressed by a vague sense of impending evil.

Chapter II

A Night's Work

For a few seconds Darrell tried vainly to recall what had awakened him. Low, confused sounds occasionally reached his ears, but they seemed part of his own troubled dreams. The heat was intolerable; he raised himself to the open window that he might get a breath of cooler air; his head whirled, but the half-sitting posture seemed to clear his brain, and he recalled his surroundings. At once he became conscious that the train was not in motion, yet no sound of trainmen's voices came through the open window; all was dead silence, and the vague, haunting sense of impending danger quickened.

Suddenly he heard a muttered oath in one of the sections, followed by an order, low, but peremptory,—

"No noise! Hand over, and be quick about it!"

Instantly Darrell comprehended the situation. Peering cautiously between the curtains, he saw, at the forward end of the sleeper, a masked man with a revolver in each hand, while the mirror behind him revealed

9

another figure at the rear, masked and armed in like manner. He heard another order; the man was doing his work swiftly. He thought at once of young Whitcomb, but no sound came from the opposite section, and he sank quietly back upon his pillow.

A moment later the curtains were quickly thrust aside, the muzzle of a revolver confronted Darrell, and the same low voice demanded,–

"Hand out your valuables!"

A man of medium height, wearing a mask and full beard, stood over him. Darrell quietly handed over his watch and purse, noting as he did so the man's hands, white, well formed, well kept. He half expected a further demand, as the purse contained only a few small bills and some change, the bulk of his money being secreted about the mattress, as was his habit; but the man turned with peculiar abruptness to the opposite section, as one who had a definite object in view and was in haste to accomplish it. Darrell, his faculties alert, observed that the section in front of Whitcomb's was empty; he recalled the actions of its occupant on the preceding afternoon, his business later at the telegraph office, and the whole scheme flashed vividly before his mind. The man had been a spy sent out by the band now holding the train, and Whitcomb's money was without doubt the particular object of the hold-up.

Whitcomb was asleep at the farther side of his berth. Leaning slightly towards him, the man shook him, and his first words confirmed Darrell's intuitions,–

"Hand over that money, young man, and no fuss about it, either!"

Whitcomb, instantly awake, gazed at the masked face without a word or movement. Darrell, powerless to aid his friend, watched intently, dreading some rash act on his part to which his impetuous nature might prompt him.

Again he heard the low tones, this time a note of danger in them,–

"No fooling! Hand that money over, lively!"

With a spring, as sudden and noiseless as a panther's, Whitcomb grappled with the man, knocking the revolver from his hand upon the bed. A quick, desperate, silent struggle followed. Whitcomb suddenly reached for the revolver; as he did so Darrell saw a flash of steel in the dim light, and the next instant his friend sank, limp and motionless, upon the bed.

"Fool!" he heard the man mutter, with an oath.

An involuntary groan escaped from Darrell's lips. Slight as was the sound, the man heard it and turned, facing him; the latter was screened by the curtains, and the man, seeing no one, returned to his work, but that brief glance had revealed enough to Darrell that he knew he could henceforth identify the murderer among a thousand. In the struggle the mask had been partially pushed aside, exposing a portion of the man's face. A scar of peculiar shape showed white against the olive skin, close to the curling black hair. But to Darrell the pre-eminently distinguishing characteristic of that face was the eyes. Of the most perfect steel blue he had ever seen, they seemed, as they turned upon him in that intense glance, to glint and scintillate like the points of two rapiers in a brilliant sword play, while their look of concentrated fury and malignity, more demon-like than human, was stamped ineffaceably upon his brain.

Having secured as much as he could find of the money, the murderer left hastily and silently, and a few moments later the guards, after a warning to the passengers not to leave their berths, took their departure.

Having partially dressed, Darrell at once sprang across the aisle and took Whitcomb's limp form in his arms. His heart still beat faintly, but he was unconscious and bleeding profusely. All had been done so silently and swiftly that no one outside of Darrell dreamed of murder, and soon the enforced silence began to be broken by hurried questions and angry exclamations. A man cursed over the loss of his money and a woman sobbed hysterically. Suddenly, Darrell's incisive tones rang through the sleeper.

"For God's sake, see if there is a surgeon aboard! Here is a man stabbed, dying; don't stop to talk of money when a life is at stake!"

Instantly all thought of personal loss was for the time forgotten, and half a dozen men responded to Darrell's appeal. When it became known throughout the train what had occurred, the greatest excitement followed. Train officials, hurrying back and forth, stopped, hushed and horror-stricken, beside the section where Darrell sat holding Whitcomb in his arms. Passengers from the other coaches crowded in, eager to offer assistance that was of no avail. A physician was found and came quickly to the scene, who, after a brief examination, silently shook his head, and Darrell, watching the weakening pulse and shortening gasps, needed no words to tell him that the young life was ebbing fast.

Just as the faint respirations had become almost imperceptible, Whitcomb opened his eyes, looking straight into Darrell's eyes with eager intensity, his face lighted with the winning smile which Darrell had already learned to love. His lips moved; Darrell bent his head still lower to listen.

"Kate,–you will see her," he whispered. "Tell her––" but the sentence was never finished.

Deftly and gently as a woman Darrell did the little which remained to be done for his young friend, closing the eyes in which the love-light kindled by his dying words still lingered, smoothing the dishevelled golden hair, wondering within himself at his own unwonted tenderness.

"An awful pity for a bright young life to go out like that!" said a voice at his side, and, turning, he saw Parkinson.

"How did it happen?" the latter inquired, recognizing Darrell for the first time in the dim light.

Briefly Darrell gave the main facts as he had witnessed them, saying nothing, however, of his having seen the face of the murderer.

"Too bad!" said Parkinson. "He ought never to have made a bluff of that sort; there were too many odds against him."

"He was impulsive and acted on the spur of the moment," Darrell replied; adding, in lower tones, "the mistake was in giving one so young and inexperienced a commission involving so much responsibility and danger."

11

"You knew of the money, then? Yes, that was bad business for him, poor fellow! I wonder, by the way, if it was all taken."

At Darrell's suggestion a thorough search was made, which resulted in the finding of a package containing fifteen thousand dollars which the thief in his haste had evidently overlooked. This, it was agreed, should be placed in Darrell's keeping until the arrival of the train at Ophir.

Gradually the crowd dispersed, most of the passengers returning to their berths. Darrell, knowing that sleep for himself was out of the question, sought an empty section in another part of the car, and, seating himself, bowed his head upon his hands. The veins in his temples seemed near bursting and his usually strong nerves quivered from the shock he had undergone, but of this he was scarcely conscious. His mind, abnormally active, for the time held his physical sufferings in abeyance. He was living over again the events of the past few hours—events which had awakened within him susceptibilities he had not known he possessed, which had struck a new chord in his being whose vibrations thrilled him with strange, undefinable pain. As he recalled Whitcomb's affectionate familiarity, he seemed to hear again the low, musical cadences of the boyish tones, to see the sunny radiance of his smile, to feel the irresistible magnetism of his presence, and it seemed as though something inexpressibly sweet, of whose sweetness he had barely tasted, had suddenly dropped out of his life.

His heart grew sick with bitter sorrow as he recalled the look of mingled appeal and trust which shot from Whitcomb's eyes into his own as his young life, so full of hope, of ambition, of love, was passing through the dim portals of an unknown world. Oh, the pity of it! that he, an acquaintance of but a few hours, should have been the only one to whom those eyes could turn for their last message of earthly love and sympathy; and oh, the impotency of any and all human love then!

Never before had Darrell been brought so near the unseen, the unknown,—always surrounding us, but of which few of us are conscious,—and for hours he sat motionless, lost in thought, grappling with problems hitherto unthought of, but which now perplexed and baffled him at every turn.

At last, with a heavy sigh, he opened his eyes. The gray twilight of dawn was slowly creeping down from the mountain-tops, dispelling the shadows; and the light of a new faith, streaming downward

> "From the beautiful, eternal hills
> Of God's unbeginning past,"

was banishing the doubts which had assailed him.

That night had brought to him a revelation of the awful solitude of a human soul, standing alone on the threshold of two worlds; but it had also revealed to him the Love—Infinite, Divine—that meets the soul when human love and sympathy are no longer of avail.

Chapter III

The Pines

As the day advanced Darrell grew gradually but steadily worse. After the excitement of the night had passed a reaction set in; he felt utterly exhausted and miserable, the pain returned with redoubled violence, and the fever increased perceptibly from hour to hour.

He was keenly observant of those about him, and he could not but note how soon the tragedy of the preceding night seemed forgotten. Some bemoaned the loss of money or valuables; a few, more fortunate, related how they had outwitted the robbers and escaped with trivial loss, but only an occasional careless word of pity was heard for the young stranger who had met so sad a fate. So quickly and completely does one human atom sink out of sight! It is like the dropping of a pebble in the sea: a momentary ripple, that is all!

About noon Parkinson, who had sought to while away the tedium of the journey by an interview with Darrell, became somewhat alarmed at the latter's condition and went in search of a physician. He returned with the one who had been summoned to Whitcomb's aid. He was an eastern practitioner, and, unfortunately for Darrell, was not so familiar with the peculiar symptoms in his case as a western physician would have been.

"He has a high fever," he remarked to Parkinson a little later, as he seated himself beside Darrell to watch the effect of the remedies administered, "but I do not apprehend any danger. I have given him something to abate the fever and induce sleep. If necessary, I will write out a prescription which he can have filled on his arrival at Ophir, but I think in a few days he will be all right."

They were now approaching the continental divide, the scenery moment by moment growing in sublimity and grandeur. Darrell soon sank into a sleep, light and broken at first, but which grew deeper and heavier. For more than an hour he slept, unconscious that the rugged scenes through which he was then passing were to become part of his future life; that each cliff and crag and mountain-peak was to be to him an open book, whose secrets would leave their indelible impress upon his heart and brain, revealing to him the breadth and length, the depth and height of life, moulding his soul anew into nobler, more symmetrical proportions.

At last the rocks suddenly parted, like sentinels making way for the approaching train, disclosing a broad, sunlit plateau, from which rose, in gracefully rounded contours, a pine-covered mountain, about whose base nestled the little city of Ophir, while in the background stretched the majestic range of the great divide.

A crowd could be seen congregated about the depot, for tidings of the night's tragedy had preceded the train by several hours, and Whitcomb from his early boyhood had been a universal favorite in Ophir, while his uncle was one of its wealthiest, most influential citizens.

As the train slackened speed Parkinson, with a few words to the physician, hastily left to make arrangements for transportation for himself, Hunter, and Darrell to a hotel. Amid the noise and confusion which ensued for the next ten minutes Darrell slept heavily, till, roused by a gentle shake, he awoke to find the physician bending over him and heard voices approaching down the now nearly deserted sleeping-car.

"Yes," said a heavy voice, speaking rapidly, "the conductor wired details; he said this young man did everything for the boy that could be done, and stayed by him to the end."

"He did; he stood by him like a brother," Parkinson's voice replied.

"And he is sick, you say? Well, he won't want for anything within my power to do for him, that's all!"

Parkinson stopped at Darrell's side. "Mr. Darrell," he said, "this is Mr. Underwood, Whitcomb's uncle, you know; Mr. Underwood, Mr. Darrell."

Darrell rose a little unsteadily; the two men grasped hands and for an instant neither spoke. Darrell saw before him a tall, powerfully built man, approaching fifty, whose somewhat bronzed face, shrewd, stern, and unreadable, was lighted by a pair of blue eyes which once had resembled Whitcomb's. With a swift, penetrating glance the elder man looked searchingly into the face of the younger.

"True as steel, with a heart of gold!" was his mental comment; then he spoke abruptly, and his voice sounded brusque though his face was working with emotion.

"Mr. Darrell, my carriage is waiting for you outside. You will go home with me, unless," he added, inquiringly, "you are expecting to meet friends or acquaintances?"

"No, Mr. Underwood," Darrell replied, "I am a stranger here, but, much as I appreciate your kindness, I could not think of intruding upon your home at such a time as this."

"Porter," said Mr. Underwood, with the air of one accustomed to command, "take this gentleman's luggage outside, and tell them out there that it is to go to 'The Pines;' my men are there and they will look after it;" then, turning to Darrell, he continued, still more brusquely:

"This train pulls out in three minutes, so you had better prepare to follow your luggage. You don't stop in Ophir outside of my house, and I don't think you'll travel much farther for a while. You look as though you needed a bed and good nursing more than anything else just now."

"I have given him a prescription, sir," said the physician, "that I think will set him right if he gets needed rest and sleep."

"Humph!" responded Mr. Underwood, gruffly; "he'll get whatever he needs, you can depend on that. You gentlemen assist him out of the car; I'll go and despatch a messenger to the house to have everything in readiness for him there."

At the foot of the car steps Darrell parted from the physician and, leaning on Parkinson's arm, slowly made his way through the crowd to the carriage, where Mr. Underwood awaited him. Parkinson having taken leave, Mr. Underwood assisted the young man into the carriage. A spasm of pain crossed Darrell's face as he saw, just ahead of them, waiting to

14

precede them on the homeward journey, a light wagon containing a stretcher covered with a heavy black cloth, a line of stalwart young fellows drawn up on either side, and he recalled Whitcomb's parting words on the previous night,–"When we reach Ophir to-morrow, you'll go directly home with me."

This was observed by Mr. Underwood, who remarked a moment later as he seated himself beside Darrell and they started homeward,–

"This is a sad time to introduce you to our home and household, Mr. Darrell, but you will find your welcome none the less genuine on that account."

"Mr. Underwood," said the young man, in a troubled voice, "this seems to me the most unwarrantable intrusion on my part to accept your hospitality at such a time––"

Before he could say more, Mr. Underwood placed a firm, heavy hand on his knee.

"You stood by my poor boy, Harry, to the last, and that is enough to insure you a welcome from me and mine. I'm only doing what Harry himself would do if he were here."

"As to what I did for your nephew, God knows it was little enough I could do," Darrell answered, bitterly. "I was powerless to defend him against the fatal blow, and after that there was no help for him."

"Did you see him killed?"

"Yes."

"Tell me all, everything, just as it occurred."

Mr. Underwood little knew the effort it cost Darrell in his condition to go over the details of the terrible scene, but he forced himself to give a clear, succinct, calm statement of all that took place. The elder man sat looking straight before him, immovable, impassive, like one who heard not, yet in reality missing nothing that was said. Not until Darrell repeated Whitcomb's dying words was there any movement on his part; then he turned his head so that his face was hidden and remained motionless and silent as before. At last he inquired, –

"Did he leave no message for me?"

"He mentioned only your daughter, Mr. Underwood; he evidently had some message for her which he was unable to give."

A long silence followed. Darrell, utterly exhausted, sank back into a corner of the carriage. The slight movement roused Mr. Underwood; he looked towards Darrell, whose eyes were closed, and was shocked at his deathly pallor. He said nothing, however, for Darrell was again sinking into a heavy stupor, but watched him with growing concern, making no attempt to rouse him until the carriage left the street and began ascending a long gravelled driveway; then putting his hand on Darrell's shoulder, he said, quite loudly,–

"Wake up, my boy! We're getting home now."

To Darrell his voice sounded faint and far away, like an echo out of a vast distance, and it was some seconds before he could realize where he was or form any definite idea of his surroundings. Gradually he became conscious that the air was no longer hot and stifling, but cool and fragrant

15

with the sweet, resinous breath of pines. Looking about him, he saw they were winding upward along an avenue cut through a forest of small, slender pines, which extended below them on one side and far above them on the other.

A moment later they came out into a clearing, whence he could see, rising directly before him, in a series of natural terraces, the slopes of the sombre-hued, pine-clad mountain which overlooked the little city. Upon one of the terraces of the mountain stood a massive house of unhewn granite, a house representing no particular style of architecture, but whose deep bay-windows, broad, winding verandas, and shadowy, secluded balconies all combined to present an aspect most inviting. To Darrell the place had an irresistible charm; he gazed at it as though fascinated, unable to take his eyes from the scene.

"You certainly have a beautiful home, Mr. Underwood," he said, "and a most unique location. I never saw anything quite like it."

"It will do," said the elder man, quietly, gratified by what he saw in his companion's face. "I built it for my little girl. It was her own idea to have it that way, and she has named it 'The Pines.' Thank God, I've got her left yet, but she is about all."

Something in his tone caused Darrell to glance quickly towards him with a look of sympathetic inquiry. They were now approaching the house, and Mr. Underwood turned, facing him, a smile for the first time lighting up his stern, rugged features, as he said,–

"You will find us what my little girl calls a 'patched-up' family. I am a widower; my widowed sister keeps house for me, and Harry, whom I had grown to consider almost a son, was an orphan. But the family, such as it is, will make you welcome; I can speak for that. Here we are!"

With a supreme effort Darrell summoned all his energies as Mr. Underwood assisted him from the carriage and into the house. But the ringing and pounding in his head increased, his brain seemed reeling, and he was so nearly blinded by pain that, notwithstanding his efforts, he was forced to admit to himself, as a little later he sank upon a couch in the room assigned to him, that his impressions of the ladies to whom he had just been presented were exceedingly vague.

Mr. Underwood's sister, Mrs. Dean, he remembered as a large woman, low-voiced, somewhat resembling her brother in manner, and like him, of few words, yet something in her greeting had assured him of a welcome as deep as it was undemonstrative. Of Kate Underwood, in whom he had felt more than a passing interest, remembering Whitcomb's love for his cousin, he recalled a tall, slender, girlish form; a wealth of golden-brown hair, and a pair of large, luminous brown eyes, whose wistful, almost appealing look haunted him strangely, though he was unable to recall another feature of her face.

Mr. Underwood, who had left the room to telephone for a physician, returned with a faithful servant, and insisted upon Darrell's retiring to bed without delay, a proposition which the latter was only too glad to follow. Darrell had already given Mr. Underwood the package of fifteen thousand dollars found on the train, and now, while disrobing, handed him the belt in which he carried his own money, saying,—

"I'll put this in your keeping for a few days, till I feel more like myself. I lost my watch and some change, but I took the precaution to have this hidden."

He stopped abruptly and seemed to be trying to recall something, then continued, slowly,—

"There was something else in connection with that affair which I wished to say to you, but my head is so confused I cannot think what it was."

"Don't try to think now; it will come to you by and by," Mr. Underwood replied. "You're in good hands, so don't worry yourself about anything, but get all the rest you can."

With a deep sigh of relief Darrell sank on the pillows, and was soon sleeping heavily.

A few moments later Mr. Underwood, coming from Darrell's room, having left the servant in charge, met his sister coming down the long hall. She beckoned, and, turning, slowly retraced her steps, her brother following, to another part of the house, where they entered a darkened chamber and together stood beside a low, narrow couch strewn with fragrant flowers. Together, without a word or a tear, they gazed on the peaceful face of this sleeper, wrapped in the breathless, dreamless slumber we call death. They recalled the years since he had come to them, the dying bequest of their youngest sister, a little, golden-haired prattler, to fill their home with the music of his childish voice and the sunshine of his smile. Already the great house seemed strangely silent without his ringing laughter, his bursts of merry song.

But of whatever bitter grief stirred their hearts, this silent brother and sister, so long accustomed to self-restraint and self-repression, gave no sign. Gently she replaced the covering over the face of the sleeper, and silently they left the room. Not until they again reached the door of Darrell's room was the silence broken; then the brother said, in low tones,—

"Marcia, we've done all for the dead that can be done; it's the living who needs our care now."

"Yes," she replied, quietly, "I was going to see what I could do for him when you had put him to bed."

"Bennett is in there now, and I'm going downstairs to wait for Dr. Bradley; he telephoned that he'd be up in twenty minutes."

"Very well; I'll sit by him till the doctor comes."

When Dr. Bradley arrived he found Darrell in a state of coma from which it was almost impossible to arouse him. From Mr. Underwood and his sister he learned whatever details they could furnish, but from the patient himself very little information could be obtained.

"He has this fever that is prevailing in the mountainous districts, and has it in its worst form," he said, when about to take leave. "Of course, having just come from the East, it would be worse for him in any event than if he were acclimated; but aside from that, the cerebral symptoms are greatly aggravated owing to the nervous shock which he received last night.

17

To witness an occurrence of that sort would be more or less of a shock to nerves in a normal state, but in the condition in which he was at the time, it is likely to produce some rather serious complications. Follow these directions which I have written out, and I'll be in again in a couple of hours."

But in two hours Darrell was delirious.

"Has he recognized any one since I was here?" Dr. Bradley inquired, as he again stood beside the patient.

"I don't think so," Mrs. Dean replied. "I could hardly rouse him enough to give him the medicine, and even then he didn't seem to know me."

"I'll be in about midnight," said the physician, as he again took leave, "and I'll send a professional nurse, a man; this is likely to be a long siege."

"Send whatever is needed," said Mr. Underwood, brusquely, "the same as if 'twere for the boy himself!"

"And, Mrs. Dean," the physician continued, "if he should have a lucid interval, you had better ascertain the address of his friends."

It was nearly midnight. For hours Darrell had battled against the darkening shadows fast settling down upon him, enveloping him with a horror worse than death itself. Suddenly there was a rift in the clouds, and the calm, sweet light of reason stole softly through. He felt a cool hand on his forehead, and, opening his eyes, looked with a smile into the face of Mrs. Dean as she bent over him. Bending still lower, she said, in low, distinct tones:

"Can you tell me the name of your people, and where they live?"

In an instant he comprehended all that her question implied; he must give his own name and the address of the far-away eastern home. He strove to recall it, but the effort was too great; before he could speak, the clouds surged together and all was blotted out in darkness.

Chapter IV

Life? or Death?

Hour by hour the clouds thickened, obscuring every ray of light, closing the avenues of sight and sound, until, isolated from the outer world by this intangible yet impenetrable barrier, Darrell was alone in a world peopled only with the phantoms of his imagination. Of the lapse of time, of the weary procession of days and nights which followed, he knew nothing. Day and night were to him only an endless repetition of the horrors which thronged his fevered brain.

Again and again he lived over the tragic scene in the sleeping-car, each iteration and reiteration growing in dreadful realism, until it was he

18

himself who grappled in deadly contest with the murderer, and the latter in turn became a monster whose hot breath stifled him, whose malign, demoniacal glance seemed to sear his eyeballs like living fire. Over and over, with failing strength, he waged the unequal contest, striving at last with a legion of hideous forms. Then, as the clouds grew still more dense about him, these shapes grew dim and he found himself, weak and trembling, adrift upon a sea of darkness whose black waves tossed him angrily, with each breath threatening to engulf him in their gloomy depths. Desperately he battled with them, each struggle leaving him weaker than the last, until at length, scarcely breathing, his strength utterly exhausted, he lay watching the towering forms as they swept relentlessly towards him, gathering strength and fury as they came. He saw the yawning abysses on each side, he heard the roar of the on-coming waves, but was powerless to move hand or foot.

But while he waited in helpless terror the waves on which he tossed to and fro grew calm; then they seemed to divide, and he felt himself going down, down into infinite depths. The sullen roar died away; the darkness was flooded with golden light, and through its ethereal waves he was still floating downward more gently than ever a roseleaf floated to earth on the evening's breath. Through the waves of golden light there came to him a faint, distant murmur of voices, and the words,–

"He is sinking fast!"

He smiled with perfect content, wondering dreamily if it would never end; then consciousness was lost in utter oblivion.

***

Three weeks had elapsed since Darrell came to The Pines. August had given place to September, but the languorous days brought no cessation of the fearful heat, no cooling rain to the panting earth, no promise of renewed life to the drought-smitten vegetation. The timber on the ranges had been reduced to masses of charred and smouldering embers, among which the low flames still crept and crawled, winding their way up and down the mountains. The pall of smoke overhanging the city grew more and more dense, until there came a morning when, as the sun looked over the distant ranges, the landscape was suffused with a dull red glare which steadily deepened until all objects assumed a blood-red hue. Two or three hours passed, and then a lurid light illumined the strange scene, brightening moment by moment, till earth and sky glowed like a mass of molten copper. The heat seemed to concentrate upon that part of the earth's surface, the air grew oppressive, and an ominous silence reigned, in which even the birds were hushed and the dumb brutes cowered beside their masters.

As the brazen glow was fading to a weird, yellow light, an anxious group was gathered about Darrell's bedside. He still tossed and moaned in delirium, but his movements had grown pathetically feeble and the moans were those of a tired child sobbing himself to sleep.

"He cannot hold out much longer," said Dr. Bradley, his fingers on the weakening pulse, "his strength is failing rapidly."

"There will be a change soon, one way or the other," said the nurse, "and there's not much of a chance left him now."

"One chance in a hundred," said Dr. Bradley, slowly; "and that is his wonderful constitution; he may pull through where ninety-nine others would die."

Dr. Bradley watched the sick man in silence, then noting that the room was darkening, he stepped to an open window and cast a look of anxious inquiry at the murky sky. As if in answer to his thought, there came the low rumble of distant thunder, bringing a look of relief and hopefulness to the face of the physician. Returning to the bedside, he gave a few directions, then, as he was leaving, remarked,–

"There will be a change in the weather soon, a change that may help to turn the tide in his favor, provided it does not come too late!"

Hours passed; the distant mutterings grew louder, while the darkness and gloom increased, and the sense of oppression became almost intolerable. Suddenly the leaden mass which had overspread the sky appeared to drop to earth, and in the dead silence which followed could be heard the roar of the wind through the gorges and down the canyons. A moment more, and clouds of dust and débris, the outriders of the coming tempest, rushed madly through the streets in whirling columns towering far above the city. From their vantage ground the dwellers at The Pines watched the course of the storm, but only for a moment; then blinding sheets of water hid even the nearest objects from view, while lightnings flashed incessantly and the thunder crashed and rolled in one ceaseless, deafening roar. The trees waved their arms in wild, helpless terror as one and another of their number were prostrated by the storm, while the dry channels on the mountain-side became raging, foaming torrents. Suddenly the winds changed, a chilling blast swept across the plateau, and to the rush of the wind, the roar of the thunder, and the crash of falling timber was added the sharp staccato of swiftly descending hail.

For nearly an hour the storm raged in its fury, then departed as suddenly as it came; but it left behind a clear atmosphere, crisp as an October morning.

As the storm clouds, touched with beauty by the rays of the setting sun, were settling below the eastern ranges, Dr. Bradley again entered the sick-room. The room was flooded with golden light, and the physician was quick to note the changes which the few hours had wrought in the sick man. The fever had gone and, his strength spent, his splendid energies exhausted, life's forces were ebbing moment by moment.

"He is sinking fast," said Mrs. Dean.

Even as she spoke a smile stole over the pallid features; then, as they watched eagerly for some token of returning consciousness, the nervous system, so long strained to its utmost tension, suddenly relaxed and utter collapse followed.

For hours Darrell lay as one dead, an occasional fluttering about the heart being the only sign of life. But late in the forenoon of the following

20

day the watchers by the bedside, noting each feeble pulsation, thinking it might be the last, felt an almost imperceptible quickening of the life current. Gradually the fluttering pulse grew calm and steady, the faint respirations grew deeper and more regular, until at length, with a long, tremulous sigh, Darrell sank into slumber sweet and restful as a child's, and the watchers knew that the crisis had passed.

Chapter V

John Britton

It was on one of those glorious October days, when every breath quickens the blood and when simply to live is a joy unspeakable, that Darrell first walked abroad into the outdoor world. Several times during his convalescence he had sunned himself on the balcony opening from his room, or when able to go downstairs had paced feebly up and down the verandas, but of late his strength had returned rapidly, so that now, accompanied by his physician, he was walking back and forth over the gravelled driveway under the pine-trees, his step gaining firmness with every turn.

Seated on the veranda were Mr. Underwood and his sister, the one with his pipe and newspaper, the other with her knitting; but the newspaper had slipped unheeded to the floor, and though Mrs. Dean's skilful fingers did not slacken their work for an instant, yet her eyes, like her brother's, were fastened upon Darrell, and a shade of pity might have been detected in the look of each, which the occasion at first sight hardly seemed to warrant.

"Poor fellow!" said Mr. Underwood, at length; "it's hard for a young man to be handicapped like that!"

"Yes," assented his sister, "and he takes it hard, too, though he doesn't say much. I can't bear to look in his eyes sometimes, they look so sort of pleading and helpless."

"Takes it hard!" reiterated Mr. Underwood; "why shouldn't he. I'm satisfied that he is a young man of unusual ability, who had a bright future before him, and I tell you, Marcia, it's pretty hard for him to wake up and find it all rubbed off the slate!"

"Well," said Mrs. Dean, with a sigh, "everybody has to carry their own burdens, but there's a look on his face when he thinks nobody sees him that makes me wish I could help him carry his, though I don't suppose anybody can, for that matter; it isn't anything that anybody feels like saying much about."

"I'm glad Jack is coming," said Mr. Underwood, after a pause; "he may

21

do him some good. He has a way of getting at those things that you and I haven't, Marcia."

"Yes, he's seen trouble himself, though nobody knows what it was."

Notwithstanding the tide of returning vitality was fast restoring tissue and muscle to Darrell's wasted limbs and firmness and elasticity to his step, it was yet evident to a close observer that some undercurrent of suffering was doing its work day by day; sprinkling the dark hair with gleams of silver, tracing faint lines in the face hitherto untouched by care, working its subtle, mysterious changes.

When a new lease of life was granted to John Darrell and he awoke to consciousness, it was to find that every detail of his past life had been blotted out, leaving only a blank. Of his home, his friends, of his own name even, not a vestige of memory was left. It was as though he had entered upon a new existence.

By degrees, as he was able to hear them, he was given the details of his arrival at Ophir, of his coming to The Pines, of the tragedy which he had witnessed in the sleeping-car, but they awoke no memories in his mind. For him there was no past. As a realization of his condition dawned upon him his mental distress was pitiable. Despite the efforts of physician and nurse to divert his mind, he would lie for hours trying to recall some fragment from the veiled and shrouded past, but all in vain. Yet, with returning physical strength, many of his former attainments seemed to return to him, naturally and without effort. Dr. Bradley one day used a Latin phrase in his hearing; he at once repeated it and, without a moment's hesitation, gave the correct rendering, but was unable to tell how he did it.

"It simply came to me," was all the explanation he could give.

From this the physician argued that the memory of his past life would sooner or later return, and it was this hope alone which at that time saved Darrell from total despair.

Aside from his professional interest in so peculiar a case, Dr. Bradley had become interested in Darrell himself; many of his leisure hours were spent at The Pines, and quite a friendship existed between the two.

In Mr. Underwood and his sister Darrell had found two steadfast friends, each seeming to vie with the other in thoughtful, unobtrusive kindness. His strange misfortune had only deepened and intensified the sympathy which had been first aroused by the peculiar circumstances under which he had come to them. But now, as then, they said little, and for this Darrell was grateful. Even the silent pity which he read in their eyes hurt him,—why, he could scarcely explain to himself; expressed in words, it would have been intolerable. Early in his convalescence Darrell had expressed an unwillingness to trespass upon their kindness by remaining after he could with safety be moved, but the few words they had spoken on that occasion had effectually silenced any further suggestion of the kind on his part. He understood that to leave them would be to forfeit their friendship, which he well knew was of a sort too rare to be slighted or thrown aside.

Of Kate Underwood Darrell knew nothing, except as her father or aunt spoke of her, for he had no recollection of her and she had left home early in his illness to return to an eastern college, from which she would graduate the following year.

With more animation than he had yet shown since his illness, Darrell returned to the veranda. He was flushed and trembling slightly from the unusual exertion, and Dr. Bradley, dropping down beside him, from force of habit laid his fingers on Darrell's wrist, but the latter shook them off playfully.

"No more of that!" he exclaimed, adding, "Doctor, I challenge you for a race two weeks from to-day. What do you say, do you take me up?"

"Two weeks from to-day!" repeated the doctor, with an incredulous smile, at the same time scrutinizing Darrell's form. "Well, yes. When you are in ordinary health I don't think I would care to do much business with you along that line, but two weeks from to-day is a safe proposition, I guess. What do you want to make it, a hundred yards?" he inquired, with a laughing glance at Mr. Underwood.

"One hundred yards," replied Darrell, following the direction of the doctor's glance. "Do you want to name the winner, Mr. Underwood?"

"I'll back you, my boy," said the elder man, quietly, his shrewd face growing a trifle shrewder.

"What!" exclaimed Dr. Bradley, rising hastily;

"I guess it's about time I was going, if that's your estimate of my athletic prowess," and, shaking hands with Darrell, he started down the driveway.

"I'll put you up at about ten to one," Mr. Underwood called after the retreating figure, but a deprecatory wave of his hand over his shoulder was the doctor's only reply.

"Oh," exclaimed Darrell, looking about him, "this is glorious! This is one of the days that make a fellow feel that life is worth living!"

Even as he spoke there came to his mind the thought of what life meant to him, and the smile died from his lips and the light from his eyes.

For a moment nothing was said, then, with the approaching sound of rhythmic hoof-beats, Mr. Underwood rose, deliberately emptying the ashes from his pipe as a fine pair of black horses attached to a light carriage appeared around the house from the direction of the stables.

"You will be back for lunch, David?" Mrs. Dean inquired.

"Yes, and I'll bring Jack with me," was his reply, as he seated himself beside the driver, and the horses started at a brisk trot down the driveway.

With a smile Mrs. Dean addressed Darrell, who was watching the horses with a keen appreciation of their good points.

"This 'Jack' that you've heard my brother speak of is his partner."

"Yes?" said Darrell, courteously, feeling slight interest in the expected guest, but glad of anything to divert his thoughts.

"Yes," Mrs. Dean continued; "they've been partners and friends for more than ten years. His name is John Britton, but it's never anything but 'Dave' and 'Jack' between the two; they're almost like two boys together."

Darrell wondered what manner of man this might be who could transform his silent, stern-faced host into anything boy-like, but he said nothing.

23

"To see them together you'd wonder at their friendship, too," continued Mrs. Dean, "for they're noways alike. My brother is all business, and Mr. Britton is not what you'd really call a practical business man. He is very rich, for he is one of those men that everything they touch seems to turn to gold, but he doesn't seem to care much about money. He spends a great deal of his time in reading and studying, and though he makes very few friends, he could have any number of them if he wanted, for he's one of those people that you always feel drawn to without knowing why."

Mrs. Dean paused to count the stitches in her work, and Darrell, whose thoughts were of the speaker more than of the subject of conversation, watching her placid face, wondered whether it were possible for any emotion ever to disturb that calm exterior. Presently she resumed her subject, speaking in low, even tones, which a slight, gentle inflection now and then just saved from monotony.

"He's always a friend to anybody in distress, and I guess there isn't a poor person or a friendless person in Ophir that doesn't know him and love him. He has had some great trouble; nobody knows what it is, but he told David once that it had changed his whole life."

Darrell now became interested, and the dark eyes fixed on Mrs. Dean's face grew suddenly luminous with the quick sympathy her words had aroused.

"He always seems to be on the lookout for anybody that has trouble, to help them; that's how he got to know my brother."

Mrs. Dean hesitated a moment. "I never spoke of this to any one before, but I thought maybe you'd be interested to know about it," she said, looking at Darrell with a slightly apologetic air.

"I am, and I think I understand and appreciate your motive," was his quiet reply.

She dropped her work, folding her hands above it, and her face wore a reminiscent look as she continued:

"When David's wife died, twelve years ago, it was an awful blow to him. He didn't say much,—that isn't our way,—but we were afraid he would never be the same again. His brother was out here at that time, but none of us could do anything for him. He kept on trying to attend to business just as usual, but he seemed, as you might say, to have lost his grip on things. It went on that way for nearly two years; his business got behind and everything seemed to be slipping through his fingers, when he happened to get acquainted with Mr. Britton, and he seemed to know just what to say and do. He got David interested in business again. He loaned him money to start with, and they went into business together and have been together ever since. They have both been successful, but David has worked and planned for what he has, while Mr. Britton's money seems to come to him. He owns property all over the State, and all through the West for that matter, and sometimes he's in one place and sometimes in another, but he never stays very long anywhere. David would like to have him make his home with us, but he told him once that he couldn't think of it; that he only stayed in a place till the pain got to be more than he could bear, and then he went somewhere else."

A long silence followed; then, as Mrs. Dean folded her work, she said, softly,–

"It's no wonder he knows just how to help folks who are in trouble, for I guess he has suffered himself more than anybody knows."

A little later she had gone indoors to superintend the preparations for lunch, but Darrell still sat in the mellow, autumn sunlight, his eyes closed, picturing to himself this stranger silently bearing his hidden burden, changing from place to place, but always keeping the pain.

It still lacked two hours of sunset when John Darrell, leaning on the arm of John Britton, walked slowly up the mountain-path to a rustic seat under the pines. They had met at lunch. Mr. Britton had already heard the strange story of Darrell's illness, and, looking into his eyes with their troubled questioning, their piteous appeal, knew at once by swift intuition how hopelessly bewildering and dark life must look to the young man before him just at the age when it usually is brightest and most alluring; and Darrell, meeting the steadfast gaze of the clear, gray eyes, saw there no pity, but something infinitely broader, deeper, and sweeter, and knew intuitively that they were united by the fellowship of suffering, that mysterious tie which has not only bound human hearts together in all ages, but has linked suffering humanity with suffering Divinity.

For more than two hours Darrell, taking little part himself in the general conversation, had watched, as one entranced, the play of the fine features and listened to the deep, musical voice of this stranger who was a stranger no longer.

He was an excellent conversationalist; humorous without being cynical, scholarly without being pedantic, and showing especial familiarity with history and the natural sciences.

At last, while walking up and down the broad veranda, Mr. Britton had paused beside Darrell, and throwing an arm over his shoulder had said,–

"Come, my son, let us have a little stroll."

Darrell's heart had leaped strangely at the words, he knew not why, and in a silence pregnant with deep emotion on both sides, they had climbed to the rustic bench. Here they sat down. The ground at their feet was carpeted with pine-needles; the air was sweet with the fragrance of the pines and of the warm earth; no sound reached their ears aside from the chirping of the crickets, the occasional dropping of a pine-cone, or the gentle sighing of the light breeze through the branches above their heads.

A glorious scene lay outspread before them; the distant ranges half veiled in purple haze, the valleys flooded with golden light, brightened by the autumnal tints of the deciduous timber which marked the courses of numerous small streams, and over the whole a restful silence, as though, the year's work ended, earth was keeping some grand, solemn holiday.

Mr. Britton first broke the silence, as in low tones he murmured, reverently,–

"'Thou crownest the year with Thy goodness!'"

Then turning to Darrell with a smile of peculiar sweetness, he said, "This is one of what I call the year's 'coronation days,' when even Nature

25

herself rests from her labors and dons her royal robes in honor of the occasion."

Then, as an answering light dawned in Darrell's eyes and the tense lines in his face began to relax, Mr. Britton continued, musingly:

"I have often wondered why we do not imitate Nature in her great annual holiday, and why we, a nation who garners one of the richest harvests of the world, do not have a national harvest festival. How effectively and fittingly, for instance, something similar to the old Jewish feast of tabernacles might be celebrated in this part of the country! In the earliest days of their history the Jews were commanded, when the year's harvest had been gathered, to take the boughs of goodly trees, of palm-trees and willows, and to construct booths in which they were to dwell, feasting and rejoicing, for seven days. In the only account given of one of these feasts, we read that the people brought olive-branches and pine-branches, myrtle-branches and palm-branches, and made themselves booths upon the roofs of their houses, in their courts, and in their streets, and dwelt in them, 'and there was very great gladness.' Imagine such a scene on these mountain-slopes and foot-hills, under these cloudless skies; the sombre, evergreen boughs interwoven with the brightly colored foliage from the lowlands; this mellow, golden sunlight by day alternating with the white, mystical radiance of the harvest moon by night."

Mr. Britton's words had, as he intended they should, drawn Darrell's thoughts from himself. Under his graphic description, accompanied by the powerful magnetism of his voice and presence, Darrell seemed to see the Oriental festival which he had depicted and to feel a soothing influence from the very simplicity and beauty of the imaginary scene.

"Think of the rest, the relaxation, in a week of such a life!" continued Mr. Britton. "Re-creation, in the true sense of the word. The simplest joys are the sweetest, but our lives have grown too complex for us to appreciate them. Our amusements and recreations, as we call them, are often more wearing and exhausting than our labors."

For nearly an hour Mr. Britton led the conversation on general subjects, carefully avoiding every personal allusion; Darrell following, interested, animated, wondering more and more at the man beside him, until the latter tactfully led him to speak—calmly and dispassionately, as he could not have spoken an hour before—of himself. Almost before he was aware, Darrell had told all: of his vain gropings in the darkness for some clue to the past; of the helpless feeling akin to despair which sometimes took possession of him when he attempted to face the situation continuously confronting him.

During his recital Mr. Britton had thrown his arm about Darrell's shoulder, and when he paused quite a silence followed.

"Did it ever occur to you," Mr. Britton said at length, speaking very slowly, "that there are hundreds—yes, thousands—who would be only too glad to exchange places with you to-day?"

"No," Darrell replied, too greatly astonished to say more.

"But there are legions of poor souls, haunted by crime, or crushed beneath the weight of sorrow, whose one prayer would be, if such a thing were possible, that their past might be blotted out; that they might be free to begin life anew, with no memories dogging their steps like spectres, threatening at every turn to work their undoing."

For a moment Darrell regarded his friend with a fixed, inquiring gaze, which gradually changed to a look of comprehension.

"I see," he said at length, "I have got to begin life anew; but you consider that there are others who have to make the start under conditions worse than mine."

"Far worse," said Mr. Britton. "Don't think for a moment that I fail to realize in how many ways you are handicapped or to appreciate the obstacles against which you will have to contend, but this I do say: the future is in your own hands—as much as it is in the hands of any mortal—to make the most of and the best of that you can, and with the negative advantage, at least, that you are untrammelled by a past that can hold you back or drag you down."

The younger man laid his hand on the knee of the elder with a gesture almost appealing. "The future, until now, has looked very dark to me; it begins to look brighter. Advise me; tell me how best to begin!"

"In one word," said Mr. Britton, with a smile. "Work! Just as soon as you are able, find some work to do. Did we but know it, work is the surest antidote for the poisonous discontent and ennui of this world, the swiftest panacea for its pains and miseries; different forms to suit different cases, but every form brings healing and blessing, even down to the humblest manual labor."

"That is just what I have wanted," said Darrell, eagerly; "to go to work as soon as possible; but what can I do? What am I fitted for? I have not the slightest idea. I don't care to work at breaking stone, though I suppose that would be better than nothing."

"That would be better than nothing," said Mr. Britton, smiling again, "but that would not be suited to your case. What you need is mental work, something to keep your mind constantly occupied, and rest assured you will find it when you are ready for it. Our Father provides what we need just when we need it. 'Day by day' we have the 'daily bread' for mental and spiritual life, as for temporal. But what you most want to do is to keep your mind pleasantly occupied, and above all things don't try to recall the past. In God's own good time it will return of itself."

"And when it does, what revelations will it bring?" Darrell queried musingly.

"Nothing that you will be afraid or ashamed to meet; of that I am sure," said Mr. Britton, confidently, adding a moment later, in a lighter tone, "It is nearing sunset, my boy, and time that I was taking you back to the house."

"You have given me new courage, new hope," said Darrell, rising. "I feel now as though there were something to live for—as though I might make something out of life, after all."

"I realize," said Mr. Britton, tenderly, as together they began the descent of the mountain path, "as deeply as you do that your life is sadly disjointed; but strive so to live that when the broken fragments are at last united they will form one harmonious and symmetrical whole. It is a difficult task, I know, but the result will be well worth the effort. In your case, my son, even more than in ordinary lives, the words of the poet are peculiarly applicable:

> "'A sacred burden is this life ye bear:
> Look on it, lift it, bear it solemnly;
> Stand up and walk beneath it steadfastly;
> Fail not for sorrow, falter not for sin,
> But onward, upward, till the goal ye win.'"

An hour later John Britton stood alone on one of the mountain terraces, his tall, lithe form silhouetted against the evening sky, his arms folded, his face lifted upward. It was a face of marvellous strength and sweetness combined. Sorrow had set its unmistakable seal upon his features; here and there pain had traced its ineffaceable lines; but the firmly set mouth was yet inexpressibly tender, the calm brow was unfurrowed, and the clear eyes had the far-seeing look of one who, like the Alpine traveller, had reached the heights above the clouds, to whose vision were revealed glories undreamed of by the dwellers in the vales below.

And to Darrell, watching from his room the distant figure outlined against the sky, the simple grandeur, the calm triumph of its pose must have brought some revelation concerning this man of whom he knew so little, yet whose personality even more than his words had taken so firm a hold upon himself, for, as the light faded and deepening twilight hid the solitary figure from view, he turned from the window, and, pacing slowly up and down the room, soliloquized:

"With him for a friend, I can meet the future with courage and await with patience the resurrection of the buried past. As he has conquered, so will I conquer; I will scale the heights after him, until I stand where he stands to-night!"

Chapter VI

Echoes from the Past

During his stay at The Pines Mr. Britton spent the greater portion of his time with Mr. Underwood, either at their offices or at the mines. Darrell, therefore, saw little of his new-found friend except as they all gathered in the evening around the glowing fire in the large family sitting-room, for, notwithstanding the lingering warmth and sunshine of the days, the nights were becoming sharp and frosty, so that an open fire added much to the evening's enjoyment. Each morning, however, before his departure, Mr. Britton stopped for a few words with Darrell; some quaint, kindly bit of humor, the pleasant flavor of which would enliven the entire day; some unhackneyed expression of sympathy whose very genuineness and sincerity made Darrell's position seem to him less isolated and solitary than before; or some suggestion which, acted upon, relieved the monotony of the tedious hours of convalescence.

At his suggestion Darrell took vigorous exercise each day in the morning air and sunshine, devoting his afternoons to a course of light, pleasant reading.

"If you are going to work," said Mr. Britton, "the first requisite is to have your body and mind in just as healthful and normal a condition as possible, in order that you may be able to give an equivalent for what you receive. In these days of trouble between employer and employed, we hear a great deal about the laborer demanding an honest equivalent for his toil, but it does not occur to him to inquire whether he is giving his employer an honest equivalent for his money. The fact is, a large percentage of working-men and working-women, in all departments of labor, are squandering their energies night after night in various forms and degrees of dissipation until they are utterly incapacitated for one honest day's work; yet they do not hesitate to take a full day's wages, and would consider themselves wronged were the smallest fraction withheld."

Darrell found himself rather restricted in his reading for the first few days, as he found but a limited number of books at The Pines, until Mrs. Dean, who had received a hint from Mr. Britton, meeting him one day in the upper hall, led him into two darkened rooms, saying, as she hastened to open the blinds,—

"These are what the children always called their 'dens.' All their books are here, and I thought maybe you'd like to look them over. If you see anything you like, just help yourself, and use the rooms for reading or writing whenever you want to."

Darrell, left to himself, looked about him with much interest. The two rooms were similar in style and design, but otherwise were as diverse as possible. The room in which he was standing was furnished in embossed leather. A leather couch stood near one of the windows, and a large reclining-chair of the same material was drawn up before the fireplace. Near the mantel was a pipe-rack filled with fine specimens of briar-wood and meerschaum pipes. Signs of tennis, golf, and various athletic sports were visible on all sides; in the centre of the room stood a large roll-top desk, open, and on it lay a briar pipe, filled with ashes, just where the owner's hand had laid it. But what most interested Darrell was a large portrait over the fireplace, which he knew must be that of Harry Whitcomb. The face was neither especially fine nor strong, but the winsome smile lurking about the curves of the sensitive mouth and in the depths of the frank blue eyes rendered it attractive, and it was with a sigh for the young life so suddenly blotted out that Darrell turned to enter the second room.

He paused at the doorway, feeling decidedly out of place, and glanced about him with a serio-comic smile. The furnishings were as unique as possible, no one piece in the room bearing any relation or similarity to any other piece. There were chairs and tables of wicker-work, twisted into the most ornate designs, interspersed among heavy, antique pieces of carving and slender specimens of colonial simplicity; divans covered with pillows of every delicate shade imaginable; exquisite etchings and dainty bric-à-brac. In an alcove formed by a large bay-window stood a writing-desk of ebony inlaid with mother-of-pearl, and on an easel in a secluded corner, partially concealed by silken draperies, was the portrait of Kate Underwood,—a childish, rather immature face, but with a mouth indicating both sweetness and strength of character, and with dark, strangely appealing eyes.

The walls of both rooms were lined with bookcases, but their contents were widely diverse, and, to Darrell's surprise, he found the young girl's library contained far the better class of books. But even in their selection he observed the same peculiarity that he had noted in the furnishing of the room; there were few complete sets of books; instead, there were one, two, or three volumes of each author, as the case might be, evidently her especial favorites.

But Darrell returned to the other room, which interested him far more, each article in it bearing eloquent testimony to the happy young life of whose tragic end he had now often heard, but of which he was unable to recall the faintest memory. Passing slowly through the room, his attention was caught by a violin case standing in an out-of-the-way corner. With a cry of joy he drew it forth, his fingers trembling with eagerness as he opened it and took therefrom a genuine Stradivarius. At that moment his happiness knew no bounds. Seating himself and bending his head over the instrument after the manner of a true violin lover, he drew the bow gently across the strings, producing a chord of such triumphant sweetness that the air seemed vibrating with the joy which at that instant thrilled his own soul.

Immediately all thought of himself or of his surroundings was lost. With eyes half closed and dreamy he began to play, without effort, almost mechanically, but with the deft touch of a master hand, while liquid harmonies filled the room, quivering, rising, falling; at times low, plaintive, despairing; then swelling exultantly, only to die away in tremulous, minor undertones. The man's pent-up feelings had at last found expression,—his alternate hope and despair, his unutterable loneliness and longing,—all voiced by the violin.

Of the lapse of time Darrell had neither thought nor consciousness until the door opened and Mrs. Dean's calm smile and matter-of-fact voice recalled him to a material world.

"I see that you have found Harry's violin," she said.

"I beg your pardon," Darrell stammered, somewhat dazed by his sudden descent to the commonplace, "I ought not to have taken it; I never thought,—I was so delighted to find the instrument and so carried away with its tones,—it never occurred to me how it might seem to you!"

"Oh, that is all right," she interposed, quietly; "use it whenever you like.

Harry bought it two years ago, but he never had the patience to learn it, so it has been used very little. I never heard such playing as yours, and I stepped in to ask you to bring it downstairs and play for us to-night. Mr. Britton will be delighted; he enjoys everything of that sort."

Around the fireside that evening Darrell had an attentive audience, though the appreciation of his auditors was manifested in a manner characteristic of each. Mr. Underwood, after two or three futile attempts to talk business with his partner, finding him very uncommunicative, gave himself up to the enjoyment of his pipe and the music in about equal proportions, indulging surreptitiously in occasional brief naps, though always wide awake at the end of each number and joining heartily in the applause.

Mrs. Dean sat gazing into the glowing embers, her face lighted with quiet pleasure, but her knitting-needles twinkled and flashed in the firelight with the same unceasing regularity, and she doubled and seamed and "slipped and bound" her stitches with the same monotonous precision as on other evenings.

Mr. Britton, in a comfortable reclining-chair, sat silent, motionless, his head thrown back, his eyes nearly closed, but in the varying expression of his mobile face Darrell found both inspiration and compensation.

For more than three hours Darrell entertained his friends; quaint medleys, dreamy waltzes, and bits of classical music following one after another, with no effort, no hesitancy, on the part of the player. To their eager inquiries, he could only answer,–

"I don't know how I do it. They seem to come to me with the sweep of the bow across the strings. I have no recollection of anything that I am playing; it seems as though the instrument and I were simply drifting."

Late in the evening, when they were nearly ready to separate for the night, Darrell sat idly strumming the violin, when an old familiar strain floated sweetly forth, and his astonished listeners suddenly heard him singing in a rich baritone an old love-song, forgotten until then by every one present.

Mrs. Dean had already laid aside her work and sat with hands folded, a smile of unusual tenderness hovering about her lips, while Mr. Britton's face was quivering with emotion. At its conclusion he grasped Darrell's hand silently.

"That is a very old song," said Mrs. Dean. "It seems queer to hear you sing it. I used to hear it sung when I was a young girl, and that," she added smiling, "was a great many years ago."

"And I have sung it many a time a great many years ago," said Mr. Britton. And he hastily left the room.

Chapter VII

At the Mines

Once fairly started on the road to health, Darrell gained marvellously. Each day marked some new acquisition in physical health and muscular vigor, while his systematic reading, the soothing influence of the music to which he devoted a considerable time each day, and, more than all, his growing intimacy with Mr. Britton, were doing much towards restoring a better mental equipoise.

The race to which he had challenged Dr. Bradley took place on a frosty morning early in November, Mr. Underwood himself measuring and marking the course for the runners and Mr. Britton acting as starter. The result was a victory for Darrell, who came out more than a yard ahead of his opponent, somewhat to the chagrin of the latter, who had won quite a local reputation as an athlete.

"You'll do," he said to Darrell, as he took leave a few moments later, "but don't pose here as an invalid any longer, or I'll expose you as a fraud. Understand, I cross your name off my list of patients to-day."

"But not off your list of friends, I hope," Darrell rejoined, as they shook hands.

When Dr. Bradley had gone, Darrell turned to Mr. Britton, who was standing near, saying, as his face grew serious,–

"Dr. Bradley is right; I'm no invalid now, and I must quit this idling. I must find what I can do and go to work."

"All in good time," said Mr. Britton, pleasantly. "We'll find something for you before I go from here. Meanwhile, I want to give you a little pleasure-trip if you are able to take it. How would you like to go out to the mines to-morrow with Mr. Underwood and myself? Do you think you could 'rough it' with us old fellows for a couple of days?"

"You couldn't have suggested anything that would please me better," Darrell answered. "I would like the change, and it's time I was roughing it. Perhaps when I get out there I'll decide to take a pick and shovel and start in at the bottom of the ladder and work my way up."

"Is that necessary?" queried Mr. Britton, regarding the younger man with close but kindly scrutiny. "Mr. Underwood tells me that you brought a considerable amount of money with you when you came here, which he has deposited to your credit."

Darrell met the penetrating gaze unwaveringly, as he replied, with quiet decision, "That money may be mine, or it may not; it may have been given me to hold in trust. In any event, it belongs to the past, and it will remain where it is, intact, until the past is unveiled."

Mr. Britton looked gratified, as he remarked, in a low tone, "I don't think you need any assurance, my boy, that I will back you with all the capital you need, if you would like to start in business."

"No, Mr. Britton," said Darrell, deeply touched by the elder man's

32

kindness; "I know, without words, that I could have from you whatever I needed, but it is useless for me to think of going into business with as little knowledge of myself as I have at present. The best thing for me is to take whatever work offers itself, until I find what I am fitted for or to what I can best adapt myself."

The next morning found Darrell at an early hour on his way to the mining camp with Mr. Underwood and Mr. Britton. The ground was white and glistening with frost, and the sun, not yet far above the horizon, shone with a pale, cold light, but Darrell, wrapped in a fur coat of Mr. Underwood's, felt only the exhilarating effect of the thin, keen air, and as the large, double-seated carriage, drawn by two powerful horses, descended the pine-clad mountain and passed down one of the principal streets of the little city, he looked about him with lively interest.

Leaving the town behind them, they soon began the ascent of a winding canyon. After two or three turns, to Darrell's surprise, every sign of human habitation vanished and only the rocky walls were visible, at first low and receding, but gradually growing higher and steeper. On they went, steadily ascending, till a turn suddenly brought the distant mountains into closer proximity, and Mr. Britton, pointing to a lofty, rugged range on Darrell's right, said,–

"There lies the Great Divide."

For two hours they wound steadily upward, the massive rocks towering on all sides, barren, grotesque in form, but beautiful in coloring,–dull reds, pale greens, and lovely blues and purples staining the sombre grays and browns.

Darrell had grown silent, and his companions, supposing him absorbed in the grandeur and beauty of the scenery, left him to his own reflections while they talked on matters of interest to themselves.

But to Darrell the surrounding rocks were full of a strange, deep significance. The colorings and markings in the gray granite were to him what the insignia of the secret orders are to the initiated, replete with mystical meaning. To him had come the sudden realization that he was in Nature's laboratory, and in the hieroglyphics traced on the granite walls he read the symbols of the mysterious alchemy silently and secretly wrought beneath their surface. The vastness of the scale of Nature's work, the multiplicity of her symbols, bewildered him, but in his own mind he knew that he still held the key to this mysterious code, and the knowledge thrilled him with delight. He gazed about him, fascinated, saying nothing, but trembling with joy and with eagerness to put himself to the test, and it was with difficulty that he controlled his impatience till the long ride should come to an end.

At last they left the canyon and followed a steep road winding up the side of a mountain, which, after an hour's hard climbing, brought them to the mining camp. As the carriage stopped Darrell was the first to alight, springing quickly to the ground and looking eagerly about him.

At a short distance beyond them the road was terminated by the large milling plant, above which the mountain rose abruptly, its sides dotted with shaft-houses and crossed and recrossed with trestle-work almost to the summit. A wooden flume clung like a huge serpent to the steep slopes, and a tramway descended from near the summit to the mill below. At a little distance from the mill were the boarding-house and bunk-houses, while in the foreground, near the road was the office building, to which the party adjourned after exchanging greetings with Mr. Hathaway, the superintendent, who had come out to meet them and to whom Darrell was duly introduced. The room they first entered was the superintendent's office. Beyond that was a pleasant reception-room, while in the rear were the private rooms of the superintendent and the assayer, who were not expected to share the bunk-houses with the miners.

Mr. Underwood and the superintendent at once proceeded to business, but Mr. Britton, mindful of Darrell's comfort, ushered him into the reception-room. A coal-fire was glowing in a small grate; a couch, three or four comfortable chairs, and a few books and magazines contributed to give the room a cosey appearance, but the object which instantly riveted Darrell's attention was a large case, extending nearly across one side of the room, filled with rare mineralogical and geological specimens. There were quartz crystals gleaming with lumps of free-milling gold, curling masses of silver and copper wire direct from the mines, gold nuggets of unusual size and brilliancy, and specimens of ores from the principal mines not only of that vicinity, but of the West.

Observing Darrell's interest in the contents of the case, Mr. Britton threw open the doors for a closer inspection, and began calling his attention to some of the finest specimens, but at Darrell's first remarks he paused, astonished, listened a few moments, then stepping to the next room, called Mr. Underwood. That gentleman looked somewhat perturbed at the interruption, but at a signal from Mr. Britton, followed the latter quietly across the room to where Darrell was standing. Here they stood, silently listening, while Darrell, unconscious of their presence, went rapidly through the specimens, classifying the different ores, stating the conditions which had contributed to their individual characteristics, giving the approximate value of each and the mode of treatment required for its reduction; all after the manner of a student rehearsing to himself a well-conned lesson.

At last, catching sight of the astonished faces of his listeners, his own lighted with pleasure, as he exclaimed, joyously,—

"I wanted to test myself and see if it would come back to me, and it has! I believed it would, and it has!"

"What has come back to you?" queried Mr. Underwood, too bewildered himself to catch the drift of Darrell's meaning.

"The knowledge of all this," Darrell answered, indicating the collection with a swift gesture; "it began to come to me as soon as I saw the rocks on our way up; it confused me at first, but it is all clear now. Take me to your mill, Mr. Underwood; I want to see what I can do with the ores there."

At that moment Mr. Hathaway entered to summon the party to dinner, and seeing Darrell standing by the case, his hands filled with specimens, he said, addressing Mr. Underwood with a pleasant tone of inquiry,—

"Mr. Darrell is a mining man?"

But Mr. Underwood was still too confused to answer intelligibly, and it was Mr. Britton who replied, as he linked his arm within Darrell's on turning to leave the room,—

"Mr. Darrell is a mineralogist."

At dinner Darrell found himself too excited to eat, so overjoyed was he at the discovery of attainments he had not dreamed he possessed, and so eager to put them to every test possible.

It had been Mr. Underwood's intention to visit the mines that afternoon, but at Darrell's urgent request, they went first to the mill. Here he found ample scope for his abilities. He fairly revelled in the various ores, separating, assorting, and classifying them with the rapidity and accuracy of an expert, and at once proceeded to assay some samples taken from a new lead recently struck, the report of which had occasioned this particular trip to the camp. He worked with a dexterity and skill surprising in one of his years, producing the most accurate results, to the astonishment and delight of both Mr. Underwood and Mr. Britton.

After an extended inspection of the different departments of the large milling plant, he was taken into a small laboratory, where the assayer in charge was testing some of the recently discovered ore for the presence of certain metals. After watching for a while in silence Darrell said, turning to Mr. Underwood,—

"I can give you a quicker and a surer test than that!"

The assayer and himself at once exchanged places, and, unheeding the many eyes fixed upon him, Darrell seated himself before the long table and deftly began operations. Not a word broke the silence as by methods wholly new to his spectators he subjected the ore to successive chemical changes, until, within an incredibly short time, the presence of the suspected metals was demonstrated beyond the shadow of a doubt.

"Mineralogist and metallurgist!" exclaimed Mr. Britton delightedly, as he congratulated Darrell upon his success.

The short November day had now nearly drawn to a close, and after supper the gentlemen adjourned to the office building, where they spent an hour or more around the open fire. Darrell, who was quite wearied with the unusual exertion and excitement of the day, retired early, the superintendent and assayer had gone out on some business at the mill, and Mr. Underwood and Mr. Britton were left together. No sooner were they by themselves than Mr. Britton, who was walking up and down the room, stopped beside his partner as he sat smoking and gazing abstractedly into the fire, and, laying a hand on his shoulder, said,—

"Well, Dave, what do you think? After what we've seen to-day, can't you make a place over there at the mill for the boy?"

"Hang it all!" answered the other, somewhat testily, secretly a little jealous of the growing intimacy between his partner and Darrell; "supposing I can, is there any need of your dipping in your oar about it? Do you think I need any suggestion from you in the way of befriending him or standing by him?"

"No, Dave," said Mr. Britton, pleasantly, dropping into a chair by Mr. Underwood's side, "I did not put my question with a view of making any

35

suggestions. I know, and Darrell knows, that he hasn't a better friend than you, and because I know this, and also because I am a friend to you both, I was interested to ask you what you intended doing for him."

"What I intended doing for him and what I probably will actually do for him are two altogether different propositions—all on account of his own pig-headedness," was the rather surly response.

"How's that?" Mr. Britton inquired.

"Why, confound the fellow! I took a liking to him from the first, coming here the way he did, and after what he did for Harry there was nothing I wouldn't have done for him. Then, after his sickness, when we found his memory had gone back on him and left him helpless as a child in some ways, I knew he'd stand no show among strangers, and my idea was to take him in, in Harry's place, give him a small interest in the business until he got accustomed to it, and then after a while let him in as partner. But when I broached the subject to him, a week ago or so, he wouldn't hear to it; said he'd rather find some work for which he was adapted and stick to that, at a regular salary. I told him he was missing a good thing, but nothing that I could say would make any difference."

"Well," said Mr. Britton, slowly, "I'm not sure but his is the wiser plan. You must remember, Dave, that his stay with us will probably be but temporary. Whenever that portion of his brain which is now dormant does awaken, you can rest assured he will not remain here long. He no doubt realizes this and wishes to be absolutely foot-loose, ready to leave at short notice. And as to the financial side of the question, if you give him the place in your mill for which he is eminently fitted, it will be fully as remunerative in the long run as the interest in the business which you intended giving him."

"What place in the mill do you refer to?" Mr. Underwood asked, quickly.

"Oh, I'm not making any 'suggestions,' Dave; you don't need them." And Mr. Britton smiled quietly into the fire.

"Go ahead and say your say, Jack," said the other, his own face relaxing into a grim smile; "that was only a bit of my crankiness, and you know me well enough to know it."

"Give him the position of assayer in charge."

"Great Scott! and fire Benson, who's been there for five years?"

"It makes no difference how long he's been there. Darrell is a better man every way,—quicker, more accurate, more scientific. You can put Benson to sorting and weighing ores down at the ore-bins."

After a brief silence Mr. Britton continued, "You couldn't find a better man for the place or a better position for the man. The work is evidently right in the line of his profession, and therefore congenial; and even though you should pay him no more salary than Benson, that, with outside work in the way of assays for neighboring camps, will be better than any business interest you would give him short of twelve or eighteen months at least."

"I guess you're right, and I'll give him the place; but hang it all! I did want to put him in Harry's place. You and I are getting along in years, Jack,

36

and it's time we had some young man getting broke to the harness, so that after a while he could take the brunt of things and let us old fellows slack up a bit."

"We could not expect that of Darrell," said Mr. Britton. "He is neither kith nor kin of ours, and when once Nature's ties begin to assert themselves in his mind, we may find our hold upon him very slight."

Both men sighed deeply, as though the thought had in some way touched an unpleasant chord. After a pause, Mr. Britton inquired,—

"You have no clue whatever as to Darrell's identity, have you?"

Mr. Underwood shook his head. "Queerest case I ever saw! There wasn't a scrap of paper nor a pen-mark to show who he was. Parkinson, the mine expert who was on the same train, said he didn't remember seeing him until Harry introduced him; he said he supposed he was some friend of Harry's. Since his sickness I've looked up the conductor on that train and questioned him, but all he could remember was that he boarded the train a little this side of Galena and that he had a ticket through from St. Paul."

"You say this Parkinson was a mine expert; what was he doing out here?"

"He was one of three or four that were here at that time, looking up the Ajax for eastern parties."

"In all probability," said Mr. Britton, musingly, "Darrell was here on the same business."

"If that was his business, he said nothing about it to me, and I would have thought he would, under the circumstances."

"I wonder whether we could ascertain from the owners of the Ajax what experts were out here or expected out here at that time?"

Mr. Underwood smiled grimly. "Not from the former owners, for nobody knows where they are, though there are some people quite anxious to know; and not from the present owners, for they are too busy looking for their predecessors in interest to think of anything else."

"Why, has the Ajax really changed owners? Did they find any one to buy it?"

"Yes, a Scotch syndicate bought it. They sent over a man one of their own number, I believe, and authorized to act for them—that I guess knew more about sampling liquors than ores. The Ajax people worked him accordingly, with the result that the mine was sold at the figure named,— one million, half down, you know. The man rushed back to New York, to meet a partner whom he had cabled to come over. About ten days later they arrived on the ground and began operations at the Ajax. The mill ran for just ten days when they discovered the condition of affairs and shut down, and they have been looking for the former owners ever since."

Both men laughed, then relapsed into silence. A little later, as Mr. Britton stirred the fire to a brighter glow, he said, while the tender curves about his mouth deepened,—

"I cannot help feeling that the coming to us of this young man, whose identity is wrapped in so much mystery, has some peculiar significance to each of us. I believe that in some way, whether for good or ill I cannot tell, his life is to be henceforth inseparably linked with our own lives. He already holds, as you know, a place in each of our hearts which no stranger has held before, and I have only this to say, David, old friend, that our mutual regard for him, our mutual efforts for his well-being, must never lead to any estrangement between ourselves. We have been stanch friends for too many years for any one at this late date to come between us; and you must never envy me my little share in the boy's friendship."

The two men had risen and now stood before the fire with clasped hands.

"I was an old fool to-night, Jack; that was all," said Mr. Underwood, rather gruffly. "I haven't the knack of saying things that you have,—never had,—but I'm with you all the time."

On the forenoon of the following day Darrell was shown the underground workings of the various mines, not excepting the Bird Mine, located almost at the summit of the mountain. This was the newest mine in camp, but, in proportion to its development, the best producer of all.

After an early dinner there was a private meeting in the reception-room beyond the office, at which were present only Mr. Underwood, Mr. Britton, and Darrell, and at which Mr. Underwood duly tendered to Darrell the position of assayer in charge at the Camp Bird mill, which the latter accepted with a frank and manly gratitude which more than ever endeared him to the hearts of his two friends. In this little proceeding Mr. Britton purposely took no part, standing before the grate, his back towards the others, gazing into the fire as though absorbed in his own thoughts. When all was over, however, he congratulated Darrell with a warmth and tenderness which filled both the heart and the eyes of the latter to overflowing. That night, after their arrival at The Pines, as Mr. Britton and Darrell took their accustomed stroll, the latter said,—

"Mr. Britton, I feel that I have you to thank for my good fortune of to-day. You had nothing to say when Mr. Underwood offered me that position, but, nevertheless, I believe the offer was made at your suggestion. It was, in reality, your kindness, not his."

"You are partly right and partly wrong," replied Mr. Britton, smiling. "Never doubt Mr. Underwood's kindness of heart towards yourself. If I had any part in that affair, it was only to indicate the channel in which that kindness should flow."

Together they talked of the strange course of events which had finally brought him and the work for which he was especially adapted together.

"Do you know," said Mr. Britton, as they paused on the veranda before entering the house, "I am no believer in accident. I believe that of the so-called 'happenings' in our lives, each has its appointed time and mission; and it is not for us to say which is trivial or which is important, until, knowing as we are known, we look back upon life as God sees it."

Chapter VIII

"Until the Day Break"

A week later Darrell was duly installed at the mining camp. Mr. Britton had already left, called on private business to another part of the State. After his departure, life at The Pines did not seem the same to Darrell. He sorely missed the companionship—amounting almost to comradeship, notwithstanding the disparity of their years—which had existed between them from their first meeting, and he was not sorry when the day came for him to exchange the comfort and luxury with which the kindness of Mr. Underwood and his sister had surrounded him for the rough fare and plain quarters of the mining camp.

Mrs. Dean, when informed of Darrell's position at the camp, had most strenuously objected to his going, and had immediately stipulated that he was to return to The Pines every Saturday and remain until Monday.

"Of course he's coming home every Saturday, and as much oftener as he likes," her brother had interposed. "This is his home, and he understands it without any words from us."

On the morning of his departure he realized as never before the depth of the affection of his host and hostess for himself, manifesting itself as it did in silent, unobtrusive acts of homely but heartfelt kindness. As the storing of Darrell's belongings in the wagon which was to convey him to the camp was about completed, Mrs. Dean appeared, carrying a large, covered basket, with snow-white linen visible between the gaping edges of the lids. This she deposited within the wagon, saying, as she turned to Darrell,—

"There's a few things to last you through the week, just so you don't forget how home cooking tastes."

And at the last moment there was brought from the stables at Mr. Underwood's orders, for Darrell's use in going back and forth between The Pines and the camp, a beautiful bay mare which had belonged to Harry Whitcomb, and which, having sadly missed her young master, greeted Darrell with a low whinny, muzzling his cheek and nosing his pockets for sugar with the most affectionate familiarity.

It was a cold, bleak morning. The ground had frozen after a heavy rain, and the wagon jolted roughly over the ruts in the canyon road, making slow progress. The sky was overcast and straggling snowflakes wandered aimlessly up and down in the still air.

Darrell, from his seat beside the driver, turned occasionally to speak to Trix, the mare, fastened to the rear end of the wagon and daintily picking her way along the rough road. Sometimes he hummed a bit of half-remembered song, but for the most part he was silent. While not attempting any definite analysis of his feelings, he was distinctly conscious of conflicting emotions. He was deeply touched by the kindness of Mr. Underwood and Mrs. Dean, and felt a sort of self-condemnation that he was not more responsive to their affection. He knew that their home and hearts were alike open to him; that he was as welcome as one of their own flesh and blood; yet he experienced a sense of relief at having escaped from the unvarying kindliness for which, at heart, he was profoundly grateful. Even late that night, in the solitude of his plainly furnished room, with the wind moaning outside and the snow tapping with muffled fingers against the window pane, he yet exulted in a sense of freedom and happiness hitherto unknown in the brief period which held all he recalled of life.

The ensuing days and weeks passed pleasantly and swiftly for Darrell. He quickly familiarized himself with the work which he had in charge, and frequently found leisure, when his routine work was done, for experiments and tests of his own, as well as for outside work which came to him as his skill became known in neighboring camps. His evenings were well filled, as he had taken up his old studies along the lines of mineralogy and metallurgy, pushing ahead into new fields of research and discovery, studying by night and experimenting by day. Meanwhile, the rocky peaks around him seemed beckoning him with their talismanic signs, as though silently challenging him to learn the mighty secrets for ages hidden within their breasts, and he promised himself that with the return of lengthening days, he would start forth, a humble learner, to sit at the feet of those great teachers of the centuries. He had occasional letters from Mr. Britton, cheering, inspiring, helpful, much as his presence had been, and in return he wrote freely of his present work and his plans for future work.

Sometimes, when books were closed or the plaintive tones of the violin had died away in silence, he would sit for hours pondering the strange problem of his own life; watching, listening for some sign from out the past; but neither ray of light nor wave of sound came to him. His physician had told him that some day the past would return, and that the intervening months or years as the case might be, would then doubtless be in turn forgotten, and as he revolved this in his mind he formed a plan which he at once proceeded to put into execution.

On his return one night from a special trip to Ophir he went to his room with more than usual haste, and opening a package in which he seemed greatly interested, drew forth what appeared to be a book, about eleven by fifteen inches in size, bound in flexible morocco and containing some five or six hundred pages. The pages were blank, however, and bound according to an ingenious device which he had planned and given the binder, by which they could be removed and replaced at will, and, if necessary, extra pages could be added.

For some time he stood by the light, turning the volume over and over with an expression of mingled pleasure and sadness; then removing some of the pages, he sat down and prepared to write. The new task to which he had set himself was the writing of a complete record, day by day, of this present life of his, beginning with the first glimmerings of memory, faint and confused, in the earliest days of his convalescence at The Pines. He dipped his pen, then hesitated; how should this strange volume be inscribed?

Only for a moment; then his pen was gliding rapidly over the spotless surface, and the first page, when laid aside, bore the following inscription:

"To one from the outer world, whose identity is hidden among the secrets of the past:
"With the hope that when the veil is lifted these pages may assist him in uniting into one perfect whole the strangely disjointed portions of his life, they are inscribed by

"John Darrell."

Below was the date, and then followed the words,—

"Until the day break, and the shadows flee away."

After penning the last words he paused, repeating them, vainly trying to recall when or where he had heard them. They seemed to ring in his ears like a strain of melody wafted from some invisible shore, and blending with the minor undertone he caught a note of triumph. They had come to him like a voice from out the past, but ringing with joyful assurance for the future; the assurance that the night, however dark, must end in a glorious dawning, in which no haunting shadow would have an abiding-place.

Chapter IX

Two Portraits

The winter proved to be mild and open, so that Darrell's weekly visits to The Pines were made with almost unbroken regularity, and to his surprise he discovered as the months slipped away that, instead of a mere obligation which he felt bound to perform, they were becoming a source of pleasure. After a week of unremitting toil and study and contact with the rough edges of human nature, there was something unspeakably restful in the atmosphere of that quiet home; something soothing in the silent, steadfast affection, the depth of which he was only beginning to fathom.

One Saturday evening in the latter part of April Darrell was, as usual, descending the canyon road on his way to The Pines. For weeks the winter had lingered as though loath to leave, and Darrell, absorbed in work and study, had gone his way, hiding his loneliness and suffering so deeply as to be ofttimes forgotten even by himself, and at all times unsuspected by those about him. Then, in one night had come the warm breath of the west

41

winds, and within a few hours the earth was transformed as though by magic, and the restless longing within his breast awoke with tenfold intensity.

As he rode along he was astounded at the changes wrought in one week. From the southern slopes of the mountains the snow had almost disappeared and the sunny exposures of the ranges were fast brightening into vivid green. The mountain streams had burst their icy fetters and, augmented by the melting snows, were roaring tumultuously down their channels, tumbling and plunging over rocky ledges in sheets of shimmering silver or foaming cascades; then, their mad frolic ended, flowing peacefully through distant valleys onward to the rivers, ever chanting the song which would one day blend in the great ocean harmonies.

The frail flowers, clinging to the rocks and smiling fearlessly up into the face of the sun, the silvery sheen of the willows along the distant water-courses, the softened outlines and pale green of budding cottonwoods in the valleys far below, all told of the newly released life currents bounding through the veins of every living thing. From the lower part of the canyon, the wild, ecstatic song of a robin came to him on the evening breeze, and in the slanting sunbeams myriads of tiny midges held high carnival. The whole earth seemed pulsating with new life, and tree and flower, bird and insect were filled anew with the unspeakable joy of living.

Amid this universal baptism of life, what wonder that he felt his own pulse quicken and the warm life-blood leaping swiftly within his veins! His heart but throbbed in unison with the great heart of Nature, but its very beating stifled him as the sense of his own restrictions came back upon him with crushing weight. For one moment he paused, his spirit struggling wildly against the bars imprisoning it; then, with a look towards the skies of dumb, appealing anguish, he rode onward, his head bowed, his heart sick with unutterable longing.

Arriving at The Pines, he received the usual welcome, but neither its undemonstrative affection nor the restful quiet of the old home could soothe or satisfy him that night. But if his host and hostess noted the gloom on his face or his restless manner they made no comments and asked no questions.

On going upstairs at a late hour he went across the hall to the libraries in search of a book with which to pass away the time, as he was unable to sleep. He had no definite book in mind and wandered aimlessly through both rooms, reading titles in an abstracted manner, until he came at last face to face with the picture of Kate Underwood.

He had seen it many times without especially observing it, but in his present mood it appealed to him as never before. The dark eyes seemed fixed upon his face with a look of entreaty from which he could not escape, and, drawing a chair in front of the easel, he sat down and became absorbed in a study of the picture. Heretofore he had considered it merely the portrait of a very young and somewhat plain girl. Now he was surprised to find that the more it was studied in detail, the more favorable was the impression produced. Though childish and immature, there was not a weak line in the face. The nose and mouth were especially fine, the former denoting distinct individuality, the latter marked strength and sweetness of character; and while the upper part of the face indicated keen perceptions and quick sympathies, the general contour showed a nature strong either to do or to endure. The eyes were large and beautiful, but it was not their beauty which riveted Darrell's attention; it was their look of wistful appeal, of unsatisfied longing, which led him at last to murmur, while his eyes moistened,–

"You dear child! How is it that in your short life, surrounded by all that love can provide, you have come to know such heart hunger as that?"

Long after he had returned to his room those eyes still haunted him, nor could he banish the conviction that some time, somewhere, in that young life there had been an unfilled void which in some degree, however slight, corresponded to the blank emptiness of his own.

The next morning Darrell attended church with Mrs. Dean. The latter was a strict church-woman, and Darrell, by way of showing equal courtesy to host and hostess, usually accompanied her in the morning, devoting the afternoon to Mr. Underwood.

After lunch he and Mr. Underwood seated themselves in one of the sunny bay-windows for their customary chat, Mrs. Dean having gone to her room for the afternoon nap which was as much a part of her Sunday programme as the morning sermon.

For a while they talked of the latest developments at the mines, but Mr. Underwood seemed preoccupied, gazing out of the window and frowning heavily. At last, after a long silence, he said, slowly,–

"I expect we're going to have trouble at the camp this season."

"How is that?" Darrell asked quickly, in a tone of surprise.

"Oh, it's some of this union business," the other answered, with a gesture of impatience, "and about the most foolish proposition I ever heard of, at that. But," he added, decidedly, "they know my position; they know they'll get no quarter from me. I've steered clear of them so far; they've let me alone and I've let them alone, but when it comes to a parcel of union bosses undertaking to run my business or make terms to me, I'll fight 'em to a finish, and they know it."

Darrell, watching the face of the speaker, saw the lines about his mouth harden and his lips settle into a grim smile that boded no good to his opponents.

"What do they want–higher wages or shorter hours?" he inquired.

"Neither," said Mr. Underwood, shortly, as he re-lighted his pipe. After a few puffs he continued:

"As I said before, it's the most foolish proposition I ever heard of. You see, there's five or six camps, all told, in the neighborhood of our camp up there. One or two of the lot, like the Buckeye group, for instance, are run by men that haven't much capital, and I suppose are working as economically as they can. Anyhow, there's been some kicking over there among the miners about the grub, and the upshot of the whole thing is that the union has taken the matter in hand and is going to open a union boarding-house and take in the men from all the camps at six bits a day for each man, instead of the regular rate of a dollar a day charged by the mining companies."

"The scale of wages to remain the same, I suppose," said Darrell; "so that means a gain to each man of twenty-five cents a day?"

"Exactly," said Mr. Underwood. "It means a gain of two bits a day to each man; it means loss and inconvenience to the companies, and it means a big pile of money in the pockets of the bosses who are running the thing."

"There are not many of the owners up there that can stand that sort of thing," said Darrell, reflectively.

"Of course they can't stand it, and they won't stand it if they've got any backbone! Take Dwight and Huntley; they've been to heavy expense in enlarging their mill and have just put up a new boarding-house, and they're in debt; they can't afford to have all that work and expenditure for nothing. Now, with us the loss wouldn't be so great as with the others, for we don't make so much out of our boarding-house. My motto has always been 'Live and let live,' and I give my men a good table,—just what I'd want for myself if I were in their places. It isn't the financial part that troubles me. What I object to is this: I won't have my men tramping three-quarters of a mile for meals that won't be as good as they can get right on their own grounds; more than that, I've got a good, likely set of men, and I won't have them demoralized by herding them in with the tough gangs from those other camps; and above all and once for all,"—here Mr. Underwood's tones became excited as he exclaimed, with an oath,—"I've always been capable of running my own business, and I'll run it yet, and no damned union boss will ever run it for me!"

"How do the men feel about it? Have you talked with them?" Darrell inquired.

"There isn't one of them that's dissatisfied or would leave of his own free will," Mr. Underwood replied, "but I don't suppose they would dare to stand out against the bosses. Why, man, if the workingmen only knew it, they are ten times worse slaves to the union bosses than ever they were to corporations. They have to pay over their wages to let those fellows live like nabobs; they have to come and go at their beck and call, and throw up good positions and live in enforced idleness because of some other fellows' grievances; they don't dare express an opinion or say their souls are their own. Humph!"

"Mr. Underwood," said Darrell, who had been smilingly listening to the other's tirade, "what will you do if this comes to a strike?"

"Strike!" he exclaimed in tones of scathing contempt. "Strike? I'll strike too, and they'll find I can strike just as hard as they can, and a little harder!"

"Will you close down?"

The shrewd face grew a bit shrewder. "If it's necessary to close down," he remarked, evasively, "I'll close down. I guess I can stand it as long as they can. Those mines have lain there in those rocks idle for centuries, for aught that I know; 'twon't hurt 'em to lie idle a few weeks or months now; nobody'll run off with 'em, I guess."

Darrell laughed aloud. "Well, one thing is certain, Mr. Underwood; I, for one, wouldn't want to quarrel with you!"

Mr. Underwood slowly shook his head. "You'd better not try it, my boy; you'd better not!"

"When do you expect this trouble to come to a head?" Darrell asked at length.

"Some time in the early part of July, probably; they expect to get their arrangements completed by that time."

A long silence followed; Mrs. Dean came softly into the room and took her accustomed seat, and, as Mr. Underwood made it a point never to talk of business matters in his sister's presence, nothing more was said regarding the prospective disturbance at the mines.

After dinner the beauty of the sunset brought them out upon the veranda. The air was warm and fragrant with the breath of spring. The buds were swelling on the lilacs near the house, and out on the lawn, beyond the driveway, millions of tiny spears of living green trembled in the light breeze.

"David," said Mrs. Dean, presently, "have you shown Mr. Darrell that picture of Katherine that came yesterday?"

"I declare! No; I had forgotten it!" Mr. Underwood exclaimed.

"It's well for you she isn't here to hear you say that!" Mrs. Dean remarked, smiling.

"Puss knows her old father well enough to know he wouldn't forget her very long. Bring the picture out, Marcia."

Darrell heard Mrs. Dean approaching, and turned, with the glory of the sunset in his eyes.

"Don't you want to see Katherine's new picture?" she inquired.

Her words instantly recalled the portrait he had studied the preceding night, and with that in his mind he took the picture she handed him and silently compared the two.

Ah, the beauty of the spring, everywhere confronting him, was in that face also; the joy of a life as yet pure, untainted, and untrammelled. It was like looking into the faces of the spring flowers which reflect only the sunshine, the purity and the sweetness of earth. There was a touch of womanly dignity, too, in the poise of the head, but the beautiful eyes, though lighted with the faint dawn of coming womanhood, were the same as those that had appealed to him the night before with their wistful longing.

"It is a fine portrait, but as I do not remember her, I cannot judge whether it is like herself or not," he said, handing the picture to Mr. Underwood, who seemed almost to devour it with his eyes, though he spoke no word and not a muscle moved in his stern, immobile face.

"She is getting to be such a young lady," remarked Mrs. Dean, "that I expect when she comes home we will feel as though she had grown away from us all."

"She will never do that, Marcia, never!" said Mr. Underwood, brusquely, as he abruptly left the group and went into the house.

There was a moment's silence, then Mrs. Dean said, in a low tone,–

45

"She is getting to look just like her mother. I haven't seen David so affected since his wife died as he was when that picture came yesterday."

Darrell bowed silently, in token that he understood.

"She was a lovely woman, but she was very different from any of our folks," she added, with a sigh, "and I guess Katherine is going to be just like her."

"When is Miss Underwood expected home?" Darrell inquired.

"About the last of June," was the reply.

Long after the sun had set Darrell paced up and down the veranda, pausing at intervals to gaze with unseeing eyes out over the peaceful scene below him, his only companions his own troubled thoughts. The young moon was shining, and in its pale radiance his set face gleamed white like marble.

Like, and yet unlike, it was to the face of the sleeper journeying westward on that summer afternoon eight months before. Experience, the mighty sculptor, was doing his work, and doing it well; only a few lines as yet, here and there, and the face was already stronger, finer. But it was the face of one hardened by his own sufferings, not softened by the sufferings of others. The sculptor's work was as yet only begun.

Chapter X

The Communion of Two Souls

Gradually the springtide crept upward into the heart of the mountains, quickening the pulses of the rocks themselves until even the mosses and lichens slumbering at their feet awakened to renewed life. Bits of green appeared wherever a grass root could push its way through the rocky soil, and fragile wild flowers gleamed, starlike, here and there, fed by tiny rivulets which trickled from slowly melting snows on the summits far above.

With the earliest warm days Darrell had started forth to explore the surrounding mountains, eager to learn the secrets which they seemed ever challenging him to discover. New conditions confronted him, sometimes baffling him, but always inciting to renewed effort. His enthusiasm was so aroused that often, when his day's work was done, taking a light lunch with him, he pursued his studies while the daylight lasted, walking back in the long twilight, and in the solitude of his room making full notes of the results of that day's research before retiring for the night.

Returning one evening from one of these expeditions he saw, pacing back and forth before the office building, a figure which he at once recognized as that of Mr. Britton. Instantly all thought of work or weariness was forgotten, and he hastened forward, while Mr. Britton, catching sight of Darrell rapidly approaching, turned and came down the road to meet him.

"A thousand welcomes!" Darrell cried, as soon as they were within speaking distance; "say, but this is glorious to see you here! How long have I kept you waiting?"

"A few hours, but that does not matter; it does us good to have to stop and call a halt on ourselves once in a while. How are you, my son?" And as the two grasped hands the elder man looked searchingly through the gathering dusk into the face of the younger. Even in the dim twilight, Darrell could feel that penetrating glance reading his inmost soul.

"I am well and doing well," he answered; "my physical health is perfect; as for the rest—your coming is the very best thing that could have happened. Are you alone?" he asked, eagerly, "or did Mr. Underwood come with you?"

"I came alone," Mr. Britton replied, with quiet emphasis, linking his arm within Darrell's as they ascended the road together.

"How long have you been in town?"

"But two days. I am on my way to the coast, and only stopped off for a few days. I shall spend to-morrow with you, go back with you Saturday to The Pines, and go on my way Monday."

Having made his guest as comfortable as possible in his own room, Darrell laid aside his working paraphernalia, his hammer, and bag of rock specimens, and donning a house coat and pair of slippers seated himself near Mr. Britton, all the time conscious of the close but kindly scrutiny with which the latter was regarding him.

"This is delightful!" he exclaimed; "but it is past my comprehension how Mr. Underwood ever let you slip off alone!"

Mr. Britton looked amused. "I told him I was coming to see you, and I think he intended coming with me till he heard me order my saddle-horse for the trip. I think that settled the matter. I believe there can be no perfect interchange of confidence except between two. The presence of a third party—even though a mutual friend—breaks the magnetic circuit and weakens the current of sympathy. Our interviews are necessarily rare, and I want to make the most of them; therefore I would come to you alone or not at all."

"Yes," Darrell replied; "your visits are so rare that every moment is precious to me, and think of the hours I lost by my absence to-day!"

"Do you court Dame Nature so assiduously every day, subsisting on cold lunches and tramping the mountains till nightfall?"

"Not every day, but as often as possible," Darrell replied, smiling.

"And I suppose if I were not here you would now be burrowing into that pile over there?" Mr. Britton said, glancing significantly towards the table covered to a considerable depth with books of reference, note-books, writing-pads, and sheets of closely written manuscript.

"Let me show you what I am doing; it will take but a moment," said Darrell, springing to his feet.

He drew forth several sets of extensive notes on researches and

47

experiments he was making along various lines of study, in which Mr. Britton became at once deeply interested.

"You have a good thing here; stick to it!" he said at length, looking up from the perusal of Darrell's geological notes, gathered from his studies of the rock formations in that vicinity. "You have a fine field in which to pursue this branch, and with the knowledge you already have on this subject and the discoveries you are likely to make, you may be able to make some very valuable contributions to the science one of these days."

"That is just what I hope to do!" exclaimed Darrell eagerly; "just what I am studying for day and night!"

"But you must use moderation," said Mr. Britton, smiling at the younger man's enthusiasm; "you are young, you have years before you in which to do this work, and this constant study, night and day, added to your regular routine work, is too much for you. You are looking fagged already."

"If I am, it is not the work that is fagging me," Darrell replied, quickly, his tones becoming excited; "Mr. Britton, I must work; I must accomplish all I can for two reasons. You say I have years before me in which to do this work. God knows I hope I haven't got to work years like this,—only half alive, you might say,—and when the change comes, if it ever does, you know, of course, I cannot and would not remain here."

"I understand you would not remain here," said Mr. Britton slowly, and laying his hand soothingly on the arm of his agitated companion, "but you can readily see that not only your education, but your natural trend of thought, is along these lines; therefore, when you are fully restored to your normal self you will be the more—not the less—interested in these things, and I predict that no matter when the time comes for you to leave, you will, after a while, return to continue this same line of work amid the same surroundings, but, we hope, under far happier conditions."

Darrell shook his head slowly. "It does not seem to me that I would ever wish to return to a place where I had suffered as I have here."

Mr. Britton smiled, one of his slow, sad, sweet smiles that Darrell loved to watch, that seemed to dawn in his eyes and gradually to spread until every feature was irradiated with a tender, beneficent light.

"I once thought as you do," he said, gently, "but after years of wandering, I find that the place most sacred to me now is that hallowed by the bitterest agony of my life."

Without replying Darrell unconsciously drew nearer to his friend, and a brief silence followed, broken by Mr. Britton, who inquired, in a lighter tone,—

"What is the other reason for your constant application to your work? You said there were two."

Darrell bowed his head upon his hands as he answered in a low, despairing tone,—

"To stop thinking, thinking, thinking; it will drive me mad!"

"I have been there, my boy; I know," Mr. Britton responded; then, after a pause, he continued:

"Something in the tenor of your last letter made me anxious to come to you. I thought I detected something of the old restlessness. Has the coming of spring, quickening the life forces all around you, stirred the life currents in your own veins till your spirit is again tugging at its fetters in its struggles for release?"

With a startled movement Darrell raised his head, meeting the clear eyes fixed upon him.

"How could you know?" he demanded.

"Because, as Emerson says, 'the heart in thee is the heart of all.' There are few hearts whose pulses are not stirred by the magic influence of the springtide, and under its potent spell I knew you would feel your present limitations even more keenly than ever before."

"Thank God, you understand!" Darrell exclaimed; then continued, passionately: "The last three weeks have been torture to me if I but allowed myself one moment's thought. Wherever I look I see life–life, perfect and complete in all its myriad forms–the life that is denied to me! This is not living,–this existence of mine,–with brain shackled, fettered, in many ways helpless as a child, knowing less than a child, and not even mercifully wrapped in oblivion, but compelled to feel the constant goading and galling of the fetters, to be reminded of them at every turn! My God! if it were not for constant work and study I would go mad!"

In the silence which followed Darrell's mind reverted to that autumn day on which he had first met John Britton and confided to him his trouble; and now, as then, he was soothed and strengthened by the presence beside him, by the magnetism of that touch, although no word was spoken.

As he reviewed their friendship of the past months he became conscious for the first time of its one-sidedness. He had often unburdened himself to his friend, confiding to him his griefs, and receiving in turn sympathy and counsel; but of the great, unknown sorrow that had wrought such havoc in his own life, what word had John Britton ever spoken? As Darrell recalled the bearing of his friend through all their acquaintance and his silence regarding his own sufferings, his eyes grew dim. The man at his side seemed, in the light of that revelation, stronger, grander, nobler than ever before; not unlike to the giant peaks whose hoary heads then loomed darkly against the starlit sky, calm, silent, majestic, giving no token of the throes of agony which, ages agone, had rent them asunder except in the mystic symbols graven on their furrowed brows. In that light his own complaints seemed puerile. At that moment Darrell was conscious of a new fortitude born within his soul; a new purpose, henceforth to dominate his life.

A heavy sigh from Mr. Britton broke the silence. "I know the fetters are galling," he said, "but have patience and hope, for, at the time appointed, the shackles will be loosened, the fetters broken."

Darrell faced his companion, a new light in his eyes but recently so dark with despair, as he asked, earnestly and tenderly,–

"Dearest and best of friends, is there no time appointed for the lifting of the burden borne so nobly and uncomplainingly, 'lo, these many years?'"

With a grave, sweet smile the elder man shook his head, and, rising,

49

began pacing up and down the room. "There are some burdens, my son, that time cannot lift; they can only be laid down at the gates of eternity."

With a strange, choking sensation in his throat Darrell rose, and, going to the window, stood looking out at the dim outlines of the neighboring peaks. Their vast solitude no longer oppressed him as at the first; it calmed and soothed him in his restless moods, and to-night those grim monarchs dwelling in silent fellowship seemed to him the embodiment of peace and rest.

After a time Mr. Britton paused beside him, and, throwing his arm about his shoulders, asked,—

"What are your thoughts, my son?"

"Only a whim, a fancy that has taken possession of me the last few days, since my wanderings among the mountains," he answered, lightly; "a longing to bury myself in some sort of a retreat on one of these old peaks and devote myself to study."

"And live a hermit's life?" Mr. Britton queried, with a peculiar smile.

"For a while, yes," Darrell replied, more seriously; "until I have learned to fight these battles out by myself, and to conquer myself."

"There are battles," said the other, speaking thoughtfully, "which are waged best in solitude, but self is conquered only by association with one's fellows. Solitude breeds selfishness."

Mr. Britton had resumed his pacing up and down, but a few moments later, as he approached Darrell, the latter turned, suddenly confronting him.

"My dear friend," he said, "you have been everything to me; you have done everything for me; I ask you to do one thing more,—forgive and answer this question: How have you conquered?"

The look of pain that crossed his companion's face filled Darrell with regret for what he had said, but before he could speak again Mr. Britton replied gently, with his old smile,—

"I doubt whether I have yet wholly conquered; but whatever victory is mine, I have won, not in solitude and seclusion, but in association with the sorrowing, the suffering, the sinning, and in sharing their burdens I found rest from my own."

He paused a moment, then continued, his glowing eyes holding Darrell as though under a spell:

"I know not why, but since our first meeting you have given me a new interest, a new joy in life. I have been drawn to you and I have loved you as I thought never again to love any human being, and some day I will tell you what I have told no other human being,—the story of my life."

On Saturday Mr. Britton and Darrell returned to The Pines. The increasing intimacy between them was evident even there. For the last day or so Mr. Britton had fallen into the habit of addressing Darrell by his Christian name, much to the latter's delight. For this Mrs. Dean laughingly called him to account, compelling Mr. Britton to come to his own defence.

"'John,'" he exclaimed; "of course I'll call him 'John.' It seems wonderfully pleasant to me. I've always wanted a namesake, and I can consider him one."

"A namesake!" ejaculated Mrs. Dean, smiling broadly; "I wonder if there's a poor family or one that's seen trouble of any kind anywhere around here that hasn't a 'John Britton' among its children! I should think you had namesakes enough now!"

"One might possibly like to have one of his own selection," he replied, dryly.

As Darrell took leave of Mr. Britton the following Monday morning the latter said,–

"By the way, John, whenever you are ready to enter upon that hermit life let me know; I'll provide the hermitage."

"Are you joking?" Darrell queried, unable to catch his meaning.

"Never more serious in my life," he replied, with such unusual gravity that Darrell forbore to question further.

Chapter XI

Impending Trouble

The five or six weeks following Mr. Britton's visit passed so swiftly that Darrell was scarcely conscious of their flight. His work at the mill, which had been increased by valuable strikes recently made in the mines, in addition to considerable outside work in the way of attests and assays, had left him little time for study or experiment. For nearly three weeks he had not left the mining camp, the last two Saturdays having found him too weary with the preceding week's work to undertake the long ride to Ophir.

During this time Mr. Underwood had been a frequent visitor at the camp, led not only by his interest in the mining developments, but also by his curiosity regarding the progress made by the union in the construction of its boarding-house, and also to watch the effect on his own employees.

Entering the laboratory one day after one of his rounds of the camp, he stood for some time silently watching Darrell at his work.

"In case of a shut-down here," he said at length, speaking abruptly, "how would you like a clerical position in my office down there at Ophir,– book-keeping or something of the sort,–just temporarily, you know?"

Darrell looked up from his work in surprise. "Do you regard a shut-down as imminent?" he inquired, smiling.

"Well, yes; there's no half-way measures with me. No man that works for me will go off the grounds for his meals. But that isn't answering my question."

Darrell's face grew serious. "You forget, Mr. Underwood, that until I am put to the test, I have no means of knowing whether or not I can do the work you wish done."

"By George! I never once thought of that!" Mr. Underwood exclaimed, somewhat embarrassed, adding, hastily, "but then, I didn't mean book-keeping in particular, but clerical work generally; copying instruments, looking up records, and so on. You see, it's like this," he continued, seating himself near Darrell; "I'm thinking of taking in a partner—not in this mining business, it has nothing to do with that, but just in my mortgage-loan business down there; and in case I do, we'll need two or three additional clerks and book-keepers, and I thought you might like to come in just temporarily until we resume operations here. Of course, the salary wouldn't be so very much, but I thought it might be better than nothing to bridge over."

"How long do you expect to be closed down here, Mr. Underwood?"

"Until the men come to their senses or we find others to take their places," the elder man answered, decidedly; "it may be six weeks or it may be six months. I was talking with Dwight, from the Buckeye Camp, this morning. He says they've been to too much expense to put up with the proposition for a moment; they simply can't stand it, and won't; they'll shut down and pull out first. I don't believe that mine is paying very well, anyway."

"Mr. Underwood," said Darrell, slowly, "if this were a question of accommodation to yourself, of coming into your office and helping you out personally, I would gladly do it; salary would be no object; but to take a merely clerical position for an indefinite time when I have a good, lucrative profession does not seem to me a very wise policy. There must be plenty of assaying to be done in Ophir; why couldn't I temporarily open an office there?"

"I guess there's no reason why you couldn't if you want to," Mr. Underwood replied, evidently disappointed by Darrell's reply and eying him sharply, "and if you want to open up an office of your own there's plenty of room for you in our building. You know the building was formerly occupied by one of Ophir's wildcat banks that collapsed in the general crash six years ago, and there's a fine lot of private offices in the rear, opening on the side street; one of those rooms fitted up would be just the place for you."

"Much obliged," said Darrell, smiling; "we'll see about it if the time comes that I need it. Possibly your prospective partner will have use for all the private offices."

"I guess I'll have some say about that," Mr. Underwood returned, gruffly; then, after a short pause, he continued: "I haven't fully decided about this partnership business. I talked it over with Jack when he was here, but he didn't seem to favor the idea; told me that at my age I had better let well enough alone. I told him that I didn't see what my age had to do with it, that I was capable of looking after my own interests, partner or no partner, but that I'd no objection to having some one else take the brunt of the work while I looked on."

"Is the man a stranger or an acquaintance?" Darrell inquired.

"I'm not personally acquainted with him, but he's not exactly a stranger, for he's lived in Ophir, off and on, for the last five years. His name is Walcott. He says his father is an Englishman and very wealthy; he himself, I should judge, has some Spanish blood in his veins. He spends part of his time in Texas, where he has heavy cattle interests; in fact, has been there for the greater part of the past year. He wants to go into the mortgage-loan business, and offers to put in seventy-five thousand and give his personal attention to the business for thirty-three and a third per cent. of the profits."

"What has been his business in Ophir all these years?"

"Life insurance mostly, I believe; had two offices, one in Ophir and one at Galena, and has also done some private loan business."

"What sort of a reputation has he?"

"First-rate. I've made a number of inquiries about him in both places, and nobody has a word to say against him; very quiet, minds his own business, a man of few words; just about my sort of a man, I should judge," Mr. Underwood concluded as he rose from his chair.

"Well, Mr. Underwood," said Darrell, "whatever arrangements you decide to make, I wish you success."

"No more than I do you, my boy, in anything your pig-headedness leads you into," Mr. Underwood replied, brusquely, but with a humorous twinkle in his eyes. "Confound you!" he added; "I'd help you if you'd give me a chance, but maybe it's best to let you 'gang your ain gait.'" And he walked out of the room before Darrell could reply.

A moment later he looked in at the door. "By the way, if you're not at The Pines by five o'clock sharp next Saturday afternoon, Marcia says she's going to send an officer up here after you with a writ of habeas corpus, or something of the sort."

"All right; I'll be there," Darrell laughed.

"You'll find the old place a bit brighter than you've seen it yet, for we had a letter from Puss this morning that she'll be home to-morrow."

With the last words the door closed and Darrell was left alone with his thoughts, to which, however, he could then give little time. But when the day's work was done he went for a stroll, and, seating himself upon a large rock, carefully reviewed the situation.

Hitherto he had given little thought to the impending trouble at the camp, supposing it would affect himself but slightly; but he now realized that a suspension of operations there would mean an entire change in his mode of living. The prospective change weighed on his sensitive spirits like an incubus. Even The Pines, he dismally reflected, would no longer seem the same quiet, homelike retreat, since it was to be invaded and dominated by a youthful presence between whom and himself there would probably be little congeniality.

But finally telling himself that these reflections were childish, he rose as the last sunset rays were sinking behind the western ranges and the rosy flush on the summits was fading, and, walking swiftly to his room, resolutely buried himself in his studies.

Chapter XII

New Life in the Old Home

On the following Saturday, as Darrell ascended the long driveway leading to The Pines, he was startled at the transformation which the place had undergone since last he was there. The rolling lawn seemed carpeted with green velvet, enlivened here and there with groups of beautiful foliage plants. Fountains were playing in the sunlight, their glistening spray tinted with rainbow lights. Flowers bloomed in profusion, their colors set off by the gray background of the stone walls of the house. The syringas by the bay-windows were bent to the ground with their burden of snowy blossoms, whose fragrance, mingled with that of the June roses, greeted him as he approached. He forgot his three weeks' absence and the rapid growth in that high altitude; the change seemed simply magical. Then, as he caught a glimpse through the pines of a slender, girlish figure, dressed in white, darting hither and thither, he wondered no longer; it was but the fit accompaniment of the young, joyous life which had come to the old place.

As he came out into the open, he saw a young girl romping up and down before the house with a fine Scotch collie, and he could not restrain a smile as he recalled Mrs. Dean's oft-repeated declaration that there was one thing she would never tolerate, and that was a dog or a cat about the house. She had not yet seen him; but when she did, the frolic ceased and she started towards the house. Then suddenly she stopped, as though she recognized some one or something, and stood awaiting his approach, her lips parted in a smile, two small, shapely hands shading her eyes from the sun. As he came nearer, he had time to note the lithe, supple figure, just rounding into the graceful outlines of womanhood; the full, smiling lips, the flushed cheeks, and the glint of gold in her brown hair; and the light, the beauty, the fragrance surrounding her seemed an appropriate setting to the picture. She was a part of the scene.

Darrell, of course, had no knowledge of his own age, but at that moment he felt very remote from the embodiment of youth before him; he seemed to himself to have been suddenly relegated to the background, among the elder members of the family.

The collie had been standing beside his mistress with his head on one side, regarding Darrell with a sharp, inquisitive look, and he now broke the silence, which threatened to prove rather embarrassing, with a short bark.

"Hush, Duke!" said the girl, in a low tone; then, as Darrell dismounted, she came swiftly towards him, extending her hand.

"This is Mr. Darrell, I know," she said, speaking quite rapidly in a clear, musical voice, without a shade of affectation, "and you probably know who I am, so we will need no introduction."

"Yes, Miss Underwood," said Darrell, smiling into the beautiful brown eyes, "I would have recognized you anywhere from your picture."

54

"And you have Trix, haven't you?" she exclaimed, turning to caress the mare. "Dear old Trix! Just let her go, Mr. Darrell; she will go to the stables of her own accord and Bennett will take care of her; that was the way Harry taught her. Go find Bennett, Trix!"

They watched Trix follow the driveway and disappear around the corner, then both turned towards the house.

"Auntie is out just now," said the girl; "she had to go down town, but I am expecting her back every minute. Will you go into the house, Mr. Darrell, or do you prefer a seat on the veranda?"

"The veranda looks inviting; suppose we sit here," Darrell suggested.

They had reached the steps leading to the entrance. On the top step the collie had seated himself and was now awaiting their approach with the air of one expecting due recognition.

"Mr. Darrell," said the young girl, with a merry little laugh, "allow me to present you to His Highness, the Duke of Argyle!"

The collie gave his head a slight backward toss, and, with great dignity, extended his right paw to Darrell, which the latter, instantly entering into the spirit of the joke, took, saying, with much gravity,—

"I am pleased to meet His Highness!"

The girl's brown eyes danced with enjoyment.

"You have made a friend of him for life, now," she said as they seated themselves, Duke stationing himself at her side in such a manner as to show his snow-white vest and great double ruff to the best possible advantage. "He is a very aristocratic dog, and if any one fails to show him what he considers proper respect, he is greatly affronted."

"He certainly is a royal-looking fellow," said Darrell, "but I cannot imagine how you ever gained Mrs. Dean's consent to his presence here. You must possess even more than the ordinary powers of feminine persuasion."

"Aunt Marcia?" laughed the girl; "oh, well, you see it was a case of 'love me, love my dog.' Wherever I go, Duke must go, so auntie had to submit to the inevitable."

Darrell found the situation far less embarrassing than he had expected. His young companion, with keen, womanly intuition, had divined something of his feeling, and tactfully avoiding any allusion to their previous meeting, of which he had no recollection, kept the conversation on subjects within the brief span of his memory. She seemed altogether unconscious of the peculiar conditions surrounding himself, and the brown eyes, meeting his own so frankly, had in their depths nothing of the curiosity or the pity he had so often encountered, and had grown to dread. She appeared so childlike and unaffected, and her joyous, rippling laughter proved so contagious, that unconsciously the extra years which a few moments before seemed to have been added to his life dropped away; the grave, tense lines of his face relaxed, and before he was aware he was laughing heartily at the account of some school-girl escapade or at some tricks performed by Duke for his especial entertainment.

In the midst of their merriment they heard the sound of hoof-beats,

55

and, turning, saw the family carriage approaching, containing both Mr. Underwood and his sister.

"You two children seem to be enjoying yourselves!" was Mr. Underwood's comment as the carriage stopped.

Darrell sprang to Mrs. Dean's assistance as she alighted, while Kate Underwood ran down the steps to meet her father. Both greeted Darrell warmly, but Mrs. Dean retained his hand a moment as she looked at him with genuine motherly interest.

"I'm glad the truant has returned," she said, with her quiet smile; "I only hope it seems as good to you to come home as it does to us to have you here!"

Darrell was touched by her unusual kindness. "You can rest assured that it does, mother," he said, earnestly. He was astonished at the effect of his words: her face flushed, her lips trembled, and as she passed on into the house her eyes glistened with tears.

Darrell looked about him in bewilderment. "What have I said?" he questioned; "how did I wound her feelings?"

"She lost a son years ago, and she's never got over it," Mr. Underwood explained, briefly.

"You did not hurt her feelings—she was pleased," Kate hastened to reassure him; "but did she never speak to you about it?"

"Never," Darrell replied.

"Well, that is not to be wondered at, for she seldom alludes to it. He died years ago, before I can remember, but she always grieves for him; that was the reason," she added, reflectively, half to herself, "that she always loved Harry better than she did me."

"Better than you, you jealous little Puss!" said her father, pinching her cheek; "don't you have love enough, I'd like to know?"

"I can never have too much, you know, papa," she answered, very seriously, and Darrell, watching, saw in the brown eyes for the first time the wistful look he had seen in the two portraits.

She soon followed her aunt, but her father and Darrell remained outside talking of business matters until summoned to dinner. On entering the house Darrell saw on every hand evidences of the young life in the old home. There was just a pleasant touch of disorder in the rooms he had always seen kept with such precision: here a bit of unfinished embroidery; there a book open, face down, just where the fair reader had left it; the piano was open and sheets of music lay scattered over it. From every side came the fragrance of flowers, and in the usually sombre dining-room Darrell noted the fireplace nearly concealed by palms and potted plants, the chandelier trimmed with trailing vines, the epergne of roses and ferns on the table, and the tiny boutonnières at his plate and Mr. Underwood's. With a smile of thanks at the happy young face opposite, he appropriated the one intended for himself, but Mr. Underwood, picking up the one beside his plate, sat twirling it in his fingers with a look of mock perplexity.

"Puss has introduced so many of her folderols I haven't got used to them yet," he said. "How is this to be taken,—before eating, or after?" he inquired, looking at her from under heavy, frowning brows.

"To be taken! Oh, papa!" she ejaculated; "why don't you put it on as Mr. Darrell has his? Here, I'll fix it for you!"

With an air of resignation he waited while she fastened the flowers in the lapel of his coat, giving the latter an approving little pat as she finished.

"There!" she exclaimed; "you ought to see how nice you look!"

"H'm! I'm glad to hear it," he grunted; "I feel like a prize steer at a county fair!"

In the laughter which followed Kate joined as merrily as the rest, and no one but Darrell observed the deepening flush on her cheek or heard the tremulous sigh when the laughter was ended.

After dinner they adjourned to the large sitting-room, Mr. Underwood with his pipe, Mrs. Dean with her knitting, and Darrell, while conversing with the former, watched with a new interest the latter's placid face, wondering at the depth of feeling concealed beneath that calm exterior.

As the twilight deepened and conversation began to flag, there came from the piano a few sweet chords, followed by one of Chopin's dreamy nocturnes. Mr. Underwood began to doze in his chair, and Darrell sat silent, his eyes closed, his whole soul given up to the spell of the music. Unconscious of the pleasure she was giving, Kate played till the room was veiled in darkness; then going to the fireplace she lighted the fire already laid—for the nights were still somewhat chilly—and sat down on a low seat before the fire, while Duke came and lay at her feet. It was a pretty picture; the young girl in white, her eyes fixed dreamily on the glowing embers, the firelight dancing over her form and face and lighting up her hair with gleams of gold; the dog at her feet, his head thrown proudly back, and his eyes fastened on her face with a look of loyal devotion seldom seen even in human eyes.

Happening to glance in Mr. Underwood's direction Darrell saw pride, pleasure, and pain struggling for the mastery in the father's face as he watched the picture in the firelight. Pain won, and with a sudden gesture of impatience he covered his eyes with his hand, as though to shut out the scene. It was but a little thing, but taken in connection with the incident before dinner, it appealed to Darrell, showing, as it did, the silent, stoical manner in which these people bore their grief.

Mrs. Dean's quiet voice interrupted his musings and broke the spell which the music seemed to have thrown around them.

"You will have some one now, Katherine, to accompany you on the violin, as you have always wanted; Mr. Darrell is a fine violinist."

Kate was instantly all animation. "Oh, that will be delightful, Mr. Darrell!" she exclaimed, eagerly; "there is nothing I enjoy so much as a violin accompaniment; it adds so much expression to the music. I think a piano alone is so unsympathetic; you can't get any feeling out of it!"

"I'm afraid, Miss Underwood, I will prove a disappointment to you," Darrell replied; "I have never yet attempted any new music, or even to play by note, and don't know what success I would have, if any. So far I have only played what drifts to me—some way, I don't know how—from out of the past."

The unconscious sadness in his voice stirred the depths of Kate's tender

57

heart. "Oh, that is too bad!" she exclaimed, quickly, thinking, not of her own disappointment, but of his trouble of which she had unwittingly reminded him; then she added, gently, almost timidly,—

"But you will, at any rate, let me hear you play, won't you?"

"Certainly, if it will give you any pleasure," he replied, with a slight smile.

"Very well; then we will arrange it this way," she continued, her cheerful manner restored; "you will play your music, and, if I am familiar with it, I will accompany you on the piano. I will get out Harry's violin to-morrow, and while auntie is taking her nap and papa is engaged, we will see what we can accomplish in a musical way."

Before Darrell could reply, Mr. Underwood, who had started from his revery, demanded,—

"What engagement are you talking about, you chatterbox?"

"I can't say, papa," she replied, playfully seating herself on the arm of his chair; "I only know that when I asked your company for a walk to-morrow afternoon, you pleaded a very important engagement. Now, how is that?" she asked archly; "have you an engagement, really, or didn't you care for my society?"

"Why, yes, to be sure; it had escaped my mind for the moment," her father answered, rather vaguely she thought; then, looking at Darrell, he said,—

"Walcott is coming to-morrow for my final decision in that matter."

Darrell bowed in token that he understood, but did not feel at liberty to inquire whether the decision was to be favorable to Mr. Walcott, or otherwise. Kate glanced quickly from one to the other, but before she could speak her father continued:

"I rather think if he consents to two or three conditions which I shall insist upon, that my answer will be in the affirmative."

"I thought that quite probable from your conversation the other day," Darrell replied.

"See here, papa!" Kate exclaimed, mischievously, "you needn't talk over my head! You used to do so when I was little, but you can't any longer, you know. Who is this 'Walcott,' and what is this important decision about?"

Mr. Underwood, who did not believe in taking what he called the "women folks" into his confidence regarding business affairs, looked quizzically into the laughing face beside him.

"Didn't I hear you arranging some sort of a musical programme with Mr. Darrell?" he inquired.

"Yes; what has that to do with your engagement?" she queried.

"Nothing whatever; only you carry out your engagement and I will mine, and we'll compare notes afterwards."

For an instant her face sobered; then catching sight of her father's eyes twinkling under their beetling brows, she laughingly withdrew from his side, saying,—

"That's all very well; you can score one this time, papa, but don't you think we won't come out pretty near even in the end!"

Upon learning from Darrell that the violin she expected him to use was in his room at the mining camp, she then proposed a stroll to the summit of the pine-clad mountain for the following afternoon, and having secured his promise that he would bring the violin with him on his next visit, she waltzed gayly across the floor, turned on the light, and seating herself at the piano soon had the room ringing with music and laughter while she sang a number of college songs.

To Darrell she seemed more child than woman, and he was constantly impressed with her unlikeness to her father or aunt. She seemed to have absolutely none of their self-repression. Warm-hearted, sympathetic, and demonstrative, every shade of feeling betrayed itself in her sensitive, mobile face and in the brown eyes, one moment pensive and wistful, the next luminous with sympathy or dancing with merriment.

As Darrell took leave of Mrs. Dean that night, he said, looking frankly into her calm, kindly face,—

"I am very sorry if I wounded your feelings this afternoon; it was wholly unintentional, I assure you."

"You did not in the least," she answered; "it is so long since I have been called by that name it took me by surprise, but it sounded very pleasant to me. My boy, if he had lived, would have been just about your age."

"It seemed pleasant to me to call you 'mother,'" said Darrell; "it made me feel less like an outsider."

"You can call me so as often as you wish; you are no outsider here; we consider you one of ourselves," she responded, with more warmth in her tones than he had ever heard before.

The following morning Darrell accompanied the ladies to church. After lunch he lounged for an hour or more in one of the hammocks on the veranda, listening alternately to Mr. Underwood's comments as he leisurely smoked his pipe, and to the faint tones of a mandolin coming from some remote part of the house. Mr. Underwood grew more and more abstracted, the mandolin ceased, and Darrell, soothed by his surroundings to a temporary forgetfulness of his troubles, swung gently back and forth in a sort of dreamy content. After a while, Kate Underwood appeared, dressed for a walk, and, accompanied by Duke, the two set forth for their mountain ramble, for the time as light-hearted as two children.

Upon their return, two or three hours later, while still at a little distance from the house, they saw Mr. Underwood and a stranger standing together on the veranda. The latter, who was apparently about to take his departure, and whom Darrell at once assumed to be Mr. Walcott, was about thirty years of age, of medium height, with a finely proportioned and rather muscular form, erect and dignified in his bearing, with a lithe suppleness and grace in all his movements. He was standing with his hat in his hand, and Darrell, who had time to observe him closely, noting his jet-black hair, close cut excepting where it curled slightly over his forehead, his black, silky moustache, and the oval contour of his olive face, remembered Mr. Underwood's remark of the probability of Spanish blood in his veins.

As they came near, Duke gave a low growl, but Kate instantly hushed him, chiding him for his rudeness. At the sound, the stranger turned towards them, and Mr. Underwood at once introduced Mr. Walcott to his daughter and Mr. Darrell. He greeted them both with the most punctilious courtesy, but as he faced Darrell, the latter saw for an instant in the half-closed, blue-black eyes, the pity tinged with contempt to which he had long since become accustomed, yet which, as often as he met it, thrilled him anew with pain. The look passed, however, and Mr. Walcott, in low, well-modulated tones, conversed pleasantly for a few moments with the new-comers, the three young people forming a striking trio as they stood there in the bright sunshine amid the June roses; then, with a graceful adieu, he walked swiftly away.

As soon as he was out of hearing Mr. Underwood, turning to Darrell, said,—

"It is decided; the papers will be drawn to-morrow."

Then taking his daughter's flushed, perplexed face between his hands, he said,—

"Mr. Walcott and I are going into partnership; how do you like the looks of my partner, Puss?"

She looked incredulous. "That young man your partner!" she exclaimed; "why, he seems the very last man I should ever expect you to fancy!" Then she added, laughing,—

"Oh, papa, I think he must have hypnotized you! Does Aunt Marcia know? May I tell her?" And, having gained his consent, she ran into the house to impart the news to Mrs. Dean.

"That's the woman of it!" said Mr. Underwood, grimly; "they always want to immediately tell some other woman! But what do you think of my partner?" he asked, looking searchingly at Darrell, who had not yet spoken.

Darrell did not reply at once; he felt in some way bewildered. All the content, the joy, the sunshine of the last few hours seemed to have been suddenly blotted out, though he could not have told why. The remembrance of that glance still stung him, but aside from that, he felt his whole soul filled with an inexplicable antagonism towards this man.

"I hardly know yet just what I do think of him," he answered, slowly; "I have not formed a definite opinion of him, but I think, as your daughter says, he somehow seems the last man whom I would have expected you to associate yourself with."

Mr. Underwood frowned. "I don't generally make mistakes in people," he said, rather gruffly; "if I'm mistaken in this man, it will be the first time."

Nothing further was said on the subject, though it remained uppermost in the minds of both, with the result that their conversation was rather spasmodic and desultory. At the dinner-table, Kate was quick to observe the unusual silence, and, intuitively connecting it in some way with the new partnership, refrained alike from question or comment regarding either that subject or Mr. Walcott, while it was a rule with Mrs. Dean never to refer to her brother's business affairs unless he first alluded to them himself.

The evening passed more pleasantly, as Kate coaxed her father into telling some reminiscences of his early western life, which greatly interested Darrell. Something of the old restlessness had returned to him, however. He spent a wakeful night, and was glad when morning came and he could return to his work.

As he came out of the house at an early hour to set forth on his long ride he found Kate engaged in feeding Trix with lumps of sugar. She greeted him merrily, and as he started down the avenue he was followed by a rippling laugh and a shower of roses, one of which he caught and fastened in his buttonhole, but on looking back over his shoulder she had vanished, and only Duke was visible.

Chapter XIII

Mr. Underwood "Strikes" First

The ensuing days were filled with work demanding close attention and concentration of thought, but often in the long, cool twilight, while Darrell rested from his day's work before entering upon the night's study, he recalled his visit to The Pines with a degree of pleasure hitherto unknown. He had found Kate Underwood far different from his anticipations, though just what his anticipations had been he did not stop to define. There was at times a womanly grace and dignity in her bearing which he would have expected from her portrait and which he admired, but what especially attracted him was her utter lack of affectation or self-consciousness. She was as unconscious as a child; her sympathy towards himself and her pleasant familiarity with him were those of a warm-hearted, winsome child.

He liked best to recall her as she looked that evening seated by the fireside: the childish pose, the graceful outlines of her form silhouetted against the light; the dreamy eyes, with their long golden lashes curling upward; the lips parted in a half smile, and the gleam of the firelight on her hair. But it was always as a child that he recalled her, and the thought that to himself, or to any other, she could be aught else never occurred to him. Of young Whitcomb's love for her, of course, he had no recollection, nor had it ever been mentioned in his hearing since his illness.

Day by day the work at the camp increased, and there also began to be indications of an approaching outbreak among the men. The union boarding-house was nearing completion; it was rumored that it would be ready for occupancy within a week or ten days; the walking delegates from the union could be frequently seen loitering about the camp, especially when the changes in shifts were made, waiting to get word with the men, and it was nothing uncommon to see occasional groups of the men engaged in argument, which suddenly broke off at the appearance of Darrell, or of Hathaway, the superintendent.

So engrossed was Mr. Underwood with the arrangement of details for the inauguration of the new firm of Underwood & Walcott that he was unable to be at the camp that week. On Saturday afternoon Darrell, having learned that Hathaway was to be gone over Sunday, and believing it best under existing circumstances not to leave the camp, sent Mr. Underwood a message to that effect, and also informing him of the status of affairs there.

Early the following week Mr. Underwood made his appearance at the camp, and if the union bosses had entertained any hope of effecting a compromise with the owner of Camp Bird, as it was known, such hope must have been blasted upon mere sight of that gentleman's face upon his arrival. Darrell himself could scarcely restrain a smile of amusement as they met. Mr. Underwood fairly bristled with defiance, and, after the briefest kind of a greeting, started to make his usual rounds of the camp. He stopped abruptly, fumbled in his pocket for an instant, then, handing a dainty envelope to Darrell, hastened on without a word. Darrell saw smiles exchanged among the men, but he preserved the utmost gravity until, having reached his desk, he opened and read the little note. It contained merely a few pleasant lines from Kate, expressing disappointment at his failure to come to The Pines on the preceding Saturday, and reminding him of his promise concerning the violin; but the postscript, which in true feminine style comprised the real gist of the note, made him smile audibly. It ran:

"Papa has donned his paint and feathers this morning and is evidently starting out on the war-path. I haven't an idea whose scalps he intends taking, but hope you will at least preserve your own intact."

At dinner Mr. Underwood maintained an ominous silence, replying in monosyllables to any question or remark addressed to him. He soon left the table, and Darrell did not see him again till late in the afternoon, when he entered the laboratory. A glance at the set lines of his face told Darrell as plainly as words that his line of action was fully determined upon, and that it would be as fixed and unalterable as the laws of the Medes and Persians.

"I am going home now," he announced briefly, in reply to Darrell's somewhat questioning look; "I'll be back here the last of the week."

"What do you think of the outlook, Mr. Underwood?" Darrell inquired.

"It is about what I expected. I have seen all the men. They are, as I supposed, under the thumb of the union bosses. A few of them realize that the whole proposition is unreasonable and absurd, and they don't want to go out, but they don't dare say so above their breath, and they don't dare disobey orders, because they are owned, body and soul, by the union."

"Have any of the leaders tried to make terms?"

"I met one of their 'walking delegates' this morning," said Mr. Underwood, with scornful emphasis; "I told him to 'walk' himself out of the camp or I'd boot him out; and he walked!"

Darrell laughed. Mr. Underwood continued: "The boarding-house opens on Thursday; on next Monday every man not enrolled in that institution will be ordered out."

"It's to be a strike then, sure thing, is it?" Darrell asked.

"Yes, there'll be a strike," Mr. Underwood answered, grimly, while a quick gleam shot across his face; "but remember one thing," he added, as he turned to leave the room, "no man ever yet got the drop or the first blow on me!"

Matters continued about the same at the camp. On Friday favorable reports concerning the new boarding-house began to be circulated, brought the preceding evening by miners from another camp. Some of the men looked sullen and defiant, others only painfully self-conscious, in the presence of Darrell and the superintendent, but it was evident that the crisis was approaching.

Late Friday night a horseman dismounted silently before the door of the office building and Mr. Underwood walked quietly into Darrell's room.

"How's the new hotel? Overrun with boarders?" he asked, as he seated himself, paying little attention to Darrell's exclamation of surprise.

"Chapman's men—about fifty in all—are the only ones there at present."

"Chapman!" ejaculated Mr. Underwood; "what is Chapman doing? He agreed to stand in with the rest of us on this thing!"

"He told Hathaway this morning he was only doing it for experiment. The boarding-house is located near his claims, you know, and he has comparatively few men. So he said he didn't mind trying it for a month or so."

"Confound him! I'll make it the dearest experiment ever he tried," said Mr. Underwood, wrathfully; "he was in our office the other day trying to negotiate a loan for twenty-five thousand dollars that he said he had got to have within ten days or go to the wall. I'll see that he doesn't get it anywhere about here unless he stands by his word with us."

After further conversation Mr. Underwood went out, saying he had a little business about the camp to attend to. He returned in the course of an hour, and Darrell heard him holding a long consultation with Hathaway before he retired for the night.

The following morning the mill men of the camp, on going to their work, were astonished to find the mill closed and silent, while fastened on the great doors was a large placard which read as follows:

NOTICE.

The entire mining and milling plant of Camp Bird is closed down for an indefinite period. All employees are requested to call at the superintendent's office and receive their wages up to and including Saturday, the 10th inst.

D. K. Underwood.

The miners found the hoist-house and the various shaft-houses closed and deserted, with notices similar to the above posted on their doors.

Darrell, upon going to breakfast, learned that Mr. Underwood and the superintendent had breakfasted at an early hour. A little later, on his way to the mill, he observed groups of men here and there, some standing, some moving in the direction of the office, but gave the matter no particular thought until he reached the mill and was himself confronted by the placard. As he read the notice and recalled the groups of idlers, certain remarks made by Mr. Underwood came to his mind, and he seemed struck by the humorous side of the situation.

"The old gentleman seems to have got the 'drop' on them, all right!" he said to himself, as, with an amused smile, he walked past the mill and out in the direction of the hoist. The ore-bins were closed and locked, the tram-cars stood empty on their tracks, the hoisting engine was still, the hoist-house and shaft-houses deserted. After the ceaseless noise and activity to which he had become accustomed at the camp the silence seemed oppressive, and he turned and retraced his steps to the office.

A crowd of men was gathered outside the office building. In single file they passed into the office to the superintendent's window, received their money silently, in almost every instance without comment or question, and passed out again. Once outside, however, there they remained, their number constantly augmented by new arrivals, for the men on the night shift had been aroused by their comrades and were now streaming down from the bunk-houses. A few laughed and joked, some looked sullen, some troubled and anxious, but all remained packed about the building, quiet, undemonstrative, and mute as dumb brutes as to their reason for staying there. They were all prepared to march boldly out of the mill and mines on the following Monday, on a strike, in obedience to orders; even to resort to violence in defence of their so-called "rights" if so ordered, but Mr. Underwood's sudden move had disarmed them; there had been no opportunity for a conference with their leaders, with the result that they acted more in accordance with their own individual instincts, and the loss of work for which they would have cared little in the event of a strike was now uppermost in their minds.

They eyed Darrell furtively and curiously, making way for him as he entered the building, but still they waited. For a few moments Darrell watched the scene, then he passed through the office into the room beyond, where he found Mr. Underwood engaged in sorting and filing papers. The latter looked up with a grim smile:

"Been down to the mill?"

"Oh, yes," Darrell answered, laughing; "I went to work as usual, only to find the door shut in my face, the same as the rest."

"H'm! What do you think of the 'strike' now?"

"I think you are making them swallow their own medicine, but I don't see why you need give me a dose of it; I haven't threatened to strike."

Mr. Underwood's eyes twinkled shrewdly as he replied, "You had better go out there and get your pay along with the rest, and then go to your room and pack up. You may not be needed at the mill again for the next six months."

"Will it be as serious as that, do you think?" Darrell inquired.

Before Mr. Underwood could reply the superintendent opened the office door hastily.

"Mr. Underwood," he said, "will you come out and speak to the men?

They are all waiting outside and I can't drive them away; they say they won't stir till they've seen you."

With a look of annoyance Mr. Underwood rose and passed out into the office; Darrell, somewhat interested, followed.

"Well, boys," said Mr. Underwood, as he appeared in the doorway, "what do you want of me?"

"If you please, sir," said one man, evidently spokesman for the crowd, and whom Darrell at once recognized as Dan, the engineer,—"if you please, sir, we would like to know how long this shut-down is going to last."

"Can't tell," Mr. Underwood replied, shortly; "can't tell anything about it at present; it's indefinite."

"Well," persisted the man, "there's some of us as thought that mebbe 'twould only be till this 'ere trouble about the meals is settled, one way or t'other; and there's some as thought mebbe it hadn't nothing to do with that."

"Well?" said Mr. Underwood, impatiently.

"Well, sir," said Dan, lowering his voice a little and edging nearer Mr. Underwood, "you know as how the most of us was satisfied with things as they was, and didn't want no change and wouldn't have made no kick, only, you see, we had to, and we felt kinder anxious to know whether if this thing got settled some way and the camp opened up again, whether we could get back in our old places?"

"Dan," said Mr. Underwood, impressively, and speaking loudly enough for every man to hear, "there can be no settlement of this question except to have things go on under precisely the same terms and conditions as they've always gone; so none of your leaders need come to me for terms, for they won't get 'em. And as to opening up the mines and mill, I'll open them up whenever I get ready, not a day sooner or later; and when I do start up again, if you men have come to your senses by that time and are ready to come back on the same terms, all right; if not," he paused an instant, then added with emphasis, "just remember there'll be others, and plenty of 'em, too."

"Yes, sir; thank ye, sir," Dan answered, somewhat dubiously; then one and all moved slowly and mechanically away.

Mr. Underwood turned to Darrell. "Get your things together as soon as you can. I'm going to send down three or four of the teams after dinner, and they can take your things along. And here's the key to the mill; go over and pick out whatever you will want in the way of an assaying outfit, and have that taken down with the rest. There's no need of your going to the expense of buying an outfit just for temporary use."

By two o'clock scarcely a man remained at the camp. Mr. Underwood and Darrell were among the last to leave. Two faithful servants of Mr. Underwood's had arrived an hour or so before, who were to act as watchmen during the shut-down. Having taken them around the camp and given them the necessary instructions, Mr. Underwood then gave them the keys of the various buildings, saying, as he took his departure,—

"There's grub enough in the boarding-house to last you two for some time, but whenever there's anything needed, let me know. Bring over some beds from the bunk-house and make yourselves comfortable."

He climbed to a seat on one of the wagons, and, as they started, turned back to the watchmen for his parting admonition:

"Keep an eye on things, boys! You're both good shots; if you catch anybody prowling 'round here, day or night, wing him, boys, wing him!"

The teams then rattled noisily down the canyon road, Darrell, with Trix, bringing up the rear, feeling himself a sort of shuttlecock tossed to and fro by antagonistic forces in whose conflicts he personally had no part and no interest. However, he wasted no moments in useless regrets, but rode along in deep thought, planning for the uninterrupted pursuit of his studies amid the new and less favorable surroundings. Thus far he had met with unlooked-for success along the line of his researches and experiments, and each success but stimulated him to more diligent study.

On their arrival at Ophir, Mr. Underwood gave directions to have the assaying outfit taken to the rooms in the rear of his own offices, after which he and Darrell, with the remaining teams, proceeded in the direction of The Pines. Trix, on finding herself headed for home, quickened her steps to such a brisk pace that on reaching the long driveway Darrell was considerably in advance of the others. He had no sooner emerged from the pines into the open, in full view of the house, than Duke came bounding down the driveway to meet him, with every possible demonstration of joyous welcome. His loud barking brought the ladies to the door just as Darrell, having quickly dismounted and sent Trix to the stables, was running up the broad stairs to the veranda, the collie close at his side.

"Just look at Duke!" Kate Underwood exclaimed, shaking hands with Darrell; "and this is only the second time he has met you! You surely have won his heart, Mr. Darrell."

"You are the only person outside of Katherine he has ever condescended to notice," said Mrs. Dean, with a smile.

"I assure you I feel immensely flattered by his friendship," Darrell replied, caressing the collie; "the more so because I know it to be genuine."

"He won't so much as look at me," Mrs. Dean added.

"That is because you objected at first to having him here," said Kate; "he knows it, and he'll not forget it. But, Mr. Darrell, where is papa?"

"He will be here directly," Darrell answered, smiling as he suddenly recalled the little note within his pocket; "he is returning from the war-path with the trophies of victory."

Kate laughed and colored slightly. "Your own scalp has not suffered, at any rate," she said.

"But he has brought me back a captive; here he comes now!"

The wagon loaded with Darrell's belongings was just coming slowly into view, with Mr. Underwood on the seat beside the driver, the other teams having been sent to the stables by another route.

Darrell noted the surprise depicted on the faces beside him, and, turning to Mrs. Dean, who stood next him, he said, in a low tone,—

"I have come back to the old home, mother, for a little while; is there room for me?"

Mrs. Dean looked at him steadily for an instant, while Kate ran to meet her father; then she replied, earnestly,–

"There will always be room in the old home for you. I only wish that I could hope it would always hold you."

Chapter XIV

Drifting

Early the following week Darrell was established in his new office. The building containing the offices of the firm of Underwood & Walcott had, as Mr. Underwood informed Darrell, been formerly occupied by one of the leading banks of Ophir, and was situated on the corner of two of its principal streets. Of the three handsome private offices in the rear Mr. Underwood occupied the one immediately adjoining the general offices; the next, separated from the first by a narrow entrance way, had been appropriated by Mr. Walcott, while the third, communicating with the second and opening directly upon the street, was now fitted up for Darrell's occupancy. The carpets and much of the original furnishing of the rooms still remained, but in the preparation of Darrell's room Kate Underwood and her aunt made numerous trips in their carriage between the offices and The Pines, with the result that when Darrell took possession many changes had been effected. Heavy curtains separated that portion of the room in which the laboratory work was to be done from that to be used as a study, and to the latter there had been added a rug or two, a bookcase in which Darrell could arrange his small library of scientific works, a cabinet of mineralogical specimens, and a pair of paintings intended to conceal some of Time's ravages on the once finely decorated walls, while palms and blooming plants transformed the large plate-glass windows into bowers of fragrance and beauty, at the same time forming a screen from the too inquisitive eyes of passers-by.

Just as Darrell was completing the arrangement of his effects, Mr. Underwood and his partner sauntered into the room from their apartments. Within a few feet of the door Mr. Underwood came to a stop, his hands deep in his trousers pockets, his square chin thrust aggressively forward, while, with a face unreadable as granite, his keen eyes scanned every detail in the room. Mr. Walcott, on the contrary, made the entire circuit of the room, his hands carelessly clasped behind him, his head thrown well back, his every step characterized by a graceful, undulatory motion, like the movements of the feline tribe.

"H'm!" was Mr. Underwood's sole comment when he had finished his survey of the room.

Mr. Walcott turned towards his partner with a smile. "Mr. Darrell is evidently a prime favorite with the ladies," he remarked, pleasantly.

"Well, they don't want to try any of their prime favorite business on me," retorted Mr. Underwood, as he slowly turned and left the room.

Both young men laughed, and Walcott, with an easy, nonchalant air, seated himself near Darrell.

"I find the old gentleman has a keen sense of humor," he said, still smiling; "but some of his jokes are inclined to be a little ponderous at times."

"His humor generally lies along the lines of sarcasm," Darrell replied.

"Ah, something of a cynic, is he?"

"No," said Darrell; "he has too kind a heart to be cynical, but he is very fond of concealing it by sarcasm and brusqueness."

"He is quite original and unique in his way. I find him really a much more agreeable man than I anticipated. You have very pleasant quarters here, Mr. Darrell. I should judge you intended this as a sort of study as well as an office."

"I do intend it so. Probably for a while I shall do more studying than anything else, as it may be some time before I get any assaying."

"I think we can probably throw quite a bit of work your way, as we frequently have inquiries from some of our clients wanting something in that line."

"Walcott," said Mr. Underwood, re-entering suddenly, "Chapman is out there; go and meet him. You can conduct negotiations with him on the terms we agreed upon, but I don't care to figure in the deal. If he asks for me, tell him I'm out."

"I see; as the ladies say, you're 'not at home,'" said Walcott, smiling, as he sprang quickly to his feet. "Well, Mr. Darrell," he continued, "I consider myself fortunate in having you for so near a neighbor, and I trust that we shall prove good friends and our relations mutually agreeable."

Darrell's dark, penetrating eyes looked squarely into the half-closed, smiling ones, which met his glance for an instant, then wavered and dropped.

"I know of no reason why we should not be friends," he replied, quietly, knowing he could say that much with all candor, yet feeling that friendship between them was an utter impossibility, and that of this Walcott was as conscious as was he himself.

"Well, my boy," said Mr. Underwood, seating himself before Darrell's desk, "I guess 'twas a good thing you took the old man's advice for once. I don't know where you would find better quarters than these."

Darrell smiled. "As to following your advice, Mr. Underwood, you didn't even give me a chance. You suggested my taking one of these rooms, and then gave orders on your own responsibility for my paraphernalia to be deposited here, and there was nothing left for me to do but to settle down. However," he added, laying some money on the desk before Mr. Underwood, "I have no complaint to make. Just kindly receipt for that."

"Receipt for this! What do you mean? What is it, anyway?" exclaimed Mr. Underwood, in a bewildered tone.

"It is the month's rent in advance, according to your custom."

"Rent!" Mr. Underwood ejaculated, now thoroughly angry; "what do I want of rent from you? Can't you let me be a friend to you? Time and time again I've tried to help you and you wouldn't have it. Now I'll give you warning, young man, that one of these days you'll go a little too far in this thing, and then you'll have to look somewhere else for friends, for when I'm done with a man, I'm done with him forever!"

"Mr. Underwood," said Darrell, with dignity, "you are yourself going too far at this moment. You know I do not refuse favors from you personally. Do I not consider your home mine? Have I ever offered you compensation for anything that you or your sister have done for me? But this is a different affair altogether."

"Different! I'd like to know wherein."

"Mr. Underwood, if, in addition to your other kindnesses, you personally offered me the use of this room gratis, I might accept it; but I will accept no favors from the firm of Underwood & Walcott."

"Humph! I don't see what difference that need make!" Mr. Underwood retorted.

He sat silently studying Darrell for a few moments, but the latter's face was as unreadable as his own.

"What have you got against that fellow?" he asked at length, curiously.

"I have nothing whatever against him, Mr. Underwood."

"But you're not friendly to him."

Darrell remained silent.

"He is friendly to you," continued Mr. Underwood; "he has talked with me considerably about you and takes quite an interest in you and in your success."

"Possibly," Darrell answered, dryly; "but you will oblige me by not talking of me to him. I have nothing against Mr. Walcott; I am neither friendly nor unfriendly to him, but he is a man to whom I do not wish to be under any obligations whatsoever."

In vain Mr. Underwood argued; Darrell remained obdurate, and when he left the office a little later he carried with him the receipt of Underwood & Walcott for office rent.

Darrell's reputation as an expert which he had already established at the mining camp soon reached Ophir, with the result that he was not long without work in the new office. For a time he devoted his leisure hours to unremitting study. The brief but intense summer season of the high altitudes was now well advanced, however, and in its stifling heat, amid the noise of the busy little city, and constantly subjected to interruptions, his scientific studies and researches lost half their charm.

And in proportion as they lost their power to interest him the home on the mountain-side, beyond reach of the city's heat and dust and clamor, drew him with increasing and irresistible force. Never before had it seemed to him so attractive, so beautiful, so homelike as now. He did not stop to ask himself wherein its new charm consisted or to analyze the sense of relief and gladness with which he turned his face homeward when the day's work was ended. He only felt vaguely that the silent, undemonstrative love which the old place had so long held for him had suddenly found expression. It smiled to him from the flowers nodding gayly to him as he passed; it echoed in the tinkling music of the fountains; the murmuring pines whispered it to him as their fragrant breath fanned his cheek; but more than all he read it in the brown eyes which grew luminous with welcome at his approach and heard it in the low, sweet voice whose wonderful modulations were themselves more eloquent than words. And with this interpretation of the strange, new joy day by day permeating his whole life, he went his way in deep content.

And to Kate Underwood this summer seemed the brightest and the fairest of all the summers of her young life; why, she could not have told, except that the skies were bluer, the sunlight more golden, and the birds sang more joyously than ever before.

In a mining town like Ophir there was comparatively little society for her, so that most of her evenings were spent at home, and she and Darrell were of necessity thrown much together. Sometimes he joined her in a game of tennis, a ride or drive or a short mountain ramble; sometimes he sat on the veranda with the elder couple, listening while she played and sang; but more often their voices blended, while the wild, plaintive notes of the violin rose and fell on the evening air accompanied by the piano or by the guitar or mandolin. Together they watched the sunsets or walked up and down the mountain terrace in the moonlight, enjoying to the full the beauty around them, neither as yet dreaming that,—more than their joy in the bloom and beauty and fragrance, in the music of the fountains or the murmuring voices of the pines, in the sunset's glory, or the moonlight's mystical radiance,—above all, deeper than all, pervading all, was their joy in each other. Hers was a nature essentially childlike; his very infirmity rendered him in experience less than a child; and so, devoid of worldly wisdom,—like Earth's first pair of lovers, without knowledge of good or evil,—all unconsciously they entered their Eden.

One sultry Sunday afternoon they sat within the vine-clad veranda, the strains of the violin and guitar blending on the languorous, perfumed air. As the last notes died away Kate exclaimed,—

"I never had any one accompany me who played with so much expression. You give me an altogether different conception of a piece of music; you seem to make it full of new meaning."

"And why not?" Darrell inquired. "Music is a language of itself, capable of infinitely more expression than our spoken language."

"Who is speaking, then, when you play as you did just now—the soul of the musician or your own?"

"The musician's; I am only the interpreter. The more perfect the harmony or sympathy between his soul, as expressed in the music, and mine, the truer will be the rendering I give. A fine elocutionist will reveal the beauties of a classic poem to hundreds who, of themselves, might never have understood it; but the poem is not his, he is only the poet's interpreter."

"If you call that piece of music which you have just rendered only an

70

interpretation," Kate answered, in a low tone, "I only wish that I could for once hear your own soul speaking through the violin!"

Darrell smiled. "Do you really wish it?" he asked, after a pause, looking into the wistful brown eyes.

"I do."

She was seated in a low hammock, swinging gently to and fro. He sat at a little distance from her feet, on the topmost of the broad stairs, his back against one of the large, vine-wreathed columns, Duke stretched full length beside him.

A slight breeze stirred the flower-scented air and set the pines whispering for a moment; then all was silent. With eyes half closed, Darrell raised the violin and, drawing the bow softly across the strings, began one of his own improvisos, the exquisite, piercing sweetness of the first notes swelling with an indescribable pathos until Kate could scarcely restrain a cry of pain. Higher and higher they soared, until above the clouds they poised lightly for an instant, then descended in a flood of liquid harmonies which alternately rose and fell, sometimes tremulous with hope, sometimes moaning in low undertones of grief, never despairing, but always with the same heart-rending pathos, always voicing the same unutterable longing.

Unmindful of his surroundings, his whole soul absorbed in the music, Darrell played on, till, as the strains sank to a minor undertone, he heard a stifled sob, followed by a low whine from Duke. He glanced towards Kate, and the music ceased instantly. Unobserved by him she had left the hammock and was seated opposite himself, listening as though entranced, her lips quivering, her eyes shining with unshed tears, while Duke, alarmed by what he considered signs of evident distress, looked anxiously from her to Darrell as though entreating his help.

"Why, my dear child, what is the matter?" Darrell exclaimed, moving quickly to her side.

"Oh," she cried, piteously, "how could you stop so suddenly! It was like snapping a beautiful golden thread!" And burying her face in her hands, her whole frame shook with sobs.

Darrell, somewhat alarmed himself, laid his hand on her shoulder in an attempt to soothe her. In a moment she raised her head, the tear-drops still glistening on her cheeks and her long golden lashes.

"It was childish in me to give way like that," she said, with a smile that reminded Darrell of the sun shining through a summer shower; "but oh, that music! It was the saddest and the sweetest I ever heard! It was breaking my heart, and yet I could have listened to it forever!"

"It was my fault," said Darrell, regretfully; "I should not have played so long, but I always forget myself when playing that way."

Kate's face grew suddenly grave and serious. "Mr. Darrell," she said, hesitatingly, "I have thought very often about the sad side of your life— since your illness, you know; but I never realized till now the terrible loneliness of it all."

She paused as though uncertain how to proceed. Darrell's face had in turn become grave.

71

"Did the violin tell you that?" he asked, gently.

She nodded silently.

"Yes, it has been lonely, inexpressibly so," he said, unconsciously using the past tense; "but I had no right to cause you this suffering by inflicting my loneliness upon you."

"Do not say that," she replied, quickly; "I am glad that you told me,—in the way you did; glad not only that I understand you better and can better sympathize with you, but also because I believe you can understand me as no one else has; for one reason why the music affected me so much was that it seemed the expression of my own feelings, of my hunger for sympathy all these years."

"Have there been shadows in your life, then, too? It looked to be all sunshine," Darrell said, his face growing tender as he saw the tear-drops falling.

"Yes, it would seem so, with this beautiful home and all that papa does for me, and sometimes I'm afraid I'm ungrateful. But oh, Mr. Darrell, if you could have known my mother, you would understand! She was so different from papa and auntie, and she loved me so! And it seems as though since she died I've had nobody to love me. I suppose papa does in a fashion, but he is too busy to show it, or else he doesn't know how; and Aunt Marcia! well, you know she's good as she can be, but if she loved you, you would never know it. I've wondered sometimes if poor mamma didn't die just for want of love; it has seemed lots of times as though I would!"

"Poor little girl!" said Darrell, pityingly. He understood now the wistful, appealing look of the brown eyes. He intended to say something expressive of sympathy, but the right words would not come. He could think of nothing that did not sound stilted and formal. Almost unconsciously he laid his hand with a tender caress on the slender little white hand lying near him, much as he would have laid it on a wounded bird; and just as unconsciously, the little hand nestled contentedly, like a bird, within his clasp.

A few days later Darrell heard from Walcott the story of Harry Whitcomb's love for his cousin. It had been reported, Walcott said, in low tones, as though imparting a secret, that young Whitcomb was hopelessly in love with Miss Underwood, but that she seemed rather indifferent to his attentions. It was thought, however, that the old gentleman had favored the match, as he had given his nephew an interest in his mining business, and had the latter lived and proved himself a good financier, it was believed that Mr. Underwood would in time have bestowed his daughter upon him.

Darrell listened silently. Of young Whitcomb, of his death, and of his own part in that sad affair he had often heard, but no mention of anything of this nature. He sat lost in thought.

"Of course, you know how sadly the romance ended," Walcott continued, wondering somewhat at Darrell's silence. "I have understood that you were a witness of young Whitcomb's tragic death."

"I know from hearsay, that is all," Darrell replied, quietly; "I have heard the story a number of times."

Walcott expressed great surprise. "Pardon me, Mr. Darrell, for referring to the matter. I had heard something regarding the peculiar nature of your malady, but I had no idea it was so marked as that. Is it possible that you have no recollection of that affair?"

"None whatever," Darrell answered, briefly, as though he did not care to discuss the matter.

"How strange! One would naturally have supposed that anything so terrible, so shocking to the sensibilities, would have left an impression on your mind never to have been effaced! But I fear the subject is unpleasant to you, Mr. Darrell; pardon me for having alluded to it."

The conversation turned, but Darrell could not banish the subject from his thoughts. Kate had often spoken to him of her cousin, but never as a lover. He recalled his portrait at The Pines; the frank, boyish face with its winning smile—a bonnie lover surely! Had she, or had she not, he wondered, learned to reciprocate his love before the tragic ending came? And if not, did she now regret it?

He watched her that evening, fearing to broach a subject so delicate, but pondering long and deeply, till at last she rallied him on his unusual seriousness, and he told her what he had heard.

"Yes," she said, in reply; "Harry loved me, or thought he did; though he was like the others—he did not understand me any better than they. But he had always been just like a brother to me, and I could never have loved him in any other way, and I told him so. Papa said I would learn in time, and I think perhaps he would have insisted upon it if Harry had lived. I was sorry I couldn't care for him as he wished; he thought I would after a while, but I never could, for I think that kind of love is far different from all others; don't you, Mr. Darrell?"

And Darrell, looking from the mountain-side where they were standing out into the deep blue spaces where the stars, one by one, were gliding into sight, answered, reverently,—

"As far above all others 'as the heaven is high above the earth.'"

To him at that instant love—the love that should exist between two who, out of earth's millions, have chosen each the other—seemed something as yet remote; a sacred temple whose golden dome, like some mystic shrine, gleamed from afar, but into which he might some day enter; unaware that he already stood within its outer court.

Chapter XV

The Awakening

As Darrell was returning home one evening, some ten days later, he heard Kate's rippling laughter and sounds of unusual merriment, and, on coming out into view of the house, beheld her engaged in executing a waltz on the veranda, with Duke as a partner. The latter, in his efforts to oblige his young mistress and at the same time preserve his own dignity, presented so ludicrous a spectacle that Darrell was unable to restrain his risibility. Hearing his peals of laughter and finding herself discovered, Kate rather hastily released her partner, and the collie, glad to be once more permitted the use of four feet, bounded down the steps to give Darrell his customary welcome, his mistress following slowly with somewhat heightened color.

Darrell at once apologized for his hilarity, pleading as an excuse Duke's comical appearance.

"We both must have made a ridiculous appearance," she replied, "but as Duke seems to have forgiven you, I suppose I must, and I think I had better explain such undignified conduct on my part. Auntie has just told me that she is going to give a grand reception for me two weeks from to-day, or, really, two of them, for there is to be an afternoon reception from three until six for her acquaintances, with a few young ladies to assist me in receiving; and then, in the evening, I am to have a reception of my own. We are going to send nearly two hundred invitations to Galena, besides our friends here. Papa is going to have the ball-room on the top floor fitted up for the occasion, and we are to have an orchestra from Galena, and altogether it will be quite 'the event of the season.' Now do you wonder," she added, archly, "that I seized hold of the first object that came in my way and started out for a waltz?"

"Not in the least," Darrell answered, his dark eyes full of merriment. "I only wish I had been fortunate enough to have arrived a little earlier."

A mischievous response to his challenge sparkled in Kate's eyes for a moment, but she only replied, demurely,—

"You shall have your opportunity later."

"When?"

"Two weeks from to-night."

"Ah! am I to be honored with an invitation?"

"Most assuredly you will be invited," Kate replied, quietly; then added, shyly, "and I myself invite you personally, here and now, and that is honoring you as no other guest of mine will be honored."

"Thank you," he replied, gently, with one of his tender smiles; "I accept the personal invitation for your sake."

She was standing on the topmost stair, slightly above him, one hand toying with a spray of blossoms depending from the vines above her head. With a swift movement Darrell caught the little hand and was in the act of carrying it to his lips, when it suddenly slipped from his grasp and its owner as quickly turned and disappeared.

Darrell seated himself with a curious expression. It was not the first time Kate had eluded him thus within the last few days. He had missed of late certain pleasant little familiarities and light, tender caresses, to which he had become accustomed, and he began to wonder at this change in his child companion, as he regarded her.

"What has come over the child?" he soliloquized; "two weeks ago if I had given her a challenge for a waltz she would have taken me up, but lately she is as demure as a little nun! We will have to give it up, won't we, Duke, old boy?" he continued, addressing the collie, whose intelligent eyes were fastened on his face with a shrewd expression, as though, aware of the trend of Darrell's thoughts, he, too, considered his beloved young mistress rather incomprehensible.

The ensuing days were so crowded with preparations for the coming event and with such constant demands upon Kate's time that Darrell seldom saw her except at meals, and opportunities for anything like their accustomed pleasant interchange of confidence were few and far between. On those rare occasions, however, when he succeeded in meeting her alone, Darrell could not but be impressed by the subtle and to him inexplicable change in her manner. She seemed in some way so remotely removed from the young girl who, but a few days before, in response to the violin's tale, had confided to him the loneliness of her own life. A shy, sweet, but impenetrable reserve seemed to have replaced the childlike familiarity. Her eyes still brightened with welcome at his approach, but their light was quickly veiled beneath drooping lids, and through the cadences of her low tones he caught at times the vibration of a new chord, to whose meaning his ear was as yet unattuned.

He did not know, nor did any other, that within that short time she had learned her own heart's secret. Child that she was, she had met Love face to face, and in that one swift, burning glance of recognition the womanhood within her had expanded as the bud expands, bursting its imprisoning calyx under the ardent glance of the sun. But Darrell, seeing only the effect and knowing nothing of the cause, was vaguely troubled.

On the day of the reception both Mr. Underwood and Darrell lunched and dined down town, returning together to The Pines in the interim between the afternoon and evening entertainments. As Darrell sprang from the carriage and ran up the stairs the servants were already turning on the lights temporarily suspended within the veranda and throughout the grounds, so that the place seemed transformed into a bit of fairyland. He heard chatter and laughter, and caught glimpses of young ladies—special guests from out of town—flitting from room to room, but Kate was nowhere to be seen.

Going to his room, he quickly donned an evening suit, not omitting a dainty boutonnière awaiting him on his dressing-case, and betook himself to the libraries across the hall, where, by previous arrangement, Kate was to call for him when it was time to go downstairs.

From below came the ceaseless hum of conversation, the constant ripple of laughter, mingled with bits of song, and the occasional strains of a waltz. Reading was out of the question. Sinking into the depths of a large arm-chair, Darrell was soon lost in dreamy reverie, from which he was roused by a slight sound.

Looking up, he saw framed in the arched doorway between the two rooms a vision, like and yet so unlike the maiden for whom he waited and who had occupied his thoughts but a moment before that he gazed in silent astonishment, uncertain whether it were a reality or part of his dreams. For a moment the silence was unbroken; then,–

"How do you like my gown?" said the Vision, demurely.

Darrell sprang to his feet and approached slowly, a new consciousness dawning in his soul, a new light in his eyes. Of the style or texture of her gown, a filmy, gleaming mass of white, he knew absolutely nothing; he only knew that its clinging softness revealed in new beauty the rounded outlines of her form; that its snowy sheen set off the exquisite moulding of her neck and arms; that its long, shimmering folds accentuated the height and grace of her slender figure; but a knowledge had come to him in that moment like a revelation, stunning, bewildering him, thrilling his whole being, irradiating every lineament of his face.

"I know very little about ladies' dress," he said apologetically, "and I fear I may express myself rather bunglingly, but to me the chief beauty of your gown consists in the fact that it reveals and enhances the beauty of the wearer; in that sense, I consider it very beautiful."

"Thank you," Kate replied, with a low, sweeping courtesy to conceal the blushes which she felt mantling her cheeks, not so much at his words as at what she read in his eyes; "that is the most delicate compliment I ever heard. I know I shall not receive another so delicious this whole evening, and to think of prefacing it with an apology!"

"I am glad to hear that voice," said Darrell, possessing himself of one little gloved hand and surveying his companion critically, from the charmingly coiffed head to the dainty white slipper peeping from beneath her skirt; "the voice and the eyes seem about all that is left of the little girl I had known and loved."

She regarded him silently, with a gracious little smile, but with deepening color and quickening pulse.

He continued: "She has seemed different of late, somehow; she has eluded me so often I have felt as though she were in some way slipping away from me, and now I fear I have lost her altogether. How is it?"

Darrell gently raised the sweet face so that he looked into the clear depths of the brown eyes.

"Tell me, Kathie dear, has she drifted away from me?"

For an instant the eyes were hidden under the curling lashes; then they lifted as she replied, with an enigmatical smile,–

"Not so far but that you may follow, if you choose."

Darrell bowed his head and his lips touched the golden-brown hair.

"Sweetheart," he said, in low tones, scarcely above a whisper, "I follow; if I overtake her, what then? Will I find her the same as in the past?"

76

Her heart was beating wildly with a new, strange joy; she longed to get away by herself and taste its sweetness to the full.

"The same, and yet not the same," she answered, slowly; then, before he could say more, she added, lightly, as a wave of laughter was borne upward from the parlors.

"But I came to see if you were ready to go downstairs; ought we not to join the others?"

"As you please," he replied, stooping to pick up the programme she had dropped; "are the guests arriving yet?"

"No; it is still early, but I want to introduce you to my friends. Oh, yes, my programme; thanks! That reminds me, I am going to ask you to put your name down for two or three waltzes; you know," she added, smiling, "I promised you two weeks ago some waltzes for this evening, so take your choice."

For an instant Darrell hesitated, and the old troubled look returned to his face.

"You are very kind," he said, slowly, "and I appreciate the honor; but it has just occurred to me that really I am not at all certain regarding my proficiency in that line."

Kate understood his dilemma. They had reached the hall; some one was at the piano below and the strains of a dreamy waltz floated through the rooms.

"I haven't a doubt of your proficiency myself," she replied, with a confident smile, "but if you would like a test, here is a good opportunity," and she glanced up and down the vacant but brightly lighted corridor. Darrell needed no second hint, and almost before she was aware they were gliding over the floor.

To Kate, intoxicated with her new-found joy, it seemed as though she were borne along on the waves of the music without effort or volition of her own. She dared not trust herself to speak. Once or twice she raised her eyes to meet the dark ones whose gaze she felt upon her face, but the love-light shining in their depths overpowered her glance and she turned her eyes away. She knew that he had seen and recognized the woman, and that as such—and not as a child—he loved her, and for the present this knowledge was happiness enough.

And Darrell was silent, still bewildered by the twofold revelation which had so suddenly come to him; the revelation of the lovely womanhood at his side, to which he had, until now, been blind, and of the love within his own heart, of which, till now, he had been unconscious.

Before they had completed two turns up and down the corridor the music ceased as suddenly as it had begun.

"Oh, that was heavenly! It seemed like a dream!" Kate exclaimed, with a sigh.

"It seemed a very blessed bit of reality to me," Darrell laughed in return, drawing her arm within his own as they proceeded towards the stairs.

"You are a superb dancer; now you certainly can have no scruples about claiming some waltzes," Kate replied, withdrawing her arm and again placing her programme in his hands.

As they paused at the head of the stairs while Darrell complied with her request, a chorus of voices was heard in the hall below.

"Kate, are you never coming?" some one called, and a sprightly brunette appeared for an instant on the first landing, but vanished quickly at sight of Darrell.

"Girls!" they heard her exclaim to the merry group below; "would you believe it? She is taking a base advantage of us; she has discovered what we did not suppose existed in this house—a young man—and is getting her programme filled in advance!"

Cries of "Oh, Kate, that's not fair!" followed. Kate leaned laughingly over the balustrade.

"He's an angel of a dancer, girls," she called, "but I'll promise not to monopolize him!"

Darrell returned the programme, saying, as they passed down the stairs together,—

"I didn't want to appear selfish, so I only selected three, but give me more if you can, later."

Kate smiled. "I think," she replied, "you will speedily find yourself in such demand that I will consider myself fortunate to have secured those three; but," she added shyly, as her eyes met his, "my first waltz was with you, and that was just as I intended it should be!"

Through the hours which followed so swiftly Darrell was in a sort of waking dream, a state of superlative happiness, unmarred as yet by phantoms from the shrouded past or misgivings as to the dim, uncertain future; past and future were for the time alike forgotten. One image dominated his mind,—the form and face of the fair young hostess moving among her guests as a queen amid her court, carrying her daintily poised head as though conscious of the twofold royal crown of womanhood and woman's love. One thought surged continuously through and through his brain,—that she was his, his by the sovereign right of love. Whatever courtesy he showed to others was for her sake, because they were her guests, her friends, and when unengaged he stationed himself in some quiet corner or dimly lighted alcove where, unobserved, he could watch her movements with their rhythmic grace or catch the music of her voice, the sight or sound thrilling him with joy so exquisite as to be akin to pain. The oft-repeated compliments of the crowd about him seemed to him empty, trite, meaningless; what could they know of her real beauty compared with himself who saw her through Love's eyes!

As he stood thus alone in a deep bay-window, shaded by giant palms, some one paused beside him.

"Our little débutante has surpassed herself to-night; she is fairest of the fair!"

Darrell turned to see at his side Walcott, faultlessly attired, elegant, nonchalant; a half-smile playing about his lips as through half-closed eyes he watched the dancers. Instantly all the antagonism in Darrell's nature rose against the man; strive as he might, he was powerless to subdue it. There was no trace of it in his voice, however, as he answered, quietly,—

"Miss Underwood certainly looks very beautiful to-night."

"She has matured marvellously of late," continued the other, in low, pleasant tones; "her development within the past few weeks has been remarkable. But that is to be expected in women of her style, and this is but the beginning. Mark my words, Mr. Darrell," Walcott faced his auditor with a smile, "Miss Underwood's beauty to-night is but the pale shining of a taper beside one of those lights yonder, compared with what it will be a few years hence; are you aware of that?"

"It had not occurred to me," Darrell replied, with studied calmness, for the conversation was becoming distasteful to him.

"Look at her now!" said Walcott, bowing and smiling as Kate floated past them, but regarding her with a scrutiny that aroused Darrell's quick resentment; "very fair, very lovely, I admit, but a trifle too slender; a little too colorless, too neutral, as it were! A few years will change all that. You will see her a woman of magnificent proportions and with the cold, neutral tints replaced by warmth and color. I have made a study of women, and I know that class well. Five or ten years from now she will be simply superb, and at the age when ordinary women lose their power to charm she will only be in the zenith of her beauty."

The look and tone accompanying the words filled Darrell with indignation and disgust.

"You will have to excuse me," he said, coldly; "you seem, as you say, to have made a study of women from your own standpoint, but our standards of beauty differ so radically that further discussion of the subject is useless."

"Ah, well, every man according to his taste, of course," Walcott remarked, indifferently, and, turning lightly, he walked away, a faint gleam of amusement lighting his dark features.

Half an hour later, as Darrell glided over the floor with Kate, some irresistible force drew his glance towards the bay-window where within the shadow of the palms Walcott was now standing alone, suave as ever. Their eyes met for an instant only, and Walcott smiled. The dance went on, but the smile, like a poisoned shaft, entered Darrell's soul and rankled there.

Both Darrell and Walcott were marked men that night and attracted universal attention and comment. Darrell's pale, intellectual face, penetrating eyes, and dark hair already streaked with gray would have attracted attention anywhere, as would also Walcott with his olive skin, his cynical smile, and graceful, sinuous movement. In addition, Darrell's peculiar mental condition and the fact that his identity was enveloped in a degree of mystery rendered him doubly interesting. In the case of each this was his introduction to the social life of Ophir. Each had been a resident of the town, the one as a student and recluse, the other as a business man, but each was a stranger to the stratum known as society. Each held himself aloof that evening from the throng: the one, through natural reserve, courteous but indifferent to the passing crowd; the other alert, watchful, studying the crowd; weighing, gauging this new element, speculating whether or not it were worth his while to court its favor, whether or not he could make of it an ally for his own future advantage.

Soon after his arrival Walcott had begged of Kate Underwood the honor of a waltz, but her programme being then nearly filled she could only give him one well towards the end. As he intended to render himself conspicuous by dancing only once, and then with the belle of the evening, it was at quite a late hour when he first made his appearance on the floor. Kate was on his arm, and at that instant his criticism, made earlier in the evening, that she was too colorless, certainly could not have applied.

As he led her out upon the floor he bent his gaze upon her with a look which brought the color swiftly to her face in crimson waves that flooded the full, snow-white throat and, surging upward, reached even to the blue-veined temples. Instinctively she shrank from him with a sensation almost of fear, but something in his gaze held her as though spell-bound. She looked into his eyes like one fascinated, scarcely knowing what he said or what reply she made. The waltz began, and as their fingers touched Kate's nerves tingled as though from an electric shock. She shivered slightly, then, angry with herself, used every exertion to overcome the strange spell. To a great extent she succeeded, but she felt benumbed, as though moving in a dream or in obedience to some will stronger than her own, while her temples throbbed painfully and her respiration grew hurried and difficult. She grew dizzy, but pride came to her rescue, and, except for the color which now ran riot in her cheeks and a slight tremor through her frame, there was no hint of her agitation. Her partner was all that could be desired, guiding her through the circling crowds, and supporting her in the swift turns with the utmost grace and courtesy, but it was a relief when it was over. At her request, Walcott escorted her to a seat near her aunt, then smilingly withdrew with much inward self-congratulation.

At that moment Darrell, seeing Kate unengaged, hastened to her side.

"You look warm and the air here is oppressive," he said, observing her flushed face and fanning her gently; "shall we go outside for a few moments?"

"Yes, please; anywhere out of this heat and glare," she answered; "my temples throb as if they would burst and my face feels as though it were on fire!"

Darrell hastened to the hall, returning an instant later with a light wrap which he proceeded to throw about Kate's shoulders.

"You are tired, Katherine," said Mrs. Dean, "more tired than you realize now; you had better not dance any more to-night."

"I have but two more dances, auntie," the young girl answered, smiling; "you surely would not wish me to forego those;" adding, in a lower tone, as she turned towards Darrell, "one of them is your waltz, and I would not miss that for anything!"

They passed through the hall and out upon a broad balcony. They could hear the subdued laughter of couples strolling through the brightly lighted grounds below, while over the distant landscape shone the pale weird light of the waning moon, just rising in the east. None of the guests had discovered the balcony opening from the hall on the third floor, so they had it exclusively to themselves.

As Darrell drew Kate's arm closer within his own he was surprised to feel her trembling slightly, while the hand lying on his own was cold as marble.

"My dear child!" he exclaimed; "your hands are cold and you are trembling! What is the matter—are you cold?"

"No, not cold exactly, only shivery," she answered, with a laugh. "My head was burning up in there, and I feel sort of hot flashes and then a creepy, shivery feeling by turns; but I am not cold out here, really," she added, earnestly, as Darrell drew her wrap more closely about her.

"Nevertheless, I cannot allow you to stay out here any longer," Darrell replied, finding his first taste of masculine authority very sweet.

For an instant Kate felt a very feminine desire to put his authority to the test, but the sense of his protection and his solicitude for her welfare seemed particularly soothing just then, and so, with only a saucy little smile, she silently allowed him to lead her into the house. At his suggestion, however, they did not return to the ball-room, but passed around through an anteroom, coming out into a small, circular apartment, dimly lighted and cosily furnished, opening upon one corner of the ball-room.

"It strikes me," said Darrell, as he drew aside the silken hangings dividing the two rooms and pushed a low divan before the open space, "this will be fully as pleasant as the balcony and much safer."

"The very thing!" Kate exclaimed, sinking upon the divan with a sigh of relief; "we will have a fine view of the dancers and yet be quite secluded ourselves."

A minuet was already in progress on the floor, and for a few moments Kate watched the stately, graceful dance, while Darrell, having adjusted her wrap lightly about her, seated himself beside her and silently watched her face with deep content.

Gradually the throbbing in her temples subsided, the nervous tremor ceased, her color became natural, and she felt quite herself again. She leaned back against the divan and looked with laughing eyes into Darrell's face.

"Mr. Darrell, do you believe in hypnotism?" she suddenly inquired.

"In hypnotism? Yes; but not in many of those who claim to practise it. Most of them are mere impostors. But why do you ask?" he continued, drawing her head down upon his shoulder and looking playfully into her eyes; "are you trying to hypnotize me?"

Kate laughed merrily and shook her head. "I'm afraid I wouldn't find you a good subject," she said; then added, slowly, as her face grew serious:

"Do you know, I believe I was hypnotized to-night by that dreadful Mr. Walcott. He certainly cast a malign spell of some kind over me from the moment we went on the floor together till he left me."

"Why do you say that?" Darrell asked, quickly; "you know I did not see you on the floor with him, for Miss Stockton asked me to go with her for a promenade. We came back just as the waltz had ended and Mr. Walcott was escorting you to your aunt. I noticed that you seemed greatly fatigued and excused myself to Miss Stockton and came over at once. What had happened?"

Kate related what had occurred. "I can't give you any idea of it," she said, in conclusion; "it seemed unaccountable, but it was simply dreadful. You know his eyes are nearly always closed in that peculiar way of his, and really I don't think I had any idea how they looked; but to-night as he looked at me they were wide open; and, do you know, I can't describe them, but they looked so soft and melting they were beautiful, and yet there was something absolutely terrible in their depths. It seemed some way like looking down into a volcano! And the worst of it was, they seemed to hold me—I couldn't take my eyes from his. He was as kind and courteous as could be, I'll admit that, but even the touch of his fingers made me shiver."

Darrell's face had darkened during Kate's recital, but he controlled his anger.

"Now, was that due to my own imagination or to some uncanny spell of his?" Kate insisted.

"To neither wholly, and yet perhaps a little of each," Darrell answered, lightly, not wishing to alarm her or lead her to attach undue importance to the occurrence. "I think Mr. Walcott has an abnormal amount of conceit, and that most of those little mannerisms of his are mainly to attract attention to himself. He was probably trying to produce some sort of an impression on your mind, and to that extent he certainly succeeded, only the impression does not seem to have been as favorable as he perhaps would have wished. No one but a conceited cad would have attempted such a thing, and with your supersensitive nature the effect on you was anything but pleasant, but don't allow yourself to think about it or be annoyed by it. At the same time I would advise you not to place yourself in his power or where he could have any advantage of you. By the way, this is our waltz, is it not?"

"It is," Kate replied, rising and watching Darrell as he removed her wrap and prepared to escort her to the ball-room. His playful badinage had not deceived her. As she took his arm she said, in a low tone,—

"You affect to treat this matter rather lightly, but, all the same, you have warned me against this man. 'Forewarned is forearmed,' you know, and no man can ever attempt to harm me or mine with impunity!"

Darrell turned quickly in surprise; there was a quality in her tone wholly unfamiliar.

"But I fear you exaggerate what I intended to convey," he said, hastily; "I do not know that he would ever deliberately seek to harm you, but he might render himself obnoxious in some way, as he did to-night."

She shook her head. "I was taken off guard to-night," she said; "but he had best never attempt anything of the kind a second time!"

They were now waiting for the waltz to begin; she continued, in the same low tone:

"I have had a western girl's education. When I was a child this place was little more than a rough mining camp, with plenty of desperate characters. My father trained me as he would have trained a boy, and," she added, significantly, with a bright, proud smile, "I am just as proficient now as I was then!"

Darrell scarcely heeded the import of her words, so struck was he by the change in her face, which had suddenly grown wonderfully like her father's,—stern, impassive, unrelenting. She smiled, and the look vanished, and for the time he thought no more of it, but as the passing cloud sometimes reveals features in a landscape unnoticed in the sunlight, so it had disclosed a phase of character latent, unguessed even by those who knew her best.

Two hours later the last carriage had gone; the guests from out of town who were to remain at The Pines for the night had retired, and darkness and silence had gradually settled over the house. A light still burned in Mr. Underwood's private room, where he paced back and forth, his brows knit in deep thought, but his stern face lighted with a smile of intense satisfaction. Darrell, who had remained below to assist Mrs. Dean in the performance of a few last duties, having accompanied her in a final tour of the deserted rooms to make sure that all was safe, bade her good-night and went upstairs. To his surprise, Kate's library was still lighted, and through the open door he could see her at her desk writing.

She looked up on hearing his step, and, as he approached, rose and came to the door.

She had exchanged her evening gown for a dainty robe de chambre of white cashmere and lace, and, standing there against the background of mellow light, her hair coiled low on her neck, while numerous intractable locks curled about her ears and temples, it was small wonder that Darrell's eyes bespoke his admiration and love, even if his lips did not.

"Writing at this time of night!" he exclaimed; "we supposed you asleep long ago."

"Sh! don't speak so loud," she protested. "You'll have Aunt Marcia up here! I have nearly finished my writing, so you needn't scold."

Glancing at the large journal lying open on her desk, Darrell asked, with a quizzical smile,—

"Couldn't that have been postponed for a few hours?"

"Not to-night," she replied, with emphasis; "ordinarily, you know, it could and would have been postponed, perhaps indefinitely, but not to-night!"

She glanced shyly into his eyes, and her own fell, as she added, in a lower tone,—

"To-night has memories so golden I want to preserve them before they have been dimmed by even one hour's sleep!"

Darrell's face grew marvellously tender; he drew her head down upon his breast while he caressed the rippling hair with its waves of light and shade.

"This night will always have golden memories for me, Kathie," he said, "and neither days nor years can ever dim their lustre; of that I am sure."

Kate raised her head, drawing herself slightly away from his embrace so that she could look him in the face.

"'Kathie!'" she repeated, softly; "that is the second time you have called me by that name to-night. I never heard it before; where did you get it?"

"Oh, it came to me," he said, smiling; "and somehow it seemed just the name for you; but I'll not call you so unless you like it."

"I do like it immensely," she replied; "I am tired of 'Kate' and 'Kittie' and Aunt Marcia's terrible 'Katherine;' I am glad you are original enough to call me by something different, but it sounds so odd; I wondered if there might have been a 'Kathie' in the past. But," she added, quickly, "I must not stay here. I just came out to say good-night to you."

"We had better say good-morning," Darrell laughed, as the clock in the hall below chimed one of the "wee, sma' hours;" "promise me that you will go to rest at once, won't you?"

"Very soon," she answered, smiling; then, a sudden impulsiveness conquering her reserve, she exclaimed, "Do you know, this has been the happiest night of my whole life. I hardly dare go to sleep for fear I will wake up and find it all a dream."

For answer Darrell folded her close to his breast, kissing her hair and brow with passionate tenderness; then suddenly, neither knew just how, their lips met in long, lingering, rapturous kisses.

"Will that make it seem more real, sweetheart?" he asked, in a low voice vibrating with emotion.

"Yes, oh yes!" she panted, half frightened by his fervor; "but let me go; please do!"

He released her, only retaining her hands for an instant, which he bent and kissed; then bidding her good-night, he hastened down the hall to his room.

At the door, however, he looked back and saw her still standing where he had left her. She wafted him a kiss on her finger-tips and disappeared. Going to her desk, she read with shining eyes and smiling lips the last lines written in her journal, then dipped her pen as though to write further, hesitated, and, closing the book, whispered,–

"That is too sacred to intrust even to you, you dear, old journal! I shall keep it locked in my own breast."

Then, locking her desk and turning off the light, she stole noiselessly to her room.

Chapter XVI

The Aftermath

As Darrell entered his room its dim solitude seemed doubly grateful after the glare of the crowded rooms he had lately left. His brain whirled from the unusual excitement. He wanted to be alone with his own thoughts–alone with this new, overpowering joy, and assure himself of its reality. He seated himself by an open window till the air had cooled his brow, and his brain, under the mysterious, soothing influence of the night, grew less confused; then, partially disrobing, he threw himself upon his bed to rest, but not to sleep.

Again he lived over the last few weeks at The Pines, comprehending at last the gracious influence which, entering into his barren, meagre life, had rendered it so inexpressibly rich and sweet and complete. Ah, how blind! to have walked day after day hand in hand with Love, not knowing that he entertained an angel unawares!

And then had followed the revelation, when the scales had fallen from his eyes before the vision of lovely maiden-womanhood which had suddenly confronted him. He recalled her as she stood awaiting his tardy recognition—recalled her every word and look throughout the evening down to their parting, and again he seemed to hold her in his arms, to look into her eyes, to feel her head upon his breast, her kisses on his lips.

But even with the remembrance of those moments, while yet he felt the pressure of her lips upon his own, pure and cool like the dewy petals of a rose at sunrise, there came to him the first consciousness of pain mingled with the rapture, the first dash of bitter in the sweet, as he recalled the question in her eyes and the half-whispered, "I wondered if there might have been a 'Kathie' in the past."

The past! How could he for one moment have forgotten that awful shadow overhanging his life! As it suddenly loomed before him in its hideous blackness, Darrell started from his pillow in horror, a cold sweat bursting from every pore. Gradually the terrible significance of it all dawned upon him,—the realization of what he had done and of what he must, as best he might, undo. It meant the relinquishment of what was sweetest and holiest on earth just as it seemed within his grasp; the renunciation of all that had made life seem worth living! Darrell buried his face in his hands and groaned aloud. So it was only a mockery, a dream. He recalled Kate's words: "I hardly dare go to sleep for fear I will wake up and find it all a dream," and self-reproach and remorse added their bitterness to his agony. What right had he to bring that bright young life under the cloud overhanging his own, to wreck her happiness by contact with his own misfortune! What would it be for her when she came to know the truth, as she must know it; and how was he to tell her? In his anguish he groaned,—

"God pity us both and be merciful to her!"

For more than an hour he walked the room; then kneeling by the bed, just as a pale, silvery streak appeared along the eastern horizon, he cried,—

"O God, leave me not in darkness; give me some clew to the vanished past, that I may know whether or not I have the right to this most precious of all thine earthly gifts!"

And, burying his face, he strove as never before to pierce the darkness enveloping his brain. Long he knelt there, his hands clinching the bedclothes convulsively, even the muscles of his body tense and rigid under the terrible mental strain he was undergoing, while at times his powerful frame shook with agony.

The silvery radiance crept upward over the deep blue dome; the stars dwindled to glimmering points of light, then faded one by one; a roseate flush tinged the eastern sky, growing and deepening, and the first golden rays were shooting upward from a sea of crimson flame as Darrell rose from his knees. He walked to the window, but even the sunlight seemed to mock him—there was no light for him, no rift in the cloud darkening his path, and with a heavy sigh he turned away. The struggle was not yet over; this was to be a day of battle with himself, and he nerved himself for the coming ordeal.

After a cold bath he dressed and descended to the breakfast-room. It was still early, but Mr. Underwood was already at the table and Mrs. Dean entered a moment later from the kitchen, where she had been giving directions for breakfast for Kate and her guests. Both were shocked at Darrell's haggard face and heavy eyes, but by a forced cheerfulness he succeeded in diverting the scrutiny of the one and the anxious solicitude of the other. Mr. Underwood returned to his paper and his sister and Darrell had the conversation to themselves.

"Last night's dissipation proved too much for me," Darrell said, playfully, in reply to some protest of Mrs. Dean's regarding his light appetite.

"You don't look fit to go down town!" she exclaimed; "you had better stay at home and help Katherine entertain her guests. I noticed you seemed to be very popular with them last night."

"I'm afraid I would prove a sorry entertainer," Darrell answered, lightly, as he rose from the table, "so you will kindly excuse me to Miss Underwood and her friends."

"Aren't you going to wait and ride down?" Mr. Underwood inquired.

"Not this morning," Darrell replied; "a brisk walk will do me good." And a moment later they heard his firm step on the gravelled driveway.

Mr. Underwood having finished his reading of the morning paper passed it to his sister.

"Pretty good write-up of last night's affair," he commented, as he replaced his spectacles in their case.

"Is there? I'll look it up after breakfast; I haven't my glasses now," Mrs. Dean replied. "I thought myself that everything passed off pretty well. What did you think of Katherine last night, David?"

The lines about his mouth deepened as he answered, quietly,—

"She'll do, if she is my child. I didn't see any finer than she; and old Stockton's daughter, with all her father's millions, couldn't touch her!"

"I had no idea the child was so beautiful," Mrs. Dean continued; "she seemed to come out so unexpectedly some way, just like a flower unfolding. I never was so surprised in my life."

"I guess the little girl took a good many of 'em by surprise, judging by appearances," Mr. Underwood remarked, a shrewd smile lighting his stern features.

"Yes, she received a great deal of attention," rejoined his sister. "I suppose," she added thoughtfully, "she'll have lots of admirers 'round here now."

"No, she won't," Mr. Underwood retorted, with decision, at the same time pushing back his chair and rising hastily; "I'll see to it that she doesn't. If the right man steps up and means business, all right; but I'll have no hangers-on or fortune-hunters dawdling about!"

His sister watched him curiously with a faint smile. "You had better advertise for the kind of man you want," she said, dryly, "and state that 'none others need apply,' as a warning to applicants whom you might consider undesirable."

Mr. Underwood turned quickly. "What are you driving at?" he demanded, impatiently. "I've no time for beating about the bush."

"And I've no time for explanations," she replied, with exasperating calmness; "you can think it over at your leisure."

With a contemptuous "Humph!" Mr. Underwood left the house. After he had gone his sister sat for a while in deep thought, then, with a sigh, rose and went about her accustomed duties. She had been far more keen than her brother to observe the growing intimacy between her niece and Darrell, and she had seen some indications on the previous evening which troubled her, as much on Darrell's account as Kate's, for she had become deeply attached to the young man, and she well knew that her brother would not look upon him with favor as a suitor for his daughter.

Meanwhile, Darrell, on reaching the office, found work and study alike impossible. The room seemed narrow and stifling; the medley of sound from the adjoining offices and from the street was distracting. He recalled the companions of his earlier days of pain and conflict,—the mountains,—and his heart yearned for their restful silence, for the soothing and uplifting of their solemn presence.

Having left a brief note on Mr. Underwood's desk he closed his office, and, leaving the city behind him, started on foot up the familiar canyon road. After a walk of an hour or more he left the road, and, striking into a steep, narrow trail, began the ascent of one of the mountains of the main range. It still lacked a little of midday when he at last found himself on a narrow bench, near the summit, in a small growth of pines and firs. He stopped from sheer exhaustion and looked about him. Not a sign of human life was visible; not a sound broke the stillness save an occasional breath of air murmuring through the pines and the trickling of a tiny rivulet over the rocks just above where he stood. Going to the little stream he caught the crystal drops as they fell, quenching his thirst and bathing his heated brow; then, somewhat refreshed, he braced himself for the inevitable conflict.

Slowly he paced up and down the rocky ledge, giving no heed to the passage of time, all his faculties centred upon the struggle between the inexorable demands of conscience on the one hand and the insatiate cravings of a newly awakened passion on the other. Vainly he strove to find some middle ground. Gradually, as his brain grew calm, the various courses of action which had at first suggested themselves to his mind appeared weak and cowardly, and the only course open to him was that of renunciation and of self-immolation.

With a bitter cry he threw himself, face downward, upon the ground. A long time he lay there, till at last the peace from the great pitying heart of

Nature touched his heart, and he slept on the warm bosom of Mother Earth as a child on its mother's breast.

The sun was sinking towards the western ranges and slowly lengthening shadows were creeping athwart the distant valleys when Darrell rose to his feet and, after silently drinking in the beauty of the scene about him, prepared to descend. His face bore traces of the recent struggle, but it was the face of one who had conquered, whose mastery of himself was beyond all doubt or question. He took the homeward trail with firm step, with head erect, with face set and determined, and there was in his bearing that which indicated that there would be no wavering, no swerving from his purpose. His own hand had closed and bolted the gates of the Eden whose sweets he had but just tasted, and his conscience held the flaming sword which was henceforth to guard those portals.

A little later, as Darrell in the early twilight passed up the driveway to The Pines, he was conscious only of a dull, leaden weight within his breast; his very senses seemed benumbed and he almost believed himself incapable of further suffering, till, as he approached the house, the sight of Kate seated in the veranda with her father and aunt and the thought of the suffering yet in store for her thrilled him anew with most poignant pain.

His face was in the shadow as he came up the steps, and only Kate, seated near him, saw its pallor. She started and would have uttered an exclamation, but something in its expression awed and restrained her. There was a grave tenderness in his eyes as they met hers, but the light and joy which had been there when last she looked into them had gone out and in their place were dark gloom and despair. She heard as in a dream his answers to the inquiries of her father and aunt; heard him pass into the house accompanied by her aunt, who had prepared a substantial lunch against his return, and, with a strange sinking at her heart, sat silently awaiting his coming out.

It had been a trying day for her. On waking, her happiness had seemed complete, but Darrell's absence on that morning of all mornings had seemed to her inexplicable, and when her guests had taken their departure and the long day wore on without his return and with no message from him, an indefinable dread haunted her. She had watched eagerly for Darrell's return, believing that one look into his face would banish her forebodings, but, instead, she had read there only a confirmation of her fears. And now she waited in suspense, longing, yet dreading to hear his step.

At last he came, and, as he faced the light, Kate was shocked at the change which so few hours had wrought. He, too, was touched by the piteous appeal in her eyes, and there was a rare tenderness in voice and smile as he suggested a stroll through the grounds according to their custom, which somewhat reassured her.

Perhaps Mr. Underwood and his sister had observed the old shadow of gloom in Darrell's face, and surmised something of its cause, for their eyes followed the young people in their walk up and down under the pines and a softened look stole into their usually impassive faces. At last, as they passed out of sight on one of the mountain terraces, Mrs. Dean said, with slight hesitation,—

"Did it ever occur to you, David, that Katherine and Mr. Darrell are thrown in each other's society a great deal?"

Mr. Underwood shot a keen glance at his sister from under his heavy brows, as he replied,—

"Come to think of it, I suppose they are, though I can't say as I've ever given the matter much thought."

"Perhaps it's time you did think about it."

"Come, Marcia," said her brother, good-humoredly, "come to the point; are you, woman-like, scenting a love-affair in that direction?"

Mrs. Dean found herself unexpectedly cornered. "I don't say that there is, but I don't know what else you could expect of two young folks like them, thrown together constantly as they are."

"Well," said Mr. Underwood, with an air of comic perplexity, "do you want me to send Darrell adrift, or shall I pack Puss off to a convent?"

"Now, David, I'm serious," his sister remonstrated, mildly. "Of course, I don't know that anything will come of it; but if you don't want that anything should, I think it's your duty, for Katherine's sake and Mr. Darrell's also, to prevent it. I think too much of them both to see any trouble come to either of them."

Mr. Underwood puffed at his pipe in silence, while the gleaming needles in his sister's fingers clicked with monotonous regularity. When he spoke his tones lacked their usual brusqueness and had an element almost of gentleness.

"Was this what was in your mind this morning, Marcia?"

"Well, maybe so," his sister assented.

"I don't think, Marcia, that I need any one to tell me my duty, especially regarding my child. I have my own plans for her future, and I will allow nothing to interfere with them. And as for John Darrell, he has the good, sterling sense to know that anything more than friendship between him and Kate is not to be thought of for a moment, and I can trust to his honor as a gentleman that he will not go beyond it. So I rather think your anxieties are groundless."

"Perhaps so," his sister answered, doubtfully, "but young folks are not generally governed much by common sense in things of this kind; and then you know, David, Katherine is different from us,—she grows more and more like her mother,—and if she once got her heart set on any one, I don't think anybody—even you—could make her change."

The muscles of Mr. Underwood's face suddenly contracted as though by acute pain.

"That will do, Marcia," he said, gravely, with a silencing wave of his hand; "there is no need to call up the past. I know Kate is like her mother, but she has my blood in her veins also,—enough that when the time comes she'll not let any childish sentimentality stand in the way of what I think is for her good."

Mrs. Dean silently folded her knitting and rose to go into the house. At

89

the door, however, she paused, and, looking back at her brother, said, in her low, even tones,—

"I have said my last word of this affair, David, no matter what comes of it. You think you understand Katherine better than I, but you may find some day that it's better to prevent trouble than to try to cure it."

Meanwhile, Darrell and Kate had reached their favorite seat beneath the pines and, after one or two futile attempts at talking, had lapsed into a constrained silence. To Kate there came a sudden realization that the merely friendly relations heretofore existing between them had been swept away; that henceforth she must either give the man at her side the concentrated affection of her whole being or, should he prove unworthy,— she glanced at his haggard face and could not complete the supposition even to herself. He was troubled, and her tender heart longed to comfort him, but his strange appearance held her back. At one word, one sign of love from him, she would have thrown herself upon his breast and begged to share his burden in true woman fashion; but he was so cold, so distant; he did not even take her hand as in the careless, happy days before either of them thought of love.

Kate could endure the silence no longer, and ventured some timid word of loving sympathy.

Darrell turned, facing her, his dark eyes strangely hollow and sunken.

"Yes," he said, in a low voice, "God knows I have suffered since I saw you, but I deserve to suffer for having so far forgotten myself last night. That is not what is troubling me now; it is the thought of the sorrow and wretchedness I have brought into your pure, innocent life,—that you must suffer for my folly, my wrong-doing."

"But," interposed Kate, "I don't understand; what wrong have you done?"

"Kathie," he answered, brokenly, "it was all a mistake—a terrible mistake of mine! Can you forgive me? Can you forget? God grant you can!"

"Forgive! Forget!" she exclaimed, in bewildered tones; "a mistake?" her voice faltered and she paused, her face growing deathly pale.

"I cannot think," he continued, "how I came to so forget myself, the circumstances under which I am here, the kindness you and your people have shown me, and the trust they have reposed in me. I must have been beside myself. But I have no excuse to offer; I can only ask your forgiveness, and that I may, so far as possible, undo what has been done."

While he was speaking she had drawn away from him, and, sitting proudly erect, she scanned his face in the waning light as though to read there the full significance of his meaning. Her cheeks blanched at his last words, but there was no tremor in her tones as she replied,—

"I understand you to refer to what occurred last night; is that what you wish undone—what you would have me forget?"

"I would give worlds if only it might be undone," he answered, "but that is an impossibility. Oh Kathie, I know how monstrous, how cruel this must seem to you, but it is the only honorable course left me after my stupidity, my cursed folly; and, believe me, it is far more of a kindness even to you to stop this wretched business right here than to carry it farther."

"It is not necessary to consider my feelings in the matter, Mr. Darrell. If, as you say, you found yourself mistaken, to attempt after that to carry on what could only be a mere farce would be simply unpardonable. A mistake I could forgive; a deliberate deception, never!"

The tones, so unlike Kate's, caused Darrell to turn in pained surprise. The deepening shadows hid the white, drawn face and quivering lips; he saw only the motionless, slender figure held so rigidly erect.

"But, Kathie—Miss Underwood—you must have misunderstood me," he said, earnestly. "I have acted foolishly, but in no way falsely. You could not, under any circumstances, accuse me of deception——"

"I beg your pardon, Mr. Darrell," she interposed, more gently; "I did not intend to accuse you of deception. I only meant that, regardless of any personal feeling, it was, as you said, better to stop this; that to carry it farther after you had found you did not care for me as you supposed—or as I was led to suppose——" She paused an instant, uncertain how to proceed.

"Kathie, Kathie! what are you saying?" Darrell exclaimed. "What have I said that you should so misunderstand me?"

"But," she protested, piteously, struggling to control her voice, "did you not say that it was all a mistake on your part—that you wished it all undone? What else could I understand?"

"My poor child!" said Darrell, tenderly; then reaching over and possessing himself of one of her hands, he continued, gravely:

"The mistake was mine in that I ever allowed myself to think of loving you when love is not for me. I have no right, Kathie, to love you, or any other woman, as I am now. I did not know until last night that I did love you. Then it came upon me like a revelation,—a revelation so overwhelming that it swept all else before it. You, and you alone, filled my thoughts. Wherever I was, I saw you, heard you, and you only. Again and again in imagination I clasped you to my breast, I felt your kisses on my lips,—just as I afterwards felt them in reality."

He paused a moment and dropped the hand he had taken. Under cover of the shadows Kate's tears were falling unchecked; one, falling on Darrell's hand, had warned him that there must be no weakening, no softening.

His voice was almost stern as he resumed. "For those few hours I forgot that I was a being apart from the rest of the world, exiled to darkness and oblivion; forgot the obligations to myself and to others which my own condition imposes upon me. But the dream passed; I awoke to a realization of what I had done, and whatever I have suffered since is but the just penalty of my folly. The worst of all is that I have involved you in needless suffering; I have won your love only to have to put it aside—to renounce it. But even this is better—far better than to allow your young life to come one step farther within the clouds that envelop my own. Do you understand me now, Kathie?"

"Yes," she replied, calmly; "I understand it from your view, as it looks to you."

"But is not that the only view?"

She did not speak at once, and when she did it was with a peculiar deliberation.

"The clouds will lift one day; what then?"

Darrell's voice trembled with emotion as he replied, "We cannot trust to that, for neither you nor I know what the light will reveal."

She remained silent, and Darrell, after a pause, continued: "Don't make it harder for me, Kathie; there is but one course for us to follow in honor to ourselves or to each other."

They sat in silence for a few moments; then both rose simultaneously to return to the house, and as they did so Darrell was conscious of a new bearing in Kate's manner,—an added dignity and womanliness. As they faced one another Darrell took both her hands in his, saying,—

"What is it to be, Kathie? Can we return to the old friendship?"

She stood for a moment with averted face, watching the stars brightening one by one in the evening sky.

"No," she said, presently, "we can never return to that now; it would seem too bare, too meagre. There will always be something deeper and sweeter than mere friendship between us,—unless you fail me, and I know you will not."

"And do you forgive me?" he asked.

She turned then, looking him full in the eyes, and her own seemed to have caught the radiance of the stars themselves, as she answered, simply,—

"No, John Darrell, for there is nothing to forgive."

Chapter XVII

"She knows her Father's Will is Law"

Though the succeeding days and weeks dragged wearily for Darrell, he applied himself anew to work and study, and only the lurking shadows within his eyes, the deepening lines on his face, the fast multiplying gleams of silver in his dark hair, gave evidence of his suffering.

And if to Kate the summer seemed suddenly to have lost its glory and music, if she found the round of social pleasures on which she had just entered grown strangely insipid, if it sometimes seemed to her that she had quaffed all the richness and sweetness of life on that wondrous first night till only the dregs remained, she gave no sign. With her sunny smile and lightsome ways she reigned supreme, both in society and in the home, and none but her aunt and Darrell missed the old-time rippling laughter or noted the deepening wistfulness and seriousness of the fair young face.

Her father watched her with growing pride, and with a visible satisfaction which told of carefully laid plans known only to himself, whose consummation he deemed not far distant.

Acting on the suggestion of his sister, he had been closely observant of both Kate and Darrell, but any conclusions which he formed he kept to himself and went his way apparently well satisfied.

At the close of an unusually busy day late in the summer Darrell was seated alone in his office, reviewing his life in the West and vaguely wondering what would yet be the outcome of it all, when Mr. Underwood entered from the adjoining room. Exultation and elation were patent in his very step, but Darrell, lost in thought, was hardly conscious even of his presence.

"Well, my boy, what are you mooning over?" Mr. Underwood asked, good-naturedly, noting Darrell's abstraction.

"Only trying to find a solution for problems as yet insoluble," Darrell answered, with a smile that ended in a sigh.

"Stick to the practical side of life, boy, and let the problems solve themselves."

"A very good rule to follow, provided the problems would solve themselves," commented Darrell.

"Those things generally work themselves out after a while," said Mr. Underwood, walking up and down the room. "I say, don't meddle with what you can't understand; take what you can understand and make a practical application of it. That's always been my motto, and if people would stick to that principle in commercial life, in religion, and everything else, there'd be fewer failures in business, less wrangling in the churches, and more good accomplished generally."

"I guess you are about right there," Darrell admitted.

"Been pretty busy to-day, haven't you?" Mr. Underwood asked, abruptly, after a short pause.

"Yes, uncommonly so; work is increasing of late."

"That's good. Well, it has been a busy day with us; rather an eventful one, in fact; one which Walcott and I will remember with pleasure, I trust, for a good many years to come."

"How is that?" Darrell inquired, wondering at the pleasurable excitement in the elder man's tones.

"We made a little change in the partnership to-day: Walcott is now an equal partner with myself."

Darrell remained silent from sheer astonishment. Mr. Underwood evidently considered his silence an indication of disapproval, for he continued:

"I know you don't like the man, Darrell, so there's no use of arguing that side of the question, but I tell you he has proved himself invaluable to me. You might not think it, but it's a fact that the business in this office has increased fifty per cent. since he came into it. He is thoroughly capable, responsible, honest,—just the sort of man that I can intrust the business to as I grow older and know that it will be carried on as well as though I was at the helm myself."

"Still, a half-interest seems pretty large for a man with no more capital in the business than he has," said Darrell, determined to make no personal reference to Walcott.

"He has put in fifty thousand additional since he came in," Mr. Underwood replied.

Darrell whistled softly.

"Oh, he has money all right; I'm satisfied of that. I'm satisfied that he could have furnished the money to begin with, only he was lying low."

"Well, he certainly has nothing to complain of; you've done more than well by him."

"No better proportionately than I would have done by you, my boy, if you had come in with me last spring when I asked you to. I had this thing in view then, and had made up my mind you'd make the right man for the place, but you wouldn't hear to it."

"That's all right, Mr. Underwood," said Darrell; "I appreciate your kind intentions just the same, but I am more than ever satisfied that I wouldn't have been the right man for the place."

Both men were silent for some little time, but neither showed any inclination to terminate the interview. Mr. Underwood was still pacing back and forth, while Darrell had risen and was standing by the window, looking out absently into the street.

"That isn't all of it, and I may as well tell you the rest," said Mr. Underwood, suddenly pausing near Darrell, his manner much like a school-boy who has a confession to make and hardly knows how to begin. "Mr. Walcott to-day asked me—asked my permission to pay his addresses to my daughter—my little girl," he added, under his breath, and there was a strange note of tenderness in the usually brusque voice.

If ever Darrell was thankful, it was that he could at that moment look the father squarely in the face. He turned, facing Mr. Underwood, his dark eyes fairly blazing.

"And you gave your permission?" he asked, slowly, with terrible emphasis on each word.

"Most assuredly," Mr. Underwood retorted, quickly, stung to self-defence by Darrell's look and tone. "I may add that I have had this thing in mind for some time—have felt that it was coming; in fact, this new partnership arrangement was made with a view to facilitate matters, and he was enough of a gentleman to come forward at once with his proposition."

Darrell gazed out of the window again with unseeing eyes. "Mr. Underwood," he said, in a low tone, "I would never have believed it possible that your infatuation for that man would have led to this."

"There is no infatuation about it," the elder man replied, hotly; "it is a matter of good, sound judgment and business calculation. I know of no man among our townspeople, or even in the State, to whom I would give my daughter as soon as I would to Walcott. There are others who may have larger means now, but they haven't got his business ability. With what I can give Puss, what he has now, and what he will make within the next few years, she will have a home and position equal to the best."

"Is that all you think of, Mr. Underwood?"

"Not all, by any means; but it's a mighty important consideration, just

94

the same. But the man is all right morally; you, with all your prejudice against him, can't lay your finger on one flaw in his character."

"Mr. Underwood," said Darrell, slowly, "I have studied that man, I have heard him talk. He has no conception of life beyond the sensual, the animal; he is a brute, a beast, in thought and act. He is no more fit to marry your daughter, or even to associate with her, than––"

"Young man," interrupted Mr. Underwood, laughing good-humoredly, "I have only one thing against you: you are not exactly practical. You are, like my friend Britton, inclined to rather high ideals. We don't generally find men built according to those ideals, and we have to take 'em as we find 'em."

"But you will, of course, allow your daughter to act according to her own judgment? You surely would not force her into any marriage distasteful to her?" Darrell asked, remembering Kate's aversion for Walcott.

"A young girl's judgment in those matters is not often to be relied upon. Kate knows that I consider only her best interests, and I think her judgment could be brought to coincide with my own. At any rate, she knows her father's will is law."

As Darrell, convinced that argument would be useless, made no reply, Mr. Underwood added, after a pause,–

"I know I can trust to your honor that you will not influence her against Walcott?"

"I shall not, of course, attempt to influence her one way or the other. I have no right; but if I had the right,–if she were my sister,–that man should never so much as touch the hem of her garment!"

"My boy," said Mr. Underwood, rather brusquely, extending one hand and laying the other on Darrell's shoulder, "I understand, and you're all right. We all consider you one of ourselves, and," he added, somewhat awkwardly, "you understand, if conditions were not just as they are––"

"But conditions are just as they are," Darrell interposed, quickly, "so there is no use discussing what might be were they different."

The bitterness in his tones struck a chord of sympathy within the heart of the man beside him, but he knew not how to express it, and it is doubtful whether he would have voiced it had he known how. The two clasped hands silently; then, without a word, the elder man left the room.

Not until now had Darrell realized how strong had been the hope within his breast that some crisis in his condition might yet reveal enough to make possible the fulfilment of his love. The pleasant relations between himself and Kate in many respects still remained practically unchanged. True, his sense of honor forbade any return to the tender familiarities of the past, but there yet existed between them a tacit, unspoken comradeship, beneath which flowed, deeply and silently, the undercurrent of love, not to be easily diverted or turned aside. But this he now felt would soon be changed, while all hope for the future must be abandoned.

With a heavy heart Darrell awaited developments. He soon noted a marked increase in the frequency of Walcott's calls at The Pines, and, not caring to embarrass Kate by his presence, he absented himself from the house as often as possible on those occasions.

Walcott himself must have been very soon aware that in his courtship Mr. Underwood was his sole partisan, but he bore himself with a confidence and assurance which would brook no thought of defeat. Mrs. Dean, knowing her brother as she did, was quick to understand the situation, and silently showed her disapproval; but Walcott politely ignored her disfavor as not worth his consideration.

At first, Kate, considering him her father's guest, received him with the same frank, winning courtesy which she extended to others, and he, quick to make the most of every opportunity, exerted himself to the utmost in his efforts to entertain his young hostess and her friends. To a certain extent he succeeded, in that Kate was compelled to admit to herself that he could be far more agreeable than she had ever supposed. He had travelled extensively and was possessed of good descriptive powers; his voice was low and musical, and his eyes, limpid and tender whenever he fixed them upon her face, held her glance by some irresistible, magnetic force, and invariably brought the deepening color to her cheeks.

With the first inkling, however, of the nature of his visits, all her old abhorrence of him returned with increased intensity, but her ill-concealed aversion only furnished him with a new incentive and spurred him to redouble his attentions.

The only opposition encountered by him that appeared in the least to disturb his equanimity, was that of Duke, which was on all occasions most forcibly expressed, the latter never failing to greet him with a low growl, meeting all overtures of friendship with an ominous gleam in his intelligent eyes and a display of ivory that made Mr. Walcott only too willing to desist.

"Really, Miss Underwood," Walcott remarked one evening when Duke had been more than usually demonstrative, "your pet's attentions to me are sometimes a trifle distracting. Could you not occasionally bestow the pleasure of his society upon some one else—Mr. Darrell, for instance? I imagine the two might prove quite congenial to each other."

"Please remember, Mr. Walcott, you are speaking of a friend of mine," Kate replied, coldly.

"Mr. Darrell? I beg pardon, I meant no offence; but since he and Duke seem to share the same unaccountable antipathy towards myself, I naturally thought there would be a bond of sympathy between them."

Kate had been playing, and was still seated at the piano, idly waiting for Walcott, who was turning the pages of a new music-book, to make another selection. She now rose rather wearily, and, leaving the piano, joined her father and aunt upon the veranda outside.

Walcott pushed the music from him, and, taking Kate's mandolin from off the piano, followed. Throwing himself down upon the steps at Kate's feet in an attitude of genuine Spanish abandon and grace, he said, lightly,—

"Since you will not favor us further, I will see what I can do."

He possessed little technical knowledge of music, but had quite a

96

repertoire of songs picked up in his travels in various countries, to which he could accompany himself upon the guitar or mandolin.

He strummed the strings carelessly for a moment, then, in a low voice, began a Spanish love-song. There was no need of an interpreter to make known to Kate the meaning of the song. The low, sweet cadences were full of tender pleading, every note was tremulous with passion, while the dark eyes holding her own seemed burning into her very soul.

But the spell of the music worked far differently from Walcott's hopes or anticipations. Even while angry at herself for listening, Kate could scarcely restrain the tears, for the tender love-strains brought back so vividly the memory of those hours—so brief and fleeting—in which she had known the pure, unalloyed joy of love, that her heart seemed near bursting. As the last lingering notes died away, the pain was more than she could endure, and, pleading a slight headache, she excused herself and went to her room. Throwing herself upon the bed, she gave way to her feelings, sobbing bitterly as she recalled the sudden, hopeless ending of the most perfect happiness her young life had ever known. Gradually the violence of her grief subsided and she grew more calm, but a dull pain was at her heart, for though unwilling to admit it even to herself, she was hurt at Darrell's absence on the occasions of Walcott's visits.

"Why does he leave me when he knows I can't endure the sight of that man?" she soliloquized, sorrowfully. "If he would stay by me the creature would not dare make love to me. Oh, if we could only just be lovers until all this dreadful uncertainty is past! I'm sure it would come out all right, and I would gladly wait years for him, if only he would let me!"

As she sat alone in her misery she heard Walcott take his departure. A little later Darrell returned and went to his room, and soon after she heard her aunt's step in the hall, followed by a quiet knock at her door.

"Come in, auntie," she called, wondering what her errand might be.

"Have you gone to bed, Katherine, or are you up?" Mrs. Dean inquired, for the room was dark.

"I'm up; why, auntie?"

"Your father said to tell you he wanted to see you, if you had not retired."

Mrs. Dean stopped a moment to inquire for Kate's headache, and as she left the room Kate heard her sigh heavily.

A happy thought occurred to Kate as she ran downstairs,—she would have her father put a stop to Walcott's attentions; if he knew how they annoyed her he would certainly do it. She entered the room where he waited with her sunniest smile, for the stern, gruff-voiced man was the idol of her heart and she believed implicitly in his love for her, even though it seldom found expression in words.

But her smile faded before the displeasure in her father's face. He scrutinized her keenly from under his heavy brows, but if he noted the traces of tears upon her face, he made no comment.

"I did not suppose, Kate," he said, slowly, for he could not bring himself to speak harshly to her,—"I did not suppose that a child of mine would treat any guest of this house as rudely as you treated Mr. Walcott to-night. I sent for you for an explanation."

"I did not mean to be rude, papa," Kate replied, seating herself on her father's knee and laying one arm caressingly about his neck, "but he did annoy me so to-night,—he has annoyed me so often of late,—I just couldn't endure it any longer."

"Has Mr. Walcott ever conducted himself other than as a gentleman?"

"Why, no, papa, he is gentlemanly enough, so far as that is concerned."

"I thought so," her father interposed; "I should say that he had laid himself out to entertain you and your friends and to make it pleasant for all of us whenever he has been here. It strikes me that his manners are very far from annoying; that he is a gentleman in every sense of the word; he certainly carried himself like one to-night in the face of the treatment you gave him."

"Well, I'm sorry if I was rude. I have no objection to him as a gentleman or as an acquaintance, if he would not go beyond that; but I detest his attentions and his love-making, and he will not stop even when he sees that it annoys me."

"No one has a better right to pay his attentions to you, for he has asked and received my permission to do so."

Kate drew herself upright and gazed at her father with eyes full of horror.

"You gave him permission to pay attention to me!" she exclaimed, slowly, as though scarcely comprehending his meaning; then, springing to her feet and drawing herself to her full height, she demanded,—

"Do you mean, papa, that you intend me to marry him?"

For an instant Mr. Underwood felt ill at ease; Kate's face was white and her eyes had the look of a creature brought to bay, that sees no escape from the death confronting it, for even in that brief time Kate, knowing her father's indomitable will, realized with a sense of despair the hopelessness of her situation.

"I suppose your marriage will be the outcome,—at least, I hope so," her father replied, quickly recovering his composure, "for I certainly know of no one to whom I would so willingly intrust your future happiness. Listen to me, Kate: have I not always planned and worked for your best interests?"

"You always have, papa."

"Have I not always chosen what was for your good and for your happiness?"

Kate gave a silent assent.

"Very well; then I think you can trust to my judgment in this case."

"But, papa," she protested, "this is different. I never can love that man; I abhor him—loathe him! Do you think there can be any happiness or good in a marriage without love? Would you and mamma have been happy together if you had not loved each other?"

No sooner had she spoken the words than she regretted them as she noted the look of pain that crossed her father's face. In his silent,

98

undemonstrative way he had idolized his wife, and it was seldom that he would allow any allusion to her in his presence.

"I don't know why you should call up the past," he said, after a pause, "but since you have I will tell you that your mother when a girl like yourself objected to our marriage; she thought that we were unsuited to each other and that we could never live happily together. She listened, however, to the advice of those older and wiser than she, and you know the result." The strong man's voice trembled slightly. "I think our married life was a happy one. It was for me, I know; I hope it was for her."

A long silence followed. To Kate there came the memory of the frail, young mother lying, day after day, upon her couch in the solitude of her sick-room, often weeping silently, while she, a mere child, knelt sadly and wistfully beside her, as silently wiping the tear-drops as they fell and wondering at their cause. She understood now, but not for worlds would she have spoken one word to pain her father's heart.

At last Mr. Underwood said, rising as though to end the interview, "I think I can depend upon you now, Kate, to carry out my wishes in this matter."

Kate rose proudly. "I have never disobeyed you, papa; I will treat Mr. Walcott courteously; but even though you force me to marry him I will never, never love him, and I shall tell him so."

Her father smiled. "Mr. Walcott, I think, has too much good sense to attach much weight to any girlish whims; that will pass, you will think differently by and by."

As she stopped for her usual good-night kiss she threw her arms about her father's neck, and, looking appealingly into his face, said,–

"Papa, it need not be very soon, need it? You are not in a hurry to be rid of your little girl?"

"Don't talk foolishly, child," he answered, hastily; "you know I've no wish to be rid of you, but I do want to see you settled in a home of your own—equal to the best, and, as I said a while ago, and told Mr. Darrell in talking the matter over with him, I know of no one in whose hands I would so willingly place you and your happiness as Mr. Walcott's. As for the date and other matters of that sort," he added, playfully pinching her cheeks, "I suppose those will all be mutually arranged between the gentleman and yourself."

Kate had started back slightly. "You have talked this over with Mr. Darrell?" she exclaimed.

"Yes, why not?"

"What did he think of it?"

"Well," said her father, slowly, "naturally he did not quite fall in with my views, for I think he is not just what you could call a disinterested party. I more than half suspect that Mr. Darrell would like to step into Mr. Walcott's place himself, if he were only eligible, but knowing that he is not, he is too much of a gentleman to commit himself in any way."

Mr. Underwood scanned his daughter's face keenly as he spoke, but it was as impassive as his own. To Kate, Darrell's absences of late were now explained; he understood it all. She kissed her father silently.

"You know, Puss, I am looking out for your best interests in all of this," said her father, a little troubled by her silence.

"I know that is your intention, papa," she replied, with gentle gravity, and left the room.

Chapter XVIII

"On the "Divide"

Summer had merged into autumn. Crisp, exhilarating mornings ushered in glorious days flooded with sunshine, followed by sparkling, frosty nights.

The strike at the mining camp had been adjusted; the union boarding-house after two months was found a failure and abandoned, and the strikers gradually returned to their work. Mr. Underwood, during the shut-down, had improved the time to enlarge the mill and add considerable new machinery; this work was now nearly completed; in two weeks the mill would again be running, and he offered Darrell his old position as assayer in charge, which the latter, somewhat to Mr. Underwood's surprise, accepted.

Although his city business was now quite well established, Darrell felt that life at The Pines was becoming unendurable. Walcott's visits were now so frequent it was impossible longer to avoid him. The latter's air of easy self-assurance, the terms of endearment which fell so flippantly from his lips, and his bold, passionate glances which never failed to bring the rich, warm blood to Kate's cheeks and brow, all to one possessing Darrell's fine chivalric nature and his delicacy of feeling were intolerable. In addition, the growing indications of Kate's unhappiness, the silent appeal in her eyes, the pathetic curves forming about her mouth, and the touch of pathos in the voice whose every tone was music to his ear, seemed at times more than he could bear.

There were hours—silent, brooding hours of the night—when he was sorely tempted to defy past and future alike, and, despite the conditions surrounding himself, to rescue her from a life which could have in store for her nothing but bitterness and sorrow. But with the dawn his better judgment returned; conscience, inexorable as ever, still held sway; he kept his own counsel as in duty bound, going his way with a heart that grew heavier day by day, and was hence glad of an opportunity to return once more to the seclusion of the mountains.

Kate, realizing that all further appeal to her father was useless, as a last resort trusted to Walcott's sense of honor, that, when he should fully understand her feelings towards himself, he would discontinue his attentions. But in this she found herself mistaken. Taking advantage of the courtesy which she extended to him in accordance with the promise given her father, he pressed his suit more ardently than ever.

"Why do you persist in annoying me in this manner?" she demanded one day, indignantly withdrawing from his attempted caresses. "The fact that my father has given you his permission to pay attention to me does not warrant any such familiarity on your part."

"Perhaps not," Walcott replied, in his low, musical tones, "but stolen waters are often sweetest. If I have offended, pardon. I supposed my love for you would justify me in offering any expression of it, but since you say I have no right to do so, I beg of you, my dear Miss Underwood, to give me that right."

"That is impossible," Kate answered, firmly.

"Why impossible?" he asked.

"Because I will not accept any expressions of a love that I cannot reciprocate."

"Love begets love," he argued, softly; "so long as you keep me at arm's length you have no means of knowing whether or not you could reciprocate my affection. Mr. Underwood has done me the great honor to consent to bestow his daughter's hand upon me, and I have no doubt of yet winning the consent of the lady herself if she will but give me a fair chance."

"Mr. Walcott," said Kate, her eyes ablaze with indignation, "would you make a woman your wife who did not love you—who never could, under any circumstances, love you?"

Walcott suddenly seized her hands in his, looking down into her eyes with his steady, dominant gaze.

"If I loved her as I love you," he said, slowly, "I would make her my wife though she hated me,—and win her love afterwards! I can win it, and I will!"

"Never!" Kate exclaimed, passionately, but he had kissed her hands and was gone before she could recover herself.

In that look she had for the first time comprehended something of the man's real nature, of the powerful brute force concealed beneath the smooth, smiling exterior. Her heart seemed seized and held in a vise-like grip, while a cold, benumbing despair settled upon her like an incubus, which she was unable to throw off for days.

It lacked only two days of the time set for Darrell's return to the mining camp when he and Kate set out one afternoon accompanied by Duke for a ride up the familiar canyon road. At first their ponies cantered briskly, but as the road grew more rough and steep they were finally content to walk quietly side by side.

For a while neither Darrell nor Kate had much to say. Their hearts were too oppressed for words. Each realized that this little jaunt into the mountains was their last together; that it constituted a sort of farewell to their happy life of the past summer and to each other. Each was thinking of their first meeting under the pines on that evening gorgeous with the sunset rays and sweet with the breath of June roses.

At last they turned into a trail which soon grew so steep and narrow

101

that they dismounted, and, fastening their ponies, proceeded up the trail on foot. Slowly they wended their way upward, pausing at length on a broad, projecting ledge a little below the summit, where they seated themselves on the rocks to rest a while. Kate's eyes wandered afar over the wonderful scene before them, wrapped in unbroken silence, yet palpitating in the mellow, golden sunlight with a mysterious life and beauty all its own.

But Darrell was for once oblivious to the scene; his eyes were fastened on Kate's face, a look in them of insatiable hunger, as though he were storing up the memory of every line and lineament against the barren days to come. He wondered if the silent, calm-faced, self-contained woman beside him could be the laughing, joyous maiden whom he had seen flitting among the trees and fountains at their first meeting little more than three months past. He recalled how he had then thought her unlike either her father or her aunt, and believed her to be wholly without their self-restraint and self-repression. Now he saw that the same stoical blood was in her veins. Already the sensitive, mobile face, which had mirrored every emotion of the impulsive, sympathetic soul within, bore something of the impassive calm of the rocks surrounding them; it might have been chiselled in marble, so devoid was it at that moment of any trace of feeling.

A faint sigh seemed to break the spell, and she turned facing him with her old-time sunny smile.

"What a regal day!" she exclaimed.

"It is," he replied; "it was on such a day as this, about a year ago, that I first met Mr. Britton. He called it, I remember, one of the 'coronation days' of the year. I have been reminded of the phrase and of him all day."

"Dear Mr. Britton," said Kate, "I have not seen him for more than two years. He has always been like a second father to me; he used to have me call him 'papa' when I was little, and I've always loved him next to papa. You and he correspond, do you not?"

"Yes; he writes rather irregularly, but his letters are precious to me. He was the first to make me feel that this cramped fettered life of mine held any good or anything worth living for. He made me ashamed of my selfish sorrow, and every message from him, no matter how brief, seems like an inspiration to something higher and nobler."

"He makes us all conscious of our selfishness," Kate answered, "for if ever there was an unselfish life,—a life devoted to the alleviation of the sufferings and sorrows of others,—it is his. I wish he were here now," she added, with a sigh; "he has more influence with papa than all the rest of us combined, though perhaps nothing even he might say would be availing in this instance."

In all their friendly intercourse of the last few weeks there had been one subject tacitly avoided by each, to which, although present in the mind of each, no reference was ever made. From Kate's last words Darrell knew that subject must now be met; he must know from her own lips the worst. He turned sick with dread and remained silent.

A moment later Kate again faced him with a smile, but her eyes glistened with unshed tears.

102

"Poor papa!" she said, softly, her lips quivering; "he thinks he is doing it all for my happiness, and no matter what wretchedness or misery I suffer, no knowledge of it shall ever pain his dear old heart!"

"Kathie, must it be?" Darrell exclaimed, each word vibrating with anguish; "is there no hope—no chance of escape for you from such a fate?"

"I cannot see the slightest reason to hope for escape," she replied, with the calmness born of despair. She clasped her small hands tightly and turned a pale, determined face towards Darrell.

"You know, you understand it all, and I know that you do," she said, "so there is no use in our avoiding this any longer. I want to talk it over with you and tell you all the truth, so you will not think, by and by, that I have been false or fickle or weak; but first there is something I want you to tell me."

She paused a moment, then, looking him full in the eyes, she asked, earnestly,—

"John Darrell, do you still love me?"

Startled out of his customary self-control, Darrell suddenly clasped her in his arms, exclaiming,—

"Kathie darling, how can you ask such a question? Do you think my love for you could ever grow less?"

For a moment her head nestled against his breast with a little movement of ineffable content, as she replied,—

"No; it was not that I doubted your love, but I wanted an assurance of it to carry with me through the coming days."

Then, gently withdrawing herself from his embrace, she continued, in the same calm, even tones:

"You ask if there is no chance of escape; I can see absolutely none; but I want you to understand, if I am forced into this marriage which papa has planned for me, that it is not through any weakness or cowardice on my part; that if I yield, it will be simply because of the love and reverence I bear my father."

Though her face was slightly averted, Darrell could see the tear-drops falling, but after a slight pause she proceeded as calmly as before:

"In all these years he has tried to be both father and mother to me, and even in this he thinks he is acting for my good. I have never disobeyed him, and were I to do so now I believe it would break his heart. I am all that he has left, and after what he has suffered in his silent, Spartan way, I must bring joy—not sorrow—to his declining years. And this will be my only reason for yielding."

"But, Kathie, dear child," Darrell interposed, "have you considered what such a life means to you—what is involved in such a sacrifice?"

She met his troubled gaze with a smile. "Yes, I know," she replied; "there is not a phase of this affair which I have not considered. I am years older than when we met three months ago, and I have thought of everything that a woman can think of."

She watched him a moment, the smile on her lips deepening. "Have you considered this?" she asked. "Only those whom we love have the power to

103

wound us deeply; one whom I do not love will have little power to hurt me; he can never reach my heart; that will be safe in your keeping."

Darrell bowed his head upon his hands with a low moan. Kate, laying her hand lightly upon his shoulder, continued:

"What I particularly wanted you to know before our parting and to remember is this: that come what may, I shall never be false to my love for you. No matter what the future may bring to you or to me, my heart will be yours."

Darrell raised his head, his face tense and rigid with emotion; she had risen and was standing beside him.

"I can never forgive myself for having won your heart, Kathie," he said, gravely; "It is the most precious gift that I could ask or you could bestow, but one to which I have no right."

"Then hold it in trust," she said, softly, "until such time as I have the right to bestow it upon you and you have the right to accept it."

Startled not only by her words but by the gravity of her tone and manner, Darrell glanced swiftly towards Kate, but she had turned and was slowly climbing the mountain path. Springing to his feet he was quickly at her side. Drawing her arm within his own he assisted her up the rocky trail, scanning her face as he did so for some clew to the words she had just spoken. But, excepting a faint flush which deepened under his scrutiny, she gave no sign, and, the trail for the next half-hour being too difficult to admit of conversation, they made the ascent in silence.

On reaching the summit an involuntary exclamation burst from Darrell at the grandeur of the scene. North, west, and south, far as the eye could reach, stretched the vast mountain ranges, unbroken, with here and there gigantic peaks, snow-crowned, standing in bold relief against the sky; while far to the eastward lay the valleys, threaded with silver streams, and beyond them in the purple distance outlines of other ranges scarcely distinguishable from the clouds against which they seemed to rest.

Kate watched Darrell, silently enjoying his surprise. "This is my favorite resort,–on the summit of the 'divide,'" she said; "I thought you would appreciate it. It involves hard climbing, but it is worth the effort."

"Worth the effort! Yes, a thousand times! What must it be to see the sunrise here!"

Lifted out of themselves, they wandered over the rocks, picking the late flowers which still lingered in the crevices, watching the shifting beauty of the scene from various points, for a time forgetful of their trouble, till, looking in each other's eyes, they read the final farewell underlying all, and the old pain returned with tenfold intensity.

Seating themselves on the highest point accessible, they talked of the future, ignoring so far as possible the one dreaded subject, speaking of Darrell's life in the mining camp, of his studies, and of what he hoped to accomplish, and of certain plans of her own.

Duke, after an extended tour among the rocks, came and lay at their feet, watching their faces with anxious solicitude, quick to read their unspoken sorrow though unable to divine its cause.

At last the little that could be said had been spoken; they paused, their hearts oppressed with the burden of what remained unsaid, which no words could express. Duke, perplexed by the long silence, rose and, coming to Kate's side, stood looking into her eyes with mute inquiry. As Kate caressed the noble head she turned suddenly to Darrell:

"John, would you like to have Duke with you? Will you take him as a parting gift from me?"

"I would like to have him above anything you could give me, Kathie," he replied; "but you must not think of giving him up to me."

"I will have to give him up," she said, simply; "Papa dislikes him already, he is so unfriendly to Mr. Walcott, and he himself absolutely hates Duke; I believe he would kill him if he dared; so you understand I could not keep him much longer. He will be happy with you, for he loves you, and I will be happy in remembering that you have him."

"In that case," said Darrell, "I shall be only too glad to take him, and you can rest assured I will never part with him."

The sinking sun warned them that it was time to return, and, after one farewell look about them, they prepared to descend. As they picked their way back to the trail they came upon two tiny streams flowing from some secret spring above them. Side by side, separated by only a few inches, they rippled over their rocky bed, murmuring to each other in tones so low that only an attentive ear could catch them, sparkling in the sunlight as though for very joy. Suddenly, near the edge of the narrow plateau over which they ran, they turned, and, with a tinkling plash of farewell, plunged in opposite directions,–the one eastward, hastening on its way to the Great Father of Waters, the other westward bound, towards the land of the setting sun.

Silently Kate and Darrell watched them; as their eyes met, his face had grown white, but Kate smiled, though the tears trembled on the golden lashes.

"A fit emblem of our loves, Kathie!" Darrell said, sadly.

"Yes," she replied, but her clear voice had a ring of triumph; "a fit emblem, dear, for though parted now, they will meet in the commingling of the oceans, just as by and by our loves will mingle in the great ocean of love. I can imagine how those two little streams will go on their way, as we must go, each joining in the labor and song of the rivers as they meet them, but each preserving its own individuality until they find one another in the ocean currents, as we shall find one another some day!"

"Kathie," said Darrell, earnestly, drawing nearer to her, "have you such a hope as that?"

"It is more than hope," she answered, "it is assurance; an assurance that came to me, I know not whence or how, out of the darkness of despair."

They had reached the trail, and here Kate paused for a moment. It was a picture for an artist, the pair standing on that solitary height! The young girl, fair and slender as the wild flowers clinging to the rocks at their feet, yet with a poise of conscious strength; the man at her side, broad-shouldered, deep-chested, strong-limbed; his face dark with despair, hers lighted with hope.

Suddenly a small white hand swept the horizon with a swift, undulatory motion that reminded Darrell of the flight of some white-winged bird, and Kate cried,—

"Did we think of the roughness and steepness of the path below when we stood here two hours ago and looked on the glory of this scene? Did we stop to think of the bruises and scratches of the ascent, of how many times we had stumbled, or of the weariness of the way? No, it was all forgotten. And so, when we come to stand together, by and by, upon the heights of love,—such love as we have not even dreamed of yet,—will we then look back upon the tears, the pain, the heartache of to-day? Will we stop to recount the sorrows through which we climbed to the shining heights? No, they will be forgotten in the excess of joy!"

Darrell gazed at Kate in astonishment; her head was uncovered and the rays of the sinking sun touched with gleams of gold the curling locks which the breeze had blown about her face, till they seemed like a golden halo; she had the look of one who sees within the veil which covers mortal faces; she seemed at that moment something apart from earth.

Taking her hand in his, he asked, brokenly, "Sweetheart, will that day ever come, and when?"

Her eyes, luminous with love and hope, rested tenderly upon his shadowed face as she replied,—

"At the time appointed,

   "'And that will be
   God's own good time, for you and me.'"

Chapter XIX

The Return to Camp Bird

The day preceding Darrell's departure found him busily engaged in "breaking camp," as he termed it. The assayer's outfit which he had brought from the mill was to be packed, as were also his books, and quantities of carefully written notes, the results of his explorations and experiments, to be embodied later in the work which he had in preparation, were to be sorted and filed.

Late in the afternoon Kate and her aunt, down town on a shopping tour, looked in upon him.

"Buried up to his ears!" Kate announced at the door, as she caught a glimpse of Darrell's head over a table piled high with books and manuscripts; "it's well we came when we did, auntie; a few minutes later and he would have been invisible!"

"Don't take the trouble to look for seats, Mr. Darrell," she added, her eyes dancing with mischief as he hastily emerged and began a futile search for vacant chairs, "we only dropped in for a minute, and 'standing room only' will be sufficient."

"Yes, don't let us hinder you, Mr. Darrell," said Mrs. Dean; "we just came in to see how you were getting on, and to tell you not to trouble yourself about the things from the house; we will send and get them whenever we want them."

"I was thinking of those a while ago," Darrell answered, glancing at the pictures and hangings which had not yet been removed; "I was wondering if I ought not to send them up to the house."

"No," said Mrs. Dean, "we do not need them there at present, and any time we should want them we can send Bennett down after them."

"We will not send for them at all, auntie," said Kate, in her impulsive way; "I shall keep the room looking as much as possible as when Mr. Darrell had it, and I shall use it as a waiting-room whenever I have to wait for papa; it will be much pleasanter than waiting in that dusty, musty old office of his."

"My room at the camp will look very bare and plain now," said Darrell, "after all the luxuries with which you have surrounded me; though I will, of course, get accustomed to it in a few days."

Kate and her aunt slyly exchanged smiles, which Darrell in his momentary abstraction failed to observe. They chatted pleasantly for a few moments, but underneath the light words and manner was a sadness that could not be disguised, and it was with a still heavier heart that Darrell returned to his work after Kate and her aunt had gone.

At last all was done, the last package was stowed away in the large wagon which was to carry the goods to camp, and the team moved up the street in the direction of The Pines, where it was to remain over night ready for an early start the next morning. Darrell, after a farewell survey of the little room, followed on foot, heartsick and weary, going directly to the stables to see the wagon safely stored for the night. He was surprised to see a second wagon, loaded with furniture, rugs, and pictures, all of which looked strangely familiar, and which on closer inspection he recognized as belonging to the room which he had always occupied at The Pines. He turned to Bennett, who was standing at a little distance, ostensibly cleaning some harness, but quietly enjoying the scene.

"Bennett, what does this mean?" he inquired. "Where are these goods going?"

"To the camp, sir."

"Surely not to the mining camp, Bennett; you must be mistaken."

"No mistake about it, sir; they goes to Camp Bird to-morrow morning; them's Mrs. Dean's orders."

Darrell was more touched than he cared to betray. He went at once to the house, and in the hall, dim with the early twilight, was met by Mrs. Dean herself.

"I'm sorry, Mr. Darrell," she began, "but you can't occupy your room to-night; you'll have to take the one adjoining on the south. Your room was torn up to-day, and we haven't got it put to rights yet."

107

"Mrs. Dean," Darrell answered, his voice slightly unsteady, "you are too kind; it breaks a fellow all up and makes this sort of thing the harder!"

Mrs. Dean turned on the light as though for a better understanding.

"I don't see any special kindness in turning you out of your room on your last night here," she remarked, quietly, "but we couldn't get it settled."

Darrell could not restrain a smile as he replied, "I'm afraid it will be some time before it is settled with the furniture packed out there in the stables."

"Have you been to the stables?" she exclaimed, in dismay.

A smile was sufficient answer.

"If that isn't too bad!" she continued; "I was going to have that wagon sent ahead in the morning before you were up and have it for a surprise when you got there, and now it's all spoiled. I declare, I'm too disappointed to say a word!"

"But, Mrs. Dean," Darrell interposed, hastily, as she turned to leave, "you need not feel like that; the surprise was just as genuine and as pleasant as though it had been as you intended; besides, I can thank you now, whereas I couldn't then."

"That's just what I didn't want, and don't want now," she answered, quickly; "if there is anything I can do for you, God knows I'll do it the same as though you were my own son, and I want no thanks for it, either." And with these words she left the room before Darrell could reply.

Everything that could be done to make the rooms look cheerful and homelike as possible had been done for that night. The dining-room was decorated with flowers, and when, after dinner, the family adjourned to the sitting-room, a fire was burning in the grate, and around it had been drawn the most comfortable seats in the room.

But to Darrell the extra touches of brightness and beauty seemed only to emphasize the fact that this was the last night of anything like home life that he would know for some time to come.

It had been agreed that he and Kate were to have some music that evening, and on the piano he saw the violin which he had not used since the summer's happy days. He lifted it with the tender, caressing manner with which he always handled it, as though it were something living and human. Turning it lovingly in his hands, he caught the gleam of something in the fire-light, and, bending over it, saw a richly engraved gold plate, on which he read the words:

TO JOHN DARRELL
A SOUVENIR OF "THE PINES"
FROM "KATHIE"

A mist rose before his eyes—he could not see, he could not trust himself to speak, but, raising the violin, his pent-up feelings burst forth in a flood of liquid music of such commingled sweetness and sadness as to hold his listeners entranced. Mr. Underwood, for once forgetful of his pipe, looked into the fire with a troubled gaze; he understood little of the power of expression, but even he comprehended dimly the sorrow that surged and

108

ebbed in those wild harmonies. Mrs. Dean, her hands folded idly above her work, sat with eyes closed, a solitary tear occasionally rolling down her cheek, while in the shadows Kate, her face buried on Duke's head and neck, was sobbing quietly.

Gradually the wild strains subsided, as the summer tempest dies away till nothing is heard but the patter of the rain-drops, and, after a few bars from a love-song, a favorite of Kate's, the music glided into the simple strains of "Home, Sweet Home." And as the oppressed and overheated atmosphere is cleared by the brief storm, so the overwrought feelings of those present were relieved by this little outburst of emotion.

A pleasant evening followed, and, except that the "good-nights" exchanged on parting were tenderer, more heartfelt than usual, there were no indications that this was their last night together as a family circle.

Darrell had been in his room but a short time, however, when he heard a light tap at his door, and, opening it, Mrs. Dean entered.

"You seem like a son to me, Mr. Darrell," she said, with quiet dignity, "so I have taken the liberty to come to your room for a few minutes the same as I would to a son's."

"That is right, Mrs. Dean," Darrell replied, escorting her to a large arm-chair; "my own mother could not be more welcome."

"You know us pretty well by this time, Mr. Darrell," she said, as she seated herself, "and you know that we're not given to expressing our feelings very much, but I felt that I couldn't let you go away without a few words with you first. I sometimes think that those who can't express themselves are the ones that feel the deepest, though I guess we often get the credit of not having any feelings at all."

"If I ever had such an impression of you or your brother, I found out my error long ago," Darrell remarked, gravely, as she paused.

"Yes, I think you understand us; I think you will understand me, Mr. Darrell, when I say to you that I haven't felt anything so deeply in years as I do your leaving us now—not so much the mere fact of your going away as the real reason of your going. I felt bad when you left for camp a year ago, but this is altogether different; then you felt, and we felt, that you were one of us, that your home was with us, and I hoped that as long as you remained in the West your home would be with us. Now, although there is no change in our love for you, or yours for us, I know that the place is no longer a home to you, that you do not care to stay; and about the hardest part of it all is, that, knowing the circumstances as I do, I myself would not ask you to stay."

"You seem to understand the situation, Mrs. Dean; how did you learn the circumstances?" Darrell asked, wonderingly.

She regarded him a moment with a motherly smile. "Did you think I was blind? I could see for myself. Katherine has told me nothing," she added, in answer to the unspoken inquiry which she read in his eyes; "she has told me no more than you, but I saw what was coming long before either you or she realized it."

"Oh, Mrs. Dean, why didn't you warn me in time?" Darrell exclaimed.

"The time for warning was when you two first met," Mrs. Dean replied;

"for two as congenial to be thrown together so constantly would naturally result just as it has; it is no more than was to be expected, and neither of you can be blamed. And," she added, slowly, "that is not the phase of the affair which I most regret. I think such love as you two bear each other would work little harm or sorrow to either of you in the end, if matters could only be left to take their own course. I may as well tell you that I think no good will come of this scheme of David's. Mr. Walcott is not a suitable man for Katherine, even if she were heart free, and loving you as she does—as she always will, for I understand the child—it would have been much better to have waited a year or two; I have no doubt that everything would come out all right. Of course, as I'm not her mother, I have no say in the matter and no right to interfere; but mark my words: David will regret this, and at no very distant day, either."

"I know that nothing but unhappiness can come of it for Kate, and that is what troubles me far more than any sorrow of my own," said Darrell, in a low voice.

"It will bring unhappiness and evil all around, but to no one so much as David Underwood himself," said Mrs. Dean, impressively, as she rose.

"Mrs. Dean," said Darrell, springing quickly to his feet, "you don't know the good this little interview has done me! I thank you for it and for your sympathy from the bottom of my heart."

"I wish I could give you something more practical than sympathy," said Mrs. Dean, with a smile, "and I will if I ever have the opportunity. And one thing in particular I want to say to you, Mr. Darrell: so long as you are in the West, whether your home is with us or not, I want you to feel that you have a mother in me, and should you ever be sick or in trouble and need a mother's care and love, no matter where you are, I will come to you as I would to my own son."

They had reached the door; Darrell, too deeply moved for speech and knowing her aversion to many words, bent over her and kissed her on the forehead.

"Thank you, mother; good-night!" he said.

She turned and looked at him with glistening eyes, as she replied, calmly,–

"Good-night, my son!"

The household was astir at an early hour the next morning. There were forced smiles and some desultory conversation at the breakfast-table, but it was a silent group which gathered outside in the early morning sunlight as Darrell was about taking his departure. He dreaded the parting, and, as he glanced at the faces of the waiting group, he determined to make it as brief as possible for their sakes as well as his own.

The heavy teams came slowly around from the stables, and behind them came Trix, daintily picking her steps along the driveway. With a word or two of instructions to the drivers Darrell sent the teams ahead; then, having adjusted saddle and bridle to his satisfaction, he turned to Mr. Underwood, who stood nearest.

"My boy," said the latter, extending his hand, "we hate to spare you from the old home, but I don't know where I would have got a man to take your place; with you up there I feel just as safe as though I were there myself."

"Much obliged, Mr. Underwood," Darrell replied, looking straight into the elder man's eyes; "I think you'll find me worthy of any trust you may repose in me—at the camp or elsewhere."

"Every time, my boy, every time!" exclaimed the old gentleman, wringing his hand.

Mrs. Dean's usually placid face was stern from her effort to repress her feelings, but there was a glance of mother-love in her eyes and a slight quivering of her lips as she bade him a quiet good-by.

But it was Kate's pale, sweet face that nearly broke his own composure as he turned to her, last of all. Their hands clasped and they looked silently into each other's eyes for an instant.

"Good-by, John; God bless you!" she said, in tones audible only to his ear.

"God bless and help you, Kathie!" he replied, and turned quickly to Trix waiting at his side.

"Look at Duke," said Kate, a moment later, as Darrell sprang into the saddle; "he doesn't know what to make of it that you haven't bade him good-by."

Duke, who had shown considerable excitement over the unusual proceedings, had bounded to Kate's side as Darrell approached her, expecting his usual recognition; not having received it, he sat regarding Darrell with an evident sense of personal injury quite pathetic.

Darrell looked at the drooping head and smiled. "Come, Duke," he said, slowly starting down the driveway.

Kate bent quickly for a final caress. "Go on, Duke!" she whispered.

Nothing loath to follow Darrell, he bounded forward, but after a few leaps, on discovering that his beloved mistress was not accompanying them, he stopped, looking back in great perplexity. At a signal from her and a word from Darrell he again started onward, but his backward glances were more than Kate could bear, and she turned to go into the house.

"What are you sending the dog after him for, anyway?" inquired her father, himself somewhat puzzled.

"I have given Duke to Mr. Darrell, papa," she replied.

Something in the unnatural calmness of her tone startled him; he turned to question her. She had gone, but in the glimpse which he had of her face he read a little of the anguish which at that moment wrung her young heart, and happening at the same time to catch his sister's eye, he walked away, silent and uncomfortable.

Chapter XX

Forging the Fetters

During the weeks immediately following Darrell's departure the daily routine of life at The Pines continued in the accustomed channels, but there was not a member of the family, including Mr. Underwood himself, to whom it did not seem strangely empty, as though some essential element were missing.

To Kate her present life, compared with the first months of her return home, was like the narrow current creeping sluggishly beneath the icy fetters of winter as compared with the same stream laughing and singing on its way under summer skies. But she was learning the lesson that all must learn; that the world sweeps relentlessly onward with no pause for individual woe, and each must keep step in its ceaseless march, no matter how weary the brain or how heavy the heart.

Walcott's visits continued with the same frequency, but he was less annoying in his attentions than formerly. It had gradually dawned upon him that Kate was no longer a child, but a woman; and a woman with a will as indomitable as her father's once it was aroused. He was not displeased at the discovery; on the contrary, he looked forward with all the keener anticipation to the pleasure of what he mentally termed the "taming" process, once she was fairly within his power. Meantime, he was content to make a study of her, sitting evening after evening either in conversation with her father or listening while she played and sang, but always watching her every movement, scanning every play of her features.

"A loose rein for the present," he would say to himself, with a smile; "but by and by, my lady, you will find whether or no I am master!"

He seldom attempted now to draw her into a tête à tête conversation, but finding her one evening sitting upon a low divan in one of the bay-windows looking out into the moonlight, he seated himself beside her and began one of his entertaining tales of travel. An hour or more passed pleasantly, and Walcott inquired, casually,—

"By the way, Miss Underwood, what has become of my four-footed friend? I have not seen him for three weeks or more, and his attentions to me were so marked I naturally miss them."

"Duke is at the mining camp," Kate answered, with a faint smile.

Walcott raised his eyebrows incredulously. "Possible! With my other admirer, Mr. Darrell?"

"He is with Mr. Darrell."

"Accept my gratitude, Miss Underwood, for having made my entrée to your home much pleasanter, not to say safer."

"I neither claim nor accept your gratitude, Mr. Walcott," Kate replied, with cool dignity, "since I did it simply out of regard for Duke's welfare and not out of any consideration whatever for your wishes in the matter."

"I might have known as much," said Walcott, with a mock sigh of

112

resignation, settling back comfortably among the pillows on the divan and fixing his eyes on Kate's face; "I might have known that consideration for any wish of mine could never by any chance be assigned as the motive for an act of yours."

Kate made no reply, but the lines about her mouth deepened. For a moment he watched her silently; then he continued slowly, in low, nonchalant tones:

"I am positive that when I at last gain your consent to marry me,"–he paused an instant to note the effect of his words, but there was not the quiver of an eyelash on her part,–"even then, you will have the audacity to tell me that you gave it for any other reason under heaven than consideration for me or my wishes."

"Mr. Walcott," said Kate, facing him with sudden hauteur of tone and manner, "you are correct. If ever I consent to marry you I can tell you now as well as then my reason for doing so: it will be simply and solely for my dear father's sake, for the love I bear him, out of consideration for his wishes, and with no more thought of you than if you did not exist."

Conflicting emotions filled Walcott's breast at these words, but he preserved a calm, smiling exterior. He could not but admire Kate's spirit; at the same time the thought flashed through his mind that this apparent slip of a girl might prove rather difficult to "tame;" but he reflected that the more difficult, the keener would be his enjoyment of the final victory.

"A novel situation, surely!" he commented, with a low, musical laugh; "decidedly unique!"

"But, my dear Miss Underwood," he continued, a moment later, "if your love for your father and regard for his wishes are to constitute your sole reasons for consenting to become my wife, why need you withhold that consent longer? I am sure his wishes in the matter will remain unchanged, as will also your love for him; why then should our marriage be further delayed?"

"After what I have just told you, Mr. Walcott, do you still ask me to be your wife?" Kate demanded, indignantly.

"I do, Miss Underwood; and, pardon me, I feel that you have trifled with me long enough; I must have your answer."

She rose, drawing herself proudly to her full height.

"Take me to my father," she said, imperiously.

Walcott offered his arm, which she refused with a gesture of scorn, and they proceeded to the adjoining room, where Mr. Underwood and his sister were seated together before the fire. As Kate advanced towards her father both looked up simultaneously, and each read in her white face and proud bearing that a crisis was at hand. Mrs. Dean at once arose and noiselessly withdrew from the room.

Walcott paused at a little distance from Mr. Underwood, assuming a graceful attitude as he leaned languidly over the large chair just vacated by Mrs. Dean, but Kate did not stop till she reached her father's side, where she bowed coldly to Walcott to proceed with what he had to say.

"Some time ago, Mr. Underwood," he began, smoothly and easily, "I asked you for your daughter's hand in marriage, and you honored me with

113

your consent. Since that time I have paid my addresses to Miss Underwood in so marked a manner as to leave her no room for doubt or misunderstanding regarding my intentions, although, finding that she was not inclined to look upon me with favor, I have hitherto refrained from pressing my suit. Feeling now that I have given her abundance of time I have this evening asked her to become my wife, and insisted that I was entitled to a decision. Instead, however, of giving me a direct answer, she has suggested that we refer the matter to yourself."

"How is this, Kate?" her father asked, not unkindly; "I supposed you and I had settled this matter long ago."

Her voice was clear, her tones unfaltering, as she replied: "Before giving my answer I wanted to ask you, papa, for the last time, whether, knowing the circumstances as you do and how I regard Mr. Walcott, it is still your wish that I marry him?"

"It is; and I expect my child to be governed by my wishes in this matter rather than by her own feelings."

"Have I ever gone contrary to your wishes, papa, or disobeyed you?"

"No, my child, no!"

"Then I shall not attempt it at this late day. I only wanted to be sure that this was still your wish."

"I desire it above all things," said Mr. Underwood, delighted to find Kate so ready to accede to his wishes, rising and taking her hand in his; "and the day that I see my little girl settled in the home which she will receive as a wedding-gift from her old father will be the proudest and happiest day of my life."

Kate smiled sadly. "No home can ever seem to me like The Pines, papa, but I appreciate your kindness, and I want you to know that I am taking this step solely for your happiness."

She then turned, facing Walcott, who advanced slightly, while Mr. Underwood made a movement as though to place her hand in his.

"Not yet, papa," she said, gently; then, addressing Walcott, she continued:

"Mr. Walcott, this must be my answer, since you insist upon having one: Out of love for him who has been both father and mother to me, out of reverence for his gray hairs frosted by the sorrows of earlier years, out of regard for his wishes, which have always been my law,–for his sake only,–I consent to become your wife upon one condition."

"Name it," Walcott replied.

"There can be no love between us, either in our engagement or our marriage, for, as I have told you, I can never love you, and you yourself are incapable of love in its best sense; you have not even the slightest knowledge of what it is. For this reason any token of love between us would be only a mockery, a farce, and true wedded love is something too holy, too sacred, to be travestied in any such manner. I consent to our marriage, therefore, only upon this condition: that we henceforth treat each other simply with kindness and courtesy; that no expressions of affection or endearment are to be used by either of us to the other, and that no word or sign of love ever pass between us."

114

"Kate," interposed her father, sternly, "this is preposterous! I cannot allow such absurdity;" but Walcott silenced him with a deprecatory wave of his hand, and, taking Kate's hand in his, replied, with smiling indifference,—

"I accept the condition imposed by Miss Underwood, since it is no more unique than the entire situation, and I congratulate her upon her decided originality. I suppose," he added, addressing Kate, at the same time producing a superb diamond ring, "you will not object to wearing this?"

"I yield that much to conventionality," she replied, allowing him to place it on her finger; "there is no need to advertise the situation publicly; besides, it is a fitting symbol of my future fetters."

"Conventionality, I believe, would require that it be placed on your hand with a kiss and some appropriate bit of sentiment, but since that sort of thing is tabooed between us, we will have to dispense with that part of the ceremony."

Then turning to Mr. Underwood, who stood looking on frowningly, somewhat troubled by the turn matters had taken, Walcott added, playfully,—

"According to the usual custom, I believe the next thing on the programme is for you to embrace us and give us a father's blessing, but my lady might not approve of anything so commonplace."

Before her father could reply Kate spoke for him, glancing at him with an affectionate smile:

"Papa is not one of the demonstrative sort, and he and I need no demonstration of our love for each other; do we, dear?"

"No, child, we understand each other," said her father, reseating himself, with Kate in her accustomed place on the arm of his chair, while Walcott took the large chair on the other side of the fire; "and you neither of you need any assurance of my good wishes or good intentions towards you; but," he continued, doubtfully, shaking his head, "I don't quite like the way you've gone about this business, Puss."

"It was the only way for me, papa," Kate answered, gravely and decidedly.

"I admit," said Walcott, "it will be quite a departure from the mode of procedure ordinarily laid down for newly engaged and newly wedded couples; but really, come to think it over, I am inclined to think that Miss Underwood's proposition will save us an immense amount of boredom which is the usual concomitant of engagements and honeymoons. That sort of thing, you know," he added, his lip curling just perceptibly, "is apt to get a little monotonous after a while."

Kate, watching him from under level brows, saw the slight sneer and inwardly rejoiced at the stand she had taken.

"Well," said Mr. Underwood, resignedly, "fix it up between you any way to suit yourselves; but for heaven's sake, don't do anything to cause comment or remarks!"

"Papa, you can depend on me not to make myself conspicuous in any way," Kate replied, with dignity. "What I have said to-night was said simply to let you and Mr. Walcott know just where I stand, and just what you may,

115

and may not, expect of me; but this is only between us three, and you can rest assured that I shall never wear my heart upon my sleeve or take the public into my confidence regarding my home life."

"I think myself you need have no fear on that score, Mr. Underwood," Walcott remarked, with a smile of amusement; "I believe Miss Underwood is entirely capable of carrying out to perfection any rôle she may assume, and if she chooses to take the part of leading lady in the little comedy of 'The Model Husband and Wife, I shall be only too delighted to render her any assistance within my power."

As Walcott bade Kate good-night at a late hour he inquired, "What do you think of the little comedy I suggested to-night for our future line of action? Does it meet with your approval?"

She was quick to catch the significance of the question, and, looking him straight in the eyes, she replied, calmly,–

"It will answer as well as any, I suppose; but it has in it more of the elements of tragedy than of comedy."

Chapter XXI

Two Crimes by the Same Hand

At Walcott's request the date of the wedding was set early in January, he having announced that business would call him to the South the first week in December for about a month, and that he wished the wedding to take place immediately upon his return.

The announcement of the engagement and speedily approaching marriage of the daughter of D. K. Underwood to his junior partner caused a ripple of excitement throughout the social circles of Ophir and Galena. Though little known, Walcott was quite popular. It was therefore generally conceded that the shrewd "mining king," as Mr. Underwood was denominated in that region, had selected a party in every way eligible as the future husband of the sole heiress of his fortune. Kate received the congratulations showered upon her with perfect equanimity, but with a shade of quiet reserve which effectually distanced all undue familiarity or curiosity.

Through the daily paper which found its way to the mining camp Darrell received his first news of Kate's engagement. It did not come as a surprise, however; he knew it was inevitable; he even drew a sigh of relief that the blow had fallen, for a burden is far more easily borne as an actual reality than by anticipation, and applied himself with an almost dogged persistency to his work.

116

The winter set in early and with unusual severity. The snowfall in the mountains was heavier than had been known in years. Much of the time the canyon road was impassable, making it impracticable for Darrell to visit The Pines with any frequency, even had he wished to do so.

The weeks passed, and ere he was aware the holidays were at hand. By special messenger came a little note from Kate informing him of Walcott's absence and begging him to spend Christmas at the old home. There had been a lull of two or three days in the storm, the messenger reported the road somewhat broken, and early on the morning preceding Christmas the trio, Darrell, Duke, and Trix, started forth, and, after a twelve hours' siege, arrived at The Pines wet, cold, and thoroughly exhausted, but all joyfully responsive to the welcome awaiting them.

Christmas dawned bright and clear; tokens of love and good will abounded on every side, but at an early hour news came over the wires which shocked and saddened all who heard, particularly the household at The Pines. There had been a hold-up on the west-bound express the preceding night, a few miles from Galena, in which the mail and express had been robbed, and the express clerk, a brave young fellow who stanchly refused to open the safe or give the combination, had been fatally stabbed. It was said to be without doubt the work of the same band that had conducted the hold-up in which Harry Whitcomb had lost his life, as it was characterized by the same boldness of plan and cleverness of execution.

The affair brought back so vividly to Mr. Underwood and the family the details of Harry's death that it cast a shadow over the Christmas festivities, which seemed to deepen as the day wore on. Outside, too, gathering clouds, harbingers of coming storm, added to the general gloom.

It was with a sense of relief that Darrell set out at an early hour the following morning for the camp. He realized as never before that the place teemed with painful memories whose very sweetness tortured his soul until he almost wished that the months since his coming to The Pines might be wrapped in the same oblivion which veiled his life up to that period. He was glad to escape from its depressing influence and to return to the camp with its routine of work and study.

This second winter of Darrell's life at camp was far more normal and healthful than the first. His love and sympathy for Kate had unconsciously drawn him out of himself, making him less mindful of his own sorrow and more susceptible to the sufferings of others. To the men at the camp he was far different, interesting himself in their welfare in numerous ways where before he had ignored them. The unusual severity of the winter had caused some sickness among them, and it was nothing uncommon for Darrell to go of an evening to the miners' quarters with medicines, newspapers, and magazines for the sick and convalescent.

He was returning from one of these expeditions late one evening about ten days after Christmas, accompanied by the collie. It had been snowing lightly and steadily all day and the snow was still falling. Darrell was whistling softly to himself, and Duke, who showed a marvellous adaptation to Darrell's varying moods, catching the cue for his own conduct, began to plunge into the freshly fallen snow, wheeling and darting swiftly towards

117

Darrell as though challenging him to a wrestling-match. Darrell gratified his evident wish and they tumbled promiscuously in the snow, emerging at length from a big drift near the office, their coats white, Duke barking with delight, and Darrell laughing like a school-boy.

Shaking themselves, they entered the office, but no sooner had they stepped within than the collie bounded to the door of the next room where he began a vigorous sniffing and scratching, accompanied by a series of short barks. As Darrell, somewhat puzzled by his actions, opened the door, he saw a figure seated by the fire, which rose and turned quickly, revealing to his astonished gaze the tall form and strong, sweet face of John Britton.

For a moment the two men stood with clasped hands, looking into each other's eyes with a satisfaction too deep for words.

After an affectionate scrutiny of his young friend Mr. Britton resumed his seat, remarking,–

"You are looking well–better than I have ever seen you; and I was glad to hear that laughter outside; it had the right ring to it."

"Duke was responsible for that," Darrell answered, with a smiling glance at the collie who had stationed himself by the fire and near Mr. Britton; "he challenged me to wrestle with him, and got rather the worst of it."

A moment later, having divested himself of his great coat, he drew a second seat before the fire, saying,–

"You evidently knew where to look for me?"

"Yes, your last letter, which, by the way, followed me for nearly six weeks before reaching me, apprised me of your return to the camp. I was somewhat surprised, too, after you had established yourself so well in town."

"It was best for me–and for others," Darrell answered; then, noting the inquiry in his friend's eyes, he added:

"It is a long story, but it will keep; there will be plenty of time for that later. Tell me of yourself first. For two months I have hungered for word from you, and now I simply want to listen to you a while."

Mr. Britton smiled. "I owe you an apology, but you know I am a poor correspondent at best, and of late business has called me here and there until I scarcely knew one day where I would be the next; consequently I have received my mail irregularly and have been irregular myself in writing."

Darrell's face grew tender, for he knew it was not business alone which drove his friend from place to place, but the old pain which found relief only in ceaseless activity and an equally unceasing beneficence. He well knew that many of his friend's journeys were purely of a philanthropic nature, and he remarked, with a peculiar smile,–

"Your travels always remind me very forcibly of the journey of the good Samaritan; when he met a case of suffering on the way he was not the one to 'pass by on the other side;' nor are you."

"Perhaps," said Mr. Britton, gravely, "he had found, as others have since, that pouring oil and wine into his neighbor's wounds was the surest method of assuaging the pain in some secret wound of his own."

118

Darrell watched his friend closely while he gave a brief account of his recent journeys along the western coast. Never before had he seen the lines of suffering so marked upon the face beside him as that night. Something evidently had reopened the old wound, causing it to throb anew.

"I need not ask what has brought you back into the mountains at this time of year and in this storm," Darrell remarked, as his friend concluded.

For answer Mr. Britton drew from his pocket an envelope which Darrell at once recognized as a counterpart of one which had come to him some weeks before, but which he had laid away unopened, knowing only too well its contents.

"I am particularly glad, for Miss Underwood's sake, that you are here," he said; "she feared you might not come, and it worried her."

"Which accounts for the importunate little note which accompanied the invitation," said Mr. Britton, with a half-smile; "but I would have made it a point to be present in any event; why did she doubt my coming?"

"Because of the season, I suppose, and the unusual storms; then, too," Darrell spoke with some hesitation, "she told me she believed you had a sort of aversion to weddings."

"She was partly right," Mr. Britton said, after a pause; "I have not been present at a wedding ceremony for more than twenty-five years—not since my own marriage," he added, slowly, in a low tone, as though making a confession.

Darrell's heart throbbed painfully; it was the first allusion he had ever heard the other make to his own past, and from his tone and manner Darrell knew that he himself had unwittingly touched the great, hidden sorrow in his friend's life.

"Forgive me!" he said, with the humility and simplicity of a child.

"I have nothing to forgive," Mr. Britton replied, gently, fixing his eyes with a look of peculiar affection upon Darrell's face. "You know more now, my son, than the whole world knows or has known in all these years; and some day in the near future you shall know all, because, for some inexplicable reason, you, out of the whole world, seem nearest to me."

A few moments later he resumed, with more of his usual manner, "I am not quite myself to-night. The events of the last few days have rather upset me, and," with one of his rare smiles, "I have come to you to get righted."

"To mc?" Darrell exclaimed.

"Yes; why not?"

"I am but your pupil,—one who is just beginning to look above his own selfish sorrows only through the lessons you have taught him."

"You over-estimate the little I have tried to do for you; but were it even as you say, I would come to you and to no one else. To whom did the Divine Master himself turn for human sympathy in his last hours of grief and suffering but to his little band of pupils—his disciples? And in proportion as they had learned of Him and imbibed His spirit, in just that proportion could they enter into his feelings and minister to his soul."

Mr. Britton had withdrawn the cards from the envelope and was regarding them thoughtfully.

"The receipt of those bits of pasteboard," he said, slowly, "unmanned

119

me more than anything that has occurred in nearly a score of years. They called up long-forgotten scenes,—little pathetic, heart-rending memories which I thought buried long ago. I don't mind confessing to you, my boy, that for a while I was unnerved. It did not seem as though I could ever bring myself to hear again the music of wedding-bells and wedding-marches, to listen to the old words of the marriage service. But for the sake of one who has seemed almost as my own child I throttled those feelings and started for the mountains, resolved that no selfishness of mine should cloud her happiness on her wedding day. I came, to find, what I would never have believed possible, that my old friend would sacrifice his child's happiness, all that is sweetest and holiest in her life, to gratify his own ambition. I cannot tell you the shock it was to me. D. K. Underwood and I have been friends for many years, but that did not prevent my talking plainly with him—so plainly that perhaps our friendship may never be the same again. But it was of no avail, and the worst is, he has persuaded himself that he is acting for her good, when it is simply for the gratification of his own pride. I could not stay there; the very atmosphere seemed oppressive; so I came up here for a day or two, as I told you, to get righted."

"And you came to me to be righted," Darrell said, musingly; "'Can the blind lead the blind?'"

Mr. Britton was quick to catch the significance of he other's query.

"Yes, John," he answered, covering Darrell's hand with his own; "I came to you for the very reason that your hurt is far deeper than mine."

Under the magnetism of that tone and touch Darrell calmly and in few words told his story and Kate's,—the story of their love and brief happiness, and of the wretchedness which followed.

"For a while I constantly reproached myself for having spoken to her of love," he said, in conclusion; "for having awakened her love, as I thought, by my own; but gradually I came to see that she had loved me, as I had her, unconsciously, almost from our first meeting, and that the awakening must in any event have come sooner or later to each of us. Then it seemed as though my suffering all converged in sorrow for her, that her life, instead of being gladdened by love, should be saddened and marred, perhaps wrecked, by it."

"Love works strange havoc with human lives sometimes," Mr. Britton remarked, reflectively, as Darrell paused.

"I was tempted at times," Darrell continued, "as I thought of what was in store for her, to rescue her at any cost; tempted to take her and go with her to the ends of the earth, if necessary; anywhere, to save her from the life she dreads."

"Thank God that you did not, my son!" Mr. Britton exclaimed, strangely agitated by Darrell's words; "you do not know what the cost might have been in the end; what bitter remorse, what agony of ceaseless regret!"

He stopped abruptly, and again Darrell felt that he had looked for an instant into those depths so sacredly guarded from the eyes of the world.

"You did well to leave as you did," Mr. Britton said, after a moment's silence, in which he had regained his composure.

"I had to; I should have done something desperate if I had remained there much longer."

Darrell spoke quietly, but it was the quiet of suppressed passion.

"It was better so—better for you both," Mr. Britton continued; "when we find ourselves powerless to save our loved ones from impending trouble, all that is left us is to help them bear that trouble as best we may. The best help you can give Kate now is to take yourself as completely as possible out of her life. How you can best help her later time alone will show."

A long silence followed, while both watched the flickering flames and listened to the crooning of the wind outside. When at length they spoke it was on topics of general interest; the outlook at the mining camp, the latest news in the town below, till their talk at last drifted to the recent hold-up.

"A dastardly piece of work!" exclaimed Mr. Britton. "The death of that young express clerk was in some ways even sadder than that of Harry Whitcomb. I knew him well; the only child of a widowed mother; a poor boy who, by indomitable energy and unswerving integrity, had just succeeded in securing the position which cost him his life. Two such brutal, cowardly murders ought to arouse the people to such systematic, concerted action as would result in the final arrest and conviction of the murderer."

"It is the general opinion that both were committed by one and the same party," Darrell remarked, as his friend paused.

"Undoubtedly both were the work of the same hand, in all probability that of the leader himself. He is a man capable of any crime, probably guilty of nearly every crime that could be mentioned, and his men are mere tools in his hands. He exerts a strange power over them and they obey him, knowing that their lives would pay the forfeit for disobedience. Human life is nothing to him, and any one who stood in the way of the accomplishment of his purposes would simply go the way those two poor fellows have gone."

"Why, do you know anything regarding this man?" Darrell asked in surprise.

"Only so far as I have made a study of him and his methods, aided by whatever information I could gather from time to time concerning him."

"Surely, you are not a detective!" Darrell exclaimed; "you spoke like one just now."

"Not professionally," his friend answered, with a smile; "though I have often assisted in running down criminals. I have enough of the hound nature about me, however, that when a scent is given me I delight in following the trail till I run my game to cover, as I hope some day to run this man to cover," he added, with peculiar earnestness.

"But how did you ever gain so much knowledge of him? To every one else he seems an utter mystery."

"Partly, as I said, through a study of him and his methods, and partly from facts which I learned from one of the band who was fatally shot a few years ago in a skirmish between the brigands and a posse of officials. The man was deserted by his associates and was brought to town and placed in a hospital. I did what I could to make the poor fellow comfortable, with the result that he became quite communicative with me, and, while in no way

121

betraying his confederates, he gave me much interesting information regarding the band and its leader. It is a thoroughly organized body of men, bound together by the most fearful oaths, possessing a perfect system of signals and passwords, and with a retreat in the mountains, known as the 'Pocket,' so inaccessible to any but themselves that no one as yet has been able even to definitely locate it—a sort of basin walled about by perpendicular rocks. The leader is a man of mixed blood, who has travelled in all countries and knows many dark secrets, and whose power lies mainly in the mystery with which he surrounds himself. No one knows who he is, but many of his men believe him to be the very devil personified."

"But how can you or any one else hope to run down a man with such powerful followers and with a hiding-place so inaccessible?" Darrell inquired.

"From a remark inadvertently dropped, I was led to infer that this man spends comparatively little time with the band. He communicates with them, directs them, and personally conducts any especially bold or difficult venture; but most of the time he is amid far different surroundings, leading an altogether different life."

"One of those men with double lives," Darrell commented.

Mr. Britton bowed in assent.

"But if that were so," Darrell persisted, his interest thoroughly aroused, as much by Mr. Britton's manner as by his words, "in the event, say, of your meeting him, how would you be able to recognize or identify him? Have you any clew to his identity?"

"Years ago," said Mr. Britton, slowly, "I formed the habit of studying people; at first as I met them; later as I heard or read of them. Facts gathered here and there concerning a person's life I put together, piece by piece, studying his actions and the probable motives governing those actions, until I had a mental picture of the real man, the 'ego' that constitutes the foundation of the character of every individual. Having that fixed in my mind I next strove to form an idea of the exterior which that particular 'ego' would gradually build about himself through his habits of thought and speech and action. In this way, by a careful study of a man's life, I can form something of an idea of his appearance. I have often put this to the test by visiting various penitentiaries in order to meet some of the noted criminals of whose careers I had made a study, and invariably, in expression, in voice and manner, in gait and bearing, in the hundred and one little indices by which the soul betrays itself, I have found them as I had mentally portrayed them."

Mr. Britton had risen while speaking and was walking back and forth before the fire.

"I see!" Darrell exclaimed; "and you have formed a mental portrait of this man by which you expect to recognize and identify him?"

"I am satisfied that I would have no difficulty in recognizing him," Mr. Britton replied, with peculiar emphasis on the last words; "the work of identification,"—he paused in front of Darrell, looking him earnestly in the face,—"that, I hope, will one day be yours."

"Mine!" exclaimed Darrell. "How so? I do not understand."

122

"Mr. Underwood has told me that soon after your arrival at The Pines and just before you became delirious, there was something on your mind in connection with the robbery and Whitcomb's death which you wished to tell him but were unable to recall; and both he and his sister have said that often during your delirium you would mutter, 'That face! I can never forget it; it will haunt me as long as I live!' It has always been my belief that amidst the horrors of the scene you witnessed that night, you in some way got sight of the murderer's face, which impressed you so strongly that it haunted you even in your delirium. It is my hope that with the return of memory there will come a vision of that face sufficiently clear that you will be able to identify it should you meet it, as I believe you will."

Darrell scrutinized his friend closely before replying, noting his evident agitation.

"You have already met this man and recognized him!" he exclaimed.

"Possibly!" was the only reply.

Chapter XXII

The Fetters Broken

Early on the morning of the third day after Mr. Britton's arrival at camp he and Darrell set forth for The Pines. But little snow had fallen within the last two days, and the trip was made without much difficulty, though progress was slow. Late in the day, as they neared The Pines, the clouds, which for hours had been more or less broken, suddenly dispersed, and the setting sun sank in a flood of gold and crimson light which gave promise of glorious weather for the morrow.

Arriving at the house, they found it filled with guests invited to the wedding from different parts of the State, the rooms resounding with light badinage and laughter, the very atmosphere charged with excitement as messengers came and went and servants hurried to and fro, busied with preparations for the following day.

Kate herself hastened forward to meet them, a trifle pale, but calm and wearing the faint, inscrutable smile which of late was becoming habitual with her. At sight of Darrell and his friend, however, her face lighted with the old-time, sunny smile and her cheeks flushed with pleasure. She bestowed upon Mr. Britton the same affectionate greeting with which she had been accustomed to meet him since her childhood's days. He was visibly affected, and though he returned her greeting, kissing her on brow and cheek, he was unable to speak. Her color deepened and her eyes grew luminous as she turned to welcome Darrell, but she only said,—

123

"I am inexpressibly glad that you came. It will be good to feel there is one amid all the crowd who knows."

"He knows also, Kathie," Darrell replied, in low tones, indicating Mr. Britton with a slight motion of his head.

"Does he know all?" she asked, quickly.

"Yes; I thought you could have no objection."

"No," she answered, after a brief pause; "I am glad that it is so."

There was no opportunity for further speech, as Mr. Underwood came forward to welcome his old friend and Darrell, and they were hurried off to their rooms to prepare for dinner.

Mr. Underwood was not a man to do things by halves, and the elaborate but informal dinner to which he and his guests sat down was all that could be desired as a gastronomic success. He himself, despite his brusque manners, was a genial host, and Walcott speedily ingratiated himself into the favor of the guests by his quiet, unobtrusive attentions, his punctilious courtesy to each and all alike.

Darrell and his friend felt ill at ease and out of place amid the gayety that filled the house that evening, and at an early hour they retired to their rooms.

"It is awful!" Darrell exclaimed, as they stood for a moment together at the door of his room listening to the sounds of merriment from below; "it is all so hollow, such a mockery; it seems like dancing over a hidden sepulchre!"

"And we are to stand by to-morrow and witness this farce carried out to the final culmination!" Mr. Britton commented, in low tones; "it is worse than a farce,–it is a crime! My boy, how will you be able to stand it?" he suddenly inquired.

Darrell turned away abruptly. "I could not stand it; I would not attempt it, except that my presence will comfort and help her," he answered. And so they parted for the night.

The following morning dawned clear and cloudless, the spotless, unbroken expanse of snow gleaming in the sunlight as though strewn with myriads of jewels; it seemed as if Earth herself had donned her bridal array in honor of the occasion.

"An ideal wedding-day!" was the universal exclamation; and such it was.

The wedding was to take place at noon. A little more than an hour before the bridal party was to leave the house Darrell was walking up and down the double libraries upstairs, whither he had been summoned by a note from Kate, begging him to await her there.

His thoughts went back to that summer night less than six months gone, when he had waited her coming in those very rooms. Not yet six months, and he seemed to have lived years since then! He recalled her as she appeared before him that night in all the grace and witchery of lovely maidenhood just opening into womanhood. How beautiful, how joyous she had been! without a thought of sorrow, and now––

A faint sound like the breath of the wind through the leaves roused him, and Kate stood before him once more. Kate in her bridal robes, their shimmering folds trailing behind her like the gleaming foam in the wake of a ship on a moonlit sea, while her veil, like a filmy cloud, enveloped her from head to foot.

There was a moment of silence in which Darrell studied the face before him; the same, yet not the same, as on that summer night. The childlike naïveté, the charming piquancy, had given place to a sweet seriousness, but it was more tender, more womanly, more beautiful.

She came a step nearer, and, raising her clasped hands, placed them within Darrell's.

"I felt that I must see you once more, John," she said, in the low, sweet tones that always thrilled his very soul; "there is something I wish to say to you, if I can only make my meaning clear, and I feel sure you will understand me. I want to pledge to you, John, for time and for eternity, my heart's best and purest love. Though forced into this union with a man whom I can never love, yet I will be true as a wife; God knows I would not be otherwise; that is farthest from my thoughts. But I have learned much within the past few months, and I have learned that there is a love far above all passion and sensuality; a love tender as a wife's, pure as a mother's, and lasting as eternity itself. Such love I pledge you, John Darrell. Do you understand me?"

As she raised her eyes to his it seemed to Darrell that he was looking into the face of one of the saints whom the old masters loved to portray centuries ago, so spiritual was it, so devoid of everything of earth!

"Kathie, darling," he said, clasping her hands tenderly, "I do understand, and, thank God, I believe I am able to reciprocate your love with one as chastened and pure. When I left The Pines last fall I did so because I could not any longer endure to be near you, loving you as I did. I felt in some blind, unreasoning way that it was wrong, and yet I knew that to cease to love you was an impossibility. But in the solitude of the mountains God showed me a better way. He showed me the true meaning of those words, 'In the resurrection they neither marry nor are given in marriage, but are as the angels of God in heaven.' Those words had always seemed to me austere and cold, as though they implied that our poor love would be superseded by higher attributes possessed by the angelic hosts, of which we knew nothing. Now I know that they mean that our human love shall be refined from all the dross of earthly passion, purified and exalted above mortal conception. I prayed that my love for you might be in some such measure refined and purified, and I know that prayer has been answered. I pledge you that love, Kathie; a love that will never wrong you even in thought; that you can trust in all the days to come as ready to defend or protect you if necessary, and as always seeking your best and highest happiness."

"Thank you, John," she said, and bowed her head above their clasped hands for a moment.

When she raised her head her eyes were glistening. "We need not be afraid or ashamed to acknowledge love such as ours," she said, proudly; "and with the assurance you have given me I shall have strength and courage, whatever may come. I must go," she added, lifting her face to his;

125

"I want your kiss now, John, rather than amid all the meaningless kisses that will be given me after the ceremony."

Their lips met in a lingering kiss, then she silently withdrew from the room.

As she crossed the hall Walcott suddenly brushed past her breathlessly, without seeing her, and ran swiftly downstairs. His evident excitement caused her to pause for an instant; as she did, she heard him exclaim, in a low, angry tone and with an oath,—

"You dog! What brings you here? How dare you come here?"

There came a low reply in Spanish, followed by a few quick, sharp words from Walcott in the same tongue, but which by their inflection Kate understood to be an exclamation and a question.

Her curiosity aroused, she noiselessly descended to the first landing, and, leaning over the balustrade, saw a small man, with dark olive skin, standing close to Walcott, with whom he was talking excitedly. He spoke rapidly in Spanish. Kate caught only one word, "Señora," as he handed a note to Walcott, at the same time pointing backward over his shoulder towards the entrance. Kate saw Walcott grow pale as he read the missive, then, with a muttered curse, he started for the door, followed by the other.

Quickly descending to the next landing, where there was an alcove window looking out upon the driveway, Kate could see a closed carriage standing before the entrance, and Walcott, holding the door partially open, talking with some one inside. The colloquy was brief, and, as Walcott stepped back from the carriage, the smaller man, who had been standing at a little distance, sprang in hastily. As he swung the door open for an instant Kate had a glimpse of a woman on the rear seat, dressed in black and heavily veiled. As the man closed the door Walcott stepped to the window for a word or two, then turned towards the house, and the carriage rolled rapidly down the driveway. Kate slowly ascended the stairs, listening for Walcott, who entered the house, but, instead of coming upstairs, passed through the lower hall, going directly to a private room of Mr. Underwood's in which he received any who happened to call at the house on business.

Kate went to her room, her pulse beating quickly. She felt intuitively that something was wrong; that here was revealed a phase of Walcott's personality which she in her innocence had not considered, had not even suspected. She knew that her father believed him to be a moral man, and hitherto she had regarded the lack of affinity between herself and him as due to a sort of mental disparity—a lack of affiliation in thought and taste. Now the conviction flashed upon her that the disparity was a moral one. She recalled the sense of loathing with which she instinctively shrank from his touch; she understood it now. And within two hours she was to have married this man! Never!

Passing a large mirror, she paused and looked at the reflection there. Was her soul, its purity and beauty symbolized by her very dress, to be united to that other soul in its grossness and deformity? Her cheek blanched with horror at the thought. No! that fair body should perish first, rather than soul or body ever be contaminated by his touch!

Her decision was taken from that moment, and it was irrevocable. Nothing—not even her father's love or anger, his wishes or his commands—could turn her now, for, as he himself boasted, his own blood flowed within her veins.

Swiftly she disrobed, tearing the veil in her haste and throwing the shimmering white garments to one side as though she hated the sight of them. Taking from her jewel casket the engagement ring which had been laid aside for the wedding ceremony, she quickly shut it within its own case, to be returned as early as possible to the giver; it seemed to burn her fingers like living fire.

A few moments later her aunt, entering her room, found her dressed in one of her favorite house gowns,—a camel's hair of creamy white. She looked at Kate, then at the discarded robes on a couch near by, and stopped speechless for an instant, then stammered,—

"Katherine, child, what does this mean?"

"It means, auntie," said Kate, putting her arms about her aunt's neck, "that there will be no wedding and no bride to-day."

Then, looking her straight in the eyes, she added: "Really, auntie, deep down in your heart, aren't you glad of it?"

Mrs. Dean gasped, then replied, slowly, "Yes; it will make me very glad if you do not have to marry that man; but, Katherine, I don't understand; what will your father say?"

Before Kate could reply there was a heavy knock at the door, which Mrs. Dean answered. She came back looking rather frightened.

"Your father wishes to see you, Katherine, in your library. Something must have happened; he looks excited and worried. I don't know what he'll say to you in that dress."

"I'm not afraid," Kate replied, brightly.

A moment later she entered the room where less than half an hour before she had left Darrell. Mr. Underwood was walking up and down. As Kate entered he turned towards her with a look of solicitude, which quickly changed to one of surprise, tinged with anger.

"What is the meaning of this?" he demanded, looking at his watch; "it is within an hour of the time set for your wedding; you don't look much like a bride. Do you expect to be married in that dress?"

"I am not to be married to-day, papa; nor any other day to Mr. Walcott," Kate answered, calmly.

"What!" he exclaimed, scarcely comprehending the full import of her words; "isn't the matter bad enough as it is without your making it worse by any foolish talk or actions?"

"I don't understand you, papa; to what do you refer?"

"Why, Mr. Walcott has just been called out of town by news that his father is lying at the point of death; it is doubtful whether he will live till his son can reach him. He has to take the first train south which leaves within half an hour; otherwise, he would have waited for the ceremony to be performed."

"Did he tell you that?" Kate asked, with intense scorn.

127

"Certainly, and he left his farewells for you, as he hadn't time even to stop to see you."

"It is well that he didn't attempt it," Kate replied, with spirit; "I would have told him to his face that he lied."

"What do you mean by such language?" her father demanded, angrily; "do you doubt his word to me?"

"I haven't a doubt that he was called away suddenly, but I saw him when he received the message, and he didn't appear like a man called by sickness. He was terribly excited,—so excited he did not even see me when he passed me; and he was angry, for he cursed both the message and the man who brought it."

"Excited? Naturally; he was excited in talking with me, and his anger, no doubt, was over the postponement of the wedding. You show yourself very foolish in getting angry in turn. This is a devilishly awkward affair, though, thank heaven, there's no disgrace or scandal attached to it, and we must make the best we can of it. I have already sent messengers to the church to disperse the guests as they arrive, and have also sent a statement of the facts to the different papers, so there will be no garbled accounts or misstatements to-morrow morning."

"Father," said Kate, drawing herself up with new dignity as he paused, "I want you to understand that this is no childish anger or pique on my part. I have not told all that I saw, nor is it necessary at present; but I saw enough that my eyes are opened to his real character. I want you to understand that I will never marry him! I will die first!"

Her father's face grew dark with anger at her words, but the eyes looking fearlessly into his own never quailed. Perhaps he recognized his own spirit, for he checked the wrathful words he was about to speak and merely inquired,—

"Are you going to make a fool of yourself and involve this affair in a scandal, or will you allow it to pass quietly and with no unpleasant notoriety?"

"You can dispose of it among outsiders as you please, papa, but I want you to understand my decision in this matter, and that it is irrevocable."

"Until you come to your senses!" he retorted, and left the room.

With comparatively little excitement the guests dispersed, and no one, not even Darrell or Mr. Britton, knew aught beyond the statement made by Mr. Underwood.

Some particular friends of Kate's, living in a remote part of the State, thinking it might be rather embarrassing for her to remain in Ophir, invited her to their home for two or three months, and she, realizing that she had incurred her father's displeasure, gladly accepted.

The next morning found Darrell on his way to the camp, looking longingly forward to his busy life amid the mountains, and firmly believing that it would be many a day before he again saw The Pines.

Chapter XXIII

The Mask Lifted

Three weeks of clear, cold weather followed, in which the snow became packed and frozen until the horses' hoofs on the mountain roads resounded as though on asphalt, and the steel shoes of the heavily laden sleds rang out a cheerful rhyme on the frosty air.

These were weeks of strenuous application to work on Darrell's part. His evenings were now spent, far into the night, in writing. He still kept the journal begun during his first winter in camp, believing it would one day prove of inestimable value as a connecting link between past and future. The geological and mineralogical data which he had collected through more than twelve months' research and experiment was now nearly complete, and he had undertaken the work of arranging it, along with copious notes, in form for publication. It was an arduous but fascinating task and one to which he often wished he might devote his entire time.

He was sitting before the fire at night, deeply engrossed in this work, when he was aroused by the sound of hoof-beats on the mountain road leading from the canyon to the camp. He listened; they came rapidly nearer; it was a horseman riding fast and furiously, and by the heavy pounding of the foot-falls Darrell knew the animal he rode was nearly exhausted. On they came past the miners' quarters towards the office building; it was then some messenger from The Pines, and at that hour—Darrell glanced at the clock, it was nearly midnight—it could be no message of trifling import.

Darrell sprang to his feet and, rushing through the outer room, followed by Duke barking excitedly, opened the door just as the rider drew rein before it. What was his astonishment to see Bennett, one of the house servants, on a panting, foam-covered horse.

"Ah, Mr. Darrell," the man cried, as the door opened, "it's a good thing that you keep late hours; right glad I was to see the light in your window, I can tell you, sir!"

"But, Bennett, what brings you here at this time of night?" Darrell asked, hastily.

"Mrs. Dean sent me, sir. Mr. Underwood, he's had a stroke and is as helpless as a baby, sir, and Mrs. Dean's alone, excepting for us servants. She sent me for you, sir; here's a note from her, and she said you was to ride right back with me, if you would, sir."

"Certainly, I'll go with you," Darrell answered, taking the note; "but that horse must not stand in the cold another minute. Ride right over into the stables yonder; wake up the stable-men and tell them to rub him down and blanket him at once, and then to saddle Trix and Rob Roy as quickly as they can. And while they're looking after the horses, you go over to the boarding-house and wake up the cook and tell him to get us up a good, substantial hand-out; we'll need it before morning. I'll be ready in a few minutes, and I'll meet you over there."

"All right, sir," Bennett responded, starting in the direction of the stables, while Darrell went back into his room. Opening the note, he read the following:

"My dear John: I am in trouble and look
to you as to a son. David has had a paralytic
stroke; was brought home helpless about five
o'clock. I am alone, as you might say, as there is
none of the family here. Will you come at
once?

Yours in sorrow, but with love,
Marcia Dean."

Darrell's face grew thoughtful as he refolded the missive. He glanced regretfully at his notes and manuscript, then carefully gathered them together and locked them in his desk, little thinking that months would pass ere he would again resume the work thus interrupted. Then only stopping long enough to write a few lines of explanation to Hathaway, the superintendent, he seized his fur coat, cap, and gloves, and hastened over to the boarding-house where a lunch was already awaiting him. Half an hour later he and Bennett were riding rapidly down the road, Duke bounding on ahead.

They reached The Pines between four and five o'clock. Darrell, leaving the horses in Bennett's care, went directly to the house. Before he could reach the door it was opened by Mrs. Dean.

"I ought not to have sent for you on such a night as this!" she exclaimed, as Darrell entered the room, his clothes glistening with frost, the broad collar turned up about his face a mass of icicles from his frozen breath; "but I felt as though I didn't know what to do, and I wanted some one here who did. I was afraid to take the responsibility any longer."

"You did just right," Darrell answered, dashing away the ice from his face; "I only wish you had sent for me earlier—as soon as this happened. How is Mr. Underwood?"

"He is in pretty bad shape, but the doctors think he will pull through. They have been working over him all night, and he is getting so he can move the right hand a little, but the other side seems badly paralyzed."

"Is he conscious?"

"Yes, he moves his hand when we speak to him, but he looks so worried. That was one reason why I sent for you; I thought he would feel easier to know you were here."

As Darrell approached the bedside he was shocked at the changes wrought in so short a time in the stern, but genial face. It had aged twenty years, and the features, partially drawn to one side, had, as Mrs. Dean remarked, a strained, worried expression. The eyes of the sick man brightened for an instant as Darrell bent over him, assuring him that he would attend to everything, but the anxious look still remained.

130

"I don't know anything about David's business affairs," Mrs. Dean remarked, as she and Darrell left the room, "but I know as well as I want to that this was brought on by some business trouble. I am satisfied something was wrong at the office yesterday, though I wouldn't say so to any one but you."

"Why do you think so?" Darrell queried, in surprise.

"Because he was all right when he went away yesterday morning, but when he came home at noon he was different from what I had ever seen him before. He had just that worried look he has now, and he seemed absent-minded. He was in a great hurry to get back, and the head book-keeper tells me he called for the books to be brought into his private office, and that he spent most of the afternoon going through them. He says that about four o'clock he went through the office, and David was sitting before his desk with his head on his hands, and he didn't speak or look up. A little while afterwards they heard the sound of something heavy falling and ran to his room, and he had fallen on the floor."

"It does look," Darrell admitted, thoughtfully, "as though this may have been caused by the discovery of some wrong condition of affairs."

"Yes, and it must be pretty serious," Mrs. Dean rejoined, "to bring about such results as these."

"Well," said Darrell, "we may not be able to arrive at the cause of this for some time. The first thing to be done is to see that you take a good rest; don't have any anxiety; I will look after everything. As soon as it is daylight it would be well to telegraph for Mr. Britton if you know his address, and possibly for Miss Underwood unless he should seem decidedly better."

But Mrs. Dean did not know Mr. Britton's address, no word having been received from him since his departure, and with the return of daylight Mr. Underwood had gained so perceptibly it was thought best not to alarm Kate unnecessarily.

For the first few days the improvement in Mr. Underwood's condition was slow, but gradually became quite pronounced. Nothing had been heard from Walcott since his sudden leave-taking, but about a week after Mr. Underwood's seizure word was received from him that he was on his way home. As an excuse for his prolonged absence and silence he stated that his father had died and that he had been delayed in the adjustment of business matters.

It was noticeable that after receiving word from Walcott the look of anxiety in Mr. Underwood's face deepened, but his improvement was more marked than ever. It seemed as though the powerful brain and indomitable will dominated the body, forcing it to resume its former activity. By this time he was able to move about his room on crutches, and on the day of Walcott's return he insisted upon being placed in his carriage and taken to the office. At his request Darrell accompanied him and remained with him.

Walcott, upon his arrival in the city, had heard of the illness of his senior partner, and was therefore greatly surprised on entering the offices to find him there. He quickly recovered himself and greeted Mr. Underwood with expressions of profound sympathy. To his words of condolence, however, Mr. Underwood deigned no reply, but his keen eyes

131

bent a searching look upon the face of the younger man, under which the latter quailed visibly; then, without any preliminaries or any inquiries regarding his absence, Mr. Underwood at once proceeded to business affairs.

His stay at the office was brief, as he soon found himself growing fatigued. As he was leaving Walcott inquired politely for Mrs. Dean, then with great particularity for Miss Underwood.

"She is out of town at present," Mr. Underwood replied, watching Walcott.

"Out of town? Indeed! Since when, may I inquire?"

"You evidently have not been in correspondence with her," Mr. Underwood commented, ignoring the other's question.

"Well, no," the latter stammered, slightly taken aback by his partner's manner; "I had absolutely no opportunity for writing, or I would have written you earlier, and then, really, you know, it was hardly to be expected that I would write Miss Underwood, considering her attitude towards myself. I am hoping that she will regard me with more favor after this little absence."

"You will probably be able to judge of that on her return," the elder man answered, dryly.

Kate, on being informed by letter of her father's condition, had wished to return home at once. She had been deterred from doing so by brief messages from him to the effect that she remain with her friends, but she was unable to determine whether those messages were prompted by kindness or anger. On the evening following Walcott's return, however, Mr. Underwood dictated to Darrell a letter to Kate, addressing her by her pet name, assuring her of his constant improvement, and that she need on no account shorten her visit but enjoy herself as long as possible, and enclosing a generous check as a present.

To Darrell and to Mrs. Dean, who was sitting near by with her knitting, this letter seemed rather significant, and their eyes met in a glance of mutual inquiry. After Mr. Underwood had retired Darrell surprised that worthy lady by an account of her brother's reception of Walcott that day, while she in turn treated Darrell to a greater surprise by telling him of Kate's renunciation of Walcott at the last moment, before she knew anything of the postponement of the wedding.

As they separated for the night Darrell remarked, "I may be wrong, but it looks to me as though the cause of Mr. Underwood's illness was the discovery of some evidence of bad faith on Walcott's part."

"It looks that way," Mrs. Dean assented; "I've always felt that man would bring us trouble, and I hope David does find him out before it's too late."

132

Chapter XXIV

Foreshadowings

During Mr. Underwood's illness and convalescence it was pathetic to watch his dependence upon Darrell. He seemed to regard him almost as a son, and when, as his health improved, Darrell spoke of returning to the camp, he would not hear of it.

Every day after Walcott's return Mr. Underwood was taken to the office, where he gradually resumed charge, directing the business of the firm though able to do little himself. As he was still unable to write, he wished Darrell to act as his secretary, and the latter, glad of an opportunity to reciprocate Mr. Underwood's many kindnesses to himself, readily acceded to his wishes. When engaged in this work he used the room which had formerly been his own office and which of late had been unoccupied.

Returning to his office after the transaction of some outside business, to await, as usual, the carriage to convey Mr. Underwood and himself to The Pines, he heard Walcott's voice in the adjoining room. A peculiar quality in his tones, as though he were pleading for favor, arrested Darrell's attention, and he could not then avoid hearing what followed.

"But surely," he was saying, "an amount so trifling, and taking all the circumstances into consideration, that I regarded myself already one of your family and looked upon you as my father, you certainly cannot take so harsh a view of it!"

"That makes no difference whatever," Mr. Underwood interposed sternly; "misappropriation of funds is misappropriation of funds, no matter what the amount or the circumstances under which it is taken, and as for your looking upon me as a father, I wouldn't allow my own son, if I had one, to appropriate one dollar of my money without my knowledge and consent. If you needed money you had only to say so, and I would have loaned you any amount necessary."

"But I regarded this in the nature of a loan," Walcott protested, "only I was so limited for time I did not think it necessary to speak of it until my return."

"You were not so limited but that you had time to tamper with the books and make false entries in them," Mr. Underwood retorted.

"That was done simply to blind the employees, so they need not catch on that I was borrowing."

"There is no use in further talk," the other interrupted, impatiently; "what you have done is done, and your talk will not smooth it over. Besides, I have already told you that I care far less for the money withdrawn from my personal account than for the way you are conducting business generally. There is not a client of mine who can say that I have ever wronged him or taken an unfair advantage of him, and I'll not have any underhanded work started here now. Everything has got to be open and above-board."

"As I have said, Mr. Underwood, in the hurry and excitement of the last week or so before my going away I was forced to neglect some business matters; but if I will straighten everything into satisfactory shape and repay that small loan, as I still regard it, I hope then that our former pleasant relations will be resumed, and that no little misapprehension of this sort will make any difference between us."

"Walcott," said Mr. Underwood, rising on his crutches and preparing to leave the room, "I had absolute confidence in you; I trusted you implicitly. Your own conduct has shaken that confidence, and it may be some time before it is wholly restored. We will continue business as before; but remember, you are on probation, sir—on probation!"

When Kate Underwood received her father's letter, instead of prolonging her visit she at once prepared to return home. She understood that the barrier between her father and herself had been swept away, and nothing could then hold her back from him.

Two days later, as Mr. Underwood was seated by the fire on his return from the office, there came a ring at the door which he took to be the postman's. Mrs. Dean answered the door.

"Any letter from Kate?" he asked, as his sister returned.

"Yes, there's a pretty good-sized one," she replied, with a broad smile, adding, as he glanced in surprise at her empty hands, "I didn't bring it; 'twas too heavy!"

The next instant two arms were thrown about his neck, a slender figure was kneeling beside him, and a fair young face was pressed close to his, while words of endearment were murmured in his ear.

Without a word he clasped her to his breast, holding her for a few moments as though he feared to let her go. Then, relaxing his hold, he playfully pinched her cheeks and stroked the brown hair, calling her by the familiar name "Puss," while his face lighted with the old genial smile for the first time since his illness. Each scanned the other's face, striving to gauge the other's feelings, but each read only that the old relations were re-established between them, and each was satisfied.

Within a day or so of her return Kate despatched a messenger to Walcott with the ring, accompanied by a brief note to the effect that everything between them was at an end, but that it was useless for him to seek an explanation, as she would give none whatever.

He at once took the note to his senior partner.

"I understood, Mr. Underwood, that everything was amicably adjusted between us; I did not suppose that you had carried your suspicions against me to any such length as this!"

Mr. Underwood read the note. "I know nothing whatever regarding my daughter's reasons for her decision, and have had nothing whatever to do with it. I knew that she had formed that decision at the last moment before the wedding ceremony was to be performed, before she was even aware of its postponement. She seemed to think she had sufficient reasons, but what those reasons were I have never asked and do not know."

"But do you intend to allow her to play fast and loose with me in this way? Is she not to fulfil her engagement?" Walcott inquired, with difficulty concealing his anger.

Mr. Underwood regarded him steadily for a moment. "Mr. Walcott, taking all things into consideration, I think perhaps we had better let things remain as they are, say, for a year or so. My daughter is young; there is no need of haste in the consummation of this marriage. I have found what she is worth to me, and I am in no haste to spare her from my home. If she is worth having as a wife, she is worth winning, and I shall not force her against her wishes a second time."

Mr. Underwood spoke quietly, but Walcott understood that further discussion was useless.

Meeting Kate a few days later in her father's office, he greeted her with marked politeness. After a few inquiries regarding her visit, he said,–

"May I be allowed to inquire who is responsible for your sudden decision against me?"

"You, and you alone, are responsible," she replied.

"But I do not understand you," he said.

"Explanations are unnecessary," she rejoined, coldly.

Walcott grew angry. "I know very well that certain of your friends are no friends of mine. If I thought that either or both of them had had a hand in this I would make it a bitter piece of work for them!"

"Mr. Walcott," said Kate, with dignity, "you only demean yourself by such threats. No one has influenced me in this matter but you yourself. You unwittingly afforded me, at the last moment, an insight into your real character. That is enough!"

Walcott felt that he had gone too far. "Perhaps I spoke hastily, but surely it was pardonable considering my grievance. I hope you will overlook it and allow me to see you at The Pines, will you not, Miss Underwood?"

"If my father sees fit to invite you to his house I will probably meet you as his guest, but not otherwise."

Although Mr. Underwood had resumed charge of the downtown offices as before his illness, it soon became evident to all that his active business life was practically over, and that some of his varied interests, involving as they did a multiplicity of cares and responsibilities, must be curtailed. It was therefore decided to sell the mines at Camp Bird at as early a date as practicable, and Mr. Britton, Mr. Underwood's partner in the mining business, was summoned from a distant State to conduct negotiations for the sale. He arrived early in April, and from that time on he and Darrell were engaged in appraising and advertising the property embraced in the great mining and milling plant, in arranging the terms of sale, and in accompanying various prospective purchasers or their agents to and from the mines.

Darrell's work as Mr. Underwood's secretary had been taken up by Kate, who now seldom left her father's side. Between herself and Darrell there was a comradeship similar to that which existed between them previous to her engagement with Walcott, only more healthful and normal, being unmixed with any regret for the past or dread of the future.

135

"You will remain at The Pines when the mines are sold, will you not?" she inquired one day on his return from a trip to the camp.

"Not unless I am needed," he replied; "your father will need me but little longer; then, unless you need me, I had better not remain."

She was silent for a moment. "No," she said, slowly, "I do not need you; I have the assurance of your love; that is enough. I know you will be loyal to me as I to you, wherever you may be."

"I will feel far less regret in going away now that I know you are free from that man Walcott," Darrell continued; "but I wish you would please answer me one question, Kathie: have you any fear of him?"

"Not for myself," she answered; "but I believe he is a man to be feared, and," she added, significantly, "I do sometimes fear him for my friends; perhaps for that reason it is, as you say, better that you should not remain."

"Have no fear for me, Kathie. I understand. That man has been my enemy from our first meeting; but have no fear; I am not afraid."

By the latter part of May negotiations for the sale of the mines had been consummated, and Camp Bird passed into the possession of strangers. It was with a feeling of exile and homelessness that Darrell, riding for the last time down the canyon road, turned to bid the mountains farewell, looking back with lingering glances into the frowning faces he had learned to love.

"What do you propose doing now?" Mr. Britton asked of him as they were walking together the evening after his return from camp.

"That is just what I have been asking myself," Darrell replied.

"Without arriving at any satisfactory conclusion?"

"Not as yet."

"What would you wish to do, were you given your choice?"

"What I wish to do, and what I intend to do if possible, is to devote the next few months to the completion of my book. I can now afford to devote my entire time to it, but I could not do the work justice unless amid the right surroundings, and the question is, where to find them. I do not care to remain here, and yet I shrink from going among strangers."

"There is no need of that," Mr. Britton interposed, quickly; after a pause he continued: "You once expressed a desire for a sort of hermit life. I think by this time you have grown sufficiently out of yourself that you could safely live alone with yourself for a while. How would that suit you for three or four months?"

"I should like it above all things," Darrell answered enthusiastically; "it would be just the thing for my work, but where or how could I live in such a manner?"

"I believe I agreed at that time to furnish the hermitage whenever you were ready for it."

"Yes, you said something of the kind, but I never understood what you meant by it."

"Settle up your business here, pack together what things you need for a few months' sojourn in the mountains, be ready to start with me next week, and you will soon understand."

136

"What is this hermitage, as you call it, and where is it?" Darrell asked, curiously.

The other only shook his head with a smile.

"All right," said Darrell, laughing; "I only hope it is as secluded and beautiful as Camp Bird; I am homesick to-night for my old quarters."

"You can spend your entire time, if you so desire, without a glimpse of a human being other than the man who will look after your needs, except as I may occasionally inflict myself upon you for a day or so."

"Good!" Darrell ejaculated.

"It is amid some of the grandest scenery ever created," Mr. Britton continued, adding, slowly, "and to me it is the most sacred spot on earth,– a veritable Holy of Holies; some day you will know why."

"I thank you, and I beg pardon for my levity," said Darrell, touched by the other's manner. And the two men clasped hands and parted for the night.

A few days later, as Darrell bade his friends at The Pines good-by, Kate whispered,–

"You think this is a parting for three or four months; I feel that it is more. Something tells me that before we meet again there will be a change—I cannot tell what—that will involve a long separation; but I know that through it all our hearts will be true to each other and that out of it will come joy to each of us."

"God grant it, Kathie!" Darrell murmured.

Chapter XXV

The "Hermitage"

Deep within the heart of the Rockies a June day was drawing to its close. Behind a range of snow-crowned peaks the sun was sinking into a sea of fire which glowed and shimmered along the western horizon and in whose transfiguring radiance the bold outlines of the mountains, extending far as the eye could reach in endless ranks, were marvellously softened; the nearer cliffs and crags were wrapped in a golden glory, while the hoary peaks against the eastern sky wore tints of rose and amethyst, and over the whole brooded the silence of the ages.

Less than a score of miles distant a busy city throbbed with ceaseless life and activity, but these royal monarchs, towering one above another, their hands joined in mystic fellowship, their heads white with eternal snows, dwelt in the same unbroken calm in which, with noiseless step, the centuries had come and gone, leaving their footprints in the granite rocks.

Amid those vast distances only two signs of human handiwork were visible. Close clinging to the sides of a rugged mountain a narrow track of shining steel wound its way upward, marking the pathway of civilization in its march from sea to sea, while near the summit of a neighboring peak a quaint cabin of unhewn logs arranged in Gothic fashion was built into the granite ledge.

On a small plateau before this unique dwelling stood John Britton and John Darrell, the latter absorbed in the wondrous scene, the other watching with intense satisfaction the surprise and rapture of his young companion. They stood thus till the sun dipped out of sight. The radiance faded, rose and amethyst deepened to purple; the mountains grew sombre and dun, their rugged outlines standing in bold relief against the evening sky. A nighthawk, circling above their heads, broke the silence with his shrill, plaintive cry, and with a sigh of deep content Darrell turned to his friend.

"What do you think of it?" the latter asked.

"It is unspeakably grand," was the reply, in awed tones.

Beckoning Darrell to follow, Mr. Britton led the way to the cabin, which he unlocked and entered.

"Welcome to the 'Hermitage!'" he said, smilingly, as Darrell paused on the threshold with an exclamation of delight.

A huge fireplace, blasted from solid rock, extended nearly across one side of the room. Over it hung antlers of moose, elk, and deer, while skins of mountain lion, bear, and wolf covered the floor. A large writing-table stood in the centre of the room, and beside it a bookcase filled with the works of some of the world's greatest authors.

Darrell lifted one book after another with the reverential touch of the true book-lover, while Mr. Britton hastily arranged the belongings of the room so as to render it as cosey and attractive as possible.

"The evenings are so cool at this altitude that a fire will soon seem grateful," he remarked, lighting the fragrant boughs of spruce and hemlock which filled the fireplace and drawing chairs before the crackling, dancing flames.

Duke, who had accompanied them, stretched himself in the firelight with a low growl of satisfaction, at which both men smiled.

It was the first time Darrell had ever seen his friend in the rôle of host, but Mr. Britton proved himself a royal entertainer. His experiences of mountain life had been varied and thrilling, and the cabin contained many relics and trophies of his prowess as huntsman and trapper. As the evening wore on Mr. Britton opened a small store-room built in the rock, and took therefrom a tempting repast of venison and wild fowl which his forethought had ordered placed there for the occasion. To Darrell, sitting by the fragrant fire and listening to tales of adventure, the time passed only too swiftly, and he was sorry when the entrance of the man with his luggage recalled them to the lateness of the hour.

"There is a genuine hermit for you," Mr. Britton remarked, as the man took his departure after agreeing to come to the cabin once a day to do whatever might be needed.

"Who is he?" Darrell asked.

138

"No one knows. He goes by the name of 'Peter,' but nothing is known of his real name or history. He has lived in these mountains for thirty years and has not visited a city or town of any size in that time. He is a trapper, but acts as guide during the summers. He is very popular with tourist and hunting parties that come to the mountains, but nothing will induce him to leave his haunts except as he occasionally goes to some small station for supplies."

"Where does he live?"

"In a cabin about half-way down the trail. He is a good cook, a faithful man every way, but you will find him very reticent. He is one of the many in this country whose past is buried out of sight."

Mr. Britton then led the way to two smaller rooms,—a kitchen, equipped with a small stove, table, and cooking utensils, and a sleeping-apartment, its two bunks piled with soft blankets and wolf-skins.

As Darrell proceeded to disrobe his attention was suddenly attracted by an object in one corner of the room which he was unable to distinguish clearly in the dim light. Upon going over to examine it more closely, what was his astonishment to see a large crucifix of exquisite design and workmanship. As he turned towards Mr. Britton the latter smiled to see the bewilderment depicted on his face.

"You did not expect to find such a souvenir of old Rome in a mountain cabin, did you?" he asked.

"Perhaps not," Darrell admitted; "but that of itself is not what so greatly surprises me. Are you a——" He paused abruptly, without finishing the question.

"I will answer the question you hesitate to ask," the other replied; "no, I am not a Catholic; neither am I, in the strict sense of the word, a Protestant, or one who protests, since, if I were, I would protest no more earnestly against the errors of the Catholic Church than against the evils existing in other so-called Christian churches."

Darrell's eyes returned to the crucifix.

"That," continued Mr. Britton, "was given me years ago by a beloved friend of mine—a priest, now an archbishop—in return for a few services rendered some of his people. I keep it for the lessons it taught me in the years of my sorrow, and whenever my burden seems greater than I can bear, I come back here and look at that, and beside the suffering which it symbolizes my own is dwarfed to insignificance."

A long silence followed; then, as they lay down in the darkness, Darrell said, in subdued tones,—

"I have never heard you say, and it never before occurred to me to ask, what was your religion."

"I don't know that I have any particular religion," Mr. Britton answered, slowly; "I have no formulated creed. I am a child of God and a disciple of Jesus, the Christ. Like Him, I am the child of a King, a son of the highest Royalty, yet a servant to my fellow-men; that is all."

The following morning Mr. Britton awakened Darrell at an early hour.

"Forgive me for disturbing your slumbers, but I want you to see the sunrise from these heights; I think you will feel repaid. You could not see it at the camp, you were so hemmed in by higher mountains."

Darrell rose and, having dressed hastily, stepped out into the gray twilight of the early dawn. A faint flush tinged the eastern sky, which deepened to a roseate hue, growing moment by moment brighter and more vivid. Chain after chain of mountains, slumbering dark and grim against the horizon, suddenly awoke, blushing and smiling in the rosy light. Then, as rays of living flame shot upward, mingling with the crimson waves and changing them to molten gold, the snowy caps of the higher peaks were transformed to jewelled crowns. There was a moment of transcendent beauty, then, in a burst of glory, the sun appeared.

"That is a sight I shall never forget, and one I shall try to see often," Darrell said, as they retraced their steps to the cabin.

"You will never find it twice the same," Mr. Britton answered; "Nature varies her gifts so that to her true lovers they will not pall."

After breakfast they again strolled out into the sunlight, Mr. Britton seating himself upon a projecting ledge of granite, while Darrell threw himself down upon the mountain grass, his head resting within his clasped hands.

"What an ideal spot for my work!" he exclaimed.

Mr. Britton smiled. "I fear you would never accomplish much with me here. I must return to the city soon, or you will degenerate into a confirmed idler."

"I have often thought," said Darrell, reflectively, "that when I have completed this work I would like to attempt a novel. It seems as though there is plenty of material out here for a strong one. Think of the lives one comes in contact with almost daily—stranger than fiction, every one!"

"Your own, for instance," Mr. Britton suggested.

"Yours also," Darrell replied, in low tones; "the story of your life, if rightly told, would do more to uplift men's souls than nine-tenths of the sermons."

"The story of my life, my son, will never be told to any ear other than your own, and I trust to your love for me that it will go no farther."

"Of that you can rest assured," Darrell replied.

As the sun climbed towards the zenith they returned to the cabin and seated themselves on a broad settee of rustic work under an overhanging vine near the cabin door.

"I have been wondering ever since I came here," said Darrell, "how you ever discovered such a place as this. It is so unique and so appropriate to the surroundings."

"I discovered," said Mr. Britton, with slight emphasis on the word, "only the 'surroundings.' The cabin is my own work."

"What! do you mean to say that you built it?"

"Yes, little by little. At first it was hardly more than a rude shelter, but I gradually enlarged it and beautified it, trying always, as you say, to keep it in harmony with its surroundings."

"Then you are an artist and a genius."

"But that is not the only work I did during the first months of my life here. Come with me and I will show you."

He led the way along the trail, farther up the mountain, till a sharp turn hid him from view. Darrell, following closely, came upon the entrance of an incline shaft leading into the mountain. Just within he saw Mr. Britton lighting two candles which he had taken from a rocky ledge; one of these he handed to Darrell, and then proceeded down the shaft.

"A mine!" Darrell exclaimed.

"Yes, and a valuable one, were it only accessible so that it could be developed without enormous expense; but that is out of the question."

The underground workings were not extensive, but the vein was one of exceptional richness. When they emerged later Darrell brought with him some specimens and a tiny nugget of gold as souvenirs.

"The first season," said Mr. Britton, "I worked the mine and built the cabin as a shelter for the coming winter. The winter months I spent in hunting and trapping when I could go out in the mountains, and hibernated during the long storms. Early in the spring I began mining again and worked the following season. By that time I was ready to start forth into the world, so I gave Peter an interest in the mine, and he works it from time to time, doing little more than the representation each year."

As they descended towards the cabin Mr. Britton continued: "I have shown you this that you may the better understand the story I have to tell you before I leave you as sole occupant of the Hermitage."

Chapter XXVI

John Britton's Story

Evening found Darrell and his friend seated on the rocks watching the sunset. Mr. Britton was unusually silent, and Darrell, through a sort of intuitive sympathy, refrained from breaking the silence. At last, as the glow was fading from earth and sky, Mr. Britton said,—

"I have chosen this day and this hour to tell you my story, because, being the anniversary of my wedding, it seemed peculiarly appropriate. Twenty-eight years ago, at sunset, on such a royal day as this, we were married—my love and I."

He spoke with an unnatural calmness, as though it were another's story he was telling.

"I was young, with a decided aptitude for commercial life, ambitious, determined to make my way in life, but with little capital besides sound health and a good education. She was the daughter of a wealthy man. We speak in this country of 'mining kings;' he might be denominated an 'agricultural king.' He prided himself upon his hundreds of fertile acres, his miles of forest, his immense dairy, his blooded horses, his magnificent barns and granaries, his beautiful home. She was the younger daughter—his especial pet and pride. For a while, as a friend and acquaintance of his two daughters, I was welcome at his home; later, as a lover of the younger, I was banished and its doors closed against me. Our love was no foolish boy and girl romance, and we had no word of kindly counsel; only unreasoning, stubborn opposition. What followed was only what might have been expected. Strong in our love for and trust in each other, we went to a neighboring village, and, going to a little country parsonage, were married, without one thought of the madness, the folly of what we were doing. We found the minister and his family seated outside the house under a sort of arbor of flowering shrubs, and I remember it was her wish that the ceremony be performed there. Never can I forget her as she stood there, her hand trembling in mine at the strangeness of the situation, her cheeks flushed with excitement, her lips quivering as she made the responses, the slanting sunbeams kissing her hair and brow and the fragrant, snowy petals of the mock-orange falling about her.

"A few weeks of unalloyed happiness followed; then gradually my eyes were opened to the wrong I had done her. My heart smote me as I saw her, day by day, performing household tasks to which she was unaccustomed, subjected to petty trials and privations, denying herself in many little ways in order to help me. She never murmured, but her very fortitude and cheerfulness were a constant reproach to me.

"But a few months elapsed when we found that another was coming to share our home and our love. We rejoiced together, but my heart reproached me more bitterly than ever as I realized how ill prepared she was for what awaited her. Our trials and privations brought us only closer to each other, but my brain was racked with anxiety and my heart bled as day by day I saw the dawning motherhood in her eyes,—the growing tenderness, the look of sweet, wondering expectancy. I grew desperate.

"From a booming western city came reports of marvellous openings for business men—of small investments bringing swift and large returns. I placed my wife in the care of a good, motherly woman and bade her good-by, while she, brave heart, without a tear, bade me God-speed. I went there determined to win, to make a home to which I would bring both wife and child later. For three months I made money, sending half to her, and investing every cent which I did not absolutely need of the other half. Then came tales from a mining district still farther west, of fabulous fortunes made in a month, a week, sometimes a day. What was the use of dallying where I was? I hastened to the mining camp. In less than a week I had 'struck it rich,' and knew that in all probability I would within a month draw out a fortune.

"Just at this time the letters from home ceased. For seven days I heard nothing, and half mad with anxiety and suspense I awaited each night the incoming train to bring me tidings. One night, just as the train was about to leave, I caught sight of a former acquaintance from a neighboring village, bound for a camp yet farther west, and, as I greeted him, he told me in few words and pitying tones of the death of my wife and child."

For a moment Mr. Britton paused, and Darrell drew instinctively nearer, though saying nothing.

"I have no distinct recollection of what followed. I was told afterwards that friendly hands caught me as the train started, to save me from being crushed beneath the wheels. For three months I wandered from one mining camp to another, working mechanically, with no thought or care as to success or failure. An old miner from the first camp who had taken a liking to me followed me in my wanderings and worked beside me, caring for me and guarding my savings as though he had been a father. The old fellow never left me, nor I him, until his death three years later. He taught me many valuable points in practical mining, and I think his rough but kindly care was all that saved me from insanity during those years.

"After his death I brooded over my grief till I became nearly frenzied. I could not banish the thought that but for my rashness and foolishness in taking her from her home my wife might still have been living. To myself I seemed little short of a murderer. I left the camp and wandered, night and day, afar into the mountains. I came to this mountain on which we are sitting and climbed nearly to the top. God was there, but, like Jacob of old, 'I knew it not.' But something seemed to speak to me out of the infinite silence, calming my frenzied brain and soothing my troubled soul. I sat there till the stars appeared, and then I sank into a deep, peaceful sleep— the first in years. When I awoke the sun was shining in my face, and, though the old pain still throbbed, I had a sense of new strength with which to bear it. I ate of the food I carried with me and drank from a mountain stream—the same that trickles past us now, only nearer its source. The place fascinated me; I dared not leave it, and I spent the day in wandering up and down the rocks. My steps were guided to the mine I showed you to-day. I saw the indications of richness there, and, overturning the earth with my pick, found gold among the very grassroots. Then followed the life of which I have already given you an outline.

"For a while I worked in pain and anguish, but gradually, in the solitude of the mountains, my spirit found peace; against their infinity my life with its burden dwindled to an atom, and from the lesson of their centuries of silent waiting I gathered strength and fortitude to await my appointed time.

"But after a time God spoke to me and bade me go forth from my solitude into the world, to comfort other sorrowing souls as I had been comforted. From that time I have travelled almost constantly. I have no home; I wish none. I want to bring comfort and help to as many of earth's sorrowing, sinning children as possible; but when the old wound bleeds afresh and the pain becomes more than I can bear I flee as a bird to my mountain for balm and healing. Do you wonder, my son, that the place is sacred to me? Do you understand my love for you in bringing you here?"

Darrell sat with bowed head, speechless, but one hand went out to Mr. Britton, which the latter clasped in both his own.

When at last he raised his head he exclaimed, "Strange! but your story has wrung my soul! It seems in some inexplicable way a part of my very life!"

"Our souls seem united by some mystic tie—I cannot explain what, unless it be that in some respects our sufferings have been similar."

"Mine have been as nothing to yours," Darrell replied. A moment later he added:

"I feel as one in a dream; what you have told me has taken such hold upon me."

Night had fallen when they returned to the cabin.

"This seems hallowed ground to me now," Darrell remarked.

"It has always seemed so to me," Mr. Britton replied; "but remember, so long as you have need of the place it is always open to you."

"'Until the day break and the shadows flee away,'" Darrell responded, in low tones, as though to himself.

Mr. Britton caught his meaning. "My son," he said, "when the day breaks for you do not forget those who still sit in darkness!"

Chapter XXVII

The Rending of the Veil

The story of Mr. Britton's life impressed Darrell deeply. In the days following his friend's departure he would sit for hours revolving it in his mind, unable to rid himself of the impression that it was in some way connected with his own life. Impelled by some motive he could scarcely explain, he recorded it in his journal as told by Mr. Britton as nearly as he could recall it.

Left to himself he worked with unabated ardor, but his work soon grew unsatisfying. The inspiring nature of his surroundings seemed to stimulate him to higher effort and loftier work, which should call into play the imaginative faculties and in which the brain would be free to weave its own creations. Stronger within him grew the desire to write a novel which should have in it something of the power, the force, of the strenuous western life,—something which would seem, in a measure at least, worthy of his surroundings. His day's work ended, he would walk up and down the rocks, sometimes far into the night, the plot for this story forming within his brain, till at last its outlines grew distinct and he knew the thing that was to be, as the sculptor knows what will come forth at his bidding from the lifeless marble. He made a careful synopsis of the plot that nothing might escape him in the uncertain future, and then began to write.

The order of his work was now reversed, the new undertaking being given his first and best thought; then, when imagination wearied and refused to rise above the realms of fact, he fell back upon his scientific work as a rest from the other. Thus employed the weeks passed with incredible swiftness, the monotony broken by an occasional visit from Mr. Britton, until August came, its hot breath turning the grasses sere and brown.

One evening Darrell came forth from his work at a later hour than usual. His mind had been unusually active, his imagination vivid, but, wearied at last, he was compelled to stop short of the task he had set for himself.

The heat had been intense that day, and the atmosphere seemed peculiarly oppressive. The sun was sinking amid light clouds of gorgeous tints, and as Darrell watched their changing outlines they seemed fit emblems of the thoughts at that moment baffling his weary brain,—elusive, intangible, presenting themselves in numberless forms, yet always beyond his grasp.

Standing erect, with arms folded, his pose indicated conscious strength, and the face lifted to the evening sky was one which would have commanded attention amid a sea of human faces. Two years had wrought wondrous changes in it. Strength and firmness were there still, but sweetness was mingled with the strength, and the old, indomitable will was tempered with gentleness. All the finer susceptibilities had been awakened and had left their impress there. Introspection had done its work. It was the face of a man who knew himself and had conquered himself. The sculptor's work was almost complete.

Not a breath stirred the air, which moment by moment grew more oppressive, presaging a coming storm. Darrell was suddenly filled with a strange unrest—a presentiment of some impending catastrophe. For a while he walked restlessly up and down the narrow plateau; then, seating himself in front of the cabin, he bowed his head upon his hands, shutting out all sight and thought of the present, for his mind seemed teeming with vague, shadowy forms of the past. Duke came near and laid his head against his master's shoulder, and the twilight deepened around them both.

Far up the neighboring mountain a mighty engine loomed out from the gathering darkness—a fiery-headed monster—and with its long train of coaches crawled serpent-like around the rocky height, then vanished as it came. The clouds which had been roving indolently across the western horizon suddenly formed in line and moved steadily—a solid battalion—upward towards the zenith, while from the east another phalanx, black and threatening, advanced with low, wrathful mutterings.

Unmindful of the approaching storm Darrell sat, silent and motionless, till a sudden peal of thunder—the first note of the impending battle—roused him from his revery. Springing to his feet he watched the rapidly advancing armies marshalling their forces upon the battle-ground. Another roll of thunder, and the conflict began. Up and down the mountain passes the winds rushed wildly, shrieking like demons. Around the lofty summits the lightnings played like the burnished swords of giants in mortal combat, while peal after peal resounded through the vast spaces, reverberated from peak to peak, echoed and re-echoed, till the rocks themselves seemed to tremble.

With quickening pulse and bated breath Darrell watched the storm,—fascinated, entranced,—while emotions he could neither understand nor control surged through his breast. More and more fiercely the battle waged; more swift and brilliant grew the sword-play, while the roar of heaven's artillery grew louder and louder. His spirit rose with the strife, filling him with a strange sense of exaltation.

Suddenly the universe seemed wrapped in flame, there was a deafening crash as though the eternal hills were being rent asunder, and then—oblivion!

When that instant of blinding light and deafening sound had passed John Darrell lay prostrate, unconscious on the rocks.

Chapter XXVIII

As a Dream when One Awaketh

As the morning sun arose over the snowy summits of the Great Divide, the sleeper on the rocks stirred restlessly; then gradually awoke to consciousness—a delightful consciousness of renewed life and vigor, a subtle sense of revivification of body and mind. The racking pain, the burning fever, the legions of torturing phantoms, all were gone; his pulse was calm, his blood cool, his brain clear.

With a sigh of deep content he opened his eyes; then suddenly rose to a sitting posture and gazed about him in utter bewilderment; above him only the boundless dome of heaven, around him only endless mountain ranges! Dazed by the strangeness, the isolation of the scene, he began for an instant to doubt his sanity; was this a reality or a chimera of his own imagination? But only for an instant, for with his first movement a large collie had bounded to his side and now began licking his hands and face with the most joyful demonstrations. There was something soothing and reassuring in the companionship even of the dumb brute, and he caressed the noble creature, confident that he would soon find some sign of human life in that strange region; but the dog, reading no look of recognition in the face beside him, drew back and began whining piteously.

Perplexed, but with his faculties thoroughly aroused and active, the young man sprang to his feet, and, looking eagerly about him, discovered at a little distance the cabin against the mountain ledge. Hastening thither he found the door open, and, after vainly waiting for any response to his knocking, entered.

The furnishings were mostly hand-made, but fashioned with

146

considerable artistic skill, and contributed to give the interior a most attractive appearance, while etchings, books and papers, pages of written manuscript, and a violin indicated its occupants to be a man of refined tastes and studious habits. The dog had accompanied him, sometimes following closely, sometimes going on in advance as though to lead the way. Once within the cabin he led him to the store-room in the rock where was an abundance of food, which the latter proceeded to divide between himself and his dumb guide.

Having satisfied his hunger, the young man took a newspaper from the table, and, going outside the cabin, seated himself to await the return of his unknown host. Sitting there, he discovered for the first time the railway winding around the sides of the lofty mountain opposite. The sight filled him with delight, for those slender rails, gleaming in the morning sunlight, seemed to connect him with the world which he remembered, but from which he appeared so strangely isolated.

Unfolding the newspaper his attention was attracted by the date, at which he gazed in consternation, his eyes riveted to the page. For a moment his head swam, he was unable to believe his own senses. Dropping the sheet and bowing his head upon his hands he went carefully over the past as he now remembered it,–the business on which he had been commissioned to come west; his journey westward; the tragedy in the sleeping-car–he shuddered as the memory of the murderer's face flashed before him with terrible distinctness; his reception at The Pines,–all was as clear as though it had happened but yesterday; it was in August, and this was August, but two years later! Great God! had two years dropped out of his life? Again he recalled his illness, the long agony, the final sinking into oblivion, the strange awakening in perfect health; yes, surely there must be a missing link; but how? where?

He rose to re-enter the cabin, and, passing the window, caught a glimpse of his face reflected there; a face like, and yet unlike, his own, and crowned with snow-white hair! In doubt and bewilderment he paced up and down within the cabin, vainly striving to connect these fragmentary parts, to reconcile the present with the past. As he passed and repassed the table covered with manuscript his attention was attracted by an odd-looking volume bound in flexible morocco and containing several hundred pages of written matter. It lay partly open in a conspicuous place, and upon the fly-leaf was written, in large, bold characters,–

"To my Other Self, should he awaken."

He could not banish the words from his mind; they drew him with irresistible magnetism. Again and again he read them, until, impelled by some power he could not explain, he seized the volume and, seating himself in the doorway of the cabin, proceeded to examine it. Lifting the fly-leaf, he read the following inscription:

"To one from the outer world, whose identity is hidden among the secrets of the past:

147

"With the hope that when the veil is lifted,
these pages may assist him in uniting into one
perfect whole the strangely disjointed portions
of his life, they are inscribed by

"John Darrell."

He smiled as he read the name and recalled the circumstances under which he had taken it, but he no longer felt any hesitation regarding the volume in his hands, and he began to read. It was written as a communication from one stranger to another, from the mountain recluse to one of whose life he had not the slightest knowledge; but he knew without doubt that it was addressed to himself, yet written by himself,— that writer and reader were one and the same.

For more than two hours he read on and on, deeply absorbed in the tale of that solitary life, his own heart responding to each note of joy or sorrow, of hope or despair, and vibrating to the undertone of loneliness and longing running through it all.

He strove vainly to recall the characters in the strange drama in which he had played his part but of which he had now no distinct recollection; dimly they passed before his vision like the shadowy phantoms of a dream from which one has just awakened. He started at the first mention of John Britton's name, eagerly following each outline of that noble character, his heart kindling with affection as he read his words of loving, helpful counsel. His face grew tender and his eyes filled at the love-story, so pathetically brief, faithfully transcribed on those pages, but of Kate Underwood he could only recall a slender girl with golden-brown hair and wistful, appealing brown eyes; he wondered at the strength of character shown by her speech and conduct, and his heart went out to this unknown love, notwithstanding that memory now showed him the picture of another and earlier love in the far East.

But it was the story of John Britton's life which moved him most. With strained, eager eyes and bated breath he read that sad recital, and at its termination, buried his face in his hands and sobbed like a child.

When he had grown calm he sat for some time reviewing the past and forming plans for future action. While thus absorbed in thought he heard a step, and, looking up, saw standing before him a man of apparently sixty years, with bronzed face and grizzled hair, whose small, piercing eyes regarded himself with keen scrutiny. In response to the younger man's greeting he only bowed silently.

"You must be Peter, the hermit," the young man exclaimed; "but whoever you are, you are welcome; I am glad to see a human face."

"And you," replied the other, slowly, "you are not the same man that you were yesterday; you have awakened, as he said you would some day."

"As who said?" the young man questioned.

"John Britton," the other replied.

"Yes, I have awakened, and my life here is like a dream. Sit down, Peter; I want to ask you some questions."

For half an hour they sat together, the younger man asking questions, the other answering in as few words as possible, his keen eyes never leaving the face of his interlocutor.

"Where is this John Britton?" the young man finally inquired.

"In Ophir—at a place called The Pines."

"I know the place; I remember it. How far is it from here?"

"Fifteen miles by rail from the station at the foot of the mountain."

"I must go to him at once; you will show me the way. How soon can we get away from here?"

Peter glanced at the sun. "We cannot get down the trail in season for to-day's train. We will start to-morrow morning."

Without further speech he then went into the cabin and busied himself with his accustomed duties. When he reappeared he again stood silently regarding the younger man with his fixed, penetrating gaze.

"What awakened you?" he asked, at length.

The abruptness of the question, as well as its tenor, startled the other; that was a phase of the mystery surrounding himself of which he had not even thought.

"I do not know," he replied, slowly; "that question had not occurred to me before. What do you think? Might it not have come about in the ordinary sequence of events?"

Peter shook his head. "Not likely," he muttered; "there must have been a shock of some kind."

The young man smiled brightly. "Well, I cannot answer for yesterday's events," he said, "having neither record nor recollection of the day; but I certainly sustained a shock this morning on awaking on the bare rocks at such an altitude as this and with no trace of a human being visible!"

"On the rocks!" Peter repeated; "where?"

"Yonder," said the young man, indicating the direction; "come, I will show you the exact spot."

He led the way to his rocky bed, near one end of the plateau, then watched his companion's movements as he knelt down and carefully inspected the rock, then, rising to his feet, looked searchingly in every direction with his ferret-like glance.

"Ah!" the latter suddenly exclaimed, with emphasis, at the same time pointing to a rock almost overhanging their heads.

Following the direction indicated, the young man saw a pine-tree on the edge of the overhanging rock, the entire length of its trunk split open, its branches shrivelled and blackened as though by fire.

Peter, notwithstanding his age, sprang up the rocks with the agility of a panther, the younger man following more slowly. As he came up Peter turned from an examination of the dead tree and looked at him significantly.

"An electric shock!" he said; "that was a living tree yesterday. There was an electric storm last night, the worst in years; it brought death to the tree, but life to you."

To the younger man the words of the old hermit seemed incredible, but that night brought him a strange confirmation of their truth. Upon

149

disrobing for the night, what was his astonishment to discover upon his right shoulder and extending downward diagonally across the right breast a long, blue mark of irregular, zigzag form, while running parallel with it its entire length, perfect as though done in India ink with an artist's pen, was the outline of the very scene surrounding him where he lay that morning–cliff and crag and mountain peak–traced indelibly upon the living flesh, an indubitable evidence of the power which had finally aroused his dormant faculties and a souvenir of the lost years which he would carry with him to his dying day.

Chapter XXIX

John Darrell's Story

On the following morning the cabin on the mountain side was closed at an early hour, and its late occupant, accompanied by Peter and the collie, descended the trail to the small station near the base of the mountain, where he took leave of the old hermit. On his arrival at Ophir he ordered a carriage and drove directly to The Pines, for he was impatient to see John Britton at as early a date as possible, and was fearful lest the latter, with his migratory habits, might escape him.

It was near noon when, having dismissed the carriage, he rang for admission. He recalled the house and grounds as they appeared to him on his first arrival, but he found it hard to realize that he was looking upon the scenes among which most of that strange drama of the last two years had been enacted. Mr. Underwood himself came to the door.

"Why, Darrell, my boy, how do you do?" he exclaimed, shaking hands heartily; "thought you'd take us by surprise, eh? Got a little tired of living alone, I guess, and thought you'd come back to your friends. Well, it's mighty good to see you; come in; we'll have lunch in about an hour."

To Mr. Underwood's surprise the young man did not immediately accept the invitation to come in, but seemed to hesitate for a moment.

"I am very glad to meet you, Mr. Underwood," he responded, pleasantly, but with a shade of reserve in his manner; "I remember you very well, indeed, and probably yours is about the only face I will be able to recall."

For a moment Mr. Underwood seemed staggered, unable to comprehend the meaning of the other's words.

The young man continued: "I understand Mr. Britton is stopping with you; is he still here, or has he left?"

"He is here," Mr. Underwood replied; "but, good God! Darrell, what does this mean?"

Before the other could reply Mr. Britton, who was in an adjoining room and had overheard the colloquy, came quickly forward. He gave a swift, penetrating glance into the young man's face, then, turning to Mr. Underwood, said,–

"It means, David, that our young friend has come to his own again. He is no longer of our world or of us."

Then turning to the young man, he said, "I am John Britton; do you wish to see me?"

The other looked earnestly into the face of the speaker, and his own features betrayed emotion as he replied,–

"I do; I must see you on especially important business."

"David, you will let us have the use of your private room for a while?" Mr. Britton inquired.

Mr. Underwood nodded silently, his eyes fixed with a troubled expression upon the young man's face. The latter, observing his distress, said,–

"Don't think, Mr. Underwood, that I am insensible to all your kindness to me since my coming here two years ago. I shall see you later and show you that I am not lacking in appreciation, though I can never express my gratitude to you; but before I can do that–before I can even tell you who I am–it is necessary that I see Mr. Britton."

"Tut! tut!" said Mr. Underwood, gruffly; "don't talk to me of gratitude; I don't want any; but, my God! boy, I had come to look on you almost as my own son!" And, turning abruptly, he left the room before either of the others could speak.

"He is a man of very strong feelings," said Mr. Britton, leading the way to Mr. Underwood's room; "and, to tell the truth, this is a pretty hard blow to each of us, although we should have prepared ourselves for it. Be seated, my son."

Seating himself beside the young man and again looking into his face, he said,–

"I see that the day has dawned; when did the light come, and how?"

Briefly the other related his awakening on the rocks and the events which followed down to his finding and reading the journal which recorded so faithfully the history of the missing years, Mr. Britton listening with intense interest. At last the young man said,–

"Of all the records of that journal, there was nothing that interested me so greatly or moved me so deeply as did the story of your own life. That is what brought me here to-day. I have come to tell you my story,–the story of John Darrell, as you have known him,–and possibly you may find it in some ways a counterpart to your own."

"I was drawn towards you in some inexplicable way from our first meeting," Mr. Britton replied, slowly; "you became as dear to me as a son, so that I gave you in confidence the story that no other human being has ever heard. It is needless to say that I appreciate this mark of your confidence in return, and that you can rest assured of my deepest interest in anything concerning yourself."

The younger man drew his chair nearer his companion. "As you already

151

know," he said, "I am a mine expert. I came out here on a commission for a large eastern syndicate, and as there was likely to be lively competition and I wished to remain incognito, I took the name of John Darrell, which in reality was a part of my own name. My home is in New York State. I was a country-bred boy, brought up on one of those great farms which abound a little north of the central part of the State; but, though country-bred, I was not a rustic, for my mother, who was my principal instructor until I was about fourteen years of age, was a woman of refinement and culture. My mother and I lived at her father's house—a beautiful country home; but even while a mere child I became aware that there was some kind of an unpleasant secret in our family. My grandfather would never allow my father's name mentioned, and he had little love for me as his child; but my earliest recollections of my mother are of her kneeling with me night after night in prayer, teaching me to love and revere the father I had never known, who, she told me, was 'gone away,' and to pray always for his welfare and for his return. At fourteen I was sent away to a preparatory school, and afterwards to college. Then, as I developed a taste for mineralogy and metallurgy, I took a course in the Columbian School of Mines. By this time I had learned that while it was generally supposed my mother was a widow, there were those, my grandfather among them, who believed that my father had deserted her. My first intimation of this was an insinuation to that effect by my grandfather himself, soon after my graduation. I was an athlete and already had a good position at a fair salary, and so great was my love and reverence for my father's name that I told the old gentleman that nothing but his white hairs saved him from a sound thrashing, and that at the first repetition of any such insinuation I would take my mother from under his roof and provide a home for her myself. That sufficed to silence him effectually, for he idolized her. After this little episode I went to my mother and begged her to tell me the secret regarding my father."

The young man paused for a moment, his dark eyes gazing earnestly into the clear gray eyes watching him intently; then, without shifting his gaze, he continued, in low tones:

"She told me that about a year before my birth she and my father were married against her father's will, his only objection to the marriage being that my father was poor. She told me of their happy married life that followed, but that my father was ambitious, and the consciousness of poverty and the fact that he could not provide for her as he wished galled him. She told me how, when there was revealed to them the promise of a new love and life within their little home, he redoubled his efforts to do for her and hers, and then, dissatisfied with what he could accomplish there, went out into the new West to build a home for his little family. She told of the brave, loving letters that came so faithfully and the generous remittances to provide for every possible need in the coming emergency. Then Fortune beckoned him still farther west, and he obeyed, daring the dangers of that strange, wild country for the love he bore his wife and his unborn child. From that country only one letter ever was received from him. Just at that time I was born, and my life came near costing hers who

152

bore me. For weeks she lay between life and death, so low that the report of her death reached her parents, bringing them broken-hearted and, as they supposed, too late to her humble home. They found her yet living and threw their love and their wealth into the battle against death. In all this time no news came from the great West. As soon as she could be moved my mother and her child were taken to her father's home. Her father forgave her, but he had no forgiveness for her husband and no love for his child. He tried to make my mother believe her husband had deserted her, but she was loyal in her trust in him as in her love for him. She named her child for his father, 'John,' but as her father would not allow the name repeated in his hearing she gave him the additional name of 'Darrell,' by which he was universally known; but in those sacred hours when she told me of my father and taught me to pray for him, she always called me by his name, 'John Britton.'"

As he ceased speaking both men rose simultaneously to their feet. The elder man placed his hands upon the shoulders of the younger, and, standing thus face to face, they looked into each other's eyes as though each were reading the other's inmost soul.

"What was your mother's name?" Mr. Britton asked, in low tones.

"Patience—Patience Jewett," replied the other.

Mr. Britton bowed his head with deep emotion, and father and son were clasped in each other's arms.

When they had grown calm enough for speech Mr. Britton's first words were of his wife.

"What of your mother, my son,—was she living when you came west?"

"Yes, but her health was delicate, and I am fearful of the effects of my long absence; it must have been a terrible strain upon her. As soon as I reached the city this morning I telegraphed an old schoolmate for tidings of her, and I am expecting an answer any moment."

They talked of the strange chain of circumstances which had brought them together and of the mysterious bond by which they had been so closely united while as yet unconscious of their relationship. The summons to lunch recalled them to the present. As they rose to leave the room Mr. Britton threw his arm affectionately about Darrell's shoulders, exclaiming,—

"My son! Mine! and I have loved you as such from the first time I looked into your eyes! If God will now only permit me to see my beloved wife again, I can ask nothing more!"

And as Darrell gazed at the noble form, towering slightly above his own, and looked into the depths of those gray eyes, penetrating, fearless, yet tender as a woman's, he felt that however sweet and sacred had been the friendship between them in the past, it was as naught compared with the infinitely sweeter and holier relationship of father and son.

They passed into the dining-room where Mr. Underwood and Mrs. Dean awaited them, a look of eager expectancy on both faces, the wistful expression of Mrs. Dean as she watched for the first token of recognition on Darrell's part being almost pathetic.

Mr. Britton, who had entered slightly in advance, paused half-way across the room, and, placing his hand on Darrell's shoulder, said, in a voice which vibrated with emotion,—

"My dear friends, Mrs. Dean and Mr. Underwood, allow me to introduce my son, John Darrell Britton!"

There, was a moment of strained silence in which only the labored breathing of Mr. Underwood could be heard.

"Do you mean that you have adopted him?" Mr. Underwood asked, slowly, seeming to speak with difficulty.

"No, David; he is my own flesh and blood—my legitimate son; I will explain later."

Mrs. Dean and Darrell had clasped hands and were scanning each other's faces.

"John, do you remember me?" she asked, with trembling lips.

Darrell bent his head and kissed her. "I do, Mrs. Dean," he replied.

She smiled, at the same time wiping away a tear with the corner of her white apron.

"I don't think I could have borne it if you hadn't," she remarked, simply; then, shaking hands with Mr. Britton, she added:

"I congratulate you, Mr. Britton; I congratulate you both. If ever there were two who ought to be father and son, you are the two."

Mr. Underwood wrung Darrell's hand. "I congratulate you, boy, and I'm mighty glad to find you're not a stranger to us, after all."

Then, grasping his old-time partner's hand, he added: "Jack, you old fraud! You've always got the best of me on every bargain, but I forgive you this time. I wanted the boy myself, but you seem to have the best title, so there's no use to try to jump your claim."

Lunch was just over as a messenger was announced, and a moment later a telegram was handed to Darrell. As he opened the missive his fingers trembled and Mr. Britton's face grew pale. Darrell hastily read the contents, then met his father's anxious glance with a reassuring smile.

"She is living and in usual health, though my friend says she is much more delicate than when I left."

"We must go to her at once, my boy," said Mr. Britton; "how soon can you leave?"

"In a very few hours, father; when do you wish to start?"

Mr. Britton consulted a time-table. "The east-bound express leaves at ten-thirty to-night; can we make that?"

"Sure!" Darrell responded, with an enthusiasm new to his western friends; "you can't start too soon for me, and there isn't a train that travels fast enough to take me to that little mother of mine, especially with the good news I have for her."

Half an hour later, as he was hastily gathering together his possessions, he came suddenly upon a picture, at sight of which he paused, then stood spellbound, all else for the time forgotten. It was a portrait of Kate Underwood, taken in the gown she had worn on that night of her first reception. It served as a connecting link between the past and present. Gazing at it he was able to understand how the young girl whom he faintly remembered had grown into the strong, sweet character delineated in the recorded story of his love. He was able to recall some of the scenes portrayed there; he recalled her as she stood that day on the "Divide," her head uncovered, her gleaming hair like a halo about her face, her eyes shining with a light that was not of earth.

He kissed the picture reverently. "Sweet angel of my dream!" he murmured; "come what may, you hold, and always will, a place in my heart which no other can ever take from you. I will lay your sweet face away, never again to be lifted from its hiding-place until I can look upon it as the face of my betrothed."

His trunk was packed, his preparations for departure nearly complete, when there came a gentle tap at his door, and Mrs. Dean entered.

"I was afraid," she said, speaking with some hesitation, "that you might think it strange if you did not see Katherine, and I wanted to explain that she is away. She went out of town, to be gone for a few days. She will be very sorry when she returns to find that she has missed seeing you."

"Thank you, Mrs. Dean," said Darrell, slowly; "on some accounts I would have been very glad to meet Kate; but on the whole I think perhaps it is better as it is."

"I don't suppose you remember her except as you saw her when you first came," Mrs. Dean added, wistfully; "I should like to have you see her as she is now. I think she has matured into a beautiful young woman."

"Yes, I remember her, Mrs. Dean; she is beautiful."

"Oh, do you? She will be glad to hear that!" Mrs. Dean exclaimed, with a happy smile.

Darrell came nearer and took her hands within his own. "Will you give her a message from me, just as I give it to you? She will understand."

"Oh, yes; gladly."

"Tell her," said Darrell, and his voice trembled slightly, "I remember her. Tell her I will see her 'at the time appointed;' and that I never forget!"

Chapter XXX

After Many Years

The evening train, as it was known,—a local from the south,—was approaching the little village of Ellisburg, winding its way over miles of rolling country dotted with farm-houses of snowy white; to the east, rough, rugged hills surmounted by a wall of forest, while far to the west could be seen the sandy beaches and blue waters of Lake Ontario.

The arrival of this train formed one of the chief events in the daily life of the little town, and each summer evening found a group of from twenty to fifty of the village folk awaiting its incoming. To them it afforded a welcome break in the monotony of their lives, a fleeting glimpse of people and things from that vague world outside the horizon bounding their own.

Amid the usual handful of passengers left at the station on this particular evening were two who immediately drew the attention of the crowd. Two men, one something over fifty years of age, tall, with erect form and dark hair well silvered, and with a grave, sweet face; the other not more than seven-and-twenty, but with hair as white as snow, while his face wore an inscrutable look, as though the dark, piercing eyes held within their depths secrets which the sphinx-like lips would not reveal. Closely following them was a splendid collie, trying in various ways to give expression to his delight at being released from the confinement of the baggage-car.

There was a sudden, swift movement in the crowd as a young man stepped quickly forward and grasped the younger of the two by the hand.

"Darrell, old boy! is this you?" he exclaimed; "Great Scott! what have you been doing to yourself these two years?"

"Plenty of time for explanations later," said Darrell, shaking hands heartily; "Ned, I want you to know my father; father, this is my old chum, now Dr. Elliott."

The young physician's face betrayed astonishment, but he shook hands with Mr. Britton with no remarks beyond the customary greeting.

"Now, Ned," continued Darrell, "get us out of this mob as quickly as you can; I don't want to be recognized here."

"Not much danger with that white pate of yours; but come this way, my carriage is waiting. I did not let out that you were coming back, for I thought you wouldn't want any demonstration from the crowd here, so I told no one but father; he's waiting for you in the carriage."

"You're as level-headed as ever," Darrell remarked.

They reached the carriage, greetings were exchanged with Mr. Elliott, and soon the party was driving rapidly towards the village.

"We will go at once to my office," Dr. Elliott remarked to Darrell, who was seated beside himself; "we can make arrangements there as to the best method of breaking this news to your mother."

"You have told her nothing, then?" Darrell inquired.

"No; life has so many uncertainties and she has already suffered so much. You had a long journey before you; if anything had happened to detain you, it was better not to have her in suspense."

"You were right," Darrell replied; "you know I left all that to your own judgment."

"Darrell, old boy," said the doctor, inspecting his companion critically, "do satisfy my curiosity: is that white hair genuine or a wig donned for the occasion?"

"What reason could I have for any such masquerading?" Darrell demanded; "when you come to know my experience for the past two years you will not wonder that my hair is white."

"I beg your pardon, old fellow; I meant no offence. We had all given you

156

up for dead—all but your mother; and your telegram nearly knocked me off my feet."

Here the doctor drew rein, and, fastening the horses outside, they entered his office, a small, one-story building standing close to the street in one corner of the great dooryard of his father's home, and sheltered alike from sun and storm by giant maples.

After brief consultation it was decided that as Dr. Elliott and his father were frequent callers at the Jewett home, the entire party would drive out there, and, in the probable event of not seeing Mrs. Britton, who was an invalid and retired at an early hour, Darrell and his father would spend the night at the old homestead, but their presence would not be known by the wife and mother until the following morning.

"You see, sir," Dr. Elliott remarked to Mr. Britton, "your coming has complicated matters a little. I would not apprehend any danger from the meeting between Mrs. Britton and her son, for she has looked for his return every day; but I cannot say what might be the result of the shock her nervous system would sustain in meeting you. We are safe, however, in going out there this evening, for she always retires to her room before this time."

Both Mr. Britton and Darrell grew silent as the old Jewett homestead came in view. It was a wide-spreading house of colonial build, snowy white with green shutters and overrun with climbing roses and honeysuckle vines. It stood back at a little distance from the street, and a broad walk, under interlacing boughs of oak, elm, and maple, led from the street to the lofty pillared veranda across its front. The full moon was rising opposite, its mellow light throwing every twig and flower into bold relief. Two figures could be seen seated within the veranda, and as the carriage stopped Dr. Elliott remarked,—

"I was right; Mr. Jewett and his elder daughter are sitting outside, but Mrs. Britton has retired."

As the four men alighted and proceeded up the walk towards the house strangely varied emotions surged through the breasts of Darrell and his father. To one this was his childhood's home, the only home of which he had any distinct memory; to the other it was the home to which long ago he had been welcomed as a friend, but from which he had been banished as a lover. But all reminiscent thoughts were suddenly put to flight.

They had advanced only about half-way up the walk when one of the long, old-fashioned windows upon the veranda was hastily thrown open and a slender figure robed in a white dressing-gown came with swift but tremulous steps down the walk to meet them, crying, in glad accents,—

"Oh, my son! my son! you have come, as I knew you would some day!"

Darrell sprang forward and caught his mother in his arms, and then, unable to speak, held her close to his breast, his tears falling on her upturned face, while she caressed him and crooned fond words of endearment as in the days when she had held him in her arms. Dr. Elliott and his father stood near, nonplussed, uncertain what to do or what course to take. The old gentleman on the veranda left his seat and took a few steps towards the group, as though to assist his daughter to the house, but Dr.

Elliott motioned him to remain where he was. Mr. Britton, scarcely able to restrain his feelings, yet fearful of agitating his wife, had withdrawn slightly to one side, but unconsciously was standing so that the moonlight fell full across his face.

At that instant Mrs. Britton raised her head, and, seeing the familiar faces of Dr. Elliott and his father, looked at the solitary figure as though to see who it might be. Their eyes met, his shining with the old-time love with which he had looked on her as she stood a bride on that summer evening crowned with the sunset rays, only a thousand-fold more tender. She gave a startled glance, then raised her arms to him with one shrill, sweet cry,– the cry of the lone night-bird for its mate,–

"John!"

"Patience!" came the responsive note, deep, resonant, tender.

He held her folded within his arms until he suddenly felt the fragile form grow limp in his clasp, then, lifting her, he bore her tenderly up the walk, past the bewildered father and sister, into the house, Dr. Elliott leading the way, and laid her on a couch in her own room.

She was soon restored to consciousness, and, though able to say little, lay feasting her eyes alternately upon the face of husband and son, her glance, however, returning oftener and dwelling longer on the face of the lover, who, after more than twenty-seven years of absence, was a lover still.

Chapter XXXI

An Eastern Home

Within a few days Darrell and his father were domiciled in the Jewett homestead, the physicians pronouncing it unwise to attempt to remove Mrs. Britton to another home.

To Experience Jewett, who reigned supreme in her father's house, it seemed as though two vandals had invaded her domain, so ruthlessly did they open up the rooms for years jealously guarded from sunshine and dust, while her cherished household gods were removed by sacrilegious hands from their time-honored niches and consigned to the ignominy of obscure back chambers or the oblivion of the garret.

Under Mr. Britton's supervision, soon after his arrival, the great double parlors, which had not been used since the funeral of Mrs. Jewett some seven years before, were thrown wide open, Sally, the "help," standing with open mouth and arms akimbo, aghast at such proceedings, while Miss Jewett executed a lively quick-step in pursuit of a moth, which, startled by the unusual light, was circling above her head.

Not only were the gayly flowered Brussels carpet and the black haircloth furniture the same as when he had been a guest in those rooms nearly thirty years before, but each piece of furniture occupied the same position as then. He smiled as he noted the arm-chair by one of the front windows, to which he had been invariably assigned and in which he had slipped and slid throughout each evening to the detriment of the crocheted "tidy" pinned upon its back. The vases and candlesticks upon the mantel were arranged with the same mathematical precision. He could detect only one change, which was that to the collection of family photographs framed and hanging above the mantel, there had been added a portrait of the late Mrs. Jewett.

Within a week the old furnishings had been relegated to other parts of the house and modern upholstery had taken their places, the soft subdued tints of which blended harmoniously, forming a general impression of warmth and light.

Most of these innovations Miss Jewett viewed with disfavor, particularly the staining of the floors preparatory to laying down two Turkish rugs of exquisite coloring and design.

"I don't see any use in being so skimping with the carpets," she remarked to Sally; "if I'd been in his place I'd have got enough to cover the whole floor while I was about it, even if I'd bought something a little cheaper. A carpet with bare floor showing all 'round it puts me in mind of Dick's hat-band that went part way 'round and stopped."

"That's jest what it does!" Sally assented.

"I wanted to lay down some strips of carpeting along the edges, but he wouldn't hear to it," Miss Jewett continued, regretfully.

"I s'pose," Sally remarked, sagely, "it's all on account of livin' out west along with them wild Injuns and cow-boys so many years. Western folks 'most always has queer ideas about things."

"I never would have believed it to see such overturnings in my house!" exclaimed Miss Jewett, with a sigh; "and if 'twas anybody but John Britton I wouldn't stand it. I wonder if he won't be telling me how to make butter and raise chickens and turkeys next!"

"Mebbe he'll bring 'round one o' them new-fangled contrivances for hatchin' chickens without hens," Sally ventured, with a laugh; adding, reflectively, "I wonder why, when they was about it, they didn't invent a machine to lay aigs as well as hatch 'em; that would 'ave been a savin', for a hen's keep don't amount to much when she's settin', but they're powerful big eaters generally."

Miss Jewett prided herself upon her thrift and economy; her well-kept house where nothing was allowed to go to waste; her spotless dairy-rooms and rolls of golden butter which never failed to bring a cent and a half more a pound than any other; her fine breeds of poultry which annually carried off the blue ribbons at the county fair. She had achieved a local reputation of which she was quite proud; she would brook no interference in her management of household affairs, and, as she said, no one but John Britton would ever have been allowed to infringe upon her established rules and regulations. There had been a time when she had shared equally with her sister John Britton's attentions. It had been the only bit of romance in her life, but a lingering sweetness from it still remained in her heart through all the commonplace years that had followed, like the faint perfume from rose-leaves, faded and shrivelled, but cherished as sacred mementos. She had not blamed him for choosing her younger and more attractive sister, and she had secretly admired her sister for braving their father's displeasure to marry him. And now she was glad that he had returned; glad for his own sake that the imputations cast upon him by her father and others were refuted; for her sister's sake, that her last days should be so brightened and glorified; but deep within her heart, glad for her own sake, because it was good to look upon his face and hear his voice again.

Sally's strident tones broke in upon her retrospection:

"There's one thing, Miss Jewett, I guess you needn't be afeard they'll meddle with, and that's your cookin'. Mr. Darrell, he was tellin' me about the prices people had to pay for meals on them eatin'-cars,–'diners' he called 'em,–and I told him there wasn't no vittles on earth worth any such price as that, and I up and asked him whether they was as good as the vittles he gets here, and he laughed and said there wasn't nobody could beat his Aunt Espey at cookin'."

Miss Jewett's eyes brightened. "Bless the boy's heart!" she exclaimed; "I'm glad they're going to be here for Thanksgiving; I'll see that they get such a dinner as they neither of them ever dreamed of!"

Darrell had won a warm place in her heart in his baby days with his earliest efforts to speak her name. "Espey" had been the result of his first attack on the formidable name of "Experience," and "Aunt Espey" she had been to him ever since.

Her father, Hosea Jewett, was a hale, hearty man of upward of seventy, hard and unyielding as the granite ledges cropping out along the hill-sides of his farm, and with a face gnarled and weather-beaten as the oaks before his door. He was scrupulously honest, but exacting, relentless, unforgiving.

He was not easily reconciled to the new order of things, but for his daughter's sake he held his peace. Then, too, though he never forgave John Britton for having married his daughter, yet John Britton as a man whose wealth exceeded even his own was an altogether different person from the ambitious but impecunious lover of thirty years before. He had never forgiven Darrell for being John Britton's son, but mingled with his long-cherished animosity was a secret pride in the splendid physical and intellectual manhood of this sole representative of his own line.

Between the sisters there had been few points of resemblance. Patience Jewett had been of an ardent, emotional nature, passionately fond of music, a great reader, and with little taste for the household tasks in which her more practical sister delighted. Having a more delicate constitution, she had little share in the busy routine of farm life, but was allowed to follow her own inclinations. She was still absorbed in her music and studies when Love found her, and the woman within her awoke at his call.

After Darrell's birth her health was seriously impaired. It seemed as though her faith in her husband, her belief that he would one day return, and her love for her son were the only ties holding soul and body together, and, with her natural religious tendencies, the spiritual nature developed at the expense of the physical. Since Darrell's strange disappearance she had failed rapidly.

With the return of her husband and son she seemed temporarily to renew her hold on life, appearing stronger than for many months. For the first few days much of her time was spent at her piano, singing with her husband the old songs of their early love, but oftenest a favorite of his which she had sung during the years of his absence, and which Darrell had sung on that night at The Pines following his discovery of the violin,– "Loyal to Love and Thee."

Her delight in the rooms newly fitted up for her was unbounded, and against the background of their subdued, warm tints she made a strikingly beautiful picture, with her sweet, spirituelle face crowned with waving silver hair.

Either Darrell or his father, or both, were constantly with her, for they realized that the time was short in which to make amends for the missing years. She loved to listen to her husband's tales of the great West or to bits which Darrell read from his journal of that strange chapter of his own life.

"You have not yet asked after your sweetheart, Darrell," his mother said one evening soon after his arrival, as they sat awaiting his father's return from a short stroll.

"You are my sweetheart now, little mother," he replied, kissing the hand that lay within his own.

"Does that mean that you care less for Marion than before you went away?" she queried.

"No," Darrell answered, slowly; "I cannot say that my regard for her has decreased. I may have changed in some respects, but not in my feelings towards Marion. I will ask you a question, mother: Do you think she still cares for me as before I left home?"

"I hardly know how to answer you, because, as you know, Marion is so silent and secretive. I never could understand the girl. To be candid, Darrell dear, I never could understand why you should care for her, and I never thought she cared for you as she ought."

"You know, mother, how I came to be attracted to her in the first place; we were schoolmates, and you know she was an exceptionally brilliant girl, and different from most of the others. We were interested in the same subjects, and naturally there sprang up quite an intimacy between us. Then we corresponded while I was at college, and her letters were so bright and entertaining that my admiration for her increased. I thought her the most brilliant and the best girl, every way, in all my acquaintance, and I think so still."

"But, my dear boy," his mother exclaimed, "admiration is not love; I don't believe you ever really loved her, and she always seemed to me to be all brains and no heart—one of those cold, silent natures incapable of loving."

"I think you are wrong there, mother. Marion is silent, but I don't believe she is cold or incapable of loving. She may, or may not, be

161

incapable of expressing it, but I believe she could love very deeply and sincerely were her love once awakened."

"You know she has taken up the study of medicine?"

"Ned Elliott told me she had been studying with Dr. Parker for about a year."

"Dr. Parker tells me she is making remarkable progress."

"I don't doubt it, mother; she will probably make a success of it; she is just the woman to do so."

"There never was any mention of love between you two, was there, or any engagement?" Darrell's mother asked, with some hesitation, after a brief silence.

"None whatever," he replied, then added, with a smile: "We considered ourselves in love at the time,—at least, I did; but as I look back now it seems a very Platonic affair; but I thought I loved her, and I think she loved me."

"You say, Darrell, that your regard for her is unchanged?"

"Yes; the same as ever."

"But you do not think now that you love her or loved her then?"

"No, mother; I know I do not, and did not."

"Then, Darrell, my boy, some one else has taught you what love really is?"

For answer Darrell bowed his head in assent over his mother's hand.

For a few moments she silently stroked his hair as in his boyish days; then she said, in low tones,—

"Answer me one question, Darrell: Was she a good, pure woman?"

Darrell raised his head, his eyes looking straight into the searching dark eyes, so like his own.

"My little mother," he replied, tenderly, "don't think that your teachings all the past years or the lessons of your own sweet life were lost in those two years; their influence lived even when memory had failed."

He bent and kissed her, then added: "She was scarcely more than a child; not so brilliant, perhaps, as Marion, but beautiful, good, and pure as the driven snow."

Hearing his father's voice outside, Darrell rose and, picking up his journal, opened it at the story of his love and Kate's. Then placing it open upon a table beside his mother, he said,—

"There, mother, is the story of my Dream-Love, as I call her. Read it, and if you should wish to know anything further regarding it, ask my father, for he knows all."

Chapter XXXII

Marion Holmes

The following day when Darrell entered his mother's rooms he found her with his journal lying open before her. Looking up with a smile, she said,–

"Darrell, my dear, I would like to meet your 'Kathie,' but that can never be in this world. But you will meet her again, and when you do, give her a mother's love and blessing from me."

Then, laying her hand on his arm, she added: "I understand now your question regarding Marion. As I told you, it is difficult to judge anything about her real feelings. For the first year after you went away she came often to see me and frequently inquired for tidings of you, but this last year she has seemed different. She has come here less frequently and seldom referred to you, and appeared so engrossed in her studies I concluded she had little thought or care for you. I may have misjudged her, but even were that so and she did care for you still, you would not marry her now, loving another as you do, would you?"

Darrell smiled as he met his mother's eager, questioning gaze. "If I had won the love of a girl like Marion Holmes," he said, "I would do nothing that would seem like trifling with that love; but, in justice to all parties concerned, herself in particular, I would never marry her without first giving her enough knowledge of the facts in the case that she would thoroughly understand the situation."

His mother seemed satisfied. "Marion has brains, whether she has a heart or not," she replied, with quiet emphasis; "and a girl of brains would never marry a man under such circumstances."

Handing him his journal she pointed with a smile to its inscription.

"'Until the day break,'" she quoted; "that has been my daily watchword all these years; strange that you, too, should have chosen it as your own."

Had Darrell gone to his aunt for a gauge of Marion Holmes's feelings towards himself she could have informed him more correctly than his mother. She, with an old love hidden so deeply in her heart that no one even suspected its existence, understood the silent, reticent girl far better than her emotional, demonstrative sister.

A few days after moving into the rooms newly fitted up for her Mrs. Britton gave what she termed "a little house-warming," to which were invited a few old-time friends of her own and Mr. Britton's, together with some of Darrell's associates. Among the latter Marion was, of course, included, but happening at the time to be out of town, she did not receive the invitation until two days afterwards. Meantime, Darrell, who was anxious to meet the syndicate from whom he had received his western commission two years before, left on the following day for New York City. Consequently when Marion, upon her return, called on Mrs. Britton to explain her absence, Darrell was away.

163

Marion Holmes was, as Mrs. Britton had said, a silent girl; not from any habitual self-repression, but from an inherent inability to express her deeper feelings. Hers was one of those dumb speechless souls, that, finding no means of communicating with others, unable to get in touch with those about them, go on their silent, lonely ways, no one dreaming of the depth of feeling or wealth of affection they really possess.

The eldest child of a widowed mother, in moderate circumstances, her life had been one of constant restriction and self-denial. Her association with Darrell marked a new epoch in the dreary years. For the first time within her memory there was something each morning to which she could look forward with pleasant anticipation; something to look back upon with pleasure when the day was done. As their intimacy grew her happiness increased, and when he returned from college with high honors her joy was unbounded. Brought up in a home where there was little demonstration of affection, she did not look for it here; she loved and supposed herself loved in return, else how could there be such an affinity between them? The depth of her love for Darrell Britton she herself did not know until his strange disappearance; then she learned the place he had filled in her heart and life by the void that remained. As months passed without tidings of him she lost hope. Unable to endure the blank monotony of her home life she took up the study of medicine, partly to divert her mind and also as a means of future self-support more remunerative than teaching.

With the news of Darrell's return, hope sprang into new life, and it was with a wild, sweet joy, which would not be stilled, pulsating through her heart, that she went to call on Mrs. Britton.

She had a nature supersensitive, and as she entered Mrs. Britton's rooms her heart sank and her whole soul recoiled as from a blow. With her limited means and her multiplicity of home duties her outings had been confined to the small towns within a short distance of her native village. These rooms, in such marked contrast to everything to which she had been accustomed, were to her a revelation of something beyond her of which she had had no conception; a revelation also that her comrade of by-gone days had grown away from her, beyond her—beyond even her reach or ken.

Quietly, with a strange, benumbing pain, she noted every detail as she answered Mrs. Britton's inquiries, but conscious of the lack of affinity between herself and Darrell's mother, it seemed to her that the dark eyes regarding her so searchingly must read with what hopes she had come, and how those hopes had died. She was glad Darrell was not at home; she could not have met him then and there. But so quiet were her words and manner, so like her usual demeanor, that Mrs. Britton said to herself, as Marion took leave,—

"I was right; she cares for Darrell only as a mere acquaintance."

On her return she entered the parlor of her own home and stood for some moments gazing silently about her. How shabby, how pitiably bare and meagre and colorless! An emblem of her own life! Throwing herself upon the threadbare little sofa where she and Darrell had spent so many happy hours reviewing their studies and talking of hopes and plans for the

164

future, she burst into such bitter, passionate weeping as only natures like hers can know.

Darrell's trip proved successful beyond his anticipations. He found the leading members of the syndicate, to whom he explained his two years' absence and into whose possession he gave the money intrusted to his keeping. So delighted were they to see him after having given him up for dead, and so pleased were they with his honesty and integrity that they tendered him his old position with them, offering to continue his salary from the date of his western commission. This offer he promptly declined, declaring that he would undertake no commissions or enter into no business agreements during his mother's present state of health.

He had taken with him the completed manuscript of his geological work, and this, through the influence of one or two members of the syndicate, he succeeded in placing with a publishing house making a specialty of scientific works.

These facts, communicated to his parents, soon reached Miss Jewett, filling her with a pride and delight that knew no bounds. Ellisburg had no daily paper, but it possessed a few individuals of the gentler sex who as advertising mediums answered almost as well, and whom Miss Jewett included among her acquaintance. She suddenly remembered a number of calls which her household duties had hitherto prevented her returning, and decided that this was the most opportune time for paying them. Ordering her carriage and donning her best black silk gown, she proceeded with due ceremony to make her round of calls, judiciously dropping a few words here and there, which, like the seed sown on good ground, brought forth fruit, thirty, sixty, and a hundred-fold. As a result Darrell, upon his return, found himself a literary star of the first magnitude,–the cynosure of all eyes.

These reports reaching Marion only widened the gulf which she felt now intervened between herself and Darrell.

Almost immediately upon his return Darrell called upon her. She was at home, but sent a younger sister to admit him while she nerved herself for the dreaded interview. As he awaited her coming he looked around him with a sort of wonder. Each object seemed familiar, and yet, was it possible this was the room that used to seem so bright and pleasant as he and Marion conned their lessons together? Had it changed, he wondered, or had he?

Marion's entrance put a stop to his musings. He sprang to meet her, she advanced slowly. She had changed very little. Her face, unless animated, was always serious, determined; it was a shade more determined, almost stern, but it had the same strong, intellectual look which had always distinguished it and for which he had admired it.

Darrell, on the contrary, was greatly changed. Marion, gazing at the snow-white hair, the dark eyes with their piercing, inscrutable look, the firmly set mouth, and noting the bearing of conscious strength and power, was unable to recognize her quondam schoolmate until he spoke; the voice and smile were the same as of old!

They clasped hands for an instant, then Darrell, as in the old days, dropped easily into one corner of the little sofa, supposing she would take her accustomed place in the other corner, but, instead, she drew a small rocker opposite and facing him, in which she seated herself. His manner was cordial and free as, after a few inquiries regarding herself, he spoke of his absence, touching lightly upon his illness and its strange consequences, and expressed his joy at finding himself at home once more.

She was kind and sympathetic, but her manner was constrained. She could not banish the remembrance of her call upon his mother, of the contrast between his home and hers; and as he talked something indefinable in his language, in his very movements and gestures, revealed to her sensitive nature a contrast, a difference, between them; he had somehow reached ground to which she could not attain. He drew her out to speak of her new studies and congratulated her upon her progress; but the call was not a success, socially or otherwise.

When Darrell left the house he believed more firmly than ever that Marion had loved him in the past. Whether she had ceased to love him he could not then determine; time would tell.

During the weeks that followed there were numerous gatherings of a social and informal nature where Darrell and Marion were thrown in each other's society, but, though he still showed a preference for her over the girls of his acquaintance, she shrank from his attentions, avoiding him whenever she could do so without causing remark.

Thanksgiving Day came, and Miss Jewett's guests were compelled to admit that she had surpassed herself. The dinner was one long to be remembered. Her prize turkey occupied the place of honor, flanked on one side by a roast duck, superbly browned, and on the other by an immense chicken pie, while savory vegetables, crisp pickles, and tempting relishes such as she only could concoct crowded the table in every direction. A huge plum-pudding headed the second course, with an almost endless retinue of pies,–mince, pumpkin, and apple,–while golden custards and jellies–red, purple, and amber, of currant, grape, and peach–brought up the rear. A third course of fruits and nuts followed, but by that time scarcely any one was able to do more than make a pretence of eating.

To this dinner were invited the minister and his wife, one or two far-removed cousins who usually put in an appearance at this season of the year, Marion Holmes, and a decrepit old lady, a former friend of Mrs. Jewett's, who confided to the minister's wife that she had eaten a very light breakfast and no lunch whatever in order that she might be able to "do justice to Experience's dinner."

Marion Holmes was not there, and Darrell, meeting her on the street the next day, playfully took her to task.

"Why were you not at dinner yesterday?" he inquired; "have you no more regard for my feelings than to leave me to be sandwiched between the parson's wife and old Mrs. Pettigrew?"

"I might have gone had I known such a fate as that awaited you," she replied, laughing; "but," she added with some spirit, thinking it best to come to the point at once, "I can see no reason for thrusting myself into your family gatherings simply because you and I were good comrades in the past."

"Were we not something more than merely good comrades, Marion?" he asked, anxious to ascertain her real feelings towards himself; "it seemed to me we were, or at least that we thought we were."

"That may be," she answered, her color rising slightly; "but if we thought so then, that is no reason for deceiving ourselves any longer."

She intended to mislead him, and she did.

"Very well," he replied; "we will not deceive ourselves; we will have a good understanding with ourselves and with each other. Is there any reason why we should not be at least good comrades now?"

"I know of none," she answered, meeting his eyes without wavering.

"Then let us act as such, and not like two silly children, afraid of each other. Is that a compact?" he asked, smiling and extending his hand.

"It is," she replied, smiling brightly in return as their hands clasped, thus by word and act renouncing her dearest hopes without his dreaming of the sacrifice.

Chapter XXXIII

Into the Fulness of Life

With the opening of cold weather the seeming betterment in Mrs. Britton's health proved but temporary. As the winter advanced she failed rapidly, until, unable to sit up, she lay on a low couch, wheeled from room to room to afford all the rest and change possible. Day by day her pallor grew more and more like the waxen petals of the lily, while the fatal rose flush in her cheek deepened, and her eyes, unnaturally large and lustrous, had in them the look of those who dwell in the borderland.

She realized her condition as fully as those about her, but there was neither fear nor regret in the eyes, which, fixed on the glory invisible to them, caught and reflected the light of the other world, till, in the last days, those watching her saw her face "as it had been the face of an angel."

No demonstration of sorrow marred the peace in which her soul dwelt the last days of its stay, for the very room seemed hallowed, a place too sacred for the intrusion of any personal grief.

Turning one day to her husband, who seldom left her side, she said,—

"My sorrow made me selfish; I see it now. Look at the good you have done, the many you have helped; what have I done, what have I to show for all these years?"

Just then Darrell passed the window before which she was lying.

"There is your work, Patience," Mr. Britton replied, tenderly; "you have that to show for those years of loneliness and suffering. Surely, love, you have done noble work there; work whose results will last for years—probably for generations—yet to come!"

Her face lighted with a rapturous smile. "I had not thought of that," she whispered; "I will not go empty-handed after all. Perhaps He will say of me, as of one of old, 'She hath done what she could.'"

From that time she sank rapidly, sleeping lightly, waking occasionally with a child-like smile, then lapsing again into unconsciousness.

One evening as the day was fading she awoke from a long sleep and looked intently into the faces gathered about her. Her pastor, who had known her through all the years of her sorrow, was beside her. Bending over her and looking into the eyes now dimmed by the approaching shadows, he said,—

"You have not much longer to wait, my dear sister."

With a significant gesture she pointed to the fading light.

"'Until the day break,'" she murmured, with difficulty.

He was quick to catch her meaning and bowed his head in token that he understood; then, raising his hand above her head, as though in benediction, in broken tones he slowly pronounced the words,—

"'Thy sun shall no more go down; neither shall thy moon withdraw itself: for the Lord shall be thine everlasting light, and the days of thy mourning shall be ended.'"

Her face brightened; a seraphic smile burst forth, irradiating every feature with a light which never faded, for, with a look of loving farewell into the faces of husband and son, she sank into a sleep from which she did not wake, and when, as the day was breaking over the eastern hill-tops, her soul took flight, the smile still lingered, deepening into such perfect peace as is seldom seen on mortal faces.

As Darrell, a few moments later, stood at the window, watching the stars paling one by one in the light of the coming dawn, a bit of verse with which he had been familiar years before, but which he had not recalled until then, recurred to him with peculiar force:

> "A soul passed out on its way toward Heaven
> As soon as the word of release was given;
> And the trail of the meteor swept around
> The lovely form of the homeward-bound.
> Glimmering, shimmering, there on high,
> The stars grew dim as one passed them by;
> And the earth was never again so bright,
> For a soul had slipped from its place that night."

After Mrs. Britton's death, deprived of her companionship and of the numberless little ministrations to her comfort in which they had delighted, both Mr. Britton and Darrell found life strangely empty. They also missed the strenuous western life to which they had been accustomed, with its ceaseless demands upon both muscle and brain. The life around them seemed narrow and restricted; the very monotony of the landscape wearied them; they longed for the freedom and activity of the West, the breadth and height of the mountains.

As both were standing one day beside the resting-place of the wife and mother, which Mr. Britton had himself chosen for her, the latter said,–

"John, there are no longer any ties to hold us here. You may have to remain here until affairs are settled, but I have no place, and want none, in Hosea Jewett's home. I am going back to the West; and I know that sooner or later you will return also, for your heart is among the mountains. But before we separate I want one promise from you, my son."

"Name it," said Darrell; "you know, father, I would fulfil any and every wish of yours within my power."

"It was my wish in the past, when my time should come to die, to be buried on the mountain-side, near the Hermitage. But life henceforth for me will be altogether different from what it has been heretofore; and I want your promise, John, if you outlive me, that when the end comes, no matter where I may be, you will bring me back to her, that when our souls are reunited our bodies may rest together here, within sound of the river's voice and shielded by the overhanging boughs from winter's storm and summer's heat."

Father and son clasped hands above the newly made grave.

"I promise you, father," Darrell replied; "but you did not need to ask the pledge."

When John Britton left Ellisburg a few days later a crowd of friends were gathered at the little depot to extend their sympathy and bid him farewell. A few were old associates of his own, some were his wife's friends, and some Darrell's. To those who had known him in the past he was greatly changed, and none of them quite understood his quaint philosophizings, his broad views, or his seeming isolation from their work-a-day, business world in which he had formerly taken so active a part. They knew naught of his years of solitary life or of how lives spent in years of contemplation and reflection, of retrospection and introspection, become gradually lifted out of the ordinary channels of thought and out of touch with the more practical life of the world. But they had had abundant evidence of his love and devotion to his wife, and of his kindness and liberality towards many of their own number, and for these they loved him.

There was not one, however, who mourned his departure so deeply as Experience Jewett, though she gave little expression to her sorrow. She had hoped that after her sister's death his home would still be with them. This, not from any weak sentimentality or any thought that he would ever be aught than as a brother to her, but because his very presence in the home was refreshing, helpful, comforting, and because it was a joy to be near him, to hear him talk, and to minister to his comfort. But he was going from them, as she well knew, never to return, and beneath the brave, smiling face she carried a sore and aching heart.

Thus John Britton bade the East farewell and turned his face towards the great West, mindful only of the grave under the elms, to which the river murmured night and day, and with no thought of return until he, too, should come to share that peaceful resting place.

169

Chapter XXXIV

A Warning

Spring had come again and Walcott's probationary year with Mr. Underwood had nearly expired. For a while he had maintained his old suavity of manner and business had been conducted satisfactorily, but as months passed and Kate Underwood was unapproachable as ever and the prospect of reconciliation between them seemed more remote, he grew sullen and morose, and Mr. Underwood began to detect signs of mismanagement. Determined to wait until he had abundance of evidence with which to confront him, however, he said nothing, but continued to watch him with unceasing vigilance.

Mr. Underwood, though able to attend to business, had never fully recovered from the illness of the preceding year. His physician advised him to retire from business, as any excitement or shock would be likely to cause a second attack far more serious than the first; but to this Mr. Underwood would not listen, clinging tenaciously to the old routine to which he had been accustomed. Kate, realizing her father's condition, guarded him with watchful solicitude from every possible worry and anxiety, spending much of her time with him, and even familiarizing herself with many details of his business in order to assist him.

In the months since Darrell's return east Kate had matured in many ways. Her tall, slender form was beginning to round out in symmetrical proportions, and her voice, always sweet, had developed wonderfully in volume and range. She had taken up the study of music anew, both vocal and instrumental, devoting her leisure hours to arduous practice, her father having promised her a thorough course of study in Europe, for which she was preparing herself with great enthusiasm.

Though no words were exchanged between Mr. Underwood and Walcott, the latter became conscious of the other's growing disfavor, and the conviction gradually forced itself upon him that all hope of gaining his partner's daughter in marriage was futile. For Kate Underwood he cared little, except as a means of securing a hold upon her father's wealth. As he found himself compelled to abandon this scheme and saw the prize he had thus hoped to gain slipping farther and farther from his grasp, his rage made him desperate, and he determined to gain all or lose all in one mad venture. To make ready for this would require weeks, perhaps months, but he set about his preparations with method and deliberation. Either the boldness of his plan or his absorption in the expected outcome made him negligent of details, however, and slowly, but surely, Mr. Underwood gathered the proofs of his guilt with which he intended to confront him when the opportune moment arrived. But even yet he did not dream the extent of his partner's frauds or the villany of which he was capable; he therefore took no one into his confidence and sought no assistance.

Kate was quick to observe the change in Walcott's manner and to note the malignity lurking in the half-closed eyes whenever they encountered her own or her father's gaze, and, while saying nothing to excite or worry the latter, redoubled her vigilance, seldom leaving him alone.

Affairs had reached this state when, with the early spring days, Mr. Britton returned from the East and stopped for a brief visit at The Pines. In a few days he divined enough of the situation to lead him to suspect that danger of some kind threatened his old friend. A hint from Kate confirmed his suspicion, and he resolved to prolong his stay and await developments.

One afternoon soon after his arrival Kate, returning from a walk, while passing up the driveway met a woman coming from The Pines. The latter was tall, dressed in black, and closely veiled,—a stranger,—yet something in her appearance seemed familiar. Suddenly Kate recalled the "Señora" who sent the summons to Walcott on that day set for their marriage, more than a year before. Though she had caught only a brief glimpse of the black-robed and veiled figure within the carriage, she remembered a peculiarly graceful poise of the head as she had leaned forward for a final word with Walcott, and by that she identified the woman now approaching her. Each regarded the other closely as they met. To Kate it seemed as though the woman hesitated for the fraction of a second, as though about to speak, but she passed on silently. On reaching a turn in the driveway Kate, looking back, saw the woman standing near the large gates watching her, but the latter, finding herself observed, passed through the gates to the street and walked away.

Perplexed and somewhat annoyed, Kate proceeded on her way to the house. She believed the woman to be in some way associated with Walcott, and that her presence there presaged evil of some sort. As she entered the sitting-room her aunt looked up with a smile from her seat before the fire.

"You have just had rather a remarkable caller, Katherine."

"That woman in black whom I just met?" Kate asked, betraying no surprise, for she felt none; she was prepared at that moment for almost any announcement.

"Who was she, Aunt Marcia? and what did she want with me?"

"She refused to give her name, but said to tell you 'a friend' called. She seemed disappointed at not seeing you, and as she was leaving she said, 'Say to her she has a friend where she least thinks it, and if she, or any one she loves, is in danger, I will come and warn her.' She was very quiet-appearing, notwithstanding her tragic language. You say you met her; what do you think of her?"

Kate had been thinking rapidly. "I have seen her once before, auntie. I am positive she is in some way connected with Mr. Walcott, and equally positive that he has some evil designs against papa; but why she should warn me against him, if that is her intention, I cannot imagine."

"Is there no way of warning your father, Katherine?" Mrs. Dean inquired, anxiously.

"Mr. Britton and I have talked it over, auntie. We think papa suspects him and is watching him, but so long as he doesn't take either of us into his confidence we don't want to excite or worry him by suggesting any danger. This woman may or may not be friendly, as she claims, but in any event, if she comes again, I must see her. Whatever danger there may be I want to know it; then I'm not afraid but that I can defend papa or myself in case of trouble."

For several days Kate scanned her horizon closely for portents of the coming storm. She saw nothing of the mysterious woman who had styled herself a friend, but on more than one occasion she had a fleeting glimpse of the man who on that memorable day brought the message from her to Walcott, and Kate felt that a dénouement of some kind was near.

Walcott's preparations were nearly perfected; another week would complete them. By that time the funds of the firm as well as large deposits held in trust, would be where he could lay his fingers on them at a moment's notice. At a given signal two trusted agents would be at the side entrance with fleet horses on which they would travel to a neighboring village, and there, where their appearance would excite no suspicion, they were to board the late express, which would carry them to a point whence they could easily reach a place of safety.

But his well-laid plans were suddenly checked by a request one afternoon from his senior partner to meet him in his private office that evening at eight o'clock. The tone in which this request was preferred aroused Walcott's suspicions that an investigation might be pending, and, enraged at being thus checkmated, he determined to strike at once.

At dinner Mr. Underwood mentioned an engagement which would, he said, detain him for an hour or so that evening, but having never since his illness gone to the offices in the evening, no one supposed it more than an ordinary business appointment with some friend.

He had left the house only a few moments when a caller was announced for Miss Underwood.

Kate's heart gave a sudden bound as, on entering the reception-hall, she saw again the woman whose coming was to be a warning of danger. She was, as usual, dressed in black and heavily veiled. Kate was conscious of no fear; rather a joy that the suspense was over, that there was at last something definite and tangible to face.

"Señorita, may I see you in private?" The voice was sweet, but somewhat muffled by the veil, while the words had just enough of the Spanish accent to render them liquid and musical.

Kate bowed in assent, and silently led the way to a small reception-room of her own. She motioned her caller to a seat, but the latter remained standing and turned swiftly, facing Kate, still veiled.

"Señorita, you do not know me?" The words had the rising inflection of a question.

"No," Kate replied, slowly; "I do not know you; but I know that this is not your first call at The Pines."

"I called some ten days since to see you."

"You called," Kate spoke deliberately, "more than a year since to see Mr. Walcott."

The woman started and drew back slightly. "How could you know?" she exclaimed; "surely he did not tell you!"

"I saw you."

172

There was a moment's silence; when next she spoke her voice was lower and more musical.

"Señorita, I come as your friend; do you believe me?"

"I want to believe you," Kate answered, frankly, "but I can tell better whether I do or not when I know more of you and of your errands here."

For answer the woman, with a sudden swift movement, threw back her veil, revealing a face of unusual beauty,–oval in contour, of a rich olive tint, with waving masses of jet-black hair, framing a low, broad forehead. But her eyes were what drew Kate's attention: large, lustrous, but dark and unfathomable as night, yet with a look in them of dumb, agonizing appeal. The two women formed a striking contrast as they stood face to face; they seemed to impersonate Hope and Despair.

"Señorita," she said, in a low, passionless voice, "I am Señor Walcott's wife."

Kate's very soul seemed to recoil at the words, but she did not start or shrink.

"I have the certificate of our marriage here," she continued, producing a paper, "signed by the holy father who united us."

Kate waved it back. "I do not wish to see it, nor do I doubt your word," she replied, gently; "I understand now why you first came to this house. What brings you here to-night?"

"I come to warn you that your father is in danger."

"My father!" Kate exclaimed, quickly, her whole manner changed. "Where? How?"

"Señor Walcott has an engagement with him at eight o'clock at their offices, and he means to do him harm, I know not just what; but he is angry with him, I know not why, and he is a dangerous man when he is angry."

Kate touched a bell to summon a servant. "I will go to him at once; but," she added, looking keenly into the woman's face, "how do you know of this? How did you learn it? Did he tell you?"

The other shook her head with a significant gesture. "He tells me nothing; he tells no one but Tony, and Tony tells me nothing; but I saw them talking together to-night, and he was very angry. I overheard some words. I heard him say he would see your father to-night and make him sorry he had not done as he agreed, and he showed Tony a little stiletto which he carries with him, and then he laughed."

Kate shuddered slightly. "Who is Tony?" she asked.

The woman smiled with another gesture. "Tony is–Tony; that is all I know. He and my husband know each other."

A servant appeared; Kate ordered her own carriage brought to the door at once. Then, turning on a sudden impulse to the stranger, she said,–

"Will you come with me? Or are you afraid of him–afraid to have him know you warned me?"

The woman laughed bitterly. "I feared him once," she said; "but I fear him no longer; he fears me now. Yes, I will go with you."

"Then wait here; I will be ready in a moment."

At twenty minutes of eight Kate and the stranger passed down the hall

173

together—the woman veiled, Kate attired in a trim walking suit. The latter stopped to look in at the sitting-room door.

"Aunt Marcia, Mr. Britton said he would be out but a few minutes. When he comes in please tell him I want to see him at papa's office; my carriage will be waiting for him here."

Her aunt looked her surprise, but she knew Kate to be enough like her father that it was useless to ask an explanation where she herself made none.

Once seated in the carriage and driving rapidly down the street Kate laid her hand on the arm of her strange companion.

"Señora," she said, "you say you are my friend; were you my friend the first time you came to the house? If not then, why are you now?"

"No, I was not your friend;" for the first time there was a ring of passion in her voice; "I hated you, for I thought he loved you—that you had stolen his heart and made him forget me. I travelled many miles. I vowed to kill you both before you should marry him. Then I found he could not marry you while I was his wife; he had told me our marriage was void here because performed in another country. I found he had told me wrong, and I told him unless he came with me I would go to the church and tell them there I was his wife."

"And he went away with you?" Kate questioned.

"Yes, and he gave me money, and then he told me——" The woman hesitated.

"Go on," said Kate.

"He told me that he did not love you; that he only wanted to marry you that he might get money from your father, and then he would leave you. So when I found he wanted to make you suffer as he had me I began to pity you. I came back to Ophir to see what you were like. He does not know that I am here. I found he was angry because you would not marry him. Then I was glad. I saw you many times that you did not know. Your face was kind and good, as though you would pity me if you knew all, and I loved you. I heard something about a lover you had a few years ago who died, and I knew your heart must have been sad for him, and I vowed he should never harm you or any one you loved."

They had reached the offices; the carriage stopped, but not before Kate's hand had sought and found the stranger's in silent token that she understood.

Chapter XXXV

A Fiend at Bay

Kate, on leaving her carriage, directed the driver to go back to The Pines to await Mr. Britton's return and bring him immediately to the office. She then unlocked the door to the room which had been Darrell's office and which opened directly upon the street, and she and her companion entered and seated themselves in the darkness. The room next adjoining was Walcott's private office, and beyond that was Mr. Underwood's private office, the two latter rooms being separated by a small entrance. They had waited but a few moments when Mr. Underwood's carriage stopped before this entrance, and an instant later Kate heard her father's voice directing the coachman to call for him in about an hour. As the key turned in the lock she heard Walcott's voice also. The two men entered and went at once into Mr. Underwood's private office.

Mr. Underwood immediately proceeded to business in his usual abrupt fashion:

"Mr. Walcott, there is no use dallying or beating about the bush; I want this partnership terminated at once. There's no use in an honest man and a thief trying to do business together, and this interview to-night is to find the shortest way of dissolving the partnership."

"I think that can be very easily and quickly done, Mr. Underwood," Walcott replied.

Kate, who had stationed herself in the entrance where she had a view of both men, saw the cruel leer that accompanied Walcott's words and understood their significance as her father did not. Her hand sought the bosom of her dress for an instant, then dropped quietly at her side, but swift as the movement was, her companion had seen in the dim light the gleam of the weapon now partially concealed by the folds of her skirt. With noiseless, cat-like step she approached Kate and touched her arm.

"You will not shoot? You will not kill him?" she breathed rather than whispered.

Kate's only reply was to lay her finger on her lips, never removing her eyes from Walcott's face, but even then, in her absorption, she noted a peculiar quality in those scarcely audible tones, something that was neither fear nor love; there seemed somehow an element of savagery in them.

Meanwhile, Mr. Underwood was going rapidly through the evidence which he had accumulated, showing mismanagement and fraud in the conduct of the business of the firm and misappropriation of some of the funds held in trust. Of the wholesale robbery, the plans for which Walcott had so nearly perfected, he knew absolutely nothing. As Walcott listened, the sneer on his face deepened.

"You seem to have gone to a vast amount of labor for nothing," he remarked, as Mr. Underwood concluded. "I could have given you that much information off-hand. You have not lived up to your part of the contract, and I see no reason why I should be expected to fulfil mine. You promised me your daughter in marriage, and then simply because she saw fit––"

"We will leave my daughter's name out of this controversy, sir," Mr. Underwood interposed, sternly. "Were it not for the fact that your name has been publicly associated with hers, I would prosecute you for the scoundrel and black-leg that you are."

"But for the sake of your daughter's name you intend to deal leniently with me," Walcott sneered. "Supposing we come at once to the point of dissolving our partnership; it cannot be done any too quickly for me. May I inquire on what terms you propose to settle?"

Mr. Underwood went briefly over the terms which he had outlined on a sheet of paper before him on his desk; Walcott, seated eight or ten feet distant, listened, his dark face paling with anger.

"Pardon me," he said, at the conclusion; "I think I missed a few details; suppose we go over that again together."

He rose and advanced towards Mr. Underwood's chair as though to look over his shoulder, at the same time thrusting his right hand within the inner pocket of his coat. Before he had covered half the space, however, a voice rang through the room with startling clearness,–

"Not a step farther, or you are a dead man!"

Both men turned, to see Kate Underwood standing in the doorway, holding a revolver levelled at Walcott with an aim which the latter's practised eye told him to be both sure and deadly. Astonishment and rage passed in quick succession over his countenance; he looked for an instant as though contemplating some desperate move.

"Stir one hair's breadth, and you are a dead man!" she repeated. He remained motionless, and the hand just withdrawn from his coat disclosed to view a tiny, glittering stiletto.

Kate's only anxious thought was for her father, who, too bewildered to move or speak, was for the time as motionless as Walcott himself; she feared lest the suddenness of the shock might prove too much for him. To her relief, she heard Mr. Britton entering. He took in the situation at a glance and sprang at once to her side.

"I am all right," she cried, brightly; "look after papa, first; then we will attend to this creature."

With the revolver still levelled at Walcott, Kate slowly advanced towards him.

"Give me that weapon!" she demanded.

He gave a sinister smile, but before she had taken another step, her companion sprang into the room with a piercing cry and intercepted her:

"No, no, Señorita!" she exclaimed; "do not touch it! Mother of God! it is poisoned; a single scratch means death!"

At sight of her, Walcott's face grew livid. "You fiend! You she-devil!" he hissed; "this is your doing, is it?" and he burst into a torrent of curses and imprecations.

"Be silent!" Mr. Britton ordered, sternly, and Kate accompanied the command with an ominous click of her revolver. The wretch cowered into silence, but his eyes glowed with fairly demoniac fury.

"Now," said Mr. Underwood, his faculties fully restored, "I want to know the meaning of this; let us sift this whole thing to the bottom."

"Search your man, first, David," said Mr. Britton, and suiting the action to the word he approached Walcott, but was warded off by the woman standing near.

"No, no, Señor, a little turn of the wrist, so slight you would not see, would cause death. I will take it from him; the viper dare not sting me!"

As she extended her hand she tauntingly held her wrist close to the tiny point, scarcely larger than a good-sized pin.

"Life and freedom are precious, Señor!" she said, in low, mocking tones, as she took the weapon from him and handed it to Mr. Britton, who laid it carefully on a table near by, and then proceeded to search Walcott's clothing, saying.–

"I want you to see what you have been dealing with, David."

To the stiletto already placed upon the table were added another of larger size, two loaded revolvers, several packages of valuable securities taken from the vaults of the firm that afternoon, and a nearly complete set of duplicate keys to the safes and deposit boxes of the offices.

Mr. Britton then relieved Kate, congratulating her warmly, and stationed himself near Walcott, who glowered like a wild beast that, temporarily restrained by the keeper's lash, only awaits opportunity for a more furious onslaught later.

Kate stepped at once to her father's side; he turned upon her a look of affectionate pride, but before he could speak, she had drawn forward her companion, saying,–

"Here is one, papa, to whom we owe much. She has saved your life to-night, for I would not have known you were in danger if she had not warned me, and she saved me from worse than death in preventing the carrying out of the farce of an illegal marriage with that villain, by giving me a glimpse of his real character before it was too late."

The change that passed over Mr. Underwood's countenance during Kate's words was fearful to see. From the kindliness and courtesy with which he had greeted the stranger his face seemed changed to granite, so hard and relentless it became.

"An illegal marriage? What do you mean?" he demanded, and there was something in his voice that no one present had ever heard there before.

"Illegal, papa, because this woman is his lawful wife." And Kate gave a brief explanation of the situation.

"Is that so?" he appealed to the woman, his tones strangely quiet.

"Yes, Señor; I have the papers to prove it."

"Do you admit it?" he demanded of Walcott, with a glance which made the latter quail, while his hand sought one of the loaded revolvers lying on the table.

"We were married years ago, but I did not know the woman was living; I swear I did not. I supposed she was dead until the day she came to me."

"How about the past year? You have known all this time that she was living, yet you have dared to press your suit for my daughter, you dog! Not another word!" he exclaimed, as Walcott strove to form some excuse.

He raised his hand and the revolver gleamed in the light. Mr. Britton grasped him by the arm.

"David, old friend, calm yourself!" he exclaimed. "Don't be rash or foolish; let the law take its course."

"The law!" interposed Mr. Underwood, fiercely; "do you think I'd take a case of this kind into the courts? Charges such as these against a man whose name has been publicly associated with my daughter's as her betrothed husband, and the principal witness against that man his own wife! Do you suppose for a moment I'll have my daughter's name dragged through such mire? No, by God! I'll blow the dog's brains out with my own hand first!"

A fierce struggle ensued for a moment between the two men, which ended in John Britton's disarming his friend, Kate meanwhile keeping Walcott at bay as he sought in the momentary confusion to effect an escape.

Once calmed, Mr. Underwood, notwithstanding Mr. Britton's protestations, sullenly refused to prosecute Walcott. Telephoning for an attorney who was an old-time and trusted friend, he had an agreement drawn and signed, whereby, upon the repayment of the funds belonging to him, after deducting an amount therefrom sufficient to replace what he had misappropriated, he was to leave the country altogether.

"You have escaped this time," were Mr. Underwood's parting words; "but remember, if you ever again seek to injure me or mine, no power on earth can save you, and I'll not go into the courts either."

As Kate and her strange companion parted, the former inquired, "Why did you ask me not to shoot him? You surely cannot love him!"

"Love him?" she exclaimed, softly. "No, but I feared you would kill him. His time has not come yet, Señorita, but when it does, this must be the hand!" She lifted her own right hand with a significant movement as she said this, and glided out into the darkness and was gone ere Kate could recall her.

When Kate and her father, with Mr. Britton's assistance, before returning home for the night, removed the articles taken from Walcott's pockets, the tiny, poisoned stiletto was nowhere to be found.

Chapter XXXVI

Senora Martinez

Although Mr. Underwood escaped the stroke which it was feared might follow the excitement of his final interview with Walcott, it was soon apparent that his nervous system had suffered from the shock. His physician became insistent in his demands that he not only retire from business, but have an entire change of scene, to insure absolute relaxation and rest. This advice was earnestly seconded by Mr. Britton, not alone for the sake of his friend's health, but more especially because he believed it unsafe for Mr. Underwood or Kate to remain in that part of the country so long as Walcott had his liberty. Their combined counsel and entreaties at length prevailed. A responsible man was found to take charge, under Mr. Britton's supervision, of Mr. Underwood's business interests. The Pines was closed, two or three faithful servants being retained to guard and care for the property, and early in April Mr. Underwood, accompanied by his sister and daughter, left Ophir ostensibly for the South. They remained south, however, only until he had recuperated sufficiently for a longer journey, and then sailed for Europe, but of this fact no one in Ophir had knowledge save Mr. Britton.

During the last days of Kate's stay in Ophir she watched in vain for another glimpse of her strange friend. On the morning of her departure, as the train was leaving the depot, she suddenly saw the olive-skinned messenger of former occasions running alongside the Pullman in which she was seated. Catching her eye, he motioned for her to raise the window; she did so, whereupon he tossed a little package into her lap, pointing at the same time farther down the platform, and lifting his ragged sombrero, vanished. An instant later the Señora came into view, standing at the extreme end of the platform, a lace mantilla thrown about her head and shoulders, the ends of which she now waved in token of farewell. Kate held up the little package with a smile; she responded with a deprecatory gesture indicative of its insignificance, then with another wave of the lace scarf and a flutter of Kate's handkerchief, they passed out of each other's sight.

Kate hastily undid the package; a little box of ebony inlaid with pearl slipped from the wrappings, which, upon touching a secret spring, opened, disclosing a small cross of Etruscan gold of the most exquisite workmanship. In her first letter to Mr. Britton Kate related the incident, and begged him to look out for the woman and render her any assistance possible.

To this Mr. Britton needed no urging. Since his first sight of her that night in Mr. Underwood's office he had been looking for her, for a twofold purpose. For a number of weeks he failed to get even a glimpse of her, nor could he obtain any clew to her whereabouts.

One night, well into the summer, he came upon her, unexpectedly, standing in front of a cheap restaurant, looking at the edibles displayed in the window. She was not veiled, her face was pale and haggard, and there was no mistaking the expression in her eyes as she finally turned away.

"My friend," said Mr. Britton, laying his hand gently on her shoulder, "are you hungry?"

She shrank from him with a start till a glance in his face reassured her, and she answered, with an expressive gesture,—

"Yes, Señor; I have had nothing to eat to-day, and but little yesterday."

"This is no fit place; come with me," Mr. Britton replied, leading the way two or three blocks down the street, to a first-class restaurant. He conducted her through the ladies' entrance into a private box, where he ordered a substantial dinner for two.

"Señor," she protested, as the waiter left the box, "I have no money, no way to repay you for this, you understand?"

"I understand," he answered, quickly; "I want no return for this. Miss Underwood wished me to find you, and help you, if I could."

"Yes, I know; you are the Señorita's friend."

"And your friend also, if I can help you."

"You saved his life that night, Señor; I do not forget," the woman said, with peculiar emphasis.

"Yes, I undoubtedly saved the scoundrel from a summary vengeance; possibly I might not have done it, had I known what the alternative would be. Where is that man now?" he asked, with sudden directness.

"I do not know, Señor; he tells me nothing, but I have heard he went south some time ago."

The entrance of the waiter with their orders put a temporary stop to conversation. The woman ate silently, regarding Mr. Britton from time to time with an expression of childlike wonder. When her hunger was appeased, and she seemed inclined to talk, he said,—

"Tell me something of yourself. When and where did you marry that man?"

"We were married in Mexico, seven years ago."

"Your home was in Mexico?"

"No, Señor, my father owned a big cattle ranch in Texas. Señor Walcott, as you call him here, worked for him. He wanted to marry me, but my father opposed the marriage. We lived close to the line, so we went across one day and were married. My father was very angry, but I was his only child, and by and by he forgave and took us back."

"Do I understand you that Walcott is not this man's real name?" Mr. Britton interposed.

"His name is José Martinez, Señor."

"But is he not a half-breed? I have understood his father was an Englishman."

"His father was an Englishman, but no one ever knew who he was, you understand, Señor? Afterwards his mother married Pablo Martinez, and her child took his name. That was why my father opposed our marriage."

"I understand," said Mr. Britton; "but he claims heavy cattle interests in the South; how did he come by them?"

180

"My father's, all of them;" she replied. "He and my father quarrelled soon after we went there to live. Then we came away north; we lived for a while in this State,"–she paused and hesitated as though fearing she had said too much, but Mr. Britton's face betrayed nothing, and she continued: "Then, in a year or so, we went south and he and my father quarrelled again. My father was found dead on the plains, trampled by the cattle, but no one knew how it came about. Then José took everything and told me I had nothing. He went north again three years ago. A year later he came back and told me I was not his wife, that our marriage was void because it was not performed in this country. I became very ill. He took me away among strangers and left me there, to die, as he thought. But he was mistaken. I had something to live for,–to follow him, as I have followed him and will follow him to the end."

The woman rose from the table; Mr. Britton rose also, and stood for a moment, facing her.

"He is a dangerous man," he said; "how is it that you do not fear him?"

She laughed softly. "He fears me, Señor; why should I fear him?"

"I understand," Mr. Britton said; "he fears you because you know him to be a criminal; because his freedom–perhaps his very life–is in your hands. Why are you not in danger on that account? What is to hinder his taking a life so inimical to his own?"

A cunning, treacherous smile crept over her face and a baleful light gleamed in her eyes, as she replied, "If I die at his hand my secret does not die with me. I have fixed that. If I die to-day, the world knows my secret to-morrow. He knows it, Señor, and I am safe."

"Did it never occur to you," said Mr. Britton, slowly, "that for the safety of others your secret should be made known now?"

The woman's whole appearance changed; she regarded Mr. Britton with a look of mingled anger and terror, as he continued:

"That man's life and freedom are a constant menace to other lives. Are you willing to take the responsibility of the results which may follow your withholding that secret, keeping it locked within your own breast?"

The woman looked quickly for a chance of escape, but Mr. Britton barred the only means of exit. Her expression was that of a creature brought to bay.

"I understand the meaning of your kindness to-night," she cried, fiercely. "You are one of the 'fly' men, and you thought to buy my secret from me. Let me tell you, you will never buy it, nor can you force it from me! So long as he does me no harm I will never make it known, and if I die a natural death, it dies with me!"

"You are mistaken," he replied, calmly; "I am no detective, no official of any sort. My bringing you here to-night was of itself wholly disinterested, done for the sake of a friend who wished me to help you. I have wished to meet you and talk with you, as I was interested to learn your story, out of sympathy for you and a desire to help you, and also to shed new light on your husband's character, of which I have made quite a study; but I am not seeking to force you into making any disclosures against your will."

Her anger had subsided as quickly as it had been aroused.

181

"Pardon me, Señor," she said; "I was wrong. Accept my gratitude for your kindness; I will not forget."

"Don't mention it. If you need help at any time, let me know; I do not forget that you saved my friend's life. But one word in parting: don't think your secret will not become known. Those things always work themselves out, and justice will overtake that man yet. When it does, your own life may not be as safe as you now think it is. If you need a friend then, come to me."

The woman regarded him silently for a moment. "Thank you, Señor," she said, gently; "I understand. Justice will yet overtake him, as you say; and when it does," she added, significantly, "I will need no help."

Chapter XXXVII

The Identification

The following September found Darrell again in Ophir and reestablished in his old-time quarters. To his old office he had added the room formerly occupied by Walcott, his increasing business demanding more office room and the presence of an assistant.

Before leaving the East he revisited the members of his old syndicate and informed them that he intended henceforth making his head-quarters in the West, and if they wished to employ him as their expert, he would execute commissions from that point. To this they readily agreed, and also gave him letters of introduction to a number of capitalists interested in western mining properties, who were only too glad to secure the services of a reliable expert who would be on the ground and familiar with existing conditions. As a result, Darrell had scarcely reopened business at his former quarters before he found himself with numerous eastern commissions to be executed, in addition to his old work as assayer.

He was prepared for the changes which had taken place during the year of his absence, his father having kept him thoroughly informed of all that had occurred.

Darrell was delighted at the story of Kate Underwood's coolness and bravery in saving her father's life, and sent her a note of hearty congratulation, which she kept among her cherished treasures. Since that time, occasional letters were exchanged between them; hers, bright, entertaining sketches of their travels here and there, with comments characteristic of herself regarding places and people; his, permeated with the fresh, exhilarating atmosphere of the mountains, and pervaded by a vigor and virility which roused Kate's admiration, yet led her to wonder if this could be the same lover who had won her childish heart in those idyllic days. Each realized the fact that notwithstanding their love, notwithstanding their stanch comradeship, at present they were little more than strangers. Darrell's love for Kate was a reality, but her personality, so far as he could recall it, was little more than a dream; each letter revealed some unexpected phase of her character; he found their correspondence an unfailing source of pleasure, and was content to await the time of their meeting, confident that he would find the real woman all and more than the ideal which he fondly cherished as his Dream-Love. And to Kate, each letter of Darrell's brought more and more forcibly the conviction that the lover whom she remembered was as a dream compared with the reality she was to meet some day.

About six months had elapsed when Darrell received, early one morning, the following telegram from his father, summoning him to Galena:

"Come over on first train. Important."

By the first train he would reach Galena a little before noon; he had not breakfasted, and had but twenty minutes in which to make it. Calling a carriage, he went directly to his office, where he left a brief explanatory note for the clerk, written on the way, then drove with all possible speed to the depot, arriving on time but without a minute to spare. He breakfasted on the train, and while running over the morning paper, his attention was caught by a despatch from Galena to the effect that one of the leading banks in that city had been entered and the safe opened and robbed on the preceding night. The robbers, of whom there were three, had been discovered by the police. A fight had ensued in which one officer and one of the robbers were killed, the second robber wounded, while the third had made his escape with most of the plunder. It was further stated that they were known to belong to the notorious band of outlaws so long the terror of that region, and it was believed the wounded man was none other than the leader himself, the murderer of Harry Whitcomb and the young express clerk, for whom there was a standing reward of twenty-five thousand dollars, dead or alive. The man was to have a preliminary examination that afternoon, and the greatest excitement prevailed in Galena, as it was rumored that others of the band would probably be present, scattered throughout the crowd, for the purpose of rescuing their leader.

In a flash Darrell understood his father's summons. He let the paper fall and, unmindful of his breakfast, gazed abstractedly out of the window. His thoughts had reverted to that scene in the sleeper on his first trip west. He seemed to see it again in all its sickening detail, the face of the assassin standing out before him with such startling distinctness and realism that he involuntarily placed his hand over his eyes to shut out the hateful sight.

At Galena he was met by his father, who took a closed carriage to his hotel, conducting Darrell immediately to his own room, where he ordered lunch served for both.

183

"Do you know why I have sent for you?" Mr. Britton inquired, as soon as they were left alone together.

"I had no idea when I started," Darrell replied, "but on reading the morning paper, on my way over, I concluded you wanted me at that trial this afternoon."

"You are correct. Are you prepared to identify that face? Is your recollection of it as distinct as ever?"

"Yes; after reading of that bank robbery this morning, the whole affair in the car that night came back to me so vividly I could see the man's face as clearly as any face on the train with me."

"Good!" Mr. Britton ejaculated.

"Do you think there is any likelihood of an attempt to rescue him, as stated by the paper?" Darrell inquired, rather incredulously.

"If the leader of the band finds himself in need of help it will be forthcoming," Mr. Britton answered, with peculiar emphasis. "The citizens are expecting trouble and have sworn in about a dozen extra deputy sheriffs, myself among the number."

When lunch was over Mr. Britton ordered a carriage at once, and they proceeded to the court-room.

"What is your opinion of this man?" Darrell asked his father, while on the way. "Would you have selected him as the murderer, from your study of him?"

"I reserve my opinions until later," Mr. Britton replied. "I want you to act from memory alone, unbiased by any outside influence."

Arriving at the court-room, they found it already well filled. Darrell was about to enter, but his father took him into a small anteroom, while he himself went to look for seats. He had a little difficulty in finding the seats he wanted, which delayed them so that proceedings had begun as he and Darrell entered from a side door and took their places in rather an obscure part of the room.

"You will have a good view here," Mr. Britton said to Darrell, as they seated themselves, "and there is little likelihood of your being recognized from this point."

"There is little probability of the man's recognizing me, even if he is here," Darrell replied, "for he did not give me a second thought that night, and if he had, I am so changed he would not know me."

"We cannot be too cautious," his father answered.

In a few moments the prisoner was brought in, and there was a general craning of necks to see him, a number of men in Darrell's vicinity standing and thus obstructing his view.

"Wait," said his father, as he was about to rise with the others; "don't make yourself conspicuous; when the man is called for examination you will have an excellent view from here."

Curiosity gradually subsided, and the men sank back into their seats as proceedings went on. Then the prisoner was called and stood up for examination. Darrell drew a quick breath and leaned eagerly forward. The man was of medium height and size, but his movements seemed heavy and

184

clumsy, whereas Darrell had been impressed by a litheness and agility in the movements of the other.

He stood facing his interlocutor, affording Darrell a three-quarter view of his face, but soon he turned in Darrell's direction, scanning the crowd slowly, as though in search of some one.

Darrell saw a squarely built, colorless face, surmounted by a shock of coarse, straight black hair, with heavy, repulsive features, and small, bullet-shaped, leaden eyes of rather light blue. The face was so utterly unlike what he had expected to see that he sank back into his seat with a smothered exclamation of disgust. His father, watching closely, smiled, seeming rather pleased than otherwise, but Darrell was half indignant.

"The idea of a lout like that being taken for the leader!" he exclaimed. "He is nothing but a tool, and a pretty clumsy one at that."

Notwithstanding his vexation, Darrell continued to watch the proceedings, and in a few moments began to grow interested, not so much in the examination as in the conduct of the prisoner. The latter evidently had found the face for which he was looking, for his eyes seemed glued to a certain spot. Occasionally he would shift them for a moment, but invariably, with each new interrogatory, they would turn to that particular spot, as the needle to the pole, not through any volition of his own, but drawn by some influence against which he was temporarily powerless.

"That man is under a spell; he is being worked by some one in the crowd," Darrell exclaimed to his father, in a low tone.

"Yes, and by some one not very far from us; I have spotted him, see if you cannot."

Following the direction of the man's glance, Darrell began to scan the faces of the crowd. Suddenly his pulses gave a bound. Seated at a little distance and partially facing them was a man of the same size and height as the prisoner, but whose every move and poise suggested alertness. He was leaning his arms on the back of the seat before him; his head was lowered so that his chin rested lightly on one hand, while the other hand played nervously with the seat on which he leaned. His whole attitude was that of a wild beast crouched, ready to spring upon his prey. He had an oval face, with deep olive skin, wavy black hair, cut close except where it curled low over his forehead, and through the half-closed eyes, fixed upon the prisoner's face, Darrell caught a glint like that of burnished steel. For an instant Darrell gazed like one fascinated; he had not expected such an exact reproduction of the face as he had seen it on that night. His father touched him lightly; he nodded significantly in reply.

"There is your man!" he exclaimed.

"You are sure? You could swear to it?" queried his father.

"Swear to it? Yes. I would have known him anywhere, but sitting there, watching that man, his face is precisely as I saw it that night. Wait a moment, look!"

The man in his agitation at some word of the prisoner's, raised one hand and brushed his forehead with a nervous gesture, which lifted his hair slightly, disclosing one end of a scar.

"Did you see that scar?" Darrell questioned, eagerly. "You will find it almost crescent shaped, rather jagged, and nearly three inches in length."

"That is all I wanted," his father replied. "I have the warrant for his arrest with me, and the examination is so nearly over I shall serve it at once."

"Can I help you?" Darrell asked, as his father moved away.

"No; stay where you are; don't let him see you until after he is under arrest."

The examination of the prisoner had just ended when Mr. Britton, accompanied by two deputies, re-entered the court-room. The man still maintained his crouching attitude, intently watching proceedings. Mr. Britton approached from the rear. Seizing the man suddenly by the arms, he pinioned him so that for an instant he was unable to move, and one of the deputies, leaning over, snapped the handcuffs on him before he fairly realized what had happened. Then, with a swift movement, Mr. Britton raised him to his feet and lifted him quickly out into the aisle, while his voice rang authoritatively through the court-room,–

"José Martinez, alias Walcott, I arrest you in the name of the State!"

The man shouted something in Spanish, evidently a signal, for it was repeated in different parts of the room. Instantly all was confusion. A shot fired from the rear wounded one of the deputies; a man seated near Darrell drew a revolver, but before he could level it Darrell knocked it from his hand and felled him to the floor. The officers rushed to the spot, and as the outbreak subsided Mr. Britton brought forward his prisoner.

A murmur of consternation rose throughout the room, for Walcott had been known years before among the business men of Galena, and there were not a few citizens present who had known him as Mr. Underwood's partner. Walcott, taking advantage of the situation, began to protest his innocence. Mr. Britton, unmoved, at once beckoned Darrell to his side. Upon seeing him Walcott's face took on a ghastly hue and he seemed for a moment on the verge of collapse, but he quickly pulled himself together, regarding Darrell meanwhile with a venomous malignity seldom seen on a human face. Not the least surprised man in the crowd was Darrell himself.

"Do you mean to say," he asked his father, "that this is the Walcott of whose villany you have been writing me, and that he and the murderer of Harry Whitcomb are one and the same?"

"So it seems," Mr. Britton replied; "but that is no more than I have suspected all along."

"Now I understand your fear of my being recognized; it seemed inexplicable to me," said Darrell.

"If he had seen you," his father replied, "he would have suspected your errand here at once."

Incredulity was apparent on many faces as Walcott's examination was begun. He was morose and silent, and nothing could be elicited from him. When Darrell was called upon, however, and gave his evidence, incredulity gave place to conviction. As he completed his testimony with a description of the scar, which, upon examination, was found correct, the crowd became angry and threats of lynching and personal violence were heard on

186

various sides. The judge therefore ordered that the prisoners be removed from the court-room to the jail before any in the audience had left their places.

In charge of the regular sheriff and four or five deputies the prisoners were led from the court-room. They had but just reached the street, however, when those inside heard shots fired in quick succession, followed by angry cries and shouts for help. The crowd surged to the doors, to see the officers surrounded by a band of the outlaws who had been lying in wait for their appearance, having been summoned by the signal given on the arrest of the leader. With the help of the citizens the fight was soon terminated, but when the mêlée was over it was discovered that the sheriff had been killed, a number of citizens and outlaws wounded, and Martinez, alias Walcott, had escaped.

Chapter XXXVIII

Within the "Pocket"

The remainder of that day and the following night were spent in fruitless efforts to determine the whereabouts of the fugitive. Telegrams were sent along the various railway lines into every part of the State; messengers were despatched to neighboring towns and camps, but all in vain. For the first thirty-six hours it seemed as though the earth must have opened and swallowed him up; there was not even a clue as to the direction in which he had gone.

The second morning after his disappearance reports began to come in from a dozen different quarters of as many different men, all answering the description given of the fugitive, who had been identified as the criminal. Four or five posses, averaging a dozen men each, all armed, set forth in various directions to follow the clews which seemed most worthy of credence. For the next few days reports were constantly received from one posse or another, to the effect that they were on the right trail, the fugitive had been seen only the preceding night at a miners' cabin where he had forced two men at the point of a revolver to surrender their supper of pork and beans; or some lonely ranchman and his wife had entertained him at dinner the day before. He was always reported as only about ten hours ahead, footsore and weary, but at the end of ten days they returned, disorganized, dilapidated, and disgusted, without even having had a sight of their man.

Other bands were sent out with instructions to separate into squads of three or four and search the ground thoroughly. Some of them were more successful, in that they did, occasionally, get sight of the fugitive, but always under circumstances disadvantageous to themselves. Three of them stood one day talking with a rancher, who only two hours before had furnished the man, under protest, with a hearty dinner and a fine rifle. The rancher pointed out the direction in which he had gone, over a rocky road leading down a steep, rough ravine; as he did so, his guest appeared on the other side of the ravine, within good rifle range. A mutual recognition followed; the men started to raise their rifles, but the other was too quick for them. Covering them with the rifle which he carried, he walked backward a distance of about forty yards and then, with a mocking salute, disappeared. Bloodhounds were next employed, but the man swam and waded streams and doubled back on his own trail till men and dogs were alike baffled. This continued for about two months; then all reports regarding the man ceased; nothing was heard of him, it was surmised that he had reached the "Pocket," and all efforts at further search were for the time abandoned.

Of all those concerned in the efforts for his capture there was not one more thoroughly disgusted with the outcome than Mr. Britton. For months he had had this man under surveillance, convinced that he was a criminal and planning to bring about his capture. Through his own efforts he had been identified, and by his coolness and presence of mind he had accomplished his arrest when nine out of ten others would have failed, and all seemed now to have been effort thrown away. He regretted the man's escape the more especially as he felt that his own life, as well as that of his son, was endangered so long as he was at liberty.

About a month after the search was abandoned Mr. Britton was one day surprised by a call from the wife of Martinez. He had not seen her since his one interview with her months before.

He was sitting in Mr. Underwood's office, looking over the books brought in for his inspection, when she entered, alone and unannounced.

She seated herself in the chair indicated by Mr. Britton and proceeded at once to the object of her visit.

"Señor, you told me when I last saw you that my secret would one day come out. You were right; it has. It is my secret no longer and José Martinez fears me no longer. You have been kind to me. You saved his life once; you fed me when I was hungry and asked no return. I will show you I do not forget. Señor, there is twenty-five thousand dollars reward for that man. The officers will never find him; but I will take you to him, the reward is then yours, and justice overtakes José Martinez, as you said it would. Do you accept?"

"Do you know where he is?" Mr. Britton queried, somewhat surprised by the woman's proposition.

"Yes, Señor; I have just come from there."

"He is in the Pocket, is he not?"

"Yes, Señor, but neither you nor your men could find the Pocket without a guide. I know it well; I have lived there."

"What is your proposition?" Mr. Britton inquired, after a brief silence; "how do you propose to do this?"

"I will start to-morrow for the Pocket. You come with me and bring the dogs. I will take you to a cabin where you can stay over night while I go on alone to the Pocket to see that all is right. I will leave you my veil for a scent. The next morning you will set the dogs on my trail and follow them till you come to a certain place I will tell you of. From there you will see me; I will watch for you and give you the signal that all is right. The dogs will bring you to the Pocket in half an hour. The rest will be easy work, Señor, I promise you."

"But isn't the place constantly guarded?"

"Not now, Señor; the men have gone away on another expedition, but José does not dare go out with them at present. Only one man is there beside José; I know him well; he will be asleep when you come."

"I shall need men with me to help in bringing him back," said Mr. Britton.

"Bring them, but I think he will give you little trouble, Señor."

As Mr. Britton cared nothing for the reward himself, he chose five men to accompany him to whom he thought the money would be particularly acceptable, and the following morning, with two blood-hounds, they started forth in three separate detachments to attract as little attention as possible. The first part of their journey was by rail, the men taking the same train as the woman herself. On their arrival at the little station which she had designated, conveyances, for which Mr. Britton had privately wired a personal friend living in that vicinity, were waiting to take them to their next stopping-place.

They reached the cabin of which the woman had spoken, late in the afternoon. Here they picketed their horses and prepared to stay over night, while she went on to the Pocket. Before leaving she gave Mr. Britton the lace scarf which she wore about her head.

"I shall not go in there until night," she said; "then I can watch and find if all is right. You start early to-morrow morning on foot. Set the dogs on my trail and follow them to the fork; then turn to the left and follow them till you come to a small tree standing in the trail, on which I will tie this handkerchief. Straight ahead of you you will see the entrance to the Pocket. Wait by the tree till you see my signal. If everything is right I will wave a white signal. If I wave a black signal, wait till you see the white one, or till I come to you."

Early the next morning Mr. Britton and his men set forth with the hounds in leash, leaving the horses in charge of their drivers. The dogs took the scent at once and started up the trail, the men following. They found it no easy task they had undertaken; the trail was rough and steep and in many places so narrow they were forced to go in single file. Some of the men, in order to be prepared for emergencies, were heavily armed, and progress was necessarily slow, but at last the fork was passed, and then the time seemed comparatively short ere a small tree confronted them, a white handkerchief fluttering among its branches.

They paused and drew back the hounds, then looked about them. Less than ten feet ahead the trail ended. The rocks looked as though they had been cut in two, the half on which they were standing falling perpendicularly a distance of some eighty feet, while across a rocky ravine

189

some forty feet in width, the other half rose, an almost perpendicular wall eighty or ninety feet in height. In this massive wall of rock there was one opening visible, resembling a gateway, and while the men speculated as to what it might be, the woman appeared, waving a white handkerchief, and they knew it to be the entrance to the Pocket.

"She evidently expects us to come over there," said one of the men, "but blamed if I can see a trail wide enough for a cat!"

"Send the dogs ahead!" ordered Mr. Britton.

The dogs on taking the scent plunged downward through the brush on one side, bringing them out into a narrow trail leading down and across the ravine. Just above, on the other side, they could see the woman watching their every move.

"I've always heard," said one of the men, "there was no getting into this place without you had a special invitation, and it looks like it. Just imagine one of those fellows up there with a gun! Holy Moses! he'd hold the place against all the men the State, or the United States, for that matter, could send down here!"

The ascent of the other side was difficult, but the men put forth their best efforts, and ere they were aware found themselves before the gateway in the rocks, where the woman still awaited them. She silently beckoned them to enter.

Emerging from a narrow pass some six feet in length, they found themselves in a circular basin, about two hundred feet in diameter, surrounded by perpendicular walls of rock from one hundred to five hundred feet in height. The bottom of the basin was level as a floor and covered with a luxuriant growth of grass, while in the centre a small lake, clear as crystal, reflecting the blue sky which seemed to rise like a dome from the rocky walls, gleamed like a sapphire in the sunlight. Sheer and dark the walls rose on all sides, but at one end of the basin, where the rocks were more rough and jagged, a silver stream fell in glistening cascades to the bottom, where it disappeared among the rocks.

For a moment the men, lost in admiration of the scene, forgot that they were in the den of a notorious band of outlaws, but a second glance recalled them to the situation, for on all sides of the basin were caves leading into the walls of rock, and evidently used as dwellings.

To one of these the woman now led the way. At the entrance a man lay on the ground, his heavy stertorous breathing proclaiming him a victim of some sleeping potion. The woman regarded him with a smile of amusement.

"I made him sleep, Señor," she said, addressing Mr. Britton, "so he will not trouble you."

Still leading the way into the farther part of the cave, she came to a low couch of skins at the foot of which she paused. Pointing to the figure outlined upon it, she said, calmly,–

"He sleeps also, Señor, but sound; so sound you will need have no fear of waking him!"

Her words aroused a strange suspicion in Mr. Britton's mind. The light was so dim he could not see the sleeper, but a lantern, burning low, hung on the wall above his head. Seizing the lantern, he turned on the light, holding it so it would strike the face of the sleeper. It was the face of José Martinez, but the features were drawn and ghastly. He bent lower, listening for his breath, but no sound came; he laid his hand upon his heart, but it was still.

Raising himself quickly, he threw the rays of the lantern full upon the woman standing before him, a small crucifix clasped in her hands. Under his searching gaze her face grew pale and ghastly as that upon the couch.

"You have killed him!" he said, slowly, with terrible emphasis.

She made the sign of the cross. "Holy Mother, forgive!" she muttered; then, though she still quailed beneath his look, she exclaimed, half defiantly, "I have not wronged you; you have your reward, and justice has overtaken him, as you said it would!"

"That is not justice," said Mr. Britton, pointing to the couch; "it is murder, and you are his murderer. You should have let the law take its course."

"The law!" she laughed, mockingly; "would your law avenge my father's death, or the wrongs I have suffered? No! My father had no son to avenge him, I had no brother, but I have avenged him and myself. I have followed him all these years, waiting till the right time should come, waiting for this, dreaming of it night and day! I have had my revenge, and it was sweet! I did not kill him in his sleep, Señor; I wakened him, just to let him know he was in my power, just to hear him plead for mercy——"

"Hush!" said Mr. Britton, firmly, for the woman seemed to have gone mad. "You do not know what you are saying. You must get ready to return with me."

She grew calm at once and her face lighted with a strange smile.

"I am ready to go with you, Señor," she said, at the same time clasping the crucifix suddenly to her breast.

With the last word she fell to the ground and a slight tremor shook her frame for an instant. Quickly Mr. Britton lifted her and bore her to the light, but life was already extinct. Within her clasped hands, underneath the crucifix, they found the little poisoned stiletto.

Chapter XXXIX

At the Time Appointed

For a year and a half Darrell worked uninterruptedly at Ophir, his constantly increasing commissions from eastern States testifying to his marked ability as a mining expert.

Notwithstanding the incessant demands upon his time, he still adhered to his old rule, reserving a few hours out of each twenty-four, which he devoted to scientific or literary study, as his mood impelled. He soon found himself again drawn irresistibly towards the story begun during his stay at the Hermitage, but temporarily laid aside on his return east. He carefully reviewed the synopsis, which he had written in detail, and as he did, he felt himself entering into the spirit of the story till it seemed once more part of his own existence. He revised the work already done, eliminating, adding, making the outlines clearer, more defined; then, with steady, unfaltering hand, carried the work forward to completion.

Eighteen months after his re-establishment at Ophir he was commissioned to go to Alaska to examine certain mining properties in a deal involving over a million dollars, and, anxious to be on the ground as early as possible, he took the first boat north that season. His story was published on the eve of his departure. He received a few copies, which he regarded with a half-fond, half-whimsical air. One he sent to Kate Underwood, having first written his initials on the fly-leaf underneath the brief petition, "Be merciful." He then went his way, his time and attention wholly occupied by his work, with little thought as to whether the newly launched craft was destined to ride the waves of popularity or be engulfed beneath the waters of oblivion.

Months of constant travel, of hard work and rough fare, followed. His report on the mines was satisfactory, the deal was consummated, and he received a handsome percentage, but not content with this, determined to familiarize himself with the general situation in that country and the conditions obtaining, he pushed on into the interior, pursuing his explorations till the return of the cold season. Touching at British Columbia on his way home and finding tempting inducements there in the way of mining properties, he stopped to investigate, and remained during the winter and spring months.

It was therefore not until the following June that he found himself really homeward bound and once more within the mountain ranges guarding the approach to the busy little town of Ophir.

He had been gone considerably over a year; he had accumulated a vast amount of information invaluable for future work along his line, and he had succeeded financially beyond his anticipations. Occasionally during his absence, in papers picked up here and there, he had seen favorable mention of his story, from which he inferred that his first venture in the realms of fiction had not been quite a failure, and in this opinion he was confirmed by a letter just received from his publishers, which had followed him for months. But all thought of these things was for the time forgotten in an almost boyish delight that he was at last on his way home.

As he came within sight of the familiar ranges his thoughts reverted again and again to Kate Underwood. His whole soul seemed to cry out for her with a sudden, insatiable longing. His mail had of necessity been irregular and infrequent; their letters had somehow miscarried, and he had not heard directly from her for months. Her last letter was from Germany; she was then still engrossed in her music, but her father's health was greatly improved and he was beginning to talk of home. His father's latest letter had stated that the Underwoods would probably return early in July. And this was June! Darrell felt a twinge of disappointment. He was now able to remember many incidents in their acquaintance. He recalled their first meeting at The Pines on that June day five years ago. How beautiful the old place must look now! But without Kate's presence the charm would be lost for him. He regretted he had started homeward quite so soon; the time would not have seemed so long among the mining camps of the great Northwest as here, where everything reminded him of her.

The stopping of the train at a health resort far up among the mountains, a few miles from Ophir, roused Darrell from his revery. With a sigh he recalled his wandering thoughts and left the car for a walk up and down the platform. The town, perched saucily on the slopes of a heavily timbered mountain, looked very attractive in the gathering twilight. Though early in the season, the hotel and sanitarium seemed well filled, while numerous pleasure-seekers were promenading the walks leading to and from the springs which gave the place its popularity.

Darrell felt a sudden, unaccountable desire to remain. Without waiting to analyze the impulse, as inexplicable as it was irresistible, which actuated him, he hastened into the sleeper and secured his grip and top coat. As the train pulled out he stepped into the station and sent a message to his father at Ophir, stating that he had decided to remain over a day or two at the Springs and asking him to look after his baggage on its arrival. He then took a carriage for the hotel. It was not without some compunctions of conscience that Darrell wired his father of his decision, and even as he rode swiftly along the winding streets he wondered what strange fancy possessed him that he should stop among strangers instead of continuing his journey home. To his father it would certainly seem unaccountable, as it did now to himself.

Mr. Britton, however, on receiving his son's message, could not restrain a smile, for only the preceding day he had received a telegram from Kate Underwood, at the same place, in which she stated that they had started home earlier than at first intended, and as her father was somewhat fatigued by their long journey, they had decided to stop for two or three days' rest at the Springs.

Darrell arrived at the hotel at a late hour for dinner; the dining-room was therefore nearly deserted when he took his place at the table. Dinner over, he went out for a stroll, and, glad to be alone with his thoughts, walked up and down the entire length of the little town. His mind was constantly on Kate. Again and again he seemed to see her, as he loved best to recall her, standing on the summit of the "Divide," her wind-tossed hair blown about her brow, her eyes shining, as she predicted their reunion and perfect love. Over and over he seemed to hear her words, and his heart burned with desire for their fulfilment. He had waited patiently, he had shown what he could achieve, how he could win, but all achievements, all victories, were worthless without her love and presence.

The moon was just rising as he returned to the hotel, but it was still early. His decision was taken; he would go to Ophir by the morning train, learn Kate's whereabouts from his father, and go to meet her and

193

accompany her home. He had chosen a path leading through a secluded portion of the grounds, and as he approached the hotel his attention was arrested by some one singing. Glancing in the direction whence the song came, he saw one of the private parlors brightly lighted, the long, low window open upon the veranda. Something in the song held him entranced, spell-bound. The voice was incomparably rich, possessing wonderful range and power of expression, but this alone was not what especially appealed to him. Through all and underlying all was a quality so strangely, sweetly familiar, which thrilled his soul to its very depths, whether with joy or pain he could not have told; it seemed akin to both.

Still held as by a spell, he drew nearer the window, until he heard the closing words of the refrain,—words which had been ringing with strange persistency in his mind for the last two or three hours,—

> "Some time, some time, and that will be
> God's own good time for you and me."

His heart leaped wildly. With a bound, swift and noiseless, he was on the veranda, just as the singer, with tender, lingering emphasis, repeated the words so low as to be barely audible to Darrell standing before the open window. But even while he listened he gazed in astonishment at the singer; could that magnificent woman be his girl-love? She was superbly formed, splendidly proportioned; the rich, warm blood glowed in her cheeks, and her hair gleamed in the light like spun gold. He stood motionless; he would not retreat, he dared not advance.

As the last words of the song died away, a slight sound caused the singer to turn, facing him, and their eyes met. That was enough; in that one glance the memory of his love returned to him like an overwhelming flood. She was no longer his Dream-Love, but a splendid, living reality, only more beautiful than his dreams or his imagination had portrayed her.

He stretched out his arms towards her with the one word, "Kathie!"

She had already risen, a great, unspeakable joy illumining her face, but at the sound of that name, vibrating with the pent-up emotion, the concentrated love of all the years of their separation, she came swiftly forward, her bosom palpitating, her eyes shining with the love called forth by his cry. He stepped through the low window, within the room. In an instant his arms were clasped about her, and, holding her close to his breast, his dark eyes told her more eloquently than words of his heart's hunger for her, while in her eyes and in the blushes running riot in her cheeks he read his welcome.

He kissed her hair and brow, with a sort of reverence; then, hearing voices in the corridor and rooms adjoining, he seized a light wrap from a chair near by and threw it about her shoulders.

"Come outside, sweetheart," he whispered, and drawing her arm within his own led her out onto the veranda and down the path along which he had just come. In the first transport of their joy they were silent, each almost fearing to break the spell which seemed laid upon them. The moon had risen, transforming the sombre scene to one of beauty, but to them

194

Love's radiance had suddenly made the world inexpressibly fair; the very flowers as they passed breathed perfume like incense in their path, and the trees whispered benedictions upon them.

Darrell first broke the silence. "I would have been in Ophir to-night, but some mysterious, irresistible impulse led me to stop here. Did you weave a spell about me, you sweet sorceress?" he asked, gazing tenderly into her face.

"I think it must have been some higher influence than mine," she replied, with sweet gravity, "for I was also under the spell. I supposed you many miles away, yet, as I sang to-night, it seemed as though you were close to me, as though if I turned I should see you–just as I did," she concluded, with a radiant smile. "But how did you find me?"

"How does the night-bird find its mate?" he queried, in low, vibrant tones; then, as her color deepened, he continued, with passionate earnestness,–

"I was here, where we are now, my very soul crying out for you, when I heard your song. It thrilled me; I felt as though waking from a dream, but I knew my love was near. Down through the years I heard her soul calling mine; following that call, I found my love, and listening, heard the very words which my own heart had been repeating over and over to itself, alone and in the darkness."

Almost unconsciously they had stopped at a turn in the path. Darrell paused a moment, for tears were trembling on the golden lashes. Drawing her closer, he whispered,–

"Kathie, do you remember our parting on the 'Divide'?"

"Do you think I ever could forget?" she asked.

"You predicted we would one day stand reunited on the heights of such love as we had not dreamed of then. I asked you when that day would be; do you remember your answer?"

"I do."

He continued, in impassioned tones: "Are not the conditions fulfilled, sweetheart? My love for you then was as a dream, a myth, compared with that I bring you to-day, and looking in your eyes I need no words to tell me that your love has broadened and deepened with the years. Kathie, is not this 'the time appointed'?"

"It must be," she replied; "there could be none other like this!"

Holding her head against his breast and raising her face to his, he said, "You gave me your heart that day, Kathie, to hold in trust. I have been faithful to that trust through all these years; do you give it me now for my very own?"

"Yes," she answered, slowly, with sweet solemnity; "to have and to hold, forever!"

He sealed the promise with a long, rapturous kiss; but what followed, the broken, disjointed phrases, the mutual pledges, the tokens of love given and received, are all among the secrets which the mountains never told.

As they retraced their steps towards the hotel, Darrell said, "We have waited long, sweetheart."

"Yes, but the waiting has brought us good of itself," she answered.

"Think of all you have accomplished,—I know better than you think, for your father has kept me posted,—and better yet, what these years have fitted you for accomplishing in the future! To me, that was the best part of your work in your story. It was strong and cleverly told, but what pleased me most was the evidence that it was but the beginning, the promise of something better yet to come."

"If only I could persuade all critics to see it through your eyes!" Darrell replied, with a smile.

"Do you wish to know," she asked, with sudden seriousness, "what will always remain to me the noblest, most heroic act of your life?"

"Most assuredly I do," he answered, her own gravity checking the laughing reply which rose to his lips.

"The fight you made and won alone in the mountains the day that you renounced our love for honor's sake. I can see now that the stand you took and maintained so nobly formed the turning-point in both our lives. I did not look at it then as you did. I would have married you then and there and gone with you to the ends of the earth rather than sacrifice your love, but you upheld my honor with your own. You fought against heavy odds, and won, and to me no other victory will compare with it, since—

'greater they who on life's battle-field
With unseen foes and fierce temptations fight.'"

Darrell silently drew her nearer himself, feeling that even in this foretaste of joy he had received ample compensation for the past.

A few days later there was a quiet wedding at the Springs. The beautiful church on the mountain-side had been decorated for the occasion, and at an early hour, while yet the robins were singing their matins, the little wedding-party gathered about the altar where John Darrell Britton and Kate Underwood plighted their troth for life. Above the jubilant bird-songs, above the low, subdued tones of the organ, the words of the grand old marriage service rang out with impressiveness.

Besides the rector and his wife, there were present only Mr. Underwood, Mrs. Dean, and Mr. Britton. It had been Kate's wish, with which Darrell had gladly coincided, thus to be quietly married, surrounded only by their immediate relatives.

"Let our wedding be a fit consummation of our betrothal," she had said to him, "without publicity, unhampered by conventionalities, so it will always seem the sweeter and more sacred."

That evening found them all at The Pines, assembled on the veranda watching the sunset, the old home seeming wonderfully restful and peaceful to the returned travellers.

The years which had come and gone since Darrell first came to the Pines told heaviest on Mr. Underwood. His hair was nearly white and he had aged in many ways, appearing older than Mr. Britton, who was considerably his senior; but age had brought its compensations, for the stern, immobile face had softened and the deep-set eyes glowed with a kindly, beneficent light. Mr. Britton's hair was well silvered, but his face bore evidence of the great joy which had come into his life, and as his eyes rested upon his son he seemed to live anew in that glorious young life. To

196

Mrs. Dean the years had brought only a few silver threads in the brown hair and an added serenity to the placid, unfurrowed brow. Calm and undemonstrative as ever, but with a smile of deep content, she sat in her accustomed place, her knitting-needles flashing and clicking with their old-time regularity. Duke, who had been left in Mr. Britton's care during Darren's absence, occupied his old place on the top stair, but even his five years of added dignity could not restrain him from occasional demonstrations of joy at finding himself again at The Pines and with his beloved master and mistress.

As the twilight began to deepen Kate suggested that they go inside, and led the way, not to the family sitting-room, but to a spacious room on the eastern side, a room which had originally been intended as a library, but never furnished as such. It was beautifully decorated with palms and flowers, while the fireplace had been filled with light boughs of spruce and fir.

As they entered the room, Kate, slipping her arm within Mr. Britton's, led him before the fireplace.

"My dear father," she said, "we have chosen this evening as the one most appropriate for your formal installation in our family circle and our home. I say formal because you have really been one of ourselves for years; you have shared our joys and our sorrows; we have had no secrets from you; but from this time we want you to take your place in our home, as you did long ago in our hearts. We have prepared this room for you, to be your sanctum sanctorum, and have placed in it a few little tokens of our love for you and gratitude to you, which we beg you to accept as such."

She bent towards the fireplace. "The hearthstone is ever an emblem of home. In lighting the fires upon this hearthstone, we dedicate it to your use and christen this 'our father's room.'"

The flames burst upward as she finished speaking, sending a resinous fragrance into the air and revealing a room fitted with such loving thought and care that nothing which could add to his comfort had been omitted. Near the centre of the room stood a desk of solid oak, a gift from Mr. Underwood; beside it a reclining chair from Mrs. Dean, while on the wall opposite, occupying nearly a third of that side of the room, was a superb painting of the Hermitage,—standing out in the firelight with wonderful realism, perfect in its bold outlines and sombre coloring,—the united gift of his son and daughter, which Darrell had ordered executed before his departure for Alaska.

With loving congratulations the rest of the group gathered about Mr. Britton, who was nearly speechless with emotion. As Mr. Underwood wrung his hand he exclaimed, with assumed gruffness,—

"Jack, old partner, you thought you'd got a monopoly on that boy of yours, but I've got in on the deal at last!"

"You haven't got any the best of me, Dave," Mr. Britton retorted, smiling through his tears, "for I've got a share now in the sweetest daughter on earth!"

"Yes, papa," Kate laughingly rejoined, "there are three of us Brittons now; the Underwoods are in the minority."

Which, though a new view of the situation to that gentleman, seemed eminently satisfactory.

Later, as Kate found Darrell at a window, looking thoughtfully out into the moonlit night, she asked,—

"Of what are you thinking, John?"

"Of what the years have done for us, Kathie; of how much better fitted for each other we are now than when we first loved."

"Yes," she whispered, as their eyes met, "'God's own good time' was the best."

THE END

www.ingramcontent.com/pod-product-compliance
Lightning Source LLC
Chambersburg PA
CBHW020634250626
47154CB00008B/2671